MW00860863

THE BOUNDLESS GARDEN

ALEXANDROS PAPADIAMANDIS

THE BOUNDLESS GARDEN

SELECTED SHORT STORIES

VOLUME I

EDITED BY

LAMBROS KAMPERIDIS

AND

DENISE HARVEY

DENISE HARVEY (PUBLISHER) ¥ LIMNI, EVIA, GREECE

First published in 2007
by Denise Harvey (Publisher
340 05 Limni, Evia, Greece

Paper bound edition reprinted in 2018
with minor amendments

Printed and bound in Greece

The Boundless Garden
Selected Short Stories by Alexandros Papadiamandis
Volume I
is the seventeenth publication in
THE ROMIOSYNI SERIES

ISBN 978-960-7120-20-5 set, cloth bound
ISBN 978-960-7120-21-2 volume, cloth bound
ISBN 978-960-7120-22-9 set, paper bound
ISBN 978-960-7120-23-6 volume, paper bound

ACKNOWLEDGEMENTS

THE EDITORS WISH TO THANK the Constantine and Emma Doxiades Foundation for the generous assistance offered at the outset of this undertaking without which it would not have been possible to put the work of translation in hand.

Throughout this volume's several years of gestation many people have helped in editorial matters, not least the translators themselves who patiently dealt with the punctiliousness of the editors and in various ways generously contributed their knowledge and skills to the work as a whole. Special thanks are also due to Nikos N. Triandaphyllopoulos and Dimitris Mavropoulos for clarification on points of interpretation, and to Christina Kamperidi, Jeany Papadionysiou and Vincent Rossi for their editorial contributions.

The late Zissimos Lorenzatos and Philip Sherrard have been instrumental in guiding, inspiring and sustaining this work from its inception.

Photograph of Alexandros Papadiamandis taken by Pavlos Nirvanas
in Athens, circa 1905.

Contents

Biographical Note

ALEXANDROS PAPADIAMANDIS was born on 4th March 1851 on the small island of Skiathos just off the north-east coast of Euboea, so named because the shadow — *skiá* — of the northerly great holy mountain of Athos cast by the rising sun stretches across the Aegean as far as the island. His father, the priest Adamandios Emmanuel — familiarly addressed as *Papa*-Diamandis — came from a nautical family which in earlier years had counted monastics and abbots amongst its members. His mother, Angeliki, was the daughter of Alexandros Moraïti who belonged to one of Skiathos's land-owning families. His parents had nine children, two of whom died at birth. Alexandros, who was named after his maternal grand-father, was their fourth child and eldest surviving son.

The young Alexandros had a diverse and sporadic education. He was schooled on his island until the age of eleven, but as there were no further classes offered he spent the next three years mainly helping his father in his pastoral duties. In 1865 he was sent to the high school on the nearby more affluent island of Skopelos. He was given the grade of 'A' for that year and described by his teacher as 'entirely praiseworthy', but because of his family's economic constraints he had to interrupt his schooling there and return to Skiathos. The following year, in 1867, his parents were able to send him to the gymnasium in Chalkis, the capital town of Euboea, which he attended for two years, and for his third year he went to the gymnasium in Piraeus, but in February of 1870, after only four months at the Piraeus school, he left and returned to Skiathos.

In 1872 he travelled to Mount Athos, the independent monastic community in northern Greece, with a childhood friend who was later to become a monk, the one referred to as Samuel in his story 'The Monk', where they stayed until the end of the year. It is understood that Papadiamandis seriously considered joining a monastery at that time but he nevertheless returned once more to his island. The following year, after taking preliminary examinations, he was enrolled in the fourth class of the Varvakeio gymnasium of Athens from which he graduated in 1874, and then registered at the Philosophical School of the University of Athens. He attended the university for two years and one of his professors remarked on him being regularly present at lectures, but he was never to obtain his degree. It was during this period that his cousin, Alexandros Moraïtidis, introduced him into various journalistic circles.

In 1877 he was recruited into the army in which he briefly served until being given a deferment as a student even though he was no longer attending the university but struggling to earn a living as a journalist and writer. Papadiamandis experienced great economic difficulties during this period and frequently had to ask for money from his father.

Following the recommendation of one of his new journalistic acquaintances, Vlasios Gavrielidis, Papadiamandis's first novel, a work of some 50,000 words entitled *The Migrant*, was printed in instalments in the Constantinopolitan newspaper *Neologos* in 1879. He was conscripted again in September of 1880, served until July of the following year, and not long after being released from the army his first literary work to be published in Greece, a poem entitled 'Supplication', appeared. A year later a more substantial second novel, *The Merchants of the Nations*, began to be published, again in instalments, in the Athenian newspaper *Mi Hanesai*, and at the same time Papadiamandis started to work as a translator for the *Ephimeris* newspaper. Two years later, in 1884, his longest novel, *The Gypsy Girl*, a work of more than 130,000 words, was published in Gavrielidis's newspaper, *The Acropolis*, and the following year his novel *Christos Milionis* was printed in the literary journal *Estia*.

It wasn't, however, until Christmas of 1887 that Papadiamandis's first short story, 'The Christmas Loaf', was to appear, marking the feast and setting a pattern for his writing. The métier of the short story subsequently became his favoured form, and no doubt it was an easier form for him to accommodate within his inordinately long working days at various newspapers. Many of these hours were spent in translating major European novels, such as *Crime and Punishment, Quo Vadis, Dracula,* and *The Manxman,* which appeared in daily instalments, as well as numerous short stories by such writers as Chekhov, Bret Harte and Jerome K. Jerome, in addition to translating works of non-fiction. He relieved the incredible strain he subjected himself to by frequenting wine shops and chain-smoking but these all too human habits did not prevent him from regularly attending church services in which he acted as chanter and beadle.

It was also in 1887 that he found what could be described as his spiritual bolt-hole in the turbulent and often harsh world of the metropolis: the small church of the Prophet Elisha, set in the courtyard of a private house in the old part of the city, under the rock of the Acropolis. There *Papa*-Nikolaos Planas, a simple priest born in the same year as Papadiamandis, a man of prayer and of great spiritual gifts, would regularly hold vigil services, gathering people from all walks of life into the crucible of the little church. *Papa*-Nikolaos was canonized in 1992.

Papadiamandis never married. He was a shy and retiring man, as the few extant photographs of him testify, a man seemingly not of this world despite his acute observations of it. He also had to provide for his unmarried sisters at home. But despite his introspective nature he had a small circle of close friends, including Pavlos Nirvanas and Yannis Vlachoyannis, well-known Athenian men of letters who on various occasions undertook the role of literary agents and helped him during hard times.

Except for two years when he returned to Skiathos, 1902–4, during which time he wrote his perhaps most powerful tale,

The Murderess, a short novel about an old woman who thought it better to kill female infants so they should not have to endure the tribulations that life brings upon women, he continued to live in Athens, writing and translating, until 1908. That year, in March, the Parnassos Literary Society held an event in his honour under the patronage of Princess Maria Bonaparte; typically, Papadiamandis was not present and spent the evening dining with the family of his grocer friend. But despite this recognition and the popularity of his stories, it would seem that none of his own writing was published in book form during his lifetime.

Shortly afterwards he returned to Skiathos where he lived from then on, cared for in turn by his sisters. In the winter of 1910 he fell ill with a severe chest infection, and died on 2nd January 1911 after having chanted the *tropárion* of the forthcoming feast of Epiphany.

INTRODUCTION

THE SHORT STORIES OF ALEXANDROS PAPADIAMANDIS are graced with an almost indefinable quality common to all great writers. This quality would seem to derive from an enthralment combined with a certain perplexity, an irresistible pull exerted by the author's descriptions of a world of beauty and marvels which at the same time is filled with predicaments, human tragedies and humble triumphs. Like his contemporaries in the great European tradition of story-telling, Papadiamandis explores the souls of men and women as they succumb to or struggle against the power of evil — the Raskolnikovs, the Uriah Heeps and the Kareninas — people living on the edge of their capacity to deal with evil and who are tragically driven, by an irrational process, to the extremes of human vulnerability.

Papadiamandis knew this European tradition intimately, learning his craft while translating many of the major authors of his time — Dostoyevsky, Chekhov, de Maupassant and Alphonse Daudet — as well as some of the minor literary figures, including Bram Stoker, Hall Caine, Bret Harte, Georges Ohnet,[1] and although he himself objected to it, he was even compared by some of his contemporaries to Edgar Allan Poe and Charles Dickens, most likely because of the tragic tenor of his work and his habit of marking Christmas and Easter by turning out a seasonal story. His literary field of reference, however, extended far beyond the nineteenth century and along with Homer,

---

[1] Lakis Proguidis, in his *La conquête du roman — de Papadiamantis à Boccace* (Paris: Les Belles Lettres, 1997), places the work of Papadiamandis in the European tradition and convincingly argues in favour of his undisputed place among the literary giants of the West. Mohammed Dib argues along the same lines in *Simorgh* (Paris: Albin Michel, 2003), pp. 239–47.

Plato and Hesiod he also drew on Dante and Shakespeare, easily integrating scenes and passages from their works into his writing.

Papadiamandis lived in the midst of an uncertain age of transition. Born in the middle of the nineteenth century (1851) in a period of post-Enlightenment turmoil and a generation after Greece's War of Independence (1821–32), his reflections on and observations of Greek life in both his native island of Skiathos and in urban Athens continue, almost a century after his death, to define the modern Greek experience in a way unattained by any of his now forgotten contemporaries.

The century that separates today's reader from the world of Papadiamandis has brought a radical transformation in the political, social and religious landscape of the world he describes. This complex landscape has undergone so many changes during the past hundred years that the way people inhabited it and related to one another, to the objects that surrounded them and to the animals and inanimate things that defined it — all of which he describes so compellingly — has utterly disappeared or has been transformed out of all recognition. These changes inevitably influence the way we view his world, a world which no longer exists. The attentive reader will realize, however, that this is not solely due to a temporal distance: Papadiamandis himself was also alienated from the literary and religious establishments of his day. Several of his stories reveal his rejection of the conventional assumptions of his time concerning such events as the liberation of Greece from the Turks, the reign of the Bavarian regent, Otho, the ideological alignment with the West, the revival of the Olympic Games, or social idées reçues like the position of unmarried women.

Nevertheless one cannot simply assert that Papadiamandis was as much misunderstood and misinterpreted in his day as he appears to have been in our times. In recent years he has acquired both enthusiasts and detractors, each group of critics focusing on its own area of interest, dividing, as it were, the seamless garment of his work into reductive, conflicting pieces, none of which fit or do justice to the whole fabric of his vision. Separated from the whole, each becomes a caricature. He has been claimed by the religious establishment as one of their own, hailed by the social ethnographers as a natural if not instinctive folklorist, decried by the Greek modernists as a reactionary, and remains a scandal to both sides of the purist versus the demotic language question.[1] Papadiamandis resists all such facile or narrow classifications.

To be more specific, the religious establishment in Greece appropriated him as its literary spokesman, ostensibly because his work so clearly expresses an unshakeable faith in a living God and in the Orthodox ecclesiastical tradition, but seemingly disregarding the fact that Papadiamandis frequently, and in no uncertain terms, criticized representatives of the religious hierarchy and exposed their uncharitable behaviour and their hypocrisy. Similarly, his detailed and realistic depiction of country life, especially of his native island Skiathos, earned him the now somewhat stereotypical designation of 'folk-chronicler', a sort of literary ethnologist[2] recording

[1] The language question was officially sanctioned as a national issue after the creation of the modern Greek state following the 1821 War of Independence from the Turks. Ironically, it was Adamandios Koraïs, a philologist living in Paris and a fervent spokesman for the introduction of the ideas of the Enlightenment in the nascent state of Greece, who promoted the idea of purifying the language from vulgar words and expressions, with a view to correcting the colloquial speech of the people so they could conform to the noble image of their ancestors; for Koraïs believed that the modern Greeks were the descendants of their ancient compatriots. This initiated the movement for the 'purist' language, *katharévousa*. The populist movement on the other hand espoused the language of the people, *demotikí*, in which it discerned a living source of pure linguistic forms and poetic sensitivity. It was this language that was taken up by the national poet Dionysios Solomos, who admirably expressed its merits as a medium for revealing the truths inherent in the worldview of the Greek people. The language debate continued until the final decades of the twentieth century.

[2] 'Literary ethnologist' renders the untranslatable Greek term *ethográphos*, which has been borrowed by the discipline of folkloric studies. *Éthoi* and *éthima* describe the popular customs related to the religious and social practices accompanying great events in the cycle of life — birth, baptism, marriage, death, religious celebrations — as well as other practices related to festive occasions, various occupations and professions, etc.

a former way of life that is irrelevant to contemporary reality, yet Papadiamandis wrote his stories long before the academic discipline of *Laographía*, the equivalent of folkloric studies, was inaugurated and established in Greece by its founding father Nikolaos Politis. Furthermore, his loving attachment to the old ways that even in his own time were fast disappearing, and his dislike of the indiscriminate adoption of western mores and ideas by an intellectual élite largely alienated from this living past, inevitably marked him out as an austere, even reactionary, conservative. This was confirmed in the eyes of his detractors by his unwavering use of an innovative form of language, a very personal and creative blend of classical, medieval and modern idioms which did not conform to the accepted norms on either side of the purist/populist Greek language question.

The glib appreciation of his work as 'religious' implied that it was endemically limited, its message irrelevant to the social and ideological complexities of the times. The 'ethnographic' label reduced it to a repository of exotic descriptions of rural lore and the superstitious beliefs of simple country people, and, therefore, unrelated to the complex challenges presented by modern life. And in the twentieth century, these factors, together with his refusal to espouse the cause of either the purists or the populists over the language question and including his indifference if not outright hostility to the ideological currents of his time and his distaste for the trend-setting intellectual milieu, led influential Greek critics to classify his work as insignificant, poor in conception and execution, and peopled with unconvincing, roughly-sketched characters, all expressed in an outmoded language. This simplistic adumbration, the result of an ideologically-motivated evaluation of Papadiamandis and his work, was epitomized by the critical work of Constantine T. Dimaras and persisted well into the 1960s.[1] Even when his work

---

[1] See *A History of Modern Greek Literature* (London: University of London Press, 1974), pp. 389–93.

was not dismissed outright, it was accorded only grudging respect, valuable for historians or folklorists as a source of knowledge about the otherwise dark past associated with the period of Turkish rule, the vanishing details of which should be treated with the same dignity paid to a corpse before it is committed to the earth.

These ill-conceived notions reveal more about particular contemporary intellectual or ideological views of Greece's past than of the past itself, and bear no relation to Papadiamandis's understanding of life and of how the spirit of the past breathes life into the present. This understanding was certainly not shared by most of his critics who, in his own words, were 'grazing on the scarred and wounded body of the East' ('The Monk'), and who, rather than recovering the inner life of the past, concerned themselves with dismantling and deconstructing both the past and what it stood for. Some isolated voices were heard, *clamantes in deserto*, in defense of Papadiamandis's work and protesting against the sarcophagos to which it had been consigned. The renowned twentieth-century poets Angelos Sikelianos and George Seferis spoke in different ways about the inner force of his writing and alluded to its timeless message. Nevertheless, although they both devoted extensive studies to other representatives of the modern Greek spirit, they did not deem Papadiamandis worthy of more than a few passing remarks, however respectful.

In the 1960s, the reductive labelings and limiting assumptions of both the admirers and the critics of Papadiamandis were disputed by a seminal short essay on Papadiamandis written by Zissimos Lorenzatos (1915–2004), a remarkable essayist who interpreted Greek letters in a new light. By placing Papadiamandis's writing in its true context and challenging its critics' preconceptions, Lorenzatos roused a new interest and appreciation of his work. 'We must decide seriously at some stage what we are going to do with Papadiamandis. At the moment, everyone acknowledges or accepts him, and no one wants anything to do with him. The Greeks do not want him as a spiritual guide, and the Christians scarcely want him as one of their number.'[1] The old arguments had run their course; the way for the *apokatátasis* — the restitution — of Papadiamandis had finally been opened.

In the 1970s, several studies were published that set about removing much of the critical clutter that had obscured his writings and which engaged in an authentic debate about the nature of his work.[2] Lorenzatos continued to pave the way by initiating and supporting the concerted effort that led to the first critical edition of Papadiamandis's *Collected Works*. Edited by Nikos D. Triandaphyllopoulos, and published with loving and meticulous care by Dimitris Mavropoulos of Domos Publications, it was completed in 1988.[3] This was followed by an unprecedented number of studies on all aspects of his work. An annual periodical devoted to his writings, *Ta Papadiamandiká Tetrádia* [*Papadiamandian Notebooks*], was established soon after. In 1977 the first English translation of his famous novella, *The Murderess*, was published, followed by another translation in 1983, and then in 1987 a selection of his short stories appeared in English.[4] The first international conference devoted to his work was held, appropriately, on his native island of Skiathos in September 1991.

*   *   *

[1] Zissimos Lorenzatos, *The Drama of Quality. Selected Essays*, translated by Liadain Sherrard (Limni: Denise Harvey, 2000), p. 20. In another 1960s essay, Lorenzatos states: 'Of all the Greek poets who have appeared until now, it is only with Solomos that one can spend a whole lifetime. Among the prose writers, the same can be said of Papadiamandis.' *The Lost Center and Other Essays on Greek Poetry*, translated by Kay Cicellis (Princeton: Princeton University Press, 1980), p. 84.

[2] This remarkable journey is meticulously explored and recorded by G. Farinou-Malamatari in her Introduction to the collected articles: *Eisagogí stin Pezographía tou Papadiamándi* [*Introduction to the Prose-writings of Papadiamandis*], edited G. Farinou-Malamatari (Herakleion: University of Crete Publications, 2005).

[3] Alexandros Papadiamandis, *Apanta*, 5 vols. (Athens: Domos Publications, 1981–88).

[4] *The Murderess*, translated by George X. Xanthopoulides (London and Athens: Doric Publications / Kathimerini); *The Murderess*, translated by Peter Levi (New York and London: Writers and Readers); *Tales from a Greek Island*, translated, with an introduction, by Elizabeth Constantinidis (Baltimore: The John Hopkins University Press).

Philip Sherrard's English translation of Papadiamandis's character-istically poignant tale of the loss of life mourned by the fallen world, 'The Seal's Lament', appeared in 1964. It was included in an anthology of texts celebrating the spiritual topography of an un-known Greece,[1] as explored by Sherrard, that original Hellenist who, by that time, had made his home in a remote part of Euboea, near the small port of Limni. It was there that I was summoned im-mediately after the 1991 conference, and the plans for an English edition of Papadiamandis's work were hatched with Philip and his wife Denise. Sherrard's enthusiasm for Papadiamandis matched the zeal of his friend Lorenzatos. At his request, Triandaphyllopoulos had already drawn up a list of stories suitable for translation. At that meeting, we resolved to present translations of Papadiaman-dis's most representative writings in three volumes, with the hope that the English reader might be offered a new understanding of the ever-changing Greek experience.

We combed the *Collected Works* with a view to assembling what we thought would be a representative anthology, one that would do justice to Papadiamandis's vision of a Greek way of life as revealed in the stories set both in his native island and in the ur-ban environment of Athens. They had to be stories which would be meaningful to an English reader without compromising the author's personal style. Moreover, they had to encompass the universal themes that best exemplify his work, recreating the Greek experi-ence as lived and explored from many perspectives: displacement, emigration, home-coming, estrangement, exile, attempts to reclaim lost innocence, visions of Paradise. His leitmotifs also encompassed the mythic past as it survived through the belief in supernatural wonders and animated the countryside with haunted ruins, nymphs and fairies, and the sea with mermaids and Tritons; themes dealing with the power of evil, the dark forces of cruelty,

---

[1] *The Pursuit of Greece, An Anthology*, selected by Philip Sherrard (London: John Murray, 1964; reprinted Limni: Denise Harvey, 1987).

beatific sainthood, urban loneliness, the fragmentation of a homogeneous world shattered by the adoption of foreign customs; the worship of new idols, the introduction of new values. We believed that these universal themes are invested with a natural propensity to move the modern reader and so compel him to consider their counterparts and ramifications within his own tradition in a different light. Lorenzatos's advice was solicited as well as that of Triandaphyllopoulos's, and after a few weeks we had four lists with mostly overlapping choices. Thereafter, it was not difficult to reach a consensus with regard to the final selection.

It was decided to present the stories chronologically but in spite of that stricture all the themes of that original selection decided upon so many years ago are present in this first volume. There are Christmas and Easter stories; a tale of displacement and alienation experienced by a young student, ironically unfolding on the last night of Carnival; a personal tragedy of loss and exile seen through the eyes of a monk who has abandoned his monastery to live as a stranger in a world that cannot contain him; details from the lives of the seafaring islanders and their fascinating, long-forgotten rites at the launching of a new ship — all these elements still reflect the inner life of a 'modern' Greece in search of its soul. With an innate sense of what is happening around him, Papadiamandis grounds his stories in the realization that something irretrievable is in the process of being lost or has already been lost. While everyone is preoccupied with new distractions, adopting ways that have not been tested and unravelling what has taken centuries of spiritual evolution to achieve, the close-knit sense of community of country life and the relationship with another reality is being destroyed. This profound loss encompassed spiritual, social and political implications. With the creation of the modern Greek state, what was gained by the liberation from the Turks was lost in the new order that accompanied the Bavarian regency. It ushered in a highly centralized, impersonal, western style of government that soon replaced the local independent and autonomous administration of neighbourhoods and communities radiating from the nucleus of church and parish life. This bureaucratic process was democratically enforced through the new phenomenon of state-run elections. Papadiamandis went so far as to question even the most nationalistic assumptions of the modern Greek state and intimated, with a subtle sense of irony, that there was little difference between the former domination of the Greeks by the Turks and the present liberation imposed upon them by the Bavarians. 'Ah, the elections! This has been our sole preoccupation for the past seventy years since we have been liberated, that is, since we exchanged tyrants, whom we believe we may replace even more frequently by the means of elections...' ('My Saint George').[1] In the face of this erosion of the spiritual and social elements which held his world together, Papadiamandis holds up the image of another reality, manifested in a belief that this world is grounded in the supernatural world and taking tangible form in the worship of God and His saints, and which relates human beings to their saintly counterparts and every temporal or material aspect of their earthly existence to the eternal.

Papadiamandis believed that the only unifying principle capable of counteracting the erosion taking place in the natural world was the Church. He saw the Church from the traditional Greek Orthodox point of view as an image of the Kingdom of God, recreated on earth in the festal cycle of the Church's liturgical year. As a living reality providing a foretaste of the Kingdom of Heaven here on earth, the Church is not solely a manifestation of metaphysical ideas; it is the living Body of Christ. The priests who appear so frequently in the stories are fully integrated into the life of the community; they are married and must look after their large families; they lead ordinary, if not mundane lives within that society; they carry out the given ecclesiastical rites and together with their flock form a cohesive, homogeneous body. Like shepherds, they lead their parishioners

---

[1] *Apanta*, op. cit., vol. 5, p. 191.

through valleys, over mountains, on perilous voyages in stormy seas, in order to reach a deserted country chapel and revive it by celebrating a liturgy, in the company of goatherds and illiterate chanters who recite the sacred texts as well as their flawed memories permit. These priests are not hermits, meditating alone in their cells; rather, their mission in life is to merge with that of the people, to give life to the community, to keep alive the memory of places threatened by extinction, to be witnesses to that unified reality which animates everything with the living breath of the Holy Spirit. The liturgy, the consummation of the eucharistic unity of the Church's flock — the work of the people — is never, as it often seems to be in western religious practice, a private matter between the priest and God: it must involve all the participants, as they clean and prepare the sanctuary and the church, light the fires that will keep all warm during the long night vigils, lay out the liturgical vessels, chant the necessary hymns and responses, and, finally, partake of a common meal, an indispensable component of the liturgy, drinking and eating with hearty rejoicing.

All the elements that contribute to the physical manifestation of the supernatural reality of this liturgical, sacramental, ever-present 'now', as recorded by Papadiamandis, survive in these sacred rites. They include pagan beliefs from a remote past, supernatural stories and fairy-tales that have been transmitted orally for generations and retold in the very places whence they arose; magic incantations, spells and charms that have even crept into liturgical practices and now form a seamless whole preserved within the life of the Church. The natural world forms a living part of the liturgical 'now'. The spirits of the past lurk and hide everywhere, the elements acquire an other-worldly aura: the moon, the stars, the Pleiades casting their faint light over the sea in the depth of the night; a rock emerging from the waters like a mysterious human figure; the translucent daylight, the animals, trees assuming the form of the nymph who inhabits them, the fruits of the earth, and a myriad of natural phenomena, are all transformed in the liturgical cosmos of Papadiamandis. These are so vividly described that it becomes possible to behold in nature the sacred, indelible stamp of the Creator, whose life-giving breath moves the natural world, both pagan and Christian, towards its eternal source.

If Papadiamandis insists on an elaborate description of the rites associated with this life, most of them of an ecclesiastical nature, it is not because he delights in recording forgotten or quaintly irrelevant rituals, but because he perceives them as the authentic expression of a collective practice that providentially unites earthly life with heavenly realities into which the people can still pour their souls and through which they can declare their instinctive desire for a traditional way of life. Whenever this sense of the breath of the Holy Spirit ceases to be acknowledged as the source of life, everything begins to disintegrate and is threatened with extinction, as described in the tragic story of 'Civilization in the Village'. Here the new ways that have been introduced into the island are the indirect cause of killing off, in an almost demonic way, its hope for the future — its children.

Papadiamandis was well aware of the universal presence and power of evil and knew that by no means can one attribute all ills to the advent of the new mores. In his determination to explore the dark depths of the human soul and its capacity for sin in the absence of God, he reveals the universal human predicament in the lives of the people and the social order that he depicts, a literary achievement far beyond mere descriptions of a traditional way of life. Nor does he espouse the heedless idealization of traditional rural customs offered by many of his contemporaries who excelled in ethnographic descriptions of country life, tinged with local colour. According to Papadiamandis, there are vestiges of human paganism that remain unredeemed by Christianity, just as there are ancient spirits lurking in the natural world. 'One touch of nature makes the whole world kin.'[1] It is interesting to note that all the heinous acts in his stories occur in the idyllic setting of Skiathos, while almost

---

[1] Shakespeare, *Troilus and Cressida*, III, iii, 176–9.

no crime is committed in the urban environment of alienation that one would more typically associate with Athens.

Papadiamandis's insistence on an authentic expression of reality — *that which we have heard, which we have seen with our eyes, which we have looked upon, and our hands have handled* [1] — extends equally to the way he presents and describes characters, events, landscapes, the ever-changing sea, a newly-launched tall ship or a run-down boat. His characters emerge from the narrative as they *are*, not as they ought to be; they merge with life rather than imposing themselves on it; they are not subjected to ethical scrutiny, neither are they judged according to their merits or failures. Their greatest worth is their humanity. They are at one with their environment: in village and city, in Skiathos and in Athens, whether they are transversing the seas of the Aegean or braving the whims of wind and wave in little boats, they are natural extensions of the world they inhabit, necessarily involved in the ebb and flow of good and evil, the constant flux of life and death. They live, they do not simply cope with life. They assume fully their commitment to life, knowing with resigned equanimity that they must be subjected to both good fortune and calamity.

It is fair to say that the growing contemporary preoccupation with and re-evaluation of the work of Papadiamandis convey a measure of its relevance for our times. Nearly a century after his death (1911), his imaginative insight of the Greek way of life, his uncompromising attitude with regard to the dilemmas plaguing the newly-created nation on the threshold of modernity, his caustic humour directed against those who vitiated the traditional ways, and his unyielding defense of ancestral values and revealed truths, would seem to have been sufficient reason a generation ago to relegate him to oblivion. The enduring relevance of his work today is a living proof of the persistent significance of its message.

*   *
*

[1] 1 John 1 : 1.

When our undertaking to produce this selection of Papadiamandis's work in translation became known, several voices were raised to question the feasibility of the enterprise. The strongest challenge was voiced by those who simply declared that a translation of Papadiamandis could never convey in any other language the rich expressiveness of his personal idiom, an idiom which can not even be rendered successfully into modern Greek. It was difficult not to acknowledge the truth of these warnings. Nevertheless, a translation may aspire to be successful up to a certain point. It must make the reader forget that it is a translation and yet at the same time convey the spirit of the original. When reading a literary work one allows oneself to be guided by the author into his world and be delighted by it, and a translation may humbly set out to accomplish this much. Each translator holds a unique view of this world which is reflected through his or her translation. It is for this reason that several voices, all with their distinctive tone and timbre, were enjoined to offer their symphonic interpretation of Papadiamandis's music in harmonies which he himself had chosen: the still voice of the breeze, the divine aura of the Creator's breath emerging from the sea, echoing the celestial music of the spheres and whispering inspiring words to His creation through the soft rustling of the spring foliage of a majestic oak-tree or the sighing branches of pines over a moonlit mountain chapel, now translated in these pages for the delight of you, his reader.

This collective effort, striving to recreate in English the world of Papadiamandis, is dedicated to the memory of our friend, Philip Sherrard, who devoted his life to the interpretation of the spiritual and material unity which animated and continues to animate the world that is expressed in these pages.

Lambros Kamperidis
Montréal, May 2007

EDITORIAL NOTE

TEXTUAL REFERENCES, words requiring a short explanation for the understanding of the text and points raised by Papadiamandis himself are given as footnotes. Longer exegetical remarks on terms, events, traditions, etc., are given in the Endnotes and are indicated by an asterisk. In some instances these notes are quite extensive and have been written for the purpose of providing a key for decoding a cryptic narrative in the absence of which certain aspects of a story may be obtuse.

Scriptural quotations are from the King James version of the Bible. Greek words in italics in the text refer the reader to the Glossary.

With regard to proper names, several translators opted to retain the Greek prefixes that are often attached to them and whose meaning can be easily inferred, such as *Kyr*-Margaritis, *Kyrá*-Kostaina, *Pápa*-Dimitris, *Bárba*-Stephanis. These forms of address are closely bound up with the names of the characters and express a combination of respect, endearment, intimacy and often irony, which is not always conveyed by their formal English counterparts of mister, missus, father, or uncle. For example, although *bárba* loosely means uncle, it is untranslatable in English since originally it indicated the venerable standing of the bearer of that title: *bárba* comes from the Italian for beard, and a person of venerable standing, in traditional societies, wore a beard. Women are usually, but not always, referred to by the feminine rendering of their husband's name, thus, *Kyrá*-Kostaina is *Kyr*-Kostas's wife. Many of the men's surnames, especially those of the islanders, can also be read in the Greek as nicknames, for instance, Yannis Ladikas as Yannis the Oil-can and Konstantos Z'marohaftis as Konstantos the Dough-scoffer (literally, someone who likes to eat uncooked dough). Given, however, that these names are mostly untranslatable it is virtually impossible to convey in English this Greek penchant for nicknames, one that still continues today in Greece, and for this reason they have, with an occasional exception, been kept as they are in the Greek.

Toponyms have mostly been rendered as in the original except for instances when the meaning of the toponym is relevant to the understanding of the story. For example, Treis Stavroi in 'Poor Saint' is translated as Three Crosses.

Monetary units as well as weights and measures present a certain difficulty. In the old Europe of the imperial powers the krone (*koróna*), franc (*fránko*, and *napoleónio fránko*), sterling pound (*líra*), the German *taler*, from which derive the dollar and the Greek *táliro*, and the Austrian *zwanziger* (*svánziko*) were in common use and all of them are used by Papadiamandis in his stories. Had he wished to be consistent he would have been so, but he is not because all these monetary units were circulating widely and were being constantly handled by the ever-moving Greek merchants of the time, who ploughed the European and the Levantine waterways with their ships, venturing as far as America and Africa, and who were confident in exchanging foreign currencies for the needs of their trade. The same can be said about weights and measures.

Accents indicating where the stress falls in Greek proper names and words have not been used in the translations so as not to detract from the flow of the text when it is read, but for clarity and scholarly reasons they have been placed on Greek words in the Prelims, Endnotes and Glossary. Some seeming inconsistencies in the transliteration of Greek words into English are due to preferences for certain established forms or because it was felt enriching to emphasize the relationship of Greek words with English. For example, the double consonant 'nt' in the Greek spelling of Papadiamandis is rendered as 'nd' not only because it is pronounced as such but also to indicate its connection with the word 'diamond'.

The five-volume critical edition of Papadiamandis's complete works, edited by N. D. Triandaphyllopoulos and referred to in the Introduction, was used for the translations. This present volume contains translations of his short stories only as they are most representative of Papadiamandis's oeuvre and comprise the major part of his output. They are presented in chronological order and span the years 1888 to 1893. In addition to further selections of his stories it is hoped that translations of his longer works in the form of the novel, such as *The Rose-tinted Shores* and *The Watchman at the Quarantine Colony*, may follow in the future.

THE STORIES

HANDMAIDEN

A CHRISTMAS STORY

O N CHRISTMAS EVE OF THE YEAR ____, Diomas's eighteen-
year-old daughter, Ouranio, a comely, dark-haired girl, shut
herself in her house early because she was alone.

Her father, the unlucky *Barba*-Diomas, an ancient, bankrupt,
merchant sea-captain, who had been reduced to plying a small boat
in his old age, had set off in his dinghy at about noon for the island
of Tsoungria, three miles distant, to convey various goods from
there for the festive town. He had promised that he would return
towards evening, but night had fallen and still he had not appeared.

The young girl's mother had died. Her only aunt on her mother's
side used to keep her company at one time, for their adjoining houses
were separated by the same wall, but she had fallen out with her
over half an acre of land and they no longer spoke to each other. The
girl sat next to the fire which she had lit in the hearth, waiting for
her father, her ears strained to catch every sound, to the merry songs
of the children in the street, impatient and uneasy about when her
father would come.

The hours passed, and there was no sign of the impoverished old
man. Ouranio had decided not to go to bed but to stay as she was,
half leaning against the fireplace.

Midnight came and the church bells began to ring out, calling
Christians to the joyful festal service. The girl's heart froze inside her.

'Midnight has passed,' she said, 'and my father . . . '

At that same moment she heard a disturbance and voices outside.
The neighbourhood had woken up and everyone was getting ready
for church. The unhappy Ouranio could hardly bear it, but she summoned up the courage to go out onto the enclosed wooden porch of

3

the house and, hidden in the dark, peeked out of the doorway.

A garrulous and loud-mouthed neighbour had emerged first and her shouting, as she attempted to wake up her husband and children, had roused all those in the vicinity who had not been woken by the clanging of the bells. Her husband, Daradimos, needed a crow-bar to get him onto his feet. The door of their house was opposite that of *Barba*-Diomas's. Ouranio saw the woman clearly, straight across from her, holding a lantern, which was compassionately lighting the dark street for passers-by and neighbours. For it was very dark, and a light wind was blowing from the snow-covered mountains just enough to transmit their chill and ice into people's veins.

At that moment someone passed by and on recognizing him it was impossible for Ouranio not to smile.

'What! Argyrakis is going to church . . . ,' she murmured.

Garophalia's Argyrakis, who had the distinction of being identified by his wife's name, had once said — and his words had become legendry — 'whenever I go to church they give out palm branches'. But this time Garophalia had woken him violently and ordered him to church because she said she'd had a bad dream. Opposite their little house were five or six huts of newly-baptized gypsies, and she was frightened that perhaps the gypsies had worked some sorcery against her. And, God forbid, if anything happened to her, who else in the neighbourhood would fire the bread-oven in the coming days, 'now on St Basil's day',[1] and after? Her whole person reminded one of that mother of the Forty Dragons in the fairy tale who stoked the fire with her bare hands and swabbed the floor of the oven with her breasts.*

The docile Argyrakis, who reached just to her shoulders, got up, put on his sailor's cap, girded himself with his red sash that was three times the width of the palm of his hand, slipped his feet into his shoes, and went out into the street.

Daradimos also came out at the same moment and began to talk to Garophalia's Argyrakis.

---

[1] The feast of St Basil is on New Year's day.

4

'Now I like you, neighbour,' he said to him. 'You mustn't be unchurched because it's *dish on a bull* (dishonourable). It isn't as if the moon is *fool abed* (full-orbed) so as to make you scared of your own shadow at night. . . .'

Such was the way Daradimos spoke Greek.

'What's to be done, neighbour, I'll be bound,' answered the humble Argyrakis.

And Daradimos, preceded by his wife who was still holding the lantern, went down to the road.

Then casting an expressive glance at *Barba*-Diomas's house, Daradimos's wife said: 'We don't know, I suppose, if our neighbour's come back.'

'Be quiet!' said Argyrakis, putting his finger to his lips. 'It's said he went down. . . .'

'What!' said Daradimos's wife.

Argyrakis was about to tell how and where he'd learnt it but at that moment a rending and heart-breaking shriek came from the silent house towards which the three speakers were looking. From the covered porch the wretched Ouranio had heard Argyrakis's words and had cried out.

The hard-hearted aunt, who for years had not said good morning to her niece, heard the pitiable cry and forgetting the half acre of land ran to help the suffering girl.

* * *

Towards noon of that day, the luckless *Barba*-Diomas had put on his ancient, straight-sided fez and pulled it down to his ears, donned his jacket and thick, felt breeches, went down to the sea-front, untied the small, insubstantial, rotting dinghy, and taking up the oars set out towards the most southerly laying islet of Tsoungria.

Ouranio stayed alone in the house, and alone *Barba*-Diomas — both seaman and skipper as well as boatswain — embarked in his boat.

A mariner from the age of twelve, *Barba*-Diomas had plied schooners, clippers and brigs, had later gone on to sailing a sloop, and had ended up as master of this small boat used for short fishing or ferrying trips. Furthermore, whatever had remained from his labours had been consumed by friends, they also having come to grief in their shipping enterprises. The only thing left to him in his old age was his iron-like health, thanks to which he could still work for his daily bread and endure the hardships of the sea.

Now and then, in the absence of someone to speak to, he told his grievances to the winds and the waves.

'I went then to Athens, to that 'miralty place,' he said, 'and they gave me two doss'ers to take to the 'ospital, to go before the Committee; and I went before the Committee, one doctor pronounced me sound, another disabled, even they didn't know... Later I went back to the Ministry, and they tell me, "Take yourself off home and we'll send you your pension." I get up, I leave, I come here, I wait, a month goes by, the papers come to the harbour-master's telling me, he says, to go back to Athens — they need to see me again. I scrounged thirty drachmas from a neighbour because I didn't have enough for the boat ticket, went back to Athens, winter it was; for ten days they made my life difficult, sending me from the Ministry to the 'miralty, and from the 'miralty to the 'ospital; later they tell me, "Off you go, and a decision will be made." I get up, I leave, I return home, I wait ... "Did you see a pension?" (addressing the hypothetical listener). "As much you did, so did I." And so I got my 'Andmaiden, and try to earn a living.' ('Andmaiden, or Handmaiden, was the name he had given to the dinghy.) And ceasing his monologue he started to sing in his rough and monotonous voice:

My tortured body! tormented youth!...

and said no more.

*   *   *

Drawing alongside the pleasant isle of Tsoungria, Barba-Diomas loaded on to his 'Handmaiden' five or six pairs of chickens, some baskets of eggs and cheese, two or three turkey-cocks, and some other items, and was getting ready to cast off the dinghy's moorings and set off. But at that moment his kinsman, Statharos, who herded the sheep on Tsoungria, arrived and begged him to do him the favour of taking on board a troublesome sailing companion, a *foal of an ass*[1] ready for breaking into harness, and to transport it to one of his numerous kin in the town.

Barba-Diomas considered the weight and threw a perplexed glance at the narrow and flimsy 'Handmaiden', but on the other hand he thought that the one drachma, the freightage for the foal, was not a negligible sum for him — it was tobacco and wine for the three non-working days of the Christmas holiday — and he decided to take it on.

His kinsman Statharos gratefully offered him a few eggs and a *myzithra* cheese, and *Barba*-Diomas loaded on the foal, took up his oars, and turned the prow towards the harbour.

At some distance out he hoisted the sail, and, after covering more than a mile, was about halfway between Tsoungria and the town. Although the wind was the Graios, the nor'wester,* it assisted the sail from the side for *Barba*-Diomas had set the dinghy on a north-westerly course. But the foal, which had grazed peacefully on grass and didn't appear to be very uneasy about the crossing, suddenly lifted a hoof and heedlessly stamped on the boards . . . and the keel of the flimsy and rotting dinghy split open.

Water began to enter the hold, the dinghy began to sink.

Quick as lightning, *Barba*-Diomas took off his heaviest garment, his reefer, which he wore only while at the tiller, leaned towards the main sheet on the left, and by hanging onto the side of the craft managed to capsize it.

Great was the lament under the overturned keel. Hens, turkey-cocks, baskets, and the cause of the disaster, the foal, all went to the bottom.

[1] Matthew 21 : 5.

Barba-Diomas, who swam like an eel, had also the overturned 'Handmaiden' to support and prevent him from sinking.

*   *   *

For about two hours *Barba*-Diomas remained laying on his stomach over the side of the craft, gripping the keel with his hands, not daring to put his full weight on the planking for the dinghy would have sunk.

Finally, at about dusk, while there was still enough light for it to be reflected by the surrounding snow-covered mountains, a sail appeared a long way off. *Barba*-Diomas began to shout with all his remaining strength.

The approaching ship was sailing under a fair wind from east to west; it was a heavily laden clipper. *Barba*-Diomas's cries went unheeded, for the wind was carrying them far to the south-west. The clipper, nevertheless, continued to approach and the small dark mass of the capsized dinghy seemed as if it were the nest of a halcyon* upon the waves.

As it came nearer, however, because the capsized vessel had been carried by the waves some tens of fathoms to the south-west, to which the old castaway had also contributed by thrashing his arms and legs, it became possible for his cries to be heard; and finally the clipper hove to and the life-boat was let down. *Barba*-Diomas heard oars splashing beside him, but that was all. Immediately afterwards he passed out. The two oarsmen hauled *Barba*-Diomas up, frozen and half dead, then lifted him on to the clipper.

After they had changed his clothes they tried to bring him back to life by breathing into his mouth and chafing his skin. The skipper ordered the prow to be turned towards the harbour so as to hand him over, dead or alive, to his family.

Eventually the poor shipwrecked man opened his eyes. The good sailors wanted to offer him punch and other warming beverages, but the first thing *Barba*-Diomas had seen when he opened his eyes were barrels: the ship was loaded with wine.

'No, not punch,' he said in a watery voice. 'Give me wine!'
The sailors brought him a flask of sweet-tasting red wine, and *Barba*-Diomas downed it in one.

* * *

Christmas Day had already dawned and the aunt was vainly trying to comfort the grief-wracked Ouranio when Daradimos's wife came in and announced that although *Barba*-Diomas had been shipwrecked he had been rescued and had returned alive and well. Argyrakis and some other villagers had, it seemed, seen the dinghy capsize far off and consequently assumed that the old man had drowned, for as night was falling they had not also seen the salvatory, wine-carrying clipper.

Barba-Diomas, arriving himself a little while after, clasped his daughter in his arms. O, the fragile but supreme happiness of the poor!

Ouranio still overflowed with tears, but with tears of joy. Her father had brought her neither eggs nor *myzithra* cheese nor hens, but his weathered and sea-beaten self and his two stalwart and horny hands that for some years yet would be able to toil for him and for her.

[1888]

Translated by Denise Harvey

THE GLEANER

A CHRISTMAS STORY

HER NEIGHBOUR ZERBINIO was most surprised that Christmas Day in 187_ when she saw Aunt Achtitsa wearing a new headscarf and both Yeros and Patrona with clean shirts and new shoes.

And rightly so, as it was very well known that Aunt Achtitsa had witnessed the sale of her daughter's dowry at public auction in order to pay off the debts of her worthless son-in-law, that she was destitute and widowed, and that she was rearing her orphaned grandchildren by resorting to odd jobs. She was one of those people who never get a lucky break. Her neighbour Zerbinio pitied the poverty of the old woman and the two orphans. But it was hardly as if she herself had the money to help them out and be their comforter.

The late *Barba*-Michalios, who had preceded his wife Achtitsa to the grave, was fortunate not to have seen the hardships that loomed after his death. He was a good soul — if only he were still alive, poor man. The two children, 'our lost ones', Yorgos and Vasilis, went down with their schooner and were drowned in the winter of 186_. The schooner was lost with all hands on board — what a tragedy, what a fate! I wouldn't wish such a dreadful thing on any good Christian woman.

Her third son, the idler, the good-for-nothing, went abroad and was living, they said, in America. He had shaken the dust from his feet. Had anyone seen him, or heard from him? Some fellow countrymen claimed that he had married in those parts and had taken, it was said, a Frankish bride, an English-speaking girl, a stranger, who did not know a word of Greek. What worse fate! But what can

10

you do? Can you curse your child, your own flesh and blood?

Her daughter died giving birth to a second child, leaving Achtit-sa to inherit two orphans. Their poor excuse for a father was still alive (how far could his endless demands go?), but, really, what a head of family, what a lazy good-for-nothing! A card-player, a drunk, and with still other virtues to boot. Rumour had it that he remarried elsewhere, in order to drag down yet another family, the scoundrel! Such men!... She'd found a husband alright, but what a husband! (a curse on his head!)...

What else could she do? She pushed herself as hard as she could, trying to make a living for the orphans. How pitiable, the poor things! Depending on the season, she collected herbs, pruned vines, picked olives, worked as a day labourer. She gathered arbutus berries to make *raki*. Some scrapings from the pressed grapes here, some maize husks there, everything was used. Then in October, once the olive presses opened, she took a fifty-dram tin scoop and a small jug and went around to the reservoirs where the dregs were deposited and gathered the oil from the sediment. By this means she saved enough oil for her lantern to last a year.

But Aunt Achtista derived her primary income from gleaning corn. Every year in June she took a boat, set sail and crossed over to Euboea. She endured the scornful name 'boat-woman' which other women hurled at her because it was still considered a disgrace for a woman to travel by sea. There, along with the other poor women, she gathered the wheat that had fallen from the sheaves of the harvesters, from the loading of the carts. Year after year, the peasants of Euboea and their womenfolk mocked them to their faces: 'Hey! Here come those skirts! The skirts are back again!'[1]

But she would bend down patiently, quietly, pick up the fallen grains of Euboea's rich harvest, fill three or four bags, an entire year's supply for herself and the two orphans, whom she had

---

[1] The fabric of the skirts worn by the women of Skiathos was more like that of the Europeans, in contrast to the heavy traditional weaves of the Euboean women.

entrusted in the meanwhile to the care of Zerbinio, and sail back to her seaside village.

*　　*　　*

Except that this year the crops had failed in Euboea. The olives failed on the little island where Aunt Achtitsa lived. The vines failed and the maize, even the arbutus berries nearly failed, all around the crops had failed.

Then, because troubles never come singly, a heavy winter set in over those northern parts. Already from November, when the south wind had hardly begun to blow or the rains to fall, the snows came. One snowfall would stop and right away another would start up. Sometimes a dry north wind blew, packing even harder the snow, which did not melt at all on the mountains. 'More was expected.'

The old woman had just managed to transport on her back a couple of armfuls of dry wood from the ravines and woods — enough to last two or three weeks — when the heavy winter descended. Round about the middle of December there was a short break in the weather, and a few timorous rays of sun appeared, shining like gold on the higher rooftops. Aunt Achtitsa rushed out to the forest in order to bring inside some firewood while she had the chance. The next day the winter pressed in on them more bitterly. Until Christmas there was not a single fine day, no clear patch of sky to be seen, no ray of sun.

A piercing north wind, the 'snow-bringer', blew on Christmas Eve. The roofs of the houses were loaded down with packed snow. The usual street games and snowball fights had stopped. That winter was not for game-playing. Dwarf crystals hung from the roof-tiles like ripe fruit, but even the neighbourhood urchins no longer had the appetite to eat them.

On the evening of the twenty-third, Yeros had come home from school full of cheer since lessons were finishing the next day. Even before taking his school satchel from under his arm, he hungrily opened the cupboard, but found not even a crust. The old woman had gone out, perhaps to find some bread. Miserable Patrona sat slumped over near the hearth, but the hearth was cold. She poked around in the ashes, thinking in her childish simplicity (she was only four, the poor girl) that the fireplace meant warmth, even if it was not alight. But the ash was wet. Drops of water from melting snow, thanks perhaps to some secret and transient sunbeam, had leaked in through the chimney. Yeros, who was just seven, was on the verge of tears not having found anything to sate his hunger. He opened the only window, which was three spans wide. The entire house, with its low ceiling, half panelling and loft of sorts, was only about two arms' breadth in height from the floor to the ceiling.

Yeros lifted a stool onto the stone window sill, climbed up onto the stool, supported himself with his left hand on the open shutter and, reaching up daringly toward the eaves, he stretched out his right hand and broke off an icicle from the 'stalagmites' which adorned the roof. He began to suck it slowly and with pleasure, and gave one also to Patrona to eat. The poor things were starving.

*   *
*

A little while later, old Achtitsa returned carrying something wrapped up in her bosom. Yeros, recognizing from experience that his grandmother's bosom was never puffed up without reason, leapt up and ran to her breast, stuck in his hand and let out a cry of joy. That evening the good, if a little strict, grandmother had 'saved' a piece of bread — who knows how much she'd had to beg and plead for it.

But what wouldn't she do, what sacrifices wouldn't she make for the love of those two children who were hers twice over, her child's children! Still, she did not want to indulge them, to be too soft with them. She called the boy 'Yeros' because he bore the name of her real 'yeros', that is to say, 'old man', the late *Barba*-Michalios, whose name it pained her to hear and to say aloud. The hapless little girl she called by the flattering name Patrona, 'as the impoverished lady that she was', since she could not endure hearing Argyro, her daughter's name which had been bequeathed to the orphan by her mother as she lay dying after giving birth to the girl. Except for these little nicknames, she bestowed no signs of tenderness on the two poor creatures, but provided for their everyday needs and protected them as she could.

The long-suffering old woman prepared a bed for the two orphans to sleep and lying down beside them herself told them to breathe down under their blanket to keep warm. Uttering an untruth, but wishing it might be true, she promised them that the next day Christ would bring wood and bread and a kettle boiling on the fire. She lay awake until past midnight, brooding over her bitter fortune.

*   *
*

In the morning, after the Liturgy (it was Christmas Eve), the parish priest, *Papa*-Dimitris, suddenly appeared at the door of the humble dwelling:

'Glad tidings!' he addressed her with a smile.

Glad tidings indeed. Who could she expect glad tidings from?

'I received a letter for you, Achtitsa,' said the old priest, brushing the snow from his cassock and shawl.

'Come in, Master!'

'If only I had a fire,' she whispered to herself, 'or a sweet and *raki* to offer him.'

The priest climbed up the four steps and went over to sit on the stool. He reached into his cassock and pulled out a large envelope covered with a variety of official seals and postage stamps.

'A letter, you said, Father?' Achtitsa repeated, just beginning to register what the priest had said.

The letter which he had pulled out from his breast appeared to be open at one end.

'The ship arrived this morning,' the priest resumed, 'and they brought me this now, just as I was leaving church.'

And putting his hand into the envelope, he pulled out a folded paper.

'The letter is addressed to me,' he added, 'but it concerns you.'
'What, me? Me?' repeated the old woman with surprise.
Papa-Dimitris unfolded the letter.

'God saw your suffering and has sent you a little relief,' said the good priest. 'Your son has written to you from America.'

'From America? Yannis! Yannis remembered me?' the old woman cried for joy, making the sign of the cross and then adding, 'Glory be to God!'

The priest put on his glasses and began trying to read:

'It is poorly written,' he said, 'and I have a hard time reading the characters they use these days, but I will try to get the sense of it.'

And he started to read, with difficulty and much stumbling:

'*Papa*-Dimitris, I kiss your hand. First of all, I trust that you are well, etc., etc. I've been away for many years and I don't know what has happened there, whether they are alive or dead. I'm far away, deep in Panama, and have no contact with other Greeks living in America. Three years ago I met (so and so) and (so and so), but they too had been abroad for many years and had no news of my family.

'If my mother or father is alive, tell them to forgive me, because even though we always struggle for the good, often things go wrong. I twice fell seriously ill with one of the nasty infections you catch here, and I spent a lot of time in hospital. I gave all my money to the doctors and I only just escaped with my life. I was married ten years ago according to the local custom, but am now a widower, and want nothing more than to get together enough money to return home in time to receive my parents' blessing. Tell them that they shouldn't hold anything against me, for it is God's will and we can't go against it. And they shouldn't hold a grudge, since, unless God desires it, man can't get anywhere.

'I am sending you the enclosed bill of exchange written in your name, Father, for your Reverence to sign and take care to cash for my father or mother, if they are still living. If, and I dearly hope it is not so, they are dead and buried, would your Reverence be so kind as to cash it and give the money to one of my siblings, if they

15

are alive, or to a nephew, or some other poor soul. And, Father, if my parents are dead, please reserve part of the money for the forty liturgies in their memory…'*

The letter had a lot to say, but it also omitted one important thing. It did not refer to the amount of money that he intended to be cashed. Noting the omission, *Papa*-Dimitris guessed that the author of the letter had assumed through oversight that he had already specified the amount of money earlier in the letter, and considered it unnecessary to repeat it again below. For that reason he wrote simply, 'this amount'.

Achtitsa's joy was ineffable, receiving news of her son after so many years. As if it had been sleeping beneath ashes for long years, the spark of maternal love rose up to her face from deep within her and the aged, shrivelled and wrinkled visage was transformed, shining forth youth and beauty.

Even if they did not understand what had transpired, the two children, seeing their grandmother's joy, began to skip and gambol about.

* * *

Kyr-Margaritis was not principally a money changer, or lender or merchant, he was all these together.* He paid tax on one trade, but practised three.

Old Achtitsa, being in urgent need, took her son's promissory note, on which there appeared black and red characters, both typed and hand-written, about which neither the parish priest nor she knew anything, and went to the shop of *Kyr*-Margaritis.

Kyr-Margaritis took a pinch of snuff, dusted off his full breeches onto which some of it always fell, lowered his cap down to his eyebrows, put on his glasses, and began to examine the promissory note at length.

'It comes from America?' he said. 'Your son remembered you, I see. Bravo. I'm happy for you.'

Then he went on: 'It has the number 10, but I don't know in what currency, ten shillings, ten rupees, ten crowns, or ten…'

He stopped before saying 'ten pounds'.

'Let's call the teacher,' muttered *Kyr*-Margaritis, 'perhaps he will know how to read it. What language is it anyway?'

The schoolmaster, who was sitting next door watching a game of *chiamo*, was summoned and walked over to the shop of *Kyr*-Margaritis. Stiff and erect in his gait, he entered and picked up the letter, asked *Kyr*-Margaritis to lend him his glasses and began to sound out the Latin characters.

'It must be English,' he said, 'unless it is German. Where does this document come from?'

'America, Sir,' answered Aunt Achtitsa.

'America? Then it is English.'

And saying this, he tried to sound out the words 'ten pounds sterling', as it was written by hand on the cheque.

'Sterling,' he said. 'Sterling would mean *taler*, I believe. The word appears to be of this derivation,' he pronounced dogmatically.

He returned the letter to the hands of *Kyr*-Margaritis.

'That will be it, then,' he said, 'and since the number ten is written at the top of the page, it must be a promissory note for ten *talers*. But to tell you the truth, I'm not an expert in financial matters. We men of letters occupy ourselves with other things.'

And with that, since he was feeling a chill in the flagstone-paved shop of *Kyr*-Margaritis, he returned to the coffee house to warm up.

*　　*　　*

Kyr-Margaritis had started rubbing his hands and appeared to be lost in thought.

'Now then, what shall we do?' he said turning to the old woman. 'Times are hard. Business sluggish. Do I accept it and cash it for you, do I know that my money is guaranteed, or whether the bill is forged? Does one expect honesty from over there, from that lost world? All the frauds, all the counterfeiters come from there. Those vagabonds — I beg your pardon, I don't include your son — roam around for so long there in the land where the sun bakes the bread and they don't bother to send home real money, proper cash, they only send worthless scraps of paper.'

He took two turns around his enormous accounting office and said: 'And it is not a slight undertaking, I'll have you know. We are talking about ten *talers*! If I had ten *talers*, I would get married.'

Then he went on: 'But what can I say? I feel sorry for you — a good woman with those orphans to look after. I'll keep a *taler* and a half for the risks I'm running and, as for the eight and a half that remain... well, to be sure, so that you don't go looking for crowns, I'll give you five francs to make it even between us... So that makes eight and a half and five francs... Oh! and I forgot!...'

To the contrary, he had not forgotten. He had been thinking about it from the start of their conversation.

'Your late husband Michalios owed me something, I don't remember what it was just now...'

And he turned to his accounts book: 'Ah yes, and I believe your good-for-nothing son-in-law made off with two *talers* from me.'

And armed with his gigantic accounts register, he added, 'It is right and proper, after all, for me to withhold this money... however much you get, it will seem a gift from heaven to you.'

He opened the register.

The densely annotated pages of that register resembled fertile fields, rich earth. Whatever was sown therein bore fruit many times over.

It was like pruning the leaves of a sapling, each time he made an outlay of money. But the root remained underground, preparing to sprout forth again.

Straightaway *Kyr*-Margaritis located the record of the two accounts.

'Your late husband owed me nine and fifteen,' he said, 'and two *talers* borrowed and not paid back by your son-in-law, that makes...'

Taking up his pen he started to add up the amount owed and the conversion from *talers* to drachmas, and then to subtract the sum from ten French *talers*.

'So it all comes out to my giving you...,' *Kyr*-Margaritis started to say.

Just then a new figure appeared on the scene.

✳   ✳
✳

It was a merchant from Syros, on their island briefly for business. With an air of confidence and self-assurance, he strode up to the desk where *Kyr*-Margaritis stood.

'What do we have here, *Kyr*-Margaritis?... What is this?' he asked with a quick glance at the poor widow's promissory note that lay on the desk.

And then, picking it up: 'A bill of exchange for ten English pounds from America,' he said in a clear voice. 'Where did this come from? You do this sort of business too, *Kyr*-Margaritis?'

'For ten pounds!' Aunt Achtitsa repeated spontaneously, having heard the word pronounced with no uncertainty.

'Why, yes, for ten English pounds,' the businessman from Hermoupolis said again, this time turning to her. 'Is it yours perhaps?'

'Indeed.'

Usually, when Aunt Achtitsa wanted to agree with something, she always said 'yes'. But this time she herself could not quite understand how it came to her to use the more formal 'indeed', or where she found this word.

'Or is it maybe for ten napoleons?' *Kyr*-Margaritis murmured, biting his lip.

'I tell you, it is for ten English pounds,' the man from Syros repeated. 'Don't you understand?'

He took another long look at the promissory note: 'It is guaranteed money, *argent comptant*,[1] I tell you. Are you going to cash it, or shall I do it here and now?' he asked, starting to get out his purse.

'Could somebody take it for nine... French pounds,' asked *Kyr*-Margaritis, hesitating.

---

[1] In other words, 'as good as cash'.

'French? I'll take it for nine English.'

And turning the sheet of paper over, he saw the good priest's signature, checked it against the name that appeared in the text, and found it to be identical.

Then, opening his purse, he counted out into the hand of the widow Aunt Achtitsa, right before her bedazzled eyes, nine shining English pounds.

* *
*

This was how it came about that on Christmas Day the poor widow was wearing a new white headscarf and the two orphans had clean shirts on their thin frames and warm shoes on their frozen little feet.

[1889]

Translated by Elizabeth Key Fowden

A VILLAGE EASTER

MEMORIES OF CHILDHOOD

U NCLE MILIOS WAS RIGHT when he said the good Christians living outside the town might end up having to celebrate Easter that year without a liturgy. In fact no prophecy
was ever closer to fulfilment, for it almost came true twice — but
happily God made the authorities see the light, and in the end the
poor villagers, local shepherd-farmers, were judged worthy to hear
the Word of God and eat the festive eggs.

The cause of all this was the busy little coaster that (supposedly) linked those unhappy islands to the inhospitable shore opposite,
and which twice a year, when the season changed in spring or autumn, would almost invariably sink, and as often as not take the
whole crew down with it. They would then put the post of captain
up for auction, and each time some poor wretch, undaunted by the
fate of his predecessor, was found to undertake this most perilous
task. And on this occasion, at the end of March, as winter was taking its leave, the coaster had gone down again.

The parish priest, Father Vangelis, who was also the abbot (and
only monk) of the small monastic establishment of St Athanasios, had
been appointed by the bishop to take charge of the villages on the
opposite shore. Though already an old man, he would take the boat
across four times a year, during each of the main fasts,* to hear the
confessions of his unfortunate parishioners — the 'hill-people' or
'mountain-scarecrows' as they were called — and give them some spiritual instruction, before he hastened back to his monastery (if it was
during Lent) to celebrate Easter there. But that year, as we have said,
the coaster had sunk, the islands were cut off for several days, and
Father Vangelis was reluctantly obliged to stay and celebrate Easter on

the far shore of the billowing, storm-tossed sea. It seemed as though his little flock in Kalivia, whose homes clustered around the monastery of St Athanasios, would end up not having any liturgy at all.

Some of them thought they should take their wives and children down into the town, to hear the Resurrection proclaimed and attend the liturgy there, but Uncle Milios, the village elder of Kalivia, wished to celebrate Easter the way he always had; Sevenmonth (so called because he had been born premature) did not want his wife being stared at by the townspeople; and Uncle Anagnostis, an old villager who knew the Easter service by heart, but could not actually read a word of it,[1] longed to chant 'Receive the body of Christ' himself. All three insisted (and many agreed) that at all costs they must get one of the priests in town to come up to Kalivia and celebrate the liturgy for them there.

Everyone felt the best choice would be Father Kyriakos: he was not of a particularly good family (he was even related to one or two of the villagers himself) and he accepted them as they were. He was even said to have some Albanian blood in him. He certainly wasn't stand-offish — in fact it was rumoured here and there that the priest had a habit of 'finishing off the husband's procreative duties' with his female parishioners. But that was just the idle talk of mischief-makers and grudge-bearers, and only fools paid any attention to it. Like most of the true clergymen of the Greek Church (with one or two exceptions), the priest was by and large of blameless character.

Though this is true, the fact remains that married priests are usually out of pocket and out of luck, and, being forever burdened by the need to feed their offspring, they can appear to be grasping individuals, who do not even trust their own colleagues fully. This was the case with Father Kyriakos, who was perfectly willing to go and celebrate Easter for the villagers, as he had a generous heart and would have liked them to enjoy Easter and the arrival of spring along with

[1] Anagnostis means reader; it is not only a Christian name but also the first office in the ecclesiastical order.

22

everyone else, but he had his suspicions about the other parish priest, and was reluctant to leave him in charge of the parish, especially on that day. Father Theodoris, the other priest, who was known as 'the Whirlwind', urged him to go, saying it would be a pity to lose the income from Kalivia, and suggesting that they share the receipts from the parish and the village equally between them.

This did not reassure Father Kyriakos at all: in fact it made him even more suspicious. However, as he had already more or less made up his mind to go to Kalivia when he asked his colleague for his opinion, he told his son Zachos — who pulled a face and grumbled — to stay in the church sanctuary as a spy, collect his half of the offerings and the priest's fee, and only come and join him in Kalivia at sunrise, when the liturgy had ended.

✳   ✳
✳

It was four hours before dawn, and the Evening Star was already high in the night sky. Uncle Anagnostis woke the priest, and before they entered the little church of St Dimitrios he improvised a bell out of a solid piece of walnut wood and a stick, and walked through the village, banging noisily to wake the sleeping inhabitants.

One after another the villagers arrived, accompanied by their wives. All were dressed in their best clothes.

The priest gave the blessing.

Uncle Anagnostis began to recite from memory, beginning with the preliminary prayer and the canon, 'On the wave of the sea'.

Father Kyriakos appeared at the sanctuary doors, chanting 'Come, receive the light'.

When they had all lit their candles, they filed out into the open air to hear the Resurrection gospel.* A sweet, contemplative Resurrection, amid the blossoming trees, the fragrant bushes swaying in a gentle breeze, and the white flowers of the wild clematis, 'neige odorante du printemps'.[1]

---

[1] 'fragant snow of spring': V. Hugo, *Les Orientales*, xxxiii, 10.

They sang 'Christ is risen', and all went back into the church. Men, women and children: no more than seventy souls, all told.

Uncle Anagnostis began to chant the Easter canon, and the priest himself (as there was no one else to do so) gave the responses from the sanctuary. He was about to come out and say the preparatory prayer, kiss the icons and begin the liturgy, when a rather tall twelve-year-old boy, flushed and panting, followed by two other boys of about the same age, suddenly walked, or rather burst, into the church. It was Zachos, Father Kyriakos's son. He rushed into the sanctuary, gasping for breath, and began speking to the priest. Though the congregation could hear his voice, they could not make out a single word of it.

This is what he was saying:

'*Papa, papa!*' (the children of priests also usually address their father as *papa*). '*Papa, papa!* ... Father Whirlwind ... by the back door ... the oblations ... from the sanctuary ... his mother-in-law ... and his wife ... carrying ... by the back door ... the oblations ... I saw them ... by the back door ... the oblations ... from the sanctuary ... and his mother-in-law ... and his wife ...'

Father Kyriakos was the only person who could have made any sense of his breathless son's disjointed words. He understood from them that Father Theodore, the Whirlwind, the other parish priest, was stealing the collection and passing it out to his wife and mother-in-law through the back door leading from the sanctuary.

Perhaps things were not exactly as Zachos suggested. Like all young boys, he loved the countryside and he loved having fun, and he had found it very difficult to obey his father's orders and stay behind in the town. He was ready to jump at any excuse to get away and set off on a nocturnal jaunt to Kalivia, especially as he had not had any difficulty finding some friends to come along with him.

But Father Kyriakos did not stop to think. He went red and flew into a rage. In a word, he sinned. Rather than giving his son a good box around the ears and calmly proceeding with his duty, he immediately stripped off his stole, removed his surplice and strode down the nave and out of the church — averting his eyes from his wife's face as she stared at him in alarm.

Uncle Milios, however, had an idea about what might have provoked this behaviour, and went out after him. A short distance from the church, between three trees and two stretches of fencing, the following conversation took place:

'*Papa, papa*, where are you going?'

'Don't worry — I'll be right back.'

He didn't know what else to say. The fact is that he had resolved to go back down to the town and confront the other priest about the theft. He honestly believed he had enough time to get back and celebrate the liturgy before the sun rose.

'Where are you going?' insisted Uncle Milios.

'Get Anagnostis to read the Acts of the Apostles. I'll be right back.'

He had forgotten that Uncle Anagnostis couldn't read anything, unless he already knew it by heart.

'After all, I'm leaving my wife here!' he added, unable to think of anything else to say. 'I'm leaving my wife here with you!'

And with these words he was gone.

Uncle Milios walked gloomily back into the church.

'I knew it,' he muttered to himself.

*   *
*

In the church great astonishment held sway. The villagers stared at each other in bewilderment. Some were whispering. The women were asking the priest's wife to tell them what was going on — but she was even more at a loss than they were.

Meanwhile, the priest ran and ran. The cold night air cooled his brow a little.

'And how am I supposed to feed all these children? Eight of them, God forgive me: the wife makes nine, and me — ten! They'll rob you as soon as look at you!...'

Five hundred paces from the church the path began to descend, and led down into a lovely valley. There was a watermill standing on the slope, by the side of the road. As the priest listened to the gentle murmuring of the stream and felt the cool breeze against his face, the fact that he was going to celebrate the Liturgy (let alone how or where he was going to celebrate it) was swept completely from his mind, and he stooped down to drink. But his lips had not yet touched the surface of the water, when he suddenly remembered, and realized what he was doing.

'I have to celebrate the liturgy,' he exclaimed, 'and I'm drinking water...?'[1]

And he did not drink.

Then he pulled himself together.

'What am I doing?' he said, 'Where am I going?'

He made the sign of the cross.

'I have sinned, Lord. I have sinned! Do not hold me to account!'

He resumed: 'If he is a thief, it is for the Lord to...forgive him...him and me. I must do my duty.'

He felt a tear run down his cheek.

'Oh Lord,' he exclaimed with all his heart, 'I have sinned, I have sinned! You gave yourself up for our sins, and in return we crucify you daily!'

He turned around and hurried back up towards the church to continue the service.

'And I was actually going to drink water! I am not fit to celebrate! But what can I do? I can't take communion! I shall say the office without taking communion — I am not worthy! "Behold the first fruits of the vine!"[2] I am not worthy!'

He re-entered the church, and the villagers greeted his return with joy.

He celebrated the divine mystery and administered the Holy Communion to the faithful, taking care that every last drop from the chalice passed through their lips. He himself abstained, vowing

[1] All communicants, including the celebrant, refrain from both food and drink prior to communion.

[2] John of Damascus, canon for the Sunday of Easter, ode 8, 1st *troparion*.

to tell all to his confessor — and ready to accept whatever penance
he might impose.*

*   *
*

Around noon, after the service of the Second Resurrection,* the
villagers laid out the feast under the plane-trees by the cooling
spring. For a carpet they had the grass and the meadow flowers and
for a table they used ferns and rushes. The cool breeze rustled in the
trees, while Sevenmonth responded with sweet sounds from his
lyre. The lovely Xanthe, his wife, sat between her mother Melachro
and Aunt Kratira, her mother-in-law, taking care to keep her cheeks
partially covered with her headscarf and staring fixedly at the trunk
of the great plane-tree so that the men would not look at her and
arouse her husband's jealousy.

Her sister, Atho, fifteen years old and still unmarried, without a
care in the world and no less of a beauty herself, kept teasing her,
saying: 'Silly girl, what did you see in him? I wouldn't have him if
you offered me the heavens and the stars... I'd rather be a nun!'

It was true that Sevenmonth was not much to look at in terms of
appearance or size, but he made up for these shortcomings with agili-
ty of body and mind, and a cheerful and good-natured disposition.

Father Kyriakos presided over the feast. His wife sat opposite
him, an irreproachable dark-haired woman, stocky and round-
faced, who once a year, almost without fail, would innocently hatch
out another little priest-child — without bothering with all those
herbs (whether for getting a child or for preventing one) that fill the
minds of other women.

To the right of the priest sat Uncle Milios, the village elder, and
devoted servant of his little community. He knew better than anyone how the lamb should be roasted, carving it carefully so that
everyone got his share, and proposing toasts as he tucked into his
food. His toasts were unrivalled. After the priest had made a short
formal toast of his own, Uncle Milios, clutching an enormous seven-
oka cask, stood up and began to greet the company one by one:

'*Christos Anesti!* Christ is risen! Truly the Lord is risen! He lives and reigns throughout the ages!'

After this preamble, he got down to business:

'Health to us all! Good health! Prosperity! Good cheer! *Papa!* May your vocation bring you joy!' And to the priest's wife: 'May your husband and all your little ones bring you joy! Cousin Thodoris! Long life and happiness! Godfather Panayiotis! Just as you baptized us with oil, may you also crown us with wedding wreaths of vine.* Kratira, my in-law! May God grant you a fine husband for your daughter! Yorgis, my nephew! May you make an honourable marriage, and may we rejoice on your wedding-day! Aunt Kyparissou! May your son marry a good woman, and gladden your heart! Raise your glasses! Cheers! Here's to us all! Your health! Cousin Xanthe! May good omens accompany the birth of your child! Your health! Here's to us all! May life be good to us, now and always!'

And the amount he drank depended on whom he was toasting.

Little Sevenmonth also wanted to propose a toast, but a more tender one. He hoped to touch his wife's heart and make her answer him:

'What's up?'

'Drink up, and pass the cup!'

'What, with wine?'

'I drink to you, O darling mine!'

When he had drunk, he passed the cask to his lovely Xanthe, and she moistened her lips.

Then they began to sing. First of all 'Christ is risen', followed by popular songs. When Uncle Milios tried to sing 'Christ is risen', it either became an Anatolian lament, or else a heroic ballad, but the most original singer of all was Uncle Kitsos, an aged gendarme from Northern Epirus — an old regular, who had been left stranded on the island since King Otho's reign.[1] He wasn't even sure

---

[1] Otho of Bavaria was appointed as the first king of independent Greece by the European powers after the Greek War of Independence. He reigned from 1832 to 1862.

whether his name was still in the official register — sometimes he received his pay, and other times he did not. He wore an open-sleeved tunic, short knee breeches and greaves around his shins. The mayor (there was also a mayor, alas!) had sent him to Kalivia for Easter, supposedly to maintain law and order, although there was not actually any need for it to be maintained. The truth is that he had sent him off to enjoy himself with the good-hearted country people, whose company Uncle Kitsos liked, even though he would call them 'poor wretches' or 'tinkers'. It is also true that if he had stayed in the town, the mayor would have been under an obligation to entertain him, for Uncle Kitsos had been spoilt by the previous mayors and treated to cakes and eggs at Easter. What customs...!

After kissing the cask three or four times, Uncle Kitsos began to chant 'Christ is risen' after his own fashion, as follows:

> *Crisis lads, Crisis risen*
> *from the dead by death*
> *chomping down death*
> *and to those, those in the tombs*
> *life most blessed!**

And yet, despite its singularity, no one ever sang a sacred song with more Christian feeling and enthusiasm, with the possible exception of that worthy old Cretan, long-famed in Athens, who sang the 'Dumb are the lips of the impious' with his own interpolation: 'Dumb are the lips of the impious and profane, *the scoundrels!*, at your revered image...'.*

Ah, the true Orthodox Greeks!

*   *
*

As the shadows lengthened, the men began to dance the *klephtiko* (the women waited till Monday and Tuesday before dancing the *syrtos* and the *kamara*),* and Father Kyriakos, his wife, and young Zachos, whom his father had let off in view of the special day (he had decided that his son was actually to blame for all the confusion), took leave of the company and went back down to the town.

Father Kyriakos gave his fellow priest his full share of the collection from Kalivia, and did not even bother to raise the subject of the supposed theft. As it turned out, Father Theodoris himself told him that his share of the parish receipts was in his own (Father Theodoris's) house. He had thought it best, he said, to take both shares out through the back door of the sanctuary, so as to keep them from the eyes of gossips with nothing better to think about, who might otherwise kick up a fuss about all the money priests receive. 'On the rare day,' he said, 'that we actually get something in the collection box, everyone has plenty to say about it — but they never stop to consider all the weeks and months that go by without harvest!'

Which was the reason for Zachos's mistake.

[1890]

Translated by Andrew Watson

BLACK SCARF ROCK

A STORY

N O ONE IN THE ENTIRE VILLAGE had a prettier garden plot than my cousin Yannios. Every day in the afternoon he would get on his little old donkey and put in his regular daily stint in the lovely garden, whence he would return in the evening bearing the fruits of his labour. The old-age pensioners sitting by the jetty, when they saw him returning slowly from his daily outing, would say:

'Look, there's Yannios coming back from his garden.'

'And his vegetables with him.'

'Yes, cauliflowers and melons.'

'How does he manage it?'

'It's as though they knew him.'

'You'd say he had them bewitched.'

My cousin Yannios paid no attention to these various, or rather invariable, comments, but passed indifferently by, after tethering his ass to a post; and when he had unloaded his 'vegetables' he would either sell them or take them home, depending on the circumstances.

And having rested in the evening from his moderate labours during the day, as he intended shortly to rest forever from the many troubles of his life, the next day again, in the afternoon, he untethered his donkey, got up on its back and went off again to his garden.

* *
*

What a glorious, boundless, magnificent garden it was! And how right immortal Homer was when he compared the waves of the sea with the waves in the undulating wheat of an unharvested field:

...The mighty numbers move.
So roll the billows to th' Icarian shore,
From east and south when winds begin to roar,
Burst their dark mansions in the clouds, and sweep
The whitening surface of the ruffled deep.
And as on corn when western gusts descend,
Before the blast the lofty harvests bend;
Thus o'er the field the moving host appears... [1]

Indeed, the grasses and plants in the garden of my cousin Yannios, vast, gigantic, wild or cultivated, had been constantly tilled and formed into furrows and smooth levels from the beginning, from the creation of the world. Their atoms mingled ceaselessly in shapes that were varied, unchanging and fluid, in rearing crests and lifting swells; they seethed, struck, thundered, sounded, smacked and crashed against their fellows. The west winds rolled playfully among them like mischievous children, and the offshore breezes and the alternating gusts disputed as to who should create the deepest furrows and the highest surges on their blue and purple surface, shot with phosphorescent gleams and garlanded with rings of foam. And the sea breeze softly caressed the rippling, unsullied expanse, creasing it into seductive, endless, innumerable lines, as on the forehead of some king's lovely bride displaying childish temper and obstinacy in a captivating interval between smiles, an interval whose deepest depths are invisible and whose still surface reflects the infinite joy of creation.

The whole dome of heaven was mirrored in this incomparable garden, and the sun burned down on it without setting fire to its depths, for he himself, when he had wearied of his day's charioteering, would plunge down to the bottom to rest, and to whet his blunted rays in the watery workplace. The moon grew more radiant when she silvered the breast of this boundless expanse, the Evening Star bathed voluptuously in its springs, and the Pleiades sparkled in

[1] *Iliad* 2, 144–9; translation by Alexander Pope.

its unexplored depths in all their sweet virginal modesty, like pene-
trating shafts seeking to sound the depth, to touch the bottom.

A myriad sounds echoed among the caves and rocks brushed by
the edges of the immaculate expanse, sometimes like the delicious
sighs of love, sometimes like the wild crashings of war, thudding
against the echoes. Sweet smells and delicate fragrances drifted
everywhere, scenting the breezes, and the brine and the sun's heat
toughened the skin, and made ruddy and dark and manly the people's faces.

My cousin's donkey plunged its feet deep among the cool petals
which waved and rustled around its hooves, and the mysterious
garden offered up its breast, submitting its treasure-house to the
skilled hands of the experienced gardener.

For everyone my cousin Yannios's garden was an open book, but
a book written in hieroglyphic characters, or with those 'emblems
of sorrow',[1] the cracked lines engraved on the naked skulls of the
dead, of which it is said that although they indicate the fate of the
dead person, you cannot read them unless you are a seer ... and
anyway it is too late then, since the dead man's life is over.

But for my unfortunate cousin it was a book written in shining
capital letters, clear, intelligible and easy to read. He was acquainted with all the mysteries, all the hollows and caverns of this territory he loved so much. One could in fact say, as the old pensioners
on the jetty said, not as a hackneyed figure of speech but almost as
a literal truth, that those caverns and hollows were, themselves,
acquainted with him.*

❆   ❆
❆

Their acquaintanceship with him went back a long way.

He was already in his sixties, and for fifty years, since the tender
age of ten, he had not ceased cultivating his garden.

Everyone works for himself on the pretext that he is working for

---

[1] *Iliad* 7, 168.

others; poor Yannios laboured for others and never for himself.

At the age of twelve, he became his mother's sole support, for she was widowed in her thirties. At the age of twenty, fatherless himself, he was the guardian of his fatherless sisters. At forty he was the guardian of a still more acute fatherlessness, that of his nieces.

All young people strive to realize some ambition, desire marriage, think of settling down. Poor Yannios did not dare even to dream of any such thing.

Unmarried though he was, he had three women in his house. They were the legacy fate had bequeathed to him.

He managed to marry off one of his sisters after a few years. But she was widowed after giving birth to two daughters.

As soon as this sister was widowed, the other one made a bad marriage. The man she married brought with him from his village his eight-year-old daughter from a first marriage, and after living with his new wife for a few months he left. He moved to some town in Greece where he worked as a manual labourer.

When he went away he didn't have a penny piece to leave her. So then for my poor cousin Yannios 'it didn't rain but it poured'. Apart from his sick old mother, his widowed sister and her fatherless children, he was obliged to help out his married sister and her step-daughter. He himself described this, graphically and with extreme vulgarity, as 'being saddled twice over'.

At other times, with reference to the general state of his domestic affairs since his father's death — the two widowhoods, the multiple fatherlessness in the family, his own lifetime of service — he would say of his fate, with complaining humour, that 'God had made a damn good job of it'.

We have omitted to say that Fate had also given him a brother — but ye gods, what a brother!

This brother was about ten years younger than him, and he had brought him up when they were left fatherless. 'He raised him, made a man of him', as their mother used to say. But he turned out to be a bad lot.

After being a sailor for several years in the Aegean on schooners and brigs, he ran away to America, and for decades he had not even sent a letter home.

Where was he? In Philadelphia. And what was he up to? He had married a Quakeress.

In Philadelphia — the irony of that name![1] And a Quakeress! He ate so many frogs, was Yannios's comment, that he ended up with a wife whose religion sounded like a frog croaking.

Yannios, it is true, was resentful on the subject of his brother; but then the old woman, his mother, never said a single word of thanks to her poor slave. The quarrels between them were exacerbated on account of this brother, for whom the old woman nourished a blind affection: she could never bear to hear anything said against him. The poor woman fancied that whatever Yannios did, he did naturally, because it was his duty to do it; but it never crossed her mind that he might desert her as the younger son had deserted her — and she was right: Yannios was one of those people who may grumble a lot but who never give up.

In the end, grief at the absence of her younger son, the deprivations and hardships she had undergone, as well as illness, brought her to her grave.

Yannios was left with the elder sister and her two daughters, and the younger one with her stepdaughter.

They all lived off Yannios's labour and a small income from the vineyard and the olive orchard.

The married sister heard no news of her husband for a long time. Finally, after six months, he remembered her and sent her four pounds. Then he forgot her for good.

In the meantime, Yannios fell ill and stopped giving her anything.

Those four pounds, in addition to the trifling income from the fruit, kept her and her stepdaughter going for three years. She loved

[1] Philadelphia in Greek means 'brotherly love'.

her stepdaughter as though she were her own child. Luckily she had no children of her own.

But poor woman! Just as St Mary in the desert beyond Jordan lived for I don't remember how many years on two loaves of bread,* so she, in this desert of human society, in the land of feelings and kind hearts, lived for three years on four pounds.

And whereas that superhuman saint had the sins of her youth to expiate, this poor woman was simple and devoted and so forgiving that when she died, out of her few possessions she bequeathed the little house and the vineyard to her stepdaughter, and left her fatherless nieces only the olive orchard.

The latter, out of respect for the memory of their aunt, merely grumbled a little under their breath.[1]

* * *

For whose sake did the Black Scarf Rock wear mourning?

Who other than my cousin, Yannios?

She stood amid the great flowing swathes, at the edge of the majestic watery plain, her jagged head only just visible a few inches above the smooth surface. She stood and seemed to challenge the bold passer-by who had the nerve to ignore her.

---

[1] [Papadiamandis's note] To avoid a tedious digression, I hope I may be permitted a brief footnote. Let no one think that I am inventing or fabricating anything in the text. Both the resignation and frugality of the wife and the tenderness of the stepmother are things which I have seen with my own eyes. Yet most people are happy to believe fictions, and the truth seems to them more incredible than a lie. In everyday life also, I have observed that whenever I have told a lie in jest, I have found my hearers so unexpectedly credulous that even when I protested afterwards that I was only joking, they would not be convinced but persisted in believing that the lie was a truth; and when I have attempted to tell the truth I have found myself the object of suspicion or of knowing smiles. But let the reader be certain that we, the writers of fiction, 'we know how to speak many false things as though they were true; but we know, when we will, to utter true things'

ἴδμεν ψεύδεα πολλὰ λέγειν ἐτύμοισιν ὁμοῖα,
ἴδμεν δ' εὖτ' ἐθέλωμεν, ἀληθέα μυθήσασθαι.

(Hesiod, *Theogony*, 27–8, trans. Hugh G. Evelyn-White)

Black Scarf Rock!

The old men remembered her as being the same for three generations: Black Scarf Rock, eternally in mourning.

So why would she wear black for Yannios and no one else? But then, why wear it for anyone else?

Neither she nor he had ever known happiness.

My cousin Yannios had experienced the joys of love to the same degree as the Black Scarf Rock.

And after all, if she *had* once been a woman, before being turned into stone and becoming a rock - who knows, as a woman she may have experienced love; whereas my cousin Yannios couldn't even hope to turn to stone and become a rock.

Poor Black Scarf Rock! And poor, luckless cousin of mine, Yannios!

*   *
*

At the western end of the beautiful triple harbour fronting the seaside town, where the sea, wrinkling under a light breeze, breaks and reveals a dark point lapped on all sides by a white fringe of water, is the spot where the Black Scarf Rock rears her head.

All the rocks stand about unmoving, gazing down with Olympian irony on the hopeless efforts of the maddened sea.

Only the Black Scarf Rock beckons from afar, beckons with her head to the bold sailor, who, mounted aboard a few wretched planks, is tossed about on the sea in his struggle to find nourishment in the ocean's depths for himself and his beloved ones.

She seems to invite him to approach her, siren-like, but voiceless and soulless.

She resembles a shipwreck which has been there for many long years, pounded by the foaming waves, waving and tossing her head, the head of a seal watching there for centuries.

Only the seal's head moves, deceptively beckoning; its tail is with the seaweed on the bottom; the root extends its fibres even deeper, thrusting into the rock.

Nevertheless, the head does not move either. It is only the waves which break and smack and lap against it. Themselves in motion, they seem to make it move.

It is said, though no one believes it — and yet just imagine if it were true! — that the Black Scarf Rock was once a woman and the mother of seven sons; and that all seven sons, experienced sailors, incurred the envy of the Mermaid and were drowned at sea; and that a merciful fate, taking pity on the mother's anguish, turned her into a reef and planted her there, not far from land, with her light-ning-blasted head just above the surface, and wearing, so to speak, a black kerchief; rejoicing from afar at the sight of the calamities and drownings that befall men at sea, accepting as a propitiatory sacrifice the shipwrecks thrown ashore by the waves, soothing her anguish in the sea. Such was the story of Black Scarf Rock.

I do not know what fate linked the Black Scarf Rock with my cousin Yannios; but always, whether near to him or distant, she beckoned him incessantly.

It seems that some mysterious bond existed between them: she was pre-eminently the Rock of the Black Scarf, and he from a young age had seen nothing around him but women wearing black headscarves.

He sailed almost every day in her waters, across the length and breadth of the fine harbour with its three entrances, visited all the inlets, explored all the underwater caves and traversed all the sea chambers.

He sailed from creek to creek, from beach to beach, from rock to rock. He knew all the lurking-places of the octopus, all the cham-bers of the conger eel, all the habitations of the lobster.

No sea-bass ever escaped him, and the bream were bewitched by his hooks.

If he ever felt like amusing himself by provoking astonishment in the large number of people who are more impressed by quantity than by quality (he rarely did this otherwise, as he was not fond of fishing inferior fish), he had his own method.

He knew that 'everything that is hunted hunts in turn and everything that is hated, hates'. He knew that just as cats wage war on fish, fish wage war on cats.

He only did this two or three time, in order to annoy the men on a foreign fishing boat who were fishing with a trammel net, and against whom he could not otherwise have competed. So he fished using bait made from the flesh of a dead and decaying cat.

The fish that he caught in this fashion (he caught more than a hundred and forty pounds all by himself, as much as his rival fishing boat) he did not want to sell to the islanders. He sold the lot to an Austrian steamship that was anchored in the harbour, supposedly 'taking soundings'. He said to his fellow-villagers: 'These fish are not for you, they are for people who eat cats as well.'

But no one understood what he meant.

He often sailed in the waters around the Black Scarf Rock, for he had a peculiar affection for this lonely reef, which barely showed its head above the foaming waves, like an exhausted swimmer resting on his back in the sea. He was familiar with all the rock's caves and secrets, where he would discover marine treasures, lobsters and prawns of prodigious size, and shellfish and limpets and other delicious edibles.

But gone was the time when Yannios was the owner of two fine boats, the *Golden Horn* and the *Saint Sophia*. Gone was the time when the stuff of his dreams was the return of the Greek Race to the shore of the Bosphorus. The people who had subscribed to the Great Idea, or those of them who were left, were totally disillusioned, and my cousin Yannios was of their number.*

Yannios had only one boat now, a dilapidated craft, almost the same age as the man who went in her. One Saturday in the middle of Great Lent he boarded his ancient skiff and began to row in the direction of the Black Scarf Rock.

Like all experienced oarsmen, Yannios had his own sculling method, and knew how to send his boat through the water without seeming to try and without sweating over it. He pulled smoothly and gently, but continually, unremittingly and with latent power.

The movement of his arms was almost imperceptible, and he leaned forwards and then backwards almost invisibly.

Apart from that, he had already started to get old and weary and ill. He was gouty and almost paralysed down the left side.

In the boat he had some fishing tackle: the long barbed harpoon for bringing up octopus, the three-pronged fork for spearing bass and lobsters, the glass for spying out cuttlefish, the oilcan with which he created an artificial calm on the surface of the sea and was able to see clearly into the depths. For in his old age he confined himself to these (in addition to the curved fork for getting hold of sea-urchins and his dip net and a few other things), leaving the drift-nets and drag-nets and trawl-lines to the younger fishermen.

After half an hour of continuous rowing he reached the neighbourhood of the Black Scarf Rock. He had gone out simply in order to cheer himself up, with no intention of fishing. He felt odd that day, filled with a great sadness. He had quarrelled at home with his sister, who had inherited some of their mother's eccentricity.

It was a lovely day, and the westering sun shone full into the face of the old fisherman, gilding his silver hair, lighting up his square broad face with the snub nose and the expression of indescribable kindliness and resignation, and his short figure with its tarred and patched breeches. It was already spring, the middle of the month of March. On the shore opposite him, with its beautiful inlets and the long stretches of sand which intersected it, he could see the scattered figures of the villagers and some women and children, returning along the path by the sea from the fields to the little town. Spring had started to deck the trees with blossom, and the sea was flinging its life-giving spray over the bushes which flourished at the feet of the picturesque cliffs, where a rough goatherd with unkempt hair and sunburned face extended his crook, accompanying the gesture with an incomprehensible monosyllabic utterance, towards a goat which had leaped on to a rock and had remained behind the rest of the herd, trying to graze where there were only pebbles and sand; while his lad, with a long sack hanging over his left shoulder down to his knees and a tall crook which was twice his height, ran with happy shouts ahead, returning to signal to the he-goats, and the dog wagged his tail and barked without stopping at the passers-by.

The reef known as the Black Scarf was not more than sixty yards out from the shore, where a delightfully pretty inlet closes round the advancing waves which race towards the beach, only to fall diminished on the sand which swallows them.

At that spot he saw a village woman stooping over the water, washing some rags where the sand ends, at the foot of a rock which juts out into the sea, curving over the water at the point where it starts getting deeper. This rock was called 'The Nose', and it was one of the rocks used by swimmers in the summertime to perform their spectacular leaps into the sea.

The son of this woman, a child of seven, had escaped his mother's attention and climbed nimbly up to the top of the rock.

Suddenly the mother, sensing the child's absence from the vague feeling of emptiness at her back, turned round, raised her head and saw him on top of the rock, his fists outstretched in front of him, his head bent, uttering childish squeals.

The little boy, who the summer before had seen swimmers jumping off the top of this rock, was pretending that he too, in imitation of the older boys, was going to 'take a header' off the Nose.

The mother started calling him to come back to her. Yannios, who was fishing about with his harpoon near the Black Scarf, heard the woman's cries: 'Come down off there, you little devil, you imp you, come down!'

But the little boy pretended not to hear. The mother, getting angry, stretched out the pestle with which she beat the clothes to get them clean in the direction of the rock and shook it threateningly at the child: 'You wait, you rascal, just you wait, the devil take you! You won't half catch it when your dad gets home from the fields this evening!'

Then, as the little boy, ignoring his mother's shouts, carried on with his imitation, he bent a little further forward, slipped, and with a stifled scream fell with a splash into the sea.

The sea at that point was twice as deep or more as the height of a man. The child went under, came to the surface again, thrashed around, struggled, and went down a second time.

The woman let out an anguished, piercing shriek, and holding her washing-pestle, ashen-faced, terror-stricken, wild, she went into the sea. She waded in up to her waist, then up to her breast, and tried with her pestle to reach the child, already drowning, who had vanished for the second time. But inevitably, from the eddy created by the stick in the water, the struggling body was carried further away instead of being brought within the mother's reach. She screamed again for help, but at that moment none of the people returning home to the village were in the vicinity. They had all gone past the low-lying beach which divided this inlet from the other neighbouring beaches, and were more than a thousand paces distant.

Yannios, however, was closer than the others, and both saw and heard what had happened. With four extra-powerful pulls on the oars, he forced his rotten old skiff so fast through the water that he had already reached the spot where the child had gone down. On seeing this, a glimmer of hope came to the woman.

*　*
*

Yannios took his harpoon and began feeling about in the sea. The bottom of the bay was uneven and irregular. Although ten yards out from the place where the woman was washing, at the base of the rock, the water got suddenly deep, further out, at the spot where Yannios now was, it became mysteriously shallow again. This was because a large stone shelf began at that point and extended into deeper water, an entire marine threshing floor, a solid mass of prehistoric pebbles and sand, harder than steel. It was over this shelf that the child had gone down the second time.

In only a few moments the old fisherman dragged the child to the surface with his harpoon, grasping him dexterously by the clothing.

The child appeared to be already unconscious. Perhaps, though, he was not completely drowned.

The mother, who persisted in wading into the sea, as though to soothe her anxiety in it, let out a cry of mingled joy and terror. She asked whether he was still alive.

'He seems to be,' answered Yannios. 'He needs to be hung upside down.'

At that moment, as he was placing the drowned child head downwards in the stern of the boat, the harpoon, which he hadn't had time to secure, slipped from his grasp and fell into the sea.

Yannios bent instinctively to catch it, but the iron went down like an arrow, and the wooden shaft was so heavy with seawater that it would not have floated even if the iron had not been attached to it.

Afraid of losing his harpoon, without which he would return to town without any 'vegetables', Yannios took hold of his lobster fork and tried to discover where the harpoon had gone. But on this occasion the harpoon had 'fallen badly'.

It had slid down at the exact base of the stone shelf mentioned above, and had caught on a point much deeper than the upper surface of the solid stone. The shaft, instead of lifting slightly upwards and waving like a dog's grateful tail at its master, lay even deeper than the iron barb.

It was out of the question for the lobster fork, still less the oar, to reach that point.

Then Yannios got irritated and angry, and lost his habitual patience. It struck him as terrible to lose his harpoon. He said to himself that he had intended to do a good deed, and it had turned sour on him. He committed an error of judgement. 'He remembered his youth.' He did not even think to bring the boat in to land first and give the half-drowned or possibly wholly-drowned child to its mother. Just as he was, he forgot his gout and his hemiplegia, he didn't think about the fact that he hadn't swum for ages, but threw off his fez, tore off his overcoat, shed his overshirt, removed his shirt, and ignoring the mother's cries of protest he threw himself headfirst into the sea and went to find his harpoon.

The impulse given to the boat by his jump was so forceful that the boat, with the half-dead child in it, was pushed yards out to sea.

And then the mother began to wail.

✳   ✳
✳

In a few moments Yannios came to the surface with his harpoon. But the boat with the drowned child was some distance away, and since it had already drifted offshore beyond the low coastline to where the sea breeze could catch it, it went further and further out. It was already a good thirty yards out in the sea in a westerly direction, directly opposite the Black Scarf Rock.

Yannios tried to swim out to it, but the boat was moving at twice his speed. As soon as he came to the surface, the old sailor felt that his left hand was heavy, while his knee was icy cold, almost paralysed. His hemiplegia plagued him. He used the harpoon as a crutch to support him in the sea. Standing on the marine shelf, where it was fairly shallow, he leaned on the shaft, like a wounded Triton who had stolen Poseidon's trident.

And Yannios proceeded in the direction of the Black Scarf Rock, following the underwater shelf, and the boat drifted out to sea at a slightly sideways angle.

And he continued to support himself on his barbed and iron-bound crutch, and the boat continued to drift, and the woman, the drowned child's mother, broke down into laments on the shore.

But Yannios felt that his left knee was frozen, and he had not the strength to keep swimming.

Fortunately he was now not far from the Black Scarf Rock; and since to get there was not difficult as he had his iron-girt staff with which to support himself on the underwater shelf, when he reached the Black Scarf Rock he threw his arms around her, as though to confirm the saying about 'one soul in two bodies'.[1]

✳   ✳
✳

[1] Gregory Nazianzus, *Funebris oratio in laudem Basilii Magni*, 43, 20.

Ah! only the Black Scarf Rock, the stony-hearted, the cold and unloved maiden, the oyster-covered bride with shells for eyes, the unbedded pebble-strewn nymph, the unwedded widow, the un-mourned mourner — she alone gave refuge to the suffering old sailor, and she alone enjoyed the embraces and the kisses of my cousin Yannios.

Poor, unfortunate Black Scarf! Poor Yannios, my even more unfortunate cousin!

*　*　*

He had not despaired of reaching the drifting boat. He thought of the Black Scarf Rock as a temporary stop. He hoped that after a short rest the feeling would come back to his numbed limb, and then he would continue the pursuit.

He thrust his harpoon into a crack in the rock that he knew was there, set his own foot on a projection, and clung with both arms around the neck of the Black Scarf Rock. But several minutes passed, and his left knee was no easier — on the contrary, it felt like lead.

Luckily, at that moment help came unlooked-for.

When the despairing mother had let out her first piercing shriek, the goatherd with the sunburned face and unkempt hair was di-rectly behind the low-lying beach and heard her cries. He threw off his cape, took his tall stick and started to run towards the place where the cries were coming from. However, he was more than a thousand paces away.

When he arrived at the top of the cliff, he stood for a moment to see what was happening. He saw the woman standing, wading into the sea up to her armpits, holding out her pestle towards the sea, and at first he thought that a sheet or a shirt had been carried out of her reach. He was just about to turn back to his goats when the second desperate scream from the woman made him realize that something worse had happened to her.

He descended the cliff at a run. He got down to the beach. He ran on and arrived at the spot where the scene was being enacted.

During this time Yannios had come with the boat, had pulled out the drowning child, his harpoon had fallen in, he had dived for it, and the boat with the child in it was drifting out to sea.

'What is it? What's going on?'

The mother turned round, and seeing the goatherd she pointed to the drifting boat.

'My child is drowned.'

The rough goatherd lost no time. He tore off his cap, his jacket and his shirt, and wearing only his trousers he leapt into the sea.

This man was the famous Gaidingos, who passed among his fellow goatherds as having 'seen the world'. He was a bit of a fisherman, he had also been a sailor, and he could swim like an eel. He swam powerfully, with such skill and speed that it was a sight to behold. As soon as Yannios saw him from his observation post in the sea, he judged, with an old sailor's sureness of eye, that 'the boat was safe'. Only the mother's fears could not be allayed, since she did not know whether her child was alive.

*   *
*

The uncouth Gaidingos reached the boat and threw himself over the side. He felt the child's chest, and it seemed to him that the heart was beating. He undressed him hastily, tearing some of his clothes in the process, and bundled him up in Yannios's overcoat which he found folded up under the prow. He took the oars and proved himself to be as good an oarsman as he was a swimmer.

He pulled towards the Black Scarf Rock, and helped Yannios to get into the boat. The fisherman's left leg was completely numb, and his left hand had frozen on to the harpoon.

Yannios proposed to Gaidingos that they should share his clothes, he getting into his shirt and overcoat and giving his overshirt to the goatherd. The latter refused, saying that his own clothes were there on the beach, and as for the child and its mother, clothes would shortly be found for them and a fire to warm them; and he pointed to the little wooded hill opposite, saying that there on the ridge was his hut, and that his wife was a hospitable woman who would look after the others and Yannios as well. 'The child just needs a bit of a rub-down,' he said, 'and he'll come round; and as for you, seeing you have trouble with your legs you would do better not to go swimming in March.' But then, as an afterthought, he added:

'It's a pity, though, that you didn't get any octopus.'

[1891]

Translated by Liadain Sherrard

POOR SAINT *

AN ISLAND TALE

I

WHEN WE WERE CHILDREN with time on our hands — there being no great supply of entertainment in our village — we often followed our mothers and aunts to the fields and olive groves or spent all the day amid picturesque coves and virgin sand beaches simply to annoy those industrious women with our unruliness while they laboured scrubbing the linen. Or if a conscientious priest went off to celebrate the liturgy in some country chapel, or a village wife set out to light the lamp of a roadside shrine for her seafaring husband's safe return, we would evade our parents' supervision and tag along behind these good Christians, who later turned with surprise to discover us their fellow pilgrims, our only provisions the crust of bread we had stolen from the kitchen cupboard.

But our favourite excursion was the one to the Kastro, the ancient citadel of our island, abandoned after the revolution of 1821.* The Kastro was a veritable gull's nest, built on an outcrop of rock hundreds of feet above the sea. A narrow strait ran between it and the shore, spanned by a wooden draw-bridge. The tale of what follows is simply the record of my childhood memories and impressions. I assure you I'm not exaggerating when I tell you this place was the wildest spot anyone could ever imagine amid the pleasant winds and smiling beaches of our island.

The modern town, colonized by my compatriots along with other settlers, lies in a quiet southern bay. The ancient Kastro stood far in the north, in a deserted spot, difficult of access. Beyond it there were two small islands, low-lying rocks really, neither of which helped shield the place from the wind as it blew in from the sea. These tiny isles could boast of hardly a handful of soil between

48

them yet, strange as it was, a unique species of wild cabbage grew there with a bitter but succulent taste. Many villagers, braving the sheer rocks, often risked their lives to gather a few florets of it. It was, in the English playwright's words, a 'dreadful trade!'[1]

The north wind blew so long and savagely in that spot that the trees there were stooped from the lashing they took, their trunks warped by the force of its breath. Here and there scanty brush clinging to the folds of rock found some miserable refuge. A visitor, standing there today, would think it impossible that anyone could actually live on such waterless, unfriendly stone. Clearly it had been a case of necessity, ever-present and all-compelling: fear of the en-croaching Algerians, Venetians and Turks had forced them to that extremity, crowding them on to that impregnable shell of nature.

When I was a child, within and around the ancient fortress there was a scattering of about thirty chapels, the relics of a pious past. Most of these were just ruins. Some had their four walls still while others had merely been looted of their icons and holy vessels. Only a few were still in use. They stood there in a striking pose on the proud rocks of a ledge above the sea, gilded in summer by the abundant light and washed in winter by the waves when the north wind shook and churned, relentlessly ploughing the grey sea, seeding the coast with wood and wreckage, grinding granite into sand, kneading sand into rock and stalactite, and winnowing the foam in a radiance of spray.

The horizon stretched on without end; the sea there a vast unfold-ing expanse. But in winter pitiless tempests muddied the horizon and vexed the sea's calm. From that spot it was impossible to get any pleas-ure from the sense of altitude, which only an observer standing secure at the very summit of that precipitous coastline could appreciate.

Everyone of my mates used to race to this land's end, especially on feast days, when the deserted landscape took on life and colour. Then, after long years of silence, the happy shouts of children and

---

[1] Shakespeare, *King Lear*, IV.6.15.

the swallow-like voices of young women echoed there once more.

Sometimes it happened that one of the younger members of our group decided to make his first reverent pilgrimage to the site (each of us having grown up with dreams of the Kastro and tales of the numberless spirits that haunted it). We watched for the moment at which the young initiate would crawl through the shaded gateway gaping and astonished, when our first brotherly concern would be to bang his head on the citadel's iron gate, crying out 'iron-head!' for good luck.

But most of us found even greater delight in pummelling the old cracked bells of the two or three churches that were still intact within the fortress. We would race to be first to the bells, despite the good priest's protests and the threatening whip of the local bailiff or village policeman.

There was also the habit among some of the younger vandals (how else can I call them?) of demolishing with fist and foot the few remaining walls of the houses there. The boys discovered unspeakable pleasure in casting the stones they dislodged into the sea which spread out below us and echoed wildly under that magnificent rock. It would take minutes sometimes for the thumping splash of these fragments dropping into the sea below to reach our ears.

*   *
*

Three or four roads led from the new town to the Kastro. The most important of these was called the Great Road. After passing through various landscapes, each with its own local history and traditional accounts of ghosts and nereids, the roadway came to a high plateau that formed a land-bridge joining the island's two peaks. This place was called The Cross.

Here stood no single wooden cross, which was otherwise quite common on the islands, but three: three ancient wooden crosses whose coating of red primer had worn away with the passing of the years and by the savage winds. One of the crosses looked east, the second west and the third faced south. About one hundred feet from this spot, where the road descended and turned in

the direction of the Kastro (which was still another half hour distant by this path), the ground amid the lentisk and heather was all
red. Our mothers and grandmothers used to regale us with stories
of that earth with its unusual reddish shade which also gave off an
inexplicable fragrance.

Perhaps someone will say that we were 'listeners of deeds and
watchers of stories'[1] (another could have changed it to 'smellers' of
stories), but for us also it really seemed as if the earth at that spot
was emitting a sweet perfume.

A man, it was said, had been 'hallowed' there, had achieved
sainthood. But how? When? With my simple, childlike curiosity I
didn't question the story and never learned the details. The traditional account, it seems, remained vague and over time the particular circumstances were forgotten. Even the name of the martyr had
passed into oblivion. And so, as it is commonly said, 'a poor saint
goes unsung'.

Some years intervened. Then, in 1872, when I was twenty years
old, I happened to spend several months in Macedonia where I met
a respected man from my village who had been away for many
years. In a simple and modest way he taught me a great deal and
recounted again some of the traditional tales from our native island. I remembered then to ask him about that sweet fragrance and
whether he'd ever heard of the man who'd been hallowed near
Three Crosses. This is the story he told me.*

II

Up at early dawn, the Poor Shepherd milked the few goats that he
kept in the pastureland of Three Crosses and woke his apprentice.
He sent the boy to carry the brimming milk-churn to his land-holder
in the village, and to return at once. If the boy saw that they were

---

[1] Thucydides 3.38.4. Cleon in the Mytilenian debate in 427 BC: 'You have become
regular speech-goers and as for action you merely listen to accounts of it.'

slow to open the drawbridge, he should call for the guard at the gate and have him hoist the milk up into the fortress with the pulley. But, on all accounts, he should not leave before receiving notice from Mr Anagnostis, the shepherd's patron and partner,* whether he wished to order anything more. The boy threw off his cape, washed his face with water from the pitcher, dried himself on the sleeve of his undershirt, grabbed the churn of milk and left at a run.

The shepherd poured most of the remaining milk into a cauldron and threw in a good handful of salt, which he'd collected himself, going from beach to beach, wandering over the rocks where he gathered limpets and barnacles. Then he lit a fire and prepared to boil the milk. He knew that if his partner neglected to send him 'a little salt fish', as was very likely, he'd be obliged to dine alone on milk, which he wasn't fond of doing. But he wasn't the kind to become a burden to others, and if his partner were in no good humour he would never sacrifice his self-respect, compelling the landholder to treat him to some savoury delicacy, or anything else. Others find a way, some means by which they maintain good relations with their partner, even though, as a general rule, it is the lambs owned in common that are eaten by the eagle whereas their own lambs escape all harm; and again it is these people, heaven help us, that get on in the world. If there were only enough milk to make cheese or *myzithra* — that would suffice. But this year the wrath of God had fallen hard on the man's flock. Half the animals had died. Only a few milk-goats were left and those few barren. God had not sent good weather to bring forth a little grass for the animals to graze on. What were the unfortunate things to do?

So the Poor Shepherd started to round up his herd, driving the animals to pasture in the adjacent valley.

'Tsou! Tsou! Barren-one! Hey! Greyhair! Oi! Oi!'

He'd gone only a few steps when two unknown men suddenly appeared in front of him, blocking his way. They wore unusual dress and their manner, though it did not seem terribly wild, was strange nonetheless. The shepherd was surprised, but not afraid.

His little sheepdog, prancing in front, harried the men with his angry growls.

Both men greeted the goatherd by gesturing with their right hand, moving it first to their chest and then to their forehead. One of the two, the elder, addressed him in a low, harsh voice speaking an unintelligible mix of Greek and barbarian:

'You, *Bellek, anaraf,* we road *souft?*'[1]

The shepherd did not understand a word. So the foreigner repeated what he'd said, accompanying his words with exaggerated gestures:

'*Bellek,* where go road . . . many, many, *elef elefin!*'[2]

The shepherd finally began to understand that the man was inquiring about the road to the Kastro. And so, without suspecting anything, he went ahead and indicated the main road, the one leading to the fortress. By means of several gestures of his own he let the two men understand that if they proceeded in that direction, after about one hundred steps they would see the Kastro in the distance, standing offshore, between land and sea.

The strangers mimed a goodbye and proceeded on their way. But a few moments later the shepherd saw another four in similar garb emerging from a neighbouring thicket, marching cautiously in the same direction as the first two. They were only visible for a moment, as they stepped briefly into the open clearing, peering about as if they feared someone might see them. Then they scrambled back into the forest.

Spontaneously, without knowing why, the shepherd rushed to catch a glimpse of them, then leapt behind the bushes. He was almost certain he'd managed to escape the notice of these four.

Now all six had disappeared.

The shepherd stood up tall on the bank of earth, straight as an

---

[1] [Papadiamandis's note] 'You, of the village, you know to us the road to show?'

[2] [Papadiamandis's note] 'To the village that leads the road . . . (where they live), many, many, thousand thousands.'

arrow, with his coarse, dirty blond hair hanging in curls. He leaned on his long shepherd's staff and began to wonder, suspicion and fear crowding his mind. The first rays of the rising sun were just beginning to touch the precocious seams on his forehead, illuminating the deep-drawn lines on his emaciated yet just forty-year-old face. His whole form was undergoing some sort of mysterious enchantment. Suddenly this rough and unrefined shepherd, the tall, sun-burned shepherd who grazed his few goats in the pastureland of Three Crosses, seemed possessed of a spiritual, nay, even tangible beauty.

A few minutes had passed when he heard, not far distant, the sound of leaves and branches being stirred underfoot. He started with fear. It was the sound of footsteps. Men were walking with great caution yet, in the midst of that green wood, they were unable to silence their progress completely.

'There are more. Others coming,' he whispered. 'My God, what could it be?'

A light suddenly shone in the eyes of his soul and a mysterious inspiration came to his mind.

'Bandits,' he said.

Without losing a moment he leapt lightly behind the bushes and started running along the road to the fortress.

'In God's name!' was all he whispered.

III

At the beginning of the previous century a pirate galley full of savage, bloodthirsty Berbers had moored off the south-western coast of the island under cover of night, near the bay called Moonless. A well-armed squad of men, fifteen or twenty in number, disembarked at dawn and began to make its way up the slopes of Anagyros, a beautiful mountain cut into countless ridges. They proceeded guardedly, moving from cleft to cleft.

As if to belie the name of the bay, a pale, crescent moon had just risen, barely lighting the bandits' nocturnal path. The bay, secret and dark, was hateful to any respectable sailor. It was used only by the sea to cast ashore the bodies of the drowned, those that the reef opposite, the 'Deliverer' (the shallow ridge which Herodotos calls the 'Ant,'[1] recounting that Xerxes had ordered a tall pillar to be set up there), had 'delivered' at various times, relieving ships of the burden of their cargo and sailors of the fleeting cares of life.

Suleiman ben-Mehmet, the elder of the group, assured the men that he'd visited the fortress before and knew where the infidels dwelt. But so many years had gone by; he could not remember with certainty which road they were to take. Long ago, when Suleiman had fought gallantly against the infidels, his moustache was a long, twisting hook, black as a raven's wing. But now the snow of old age had begun to brindle his wealth of hair.

On that occasion old Suleiman had land-marked the island's summit of Mount Karafiltzanaka and, guided by that, he proceeded northwards. In that direction stood the bird's nest they hoped to plunder.

The Algerians' plan was simple. Their ship was small and did not have many sailors. Two thirds of the crew had remained on board. They had dropped anchor overnight at Moonless Bay to avoid being discovered. If they had sailed anywhere near the island's fortress they'd have given warning to the infidels to close the iron gate and raise the drawbridge. Fifteen to eighteen men went ahead on land as scouts to take the infidels by surprise, giving them no time to protect themselves. In the meantime the light galley with the rest of the crew, protected from the southerly wind, would sail at first light to St Saviour's, directly opposite the fortress, and with surprise on their side that small force would be able to take the town.

The island, situated on the trade route from Cassandra on toward Mount Olympus and the White Aegean Sea, had frequently been used as a base for wars and campaigns. It was rumoured that the

[1] Herodotus 7.183.

wealth of Venetians and Turks and the booty of Greek highwaymen, all those who had ever set foot on the little island, were hidden in unknown caves, in the cellars of the Kastro, and throughout the whole island. In addition, the island women were no soft dainties like Muslim girls, but industrious, dark and delectable, judged worthy to adorn as slaves the harems of those who followed the True Faith.

By the time the scouts had arrived at the summit of St Constantine the dawn had purpled the eastern horizon with her rosy mantle. Two separate seas, east and west, branched out below. The one, like a cloth of blue weft and saffron warp, bathed in the rays of the all-brightening east; the other, like newly-furrowed earth, lay with the rust of darkness strewn along its folds.

The barbarians halted on a pass, hidden by the pines that clothed the whole mountainside, and their captain commanded their dispersal into three brigades. Each of these was to proceed separately, at a distance of five hundred paces, so as not to arouse the suspicion of any country dweller, someone who might wake at dawn amid the hills and descry them at a distance. They hid their weapons carefully under their wide caftans and unwound the turbans from their tall fezzes, trying to impersonate merchants from the east or wandering peddlers.

The distance to the Kastro could have been covered much more quickly if they had descended straight down from the peak of St Constantine into the valley called Arvanitis. But since old Suleiman had land-marked the higher peak called Karafiltzanaka, he led his men further east and descended into the picturesque locale of Prophet Elias. Here they drank fresh water from a clear spring shadowed by giant plane-trees. It was already near the end of April, and the evening dew was abundant. The air held a perfect calm and the day showed every indication of imminent warmth, even though the sun had not yet risen.

From there they turned to the north-east and ran across a long sloping plain where the view stretched over the vast Aegean sea, between the lofty Mount Athos and Euboea and the other islands. At the foot of Karafiltzanaka they began to climb, veering to the north-west.

They came to a shady, wooded stream, to a place called Cold Well, adjacent to Three Crosses. Here stood an ancient well, haunted, it was said, by ghosts that were known to rise from its wellhead. One of these was a Negro with pipe in hand, not of brown Arab hue like themselves, but Nubian, dark as ebony. Old Suleiman, who knew the place, suggested that, with the sun now creeping over the horizon's rim, all should reverently pray, striking their foreheads thrice against the flag stones of the path, invoking mercy from the shade of their ancient co-religionist, whose spirit, due to some unknown sin, had remained outside the gates of paradise and continued even now after so many years to wander in that melancholic spot.

IV

The Poor Shepherd had abandoned his goats just as they were to the mercy of God. There had been no time to lead them back to the fold and make them safe. There was no other shepherd at hand to replace him. His apprentice hadn't yet returned from the fortress. The little villain had probably found the gates wide open and afterwards had followed his friends to a wine shop. Who knows if he hadn't gone and sold half the contents of the milk-churn intended for the associate for half a dozen salted fish?

The shepherd ran a few steps along the main road then turned to the left and plunged into a clump of brush. He had not been so foolish as to take the main road to the Kastro, the same road he had just indicated to the bandits. There were numerous indirect tracks and pathways, known only to men of his occupation.

From among the bushes there began a path which he was utterly familiar with; he'd run it a thousand times. On this track he had a head start of at least a thousand paces. He had time to run to the fortress and return long before they would have arrived.

The path snaked along a steep bank, like the 'beetling crag' familiar from folk songs. But this man knew his way along such crags. He didn't break out into a sweat at such a challenge. He made his way so lightly over the earth that he passed almost without leaving a trace. Over the level ground his feet moved like wheels; on the precipitous bank they held like grappling irons. The leather straps of his sandals, wound tightly from his ankles to the top of his shins, were like wings on his feet.

He ran, scaling rocks, leaping over gullies, rushing down the precipitous shore, keeping his balance on slopes where only wild flowers, dead bushes and leafless asphodel grow. He ran as if suspended above the sea that played softly with the rocks lying sheer beneath. And as he ran he conceived a plan in his mind. The people in the fortress had the habit, born of necessity, of raising the drawbridge every day just before sunset and lowering it again the next morning at sunrise. If the shepherd should find the bridge in its raised position, even if the day had already begun, he would shout to the gatekeeper not to let it down, in God's name. But if he should find the bridge down, as was likely, he would plead with the guard to raise the bridge, to hoist it up, severing all communication with the land, for the love of God, or the Kastro was lost.

These were the thoughts he turned over in his mind and the fears he entertained as he ran down that wild northwestern coast, where only goats typically plant their hooves.

He arrived across from the chapel of St Saviour situated idiorrhythmically on a reef just a few yards from the shore, made the sign of the cross three times and called on the saint not to belie his name.

For safety, he came down to the shore and continued his approach, stepping lightly, climbing towards the citadel's drawbridge until he stood before it, facing the fortress. Between there lay the terrifying, rocky chasm: trembling and dizziness overcomes anyone who gazes over the sandy abyss and the watery depths that yawn beneath the bridge.

The bridge had not yet been lowered, even though the sun was rising.

The shepherd suddenly wondered about his apprentice, if he had suffered anything, if he'd fallen (God forbid!) into the hands of the corsairs. Maybe they'd captured him that morning and enslaved him? The shepherd understood that the barbarians had only spared him out of caution, of their fear of being discovered before they arrived at the Kastro. But his apprentice, it turned out, had not suffered any harm. The shepherd would be freed of his doubt before he even had a chance to ask.

Breathing hard the poor goatherd stood on the left, at the base of the bridge's stone rampart and cried out to the gatekeeper of the fortress:

'You there! In the Kastro! Hey! Gatekeeper!'

No answer came.

The shepherd screamed with all his strength, in his loudest, strongest voice:

'Hey! Gatekeeper! Hey! On the terrace! Hey! In the kiosk!'

The terrace stood above the iron gate, a tall structure with slits in the walls for guns and the essential 'hot room' with its even larger slit from which, as a weapon of last resort, the men inside could threaten and scald with boiling water any aggressors attempting to breach the gate below. The kiosk was a small pavilion where the elders gathered and deliberated or simply just sat and talked idly amid their long, snaking water pipes, with their ornate sleeves and their embroidered belts.

A third time he repeated:

'Hey! Gatekeeper! Hey! You elders!'

This time he was answered by the deep gnashing of the iron levers and gears. But then, even more inexplicably, the gate remained closed, as if the man who was about to open it had suffered a change of heart.

At the same time a voice reached him through one of the apertures in the high fortification:

'Ah! You. Why in such a rush there, Shepherd? Will you wait, or no, until the bridge is lowered? Or do you want me to lift you with the hoist, the way I did your apprentice earlier today?'

'You lifted him with the hoist?' the shepherd automatically replied.

'He had the elder's milk, Mr Anagnostis's, and Mr Anagnostis likes it fresh, you know. I dropped the hoist for him to tie on the milk-churn, but he went and hooked himself on it, without saying a word. "The milk sure is heavy today," I say to myself as I'm hauling it up. Then, when I get it halfway up, there's your boy's mug staring at me, laughing like a monkey. I told him I'd show him a nice trick, scare the wits out of him, let go the rope, and pound him into cheese. But, luckily for him, I took pity on Mr Anagnostis's milk. Besides, one shepherd-boy less or one more makes no difference.'

'I don't care about that,' the shepherd yelled up from below, growing tired of the wordy gatekeeper who stood unseen behind the wall. The keeper, smoking his pipe and enjoying his performance, kept watching the shepherd through the embrasure. He had pretensions to some status within the village and nourished contempt for the whole race of shepherds.

'What *do* you care about then, ay?' the gatekeeper replied, imitating the nasal voice of the shepherd.

'Listen and I'll tell you!' he cried out impatiently. 'Run and tell the elders. For your own sake, don't lower the bridge! It's for your own good! Do you hear?'

'Don't lower the bridge?' the gatekeeper mechanically cried from behind the gun-slits.

'That's right, don't lower it,' the shepherd yelled more emphatically.

'And why's that? Are you giving the orders now? Did you have a bad dream?'

Then, just as he'd earlier postponed opening the gate just to torture the shepherd, thinking he was demanding entry for some personal matter, so now the guard was ready to open the gate and lower the bridge merely to antagonize the man who asked that it remain closed. *Barba*-Dimos, for that was the name of the keeper, was the embodiment of caprice and contrariness.

'Bandits are here!' the shepherd's voice repeated. 'Corsairs are coming! I saw them with my own eyes!'

'Bandits? Corsairs?' *Barba*-Dimos repeated to himself.

'Run, tell the elders, and give many greetings for me to Mr Anagnosti, my associate. Corsairs are here! I saw them up at the Cross. As heaven is my judge, I saw more than ten, twelve maybe. The others must be hiding. I don't know where they've anchored their boat, but I saw them. They asked me which road to take to the Kastro...'

Barba-Dimos suddenly began to take the matter a bit more seriously. But he couldn't completely refrain from banter:

'Are you sure it wasn't a dream, my man? Where are these Corsairs of yours?'

'I saw them with my own eyes I tell you. They will be here any moment now. Don't lower the bridge before the elders give you permission. Set guards at Pregadi and elsewhere, otherwise they may take you at night!'

And with this the shepherd started to move away from the bridge.

'Are you out of your mind, man,' Barba-Dimos yelled for the last time.

'My mind is fine, rest assured. You'll see.'

'And you, where will you go?' the gatekeeper asked.

'I have my goats to tend, and besides, I know all the island's caves where I can hide,' the shepherd replied.

Indeed, the question had finally worked its way into Barba-Dimos's mind: if, in fact, pirates had invaded, the shepherd had taken no thought for his own safety. Meanwhile the Shepherd faded into the distance and soon had disappeared completely.

Barba-Dimos started crossing himself prodigally from behind the gun-slit. He hurried down from the terrace and entered the kiosk where he relayed the news to the elders of the Kastro.

V

It was true. It had never occurred to the humble goatherd who grazed his few goats in the pastureland of Three Crosses to ask Barba-Dimos to throw him the rope-ladder or to let down the hook and hoist by which, as the keeper reported, his apprentice had ascended to the terrace. He hoped, first of all, that the pirates wouldn't suspect what he had done. But in any case, just as he knew the islands crags and hidden paths, so he knew all the coves and hollows along the rocky northern perimeter of the island. Yet he was saddened to think how his poor goats would manage, these animals that parsimonious fate had entrusted to his care.

His partner, Mr Anagnostis, the elder, was not a generous-handed man, you see, and should the Poor Shepherd lose his goats he would be destroyed, for he had little hope of raising capital enough to replace them. Consequently, everyone would say he was no good. He understood how the world works, even if he was a mere herder of goats. If things are going well for you, they put on a good face while digging your grave behind your back, and when things are not going well they simply kick you when you're down. Nor did the shepherd indulge in any wild reveries about a reward or other compensation for having announced the impending danger and saving the whole village from slaughter and plunder. These things are, how do we call them, 'sacred matters', and if there were any reward for them it would lie elsewhere; the shepherd had a vague understanding of such things.

*   *   *

The poor herdsman who grazed his few goats in the pastureland of Three Crosses was thinking of all this as he returned along the same path he had taken to the fortress.

When he reached the level of the precipice where the path had first begun, three men who were hiding in the bushes jumped out and seized him. The shepherd let out a strangled cry. The armed men quickly muzzled and bound him, and brought him to their companions.

They were members of the rearguard of the Muslims. After they had reached the valley near the approach to Three Crosses, they had found the untended goats of the Poor Shepherd to be tempting prey. The barbarians promptly slaughtered three fat billy goats and as many kids as were there, then flayed and spitted them.

The men had been waiting there for the signal they'd agreed on with their other companions: five gunshots. Until the Kastro was taken they would have time to roast the slaughtered animals and have a small feast. One of them lit a fire and started cooking the most tender of the kids.

Three or four of them had taken a seat by the precipice looking out toward St Saviour. They were watching for their ship to appear.

These were the captors of the humble shepherd.

They bound him but left him otherwise unharmed. They were clearly ignorant of the shepherd's deeds, his race to the fortress and his betrayal of their arrival to his compatriots.

As time went by the pirates grew concerned. Finally, the ship cautiously appeared beyond the peninsula of St Helen and came to rest not far from St Saviour. But still no gunshots were heard from the fortress.

At last, at around eleven in the morning, with the sun nearly at the sky's meridian, the twelve scouts who'd gone ahead arrived back empty-handed. They were breathing hard and sweating.

The captive shepherd understood from their angry looks and the wild expressions on their faces (without knowing a word of that barbaric tongue) that they had found the fortress gate closed and the bridge raised. St Saviour had accomplished his miracle. Suddenly one of the barbarians, broad-shouldered and striking, who seemed to wield some power among the others, raised his eyes to the east and cried out in Arabic:

'I swear by Allah, if the traitor should fall into my hands, I will sacrifice him like these goats!'

'What traitor?' asked one of his colleagues.

But at that moment, the man who first spoke, the man with old Suleiman who had used that strange Greco-barbarian tongue when he had asked the shepherd about the road to the fortress, turned his eye to the place where the captive shepherd lay beside the lentisk.

'What's this?' he asked.

And bending down he examined the face of the shepherd.

'Behold the traitor, my friend!' replied the thickset foreigner to the previous questioner.

He began to explain briefly to the pirates that, with his practised eye, from the kind of movement he had discerned in the fortress, from the sort of looks he guessed were being directed at them from the gun-slits in the fortifications over the gate, someone had warned the infidels of the arrival of his Muslim band.

He then asked them where they had found this infidel. His men explained that they had captured him as he made his way along the precipice, while they sat lying in wait for the signal.

And then, as has happened so many times before, the Lord's word came to pass and another barbarian, a sworn defender of the Faith, thought *that he doeth God service.*[1]

＊　＊　＊

He was taken between the heather and the lentisk, where the shy spring flowers broidered the earth's verdant carpet. There he was dragged off by the Algerians, cheering wildly; there he washed the flowers and green branches with his blood; and there a burning stream reddened the earth, which gratefully received it. Then, as a feathered wing, a gentle breeze took up his breath and there he fell asleep in paradise, Poor Shepherd! in the image of *the good shepherd* who *giveth his life for his sheep.*[2]

And after that, how could the earth not give off such fragrance?

[1891]

Translated by Avi Sharon

---

[1] John 16 : 2.　　　　[2] John 10 : 11.

CIVILIZATION IN THE VILLAGE

A CHRISTMAS STORY

F
OR THE SECOND MRS STERGIOS, the saying that 'the first wife is a slave, the second a fine lady' did not, unfortunately, hold true. Poor Thodoria had to endure all the hard work that her husband inflicted on her. He was a lime-burner, she had a bakery. Their poor little son, Eleftheris, had not had enough of his mother's milk. She looked old already, although she had only just turned thirty-five. Old Stergios, who was fifteen years her senior, had taken her as his second wife — in fact he had abducted her, at swordpoint as it were. Little Eleftheris, now four years old, was a pinched, pale, sickly child, and his mother could neither feed him nor wean him. Her breasts, as though charred in the glare of the oven, hung withered on her chest, and the child could scarcely find a drop of milk in them to suck.

Her first two children, one a girl and the other a little boy, had both died, and now all her hopes were pinned on Eleftheris. But a great fear had her in its grip, because he too was ill. She was sick to the bottom of her heart — oh how much better it would be not to be born into the world at all! She recalled with anguish the moment when her little girl 'went to heaven'. She had gone to the cradle and found her stiff, blue, half-dead. At her screams two of the neighbours came running. 'What is the matter? What has happened?' 'My child! My child!' They called the doctor. By the time the doctor arrived, the girl had breathed her last. And all in one hour, just one hour! Her neighbour, Katerina the Midwife, came and laid the child in its shroud, while Thodoria looked for the little garments to dress it in; she bent over the chest to find them, keening quietly as she did so, and Katerina rebuked her, saying that you don't keen over the dead before you have dressed them. They attired the body as prettily as possible, laid it on the bedspread and covered it up in case the little boy saw it and started to cry. Little Charalambos was two years older and able to understand; the neighbours took him away until the body had left the house. Later that evening, when little Charalambos asked, 'Where is Chrysso, mother where has Chrysso gone?', they answered that she had gone to sleep 'among the flowers'. And Katerina the Midwife told him that she had gone 'to the priest's threshing-floor, down in the orchard'. And the child went on asking, 'When will she come back, mother, when will our Chrysso come?' until three days had passed and he forgot her.

Who could have guessed that he would join her so soon! A year later little Charalambos fell ill. Get the doctor, quick — they rushed to get the doctor in case the same thing happened. The doctor came and looked at him: 'It's nothing.' He sent them some medicine, then he sent them some more medicine. The more medicine the child took, the higher his burning temperature climbed. The doctor came and looked at him again. 'He'll be better in three days.' In three days he was dead. How could she find it in her heart to search out his little garments, how could her hands bear to deck him out in them! Luckily Katerina the Midwife was there, with her unfailing willingness, her white gauze scarf under the Constantinoplitan head-dress, her upper lip faintly shadowed by a moustache, and took over the task from her. Her voice should be keening over him, but how? What songs could she sing for him? The priests came and took him, too; they sang over him and brought him 'to the flowers', where they had brought little Chrysso a year ago.

Now all that was left to her was this child, Eleftheris. She lay beside him, her head resting on her arm which was stretched out across the child's pillow, and the child's head in the crook of her left arm. She was unable to get to sleep with thinking of all she had been through. On the hearth, the few remaining embers still smouldered among the ashes. Above her head the oil-lamp burned in front of the icons, casting a line of light across the melancholy faces of the saints.* Her husband, stretched out on her right, had been snoring since nine o'clock. He had already turned over twice, and he breathed heavily, muttering something, and sometimes he let out a mooing sound in his sleep. Poor old Stergios! He wasn't such a bad man, even though he did tend to eat the bread from the bakery, saying that by running a bakery in the neighbourhood his wife had got out of the chore of making bread at home. He brought her plenty of wood on his donkey, all the wood left over from firing the lime-kiln. But he was hard-working, and he didn't really give his wife such a bad time. Except that when he sold a lot of lime all at once and had a bit of money, he never came home with his purse full or his belly empty. Usually he went off to 'refresh the inner man'. And if it happened to be a Saturday night, he had a three-day holiday, as Thodoria put it, and was 'in glorious heaven' until Monday morning. But she knew his ways, and when she saw that he was under the influence she never commented, as he might then lay into her. But on the Monday morning, before he left for the kiln, she would ask him to give her some money if there was any left over, and he would come somewhat to his senses.

In the days before Christmas, he had 'rejoiced in the Lord', having sold a lot of cans of lime and got some money in his pocket. Now Christmas was over and the New Year, the feast of St Basil, was coming,* and because there was a Sunday in between he hadn't yet pulled himself together. This evening he had got a bit merry again, but luckily he had come back early, whence Thodoria concluded that there was no money left over from the last sale. However, what she did not know was that in the course of the day old Stergios had sold some more lime. And the reason he had come back early was because he had got a bit bored of being tipsy, and also he had a bad headache. Even so, Thodoria was glad because, seeing that her child was ill, at least she would have her husband for company, even though he was asleep; and his snores were somehow a comfort to her in her anxiety.

But the child was getting worse. Thodoria, sleepless from

watching over the patient, suddenly saw that her son was struggling, gasping for breath and coughing. His forehead was pale, his lips dry, his eyes were dim, and a faint flush was spreading from his cheeks to his temples. The woman, aghast, remembered the symptoms shown by the other children and was seized with panic. Hastily she shook her husband awake.

'Stergios, get up!... are you asleep, husband?'

Old Stergios, drowsing, stretched and yawned.

'What's up?... What d'you want? Can't you sleep, Thodoria?'

And he turned over.

His wife shook him more roughly.

'Can't you hear, husband? Have you gone to sleep again? For heaven's sake!'

'What're you talking about, woman?'

'Get up, the child is ill.'

'And what d'you expect me to do about it?... If he's ill, he'd better get well, that's all...'

He was floating away as if over an abyss that yawned to swallow him, that he imagined to be his wife's mouth, and he pressed himself into the pillow as if against the edge of a gently, deliciously swaying swing, the image, it seemed to him, of sleep; and like a swimmer preparing to plunge, he made ready to immerse himself once more in slumber.

'Are you going to get up, father?'

Thodoria pronounced the word 'father' as if it came from the lips of the sick child. Then, unable to keep back her tears, she said again:

'Are you going to get up, father, or are you going to let me die too, as our Chrysso and little Charalambos died? Those two are "among the flowers", father, in the other world, in the true life, where all children have a father... In this world here, I have no other father but you, and you have no other child but me...'

Hearing this complaint, old Stergios was touched, and pushing back the coverlet he sat up in bed, rubbed his eyes and turned towards the child's cot. His wife fetched a jugful of water and washed his eyes with it.

'Won't you go and get the doctor, Stergios dear?'

'Doctors, doctors... There's no trusting doctors, they've no human feelings... Do you really think they care, wife? Alright, so I'll go, I'll call him, I'll throw stones at his window, and he'll pretend he hasn't heard me, or else he'll get up and shout curses at me, send me packing. "Couldn't you have come earlier? What kind of time is this to be waking up the doctor?" Ah wife, you have no idea how hard these people's hearts are!'

'Never mind, just go, and blame me for it. Say that your wife didn't tell you earlier in the evening that the child was ill.'

Old Stergios got up, dressed himself in his breeches and jacket, tied his broad yellow-fringed sash around his waist, put on his shoes, picked up his faded fez with its short frayed tassel, slung his cape over his shoulders, took the lantern which his wife had lit for him, and went outside. The night was very dark; a few stars twinkled here and there, and the sky had a misty look. The icy north wind which had been raging for three days had dropped an hour ago, and the weather was strangely mild, a mildness which old Stergios immediately knew to be a forecast of snow — indeed, the first sparse flakes had already begun to fall. 'And Thodoria expects me to fetch the doctor,' muttered the lime-burner, yawning, 'as if it's likely that the doctor would come in the middle of the night, when it's snowing!'

Nevertheless he turned right, walked the two hundred paces to the next part of the village, and when he eventually reached the doctor's house, he did exactly as he had said. He knocked on the door, but in vain. Then he threw pebbles at the window of what he knew to be the doctor's bedroom. There was no reply. Finally a shutter was half-opened in the basement, and the maidservant, a lock of her loosened hair falling forwards as she leaned out of the window, said:

'The doctor's not here.'

'Where is he?' asked old Stergios.

'He's out.'

'Out where?'

'He's not back yet. He probably went to see a patient.'

'At this hour?'

'Well, you want him at this hour, so why shouldn't other people?'

Old Stergios stood there, undecided. Suddenly the maidservant, as if wishing to display greater confidence than usual, added:

'Have a look and see if any of the wine shops are open in the square, in case there's some card-playing going on somewhere. Don't say I said so.'

And she shut the shutter at once and vanished.

Old Stergios suspected that the artful girl had been making fun of him. 'Ah yes,' he said, 'they laugh at us old men nowadays, these maidservants, they look at us as though we're completely useless. But I'm not as old as all that, and I've only been married twice, and if Thodoria ever died on me...' He didn't complete his thought, which was only the final upsurge, as it were, of his drunkenness that day; and the image of the pale, feebly-breathing child, and of the tearful mother, rose up before him and cooled his sudden youthful ardour. He remembered the maidservant's words, 'in case there's some card-playing going on somewhere'. And because he was no longer sleepy, and felt ashamed to return home empty-handed, he decided to go back via the market-place, just in case he came across the doctor.

✵   ✵
✵

Along with all the other ills, this village by the sea had been infected by the mania, rampant among its young people, for card-playing. Of all the civil servants, only the assistant customs director, who was bound by a promise, and the magistrate, who was concerned about his reputation, and the teacher of ancient Greek, did not participate in the evening gatherings which took place on a regular basis in one or other of the officials' houses. All the rest — the

assistant harbour-master, the health officer, the two aides or ac-
countants from the assistant harbour-master's office, the court
secretary, the telegraphist — everyone, every evening, threw away
their money at cards.

But the disease was not entirely a foreign importation, as was
proved by the fact that, particularly during these last days, when
the evening gatherings were being held in the smart, well-kept wine
shop owned by Thanasis Moreyios, a good number of local people
took part, including the secretary of the local council, two young
butchers who had served in the army, the tailor who made western-
style clothes (but who spent most of his time acting as a solicitor),
a barber, and two sailors. The primary school teacher came regularly each evening, and would lay a couple of penny pieces on the
six: if he lost, he would leave without saying anything, without even
drinking a tot of rum; but if he won, he would sit with one leg outstretched along the bench and the other on the floor, smoking the
short pipe which he kept permanently alight, and drink two or
three tots of rum, to the value of his winnings; and when the clock
struck twelve, he went home to bed.

The others usually stayed up most of the night, sometimes till
three o'clock, sometimes till four. The wine shop keeper, Thanasis
Moreyios, was highly delighted to have this custom, because apart
from the 'official kitty', he did a brisk trade in muscat wine and
other drinks. The party played cards and drank. Whoever won
would willingly stand the others a drink, except that it was rare for
anyone to admit that they had won. And perhaps they were being
honest, for it is a card-player's axiom that two people win at cards:
the man who never plays at all, and the man who gets to be
'banker'. A member of the first category came in every evening: he
was Captain Yorgos Asproudakis, who never played, yet who was
never absent from the gathering. Two or three others would come
and stand behind the players like spectres turned to stone, living
personifications of good and bad luck. *Barba*-Antonis Priftis, an
aged boatman, also used to come, and stay until someone decided

to stand drinks 'all round'; then, having drunk his rum, he would leave, shepherding off with him the men who stood as though glued to the backs of the players; but if he saw that the drinks were late in arriving he would slip out quietly, or go to his boat to sleep.

Sometimes, though, *Barba*-Antonis Priftis, always partnered by Captain Yorgos Asproudakis, and two others, would go into a corner apart and play Slapjack for the customary rounds of drinks rather than for money. Captain Yorgos always dealt, and if they happened to lose, the two would stay up playing each other until two in the morning. OAntonis was usually the last to lose, and always protested that Captain Yorgos had robbed him.

That evening, when the party had gathered in the smart wine shop, snow began suddenly to fall, but so gently and so softly that it was as if God were laying out white sheets on the road for the poor and the homeless. The wind had dropped all at once, and it did not feel cold. Delicately, silently, suddenly, the earth was covered in broad swathes of whiteness. One of the card-players, getting up from the table to stretch his legs (it was now half past midnight), went to the window to look out through the dim panes. But he could hardly see anything except a boundless whitish gloom. At that moment a knock came on the door of the wine shop, which was bolted from within.

'Open up, Mister Thanasis!'

'Who is it?' shouted the landlord, whose voice sounded as though he had a cold, and who was sitting beside the table and keeping a watchful eye on the players.

'Open up, it's snowing.'

More by coincidence than in response to the appeals of the man who knocked, the player who had got up to look through the window, unable to make anything out distinctly and wanting to see whether it was snowing, opened the door and old Stergios came in, shaking out his cape, which was white on this occasion with something other than lime. For by the time he had gone from his house to the doctor's and from the doctor's to the market-place, where he saw a light on in the wine shop of Thanasis Moreyios, the snow was falling thickly, and in a few minutes lay inch-deep on the ground.

'It's snowing, it's snowing!' they all said on seeing old Stergios white with it, and those who were standing went towards the door, while those who were seated playing solitaire shouted:

'Shut the door!'

'Where have you sprung from, old Stergios?'

'What a time to turn up!'

'Have you left the kiln in the middle of the night to come here?'

Old Stergios made no answer to these comments, but having spotted the doctor immediately, sitting between the assistant harbour-master and the court secretary, he approached him and bending down, spoke into his ear:

'Will you do me a favour, your honour, and come to my house? Someone's ill at home.'

'Who is ill? Your wife?'

'No, my son.'

'And you come now?'

'The blessed woman didn't tell me about it. But the boy was alright earlier on, he's got worse during the night.'

'Can't you see it's snowing? How can we go?'

'Come and sit down, old Stergios,' said another voice. 'Thanasis, bring a glass of muscat for old Stergios. Have some muscat to warm you up. Come and sit here, next to me.'

It was the secretary of the court, a tall, fair young man with large tow-coloured side whiskers and eyes which bulged out of his face. He happened to be banker at the time, and when he saw old Stergios his whiskers twitched like a cat's when it scents a mouse.

He grasped him by the elbow with his strong hand and, with that friendly force which certain people like to exert towards others of a weaker character, made him sit down beside himself. His name was Aristidis Manganopoulos, and with the change in the ministry (it was around 188_) he had been pitchforked into here from the other end of the Kingdom. He was pleasure-loving, a tippler, a decent enough chap; but who could live on sixty drachmas a month?

Old Stergios drank the glass of muscat and then, leaning round behind the secretary, said once more into the doctor's ear:

'Do me this favour, doctor, and God will reward you. My wife sent me and she'll be waiting for me. The child is in danger.'

The doctor was a good-hearted young man, approaching forty, tall, slim, well-disposed, neither callous nor greedy. He had graduated from the university of Athens and, although he could have gone if he chose to Europe for further education, he had no inclination to do so. Sometimes, however, he got bored, and that evening he blamed himself for having been lured into playing cards with the party. He thought that if he had gone early to bed, old Stergios's son wouldn't have fallen ill, and old Stergios wouldn't have come to invade his peace.

'How did you know I was here?' he asked him suddenly.

Old Stergios immediately remembered the maidservant's instructions and answered:

'I was on my way to your house and I went along by the beach, where it's more sheltered... When I saw a light on in the wine shop, I said to myself, I might as well go in, just in case the doctor's there.'

'And what reason did you have to think I might be here?'

'I don't know why it occurred to me ... I somehow felt you would be... and anyway I wanted a spot of rum to warm me up.'

'And instead of rum you've been drinking muscat...'

'That's thanks to Mister Secretary here, he offered me a drink.'

Aristidis Manganopoulos had not forgotten about old Stergios, but he was at a loss as to how to keep him there. On hearing the limeburner's words, however, he hastened to join in the conversation.

'Well now, old Stergios, aren't you going to have a little bet, to pass the time?'

Old Stergios was not totally unacquainted with cards. In his youth he had been a corporal in the army, and had spent four years living in different cities in Greece.

To please the secretary, he bet a penny and lost. But in a few minutes he took out all the coins he had in his pocket, amounting to more than ten pennies, and he lost them all.

To console him, Aristidis Manganopoulos stood him a penny's worth of muscat. Old Stergios knocked it back, and then, bending once more to the doctor's ear:

'Let's go now, doctor... The snow must have stopped.'

'It's stopped, but it hasn't melted,' murmured the secretary under his breath.

'Alright, let's go and look ... we'll see if we can, old Stergios,' said the doctor. 'Dammit, did your child have to get ill now?'

'Please, doctor, may God reward you...'

The secretary, turning towards old Stergios, said:

'Come on, old Stergios, what's on your mind?... Have a bit of a play, to pass the time... get your money back, too...'

'I haven't any money left, Mister Secretary.'

'Don't tell fibs, old Stergios. Do you think I don't know that you sold some lime today?'

The simple old man leaned over and said surreptitiously into the secretary's ear:

'You speak to the doctor too, see if you can persuade him to come.'

'Come where?'

'Come home with me — my son is ill.'

'There's nothing wrong with him,' said the secretary, 'don't you worry. He'll be alright.'

'My wife's waiting for me, she's all on her own... just think, Mister Secretary.'

'Come off it, old Stergios, cheer up!... don't be afraid, nothing's going to happen to the child.'

Old Stergios bowed his head, and at that moment there rose before him the fearful image of the child in agony, coughing and gasping, its forehead deathly pale, and of the suffering mother, wringing her hands and begging for mercy.

'Bring two glasses of muscat for myself and old Stergios, Thanasis,' ordered the secretary.

The landlord brought the two glasses. Manganopoulos poured most of the contents of his into that of his companion.

'I'm not drinking,' said the old lime-burner, 'it'll be too much for me... besides, I drank earlier this evening.'

'Drink up and stop worrying... Don't think about it... The child will be fine.'

Old Stergios drank down the fragrant liquor, and gradually the fumes started to rise to his head.

'You're a good friend,' he said to the secretary. 'You've put some heart into me... I was so afraid about my child.'

'Bring out a little something and I'll change it for you, old Stergios,' said the secretary, pushing the penny coins around on the table. 'See all these?... I lost them earlier this evening... I can't even get my money back...'

Old Stergios pulled out his cloth purse, greasy and filthy, which was tied round the mouth with string, opened it, extracted a five-drachma piece, and gave it to the secretary, who changed it for him. One of the party had gone outside, and now came back in.

'The snow's more than knee-deep... How are we going to get home, lads?'

'Has it stopped falling at least?' asked the doctor.

'No, it's still falling.'

'Hell.'

'D'you hear that, old Stergios?' said the secretary. 'It's still snowing... Stay here until it stops, and then you and the doctor can go.'

'Oh... alright then, Mister Secretary.'

'Won't you bet a little something?'

Old Stergios started by betting a little something, then another, and then another, and then went on to higher stakes, and then it was double or quits, and then paroli,[1] and at every double or

---

[1] Paroli: a gambling term denoting that the winner is not withdrawing his winnings but places them in their entirety on the next round of the game.

quits the secretary stood him a glass of muscat, and at every paroli a penny piece. And in half an hour he had lost every last half penny of his fifty. So he took out a second five-drachma piece, and in fifteen minutes he lost that; and he took out a third, the last he had left, and in ten minutes the secretary with his bank had mopped it up.

It was now three hours after midnight.

Suddenly there was a knock on the wine shop door.

'Open up! open up!'

'It must be a lunatic, in this snow,' said the landlord.

'Open up please, Mister Thanasis!'

'Who are you?'

'It's me, Yorgis Sefertzis.'

'What do you want?'

'Is old Stergios the lime-burner there?'

'What d'you want him for?'

Everyone turned in the direction of old Stergios, who, drunk on the muscat, was smiling foolishly at the secretary's side-whiskers and saying:

'I don't care! Take the lot! to hell with being poor!... I'm not bothered about money!... It's friendship I care about!... You're a real friend, you are!'

The door was opened and Yorgis Sefertzis came in.

*   *
*

Thodoria leant against the pillow, feeling the child's hot breath on her cheek, and counted the minutes and the hours that had passed since her husband left, saying: 'He'll come now, he's coming... he'll be here any minute... he'll bring the doctor with him, to make my child better... you can't blame the doctors, it's the parents' fault for not realizing... If I'd called the doctor in time, little Charalambos wouldn't have died.' She listened for the sound of her husband arriving with the doctor, but there was nothing to be heard. God was snowing silently, shedding snowflakes to intoxicate the earth, for the living to eat of its fruits, and as a white shroud for the dead, burying them yet deeper under the ground.

But time was passing, and there was no sign of old Stergios. Thodoria got up, threw some sticks into the fireplace, stirred up the fire, and went back to lie down beside the cot where little Eleftheris was. The child moaned and whimpered piteously, slept uneasily and woke again, cried and coughed convulsively. 'Hush, my darling, hush, my little lamb, you'll be better tomorrow. Daddy's gone to buy you some pretty toys for the New Year, so you can have a lovely time playing with them. And I'll make you a beautiful doll out of dough, brushed over with egg yolk; and your godmother will bring you another doll, a lovely great big one, all bright and shiny, embroidered all over with little birds and nightingales, like no other little boy has.' The child had lost consciousness, perhaps, of his surroundings, and had not spoken since the evening. Thodoria asked him over and over: 'Where does it hurt, Leftheris my lovey, where does it hurt?', but by way of answer the little boy only moaned and gasped for breath.

In the fireplace a piece of wood suddenly flared up with a crackle of sparks, and Thodoria, reminded of the popular rhyme, started to recite it:

> *If it's a friend, God give him joy,*
> *if it's a foe, God give him pain,*
> *but if it's someone of this house,*
> *God bring him quickly home again.*

But the sputtering went on for a long time; the rhyme, seemingly, had no power to put an end to it, perhaps because this time it was both friend and enemy, both of the house and not of it...

Finally the sputtering stopped, but old Stergios did not come back. Thodoria had not had a wink of sleep since the evening before. How slowly the hours passed! The poor woman's eyes closed involuntarily and for a few moments she drifted off into that condition in which the soul approaches the threshold of the fantastical palace of dreams, even though sleep has not entirely overwhelmed the body. But after a moment she was woken by another sputtering noise, not unlike the one which had just ceased: the sound of the wick in the oil-lamp before the icons struggling, with the last drop of its oil, to save itself from the water on which it floated, like a drowning man clinging to a plank, or like the soul floundering in pain and bitter anguish before it leaves the body. What a mysterious, mournful sound that sputtering was! It sent a shudder of fear through one. The oil-lamp seemed alive, presageful, prophetic. What was it recalling? seeing? foretelling? It seemed to want to go out, as though weary of being both sacred and profane, of illuminating the tranquil dispassion of the Byzantine saints, the soul's passions and affections, the sins of mankind... The lamp wished to go out, but the wick resisted and flickered on... *

Thodoria sat up, raised her head, and remained for some moments listening to the sputterings of the wick. Her face, chin and throat took on that expressiveness which we so admire in the paintings of the great European masters. She was tall, dark, attractive, pleasing, almost beautiful. Although she was only thirty-five, her black hair was plentifully sprinkled with white at the temples, as though scorched by the oven or whitened with lime. Poor unfortunate woman, lime-burner's wife, village breadmaker!...

Thodoria took out the oil-can from a cupboard and lowered the oil-lamp; the sound of the cord as it grated in its pulley made her wince. She poured oil into the lamp, raised it, crossed herself three times before the icons of the saints, and prayed to the Virgin to help her. 'My husband is a long time away, though,' she said afterwards. 'Dear God, what can have happened to him!' She thought that if she opened the window to look out, she would see him coming, together with the doctor. She went to the window, opened it, and saw with amazement that the street was white in the darkness, and all the roofs white as well.

'It's been snowing! Good heavens, when did all this snow fall?'

She clasped her hands together, overcome by this added distress. Up until now she had feared for her sick child, now she began to worry about her husband as well. What had become of him? Was he somewhere under the snow? Had he fallen over? Had he frozen to death? Had he had a heart attack? Oh dear God! She reproached herself for sending him out at such an hour to get the doctor. It would have been better to leave the child in God's hands. Christ and the Blessed Virgin help us! What had happened to old Stergios? He must be ill. Suppose they brought him to her in the morning frozen, suffering from heart failure, dead! Oh heavens!

She shut the window and thought for a moment what to do. It crossed her mind to go herself, as she was, and find out what had happened to her husband. But the child, how could she leave the child? And anyway, how could she, a woman, go running around at night in the snow? It was probably impassable. She searched about in her mind for reassurance. Perhaps old Stergios hadn't managed to persuade the doctor, perhaps the doctor had been adamant, and old Stergios had been ashamed to come back empty-handed, had got into a temper and... might he have found a wine shop open at this time of night, or he'd met up with some friends and they'd started drinking?... But what time was it now?... He'd been gone a long while. There couldn't be a wine shop open at this hour. A bad thing if there was. She hesitated a little longer, then went across to the other side of the house and opened the other window, which faced west. Right up against it was the house of Yorgis Sefertzis, a neighbour with whom they hadn't quarrelled for a long time.

'Neighbour!' she called. 'Mrs Yorgis! Neighbour!'

She waited a few moments. No answer.

'Neighbour!' she called again. 'Yorgis!'

A few more seconds passed, then a woman's voice said:

'What are you shouting about, Mrs Stergios?'

'Is Yorgis asleep?' said Thodoria, recognizing her neighbour's voice.

'Yes, he is.'

'Will you do me a favour and wake him up?'

'What's going on?'

Mrs Yorgis had opened her window. Thodoria explained briefly what had happened.

'And what do you want him for?'

'If he'd be kind enough to go and find out what's happened to my husband.'

'How can he, when the snow is over his head?'

'Over his head?... oh dear oh dear, what am I going to do?

Meanwhile Yorgis had woken up, and after objecting for a while he gave in to the pleading of the unhappy woman and decided to go out and look for her husband. In places the snow was actually more than knee-deep, while in the more sheltered spots it did not exceed two inches. Luckily Yorgos Sefertzis, a former sailor turned farmer, had a pair of old boots which came over the knee.

*　　*　　*

At the end of the street that goes up beside the sea, next to the cobbled way leading to the higher part of the village, neither in nor altogether out of the market-place, stood the shop belonging to Master Argyros Sirmatenios.* If the tax inspector or the president of the Local Council or anyone else had wanted to make a correct assessment of the taxes to which his business was liable, they would have been puzzled as to what category of tradesman he belonged to, since to all appearances he sold nothing at all. Inside the shop, which was actually open from morning until eight o'clock at night, there was nothing to be seen except brackets and chests, empty showcases, two or three permanently empty barrels, a pair of scales of questionable usefulness, and next to the scales a small jar whose cover was frequently lifted by people who supposed it to contain snuff, but whose hopes were dashed when they found it empty. True, on such occasions they were generously offered the snuff-box of Master Argyros Sirmatenios, who spent all day sitting on his stool, inhaling snuff and discussing the day's politics or local affairs with a few friends.

Master Argyros, tall, pale, stout, sixtyish, with light brown hair, very fine-featured, his small eyes hidden behind spectacles, had lately decided to adopt European dress in deference to the times, but still wore an ankle-length fur cloak over his European clothes, and on his head an embroidered cap. The thumb and forefinger of his left hand were permanently joined, practically stuck, together, holding his eternal pinch of snuff. He took snuff as all old misers do, who feel the need to replace all the passions — tobacco, wine, cards, billiards, travel, banquets, love itself — with one, the cheapest of all. And despite the fact that the jar was empty, Master Argyros was happy to pass round his snuff-box, thinking perhaps that at the cost of fifteen or twenty penny pieces a month, he earned a great many people's gratitude and made a lot of friends.

And while downstairs in the shop the law-abiding Master Argyros spent his days in this monotonous fashion, often lavishing good advice as well on all and sundry, upstairs in the house his wife, a woman of his own age, ran the main business, which consisted in the sale of silk material and gold thread of varying quality to those women in the village who had daughters to marry off and had to embroider the bride's trousseau. Out of this business, very scrupulously, Master Argyros would make a profit of up to seventy-five per cent.

It was said, however, that he also sometimes lent money to close friends, on security, which always represented three times the value of the sum loaned, and at an annual interest rate not exceeding eighty per cent. 'Times are hard, bless you. Money these days is not easy to come by. And anyway, look, if you go and squander your money like a good-for-nothing, that's no one's fault but your own, is it? And if you go and drink it all away, well, why take it out on someone else, may I ask? Why expect someone else to fork out money, if you get my meaning? If you, God forbid, can't make a living, you're to blame for being so lazy. And Lord love us, who's got enough money to go around helping others? I can't afford to throw it away, as God is my witness...'

On the morning of the following day it had stopped snowing, and the risen sun, dispersing the clouds, shone mildly on the earth, melting the occasional patch of snow where it lay more lightly. Many of the villagers, street by street, in high boots and equipped with spades, were labouring to clear away the snow and open a way through, when old Stergios, wearing his cape and looking sad and mournful, appeared in Master Argyros's shop at nine o'clock.

'What's up, Stergios?' asked the latter. 'You look pensive.'

'Ah, Master Argyros,' replied old Stergios with a sigh, 'don't even ask... I'm not well.'

'What's wrong?'

'My child died this morning, my only child...'

Tears fell from his eyes as he said this.

'How is that?... Had he been ill a long time?'

'Only a few days, but... yesterday evening he got worse... I went at midnight to call the doctor, but then it started snowing... I couldn't wake the doctor up, so I turned back, I was in tears...and by morning the child was dead.'

'Well, why didn't you wake the doctor, since it was urgent?'

'He wasn't at home.'

'Not at home? At that hour of night?'

'Either he wasn't home, or they weren't letting on,' said old Stergios, avoiding telling the whole truth.

After a moment of silence, old Stergios went on:

'Master Argyros, I've come to you... I'm so ashamed...but I'm really desperate... I've brought you this jewellery...if you could see your way to lending me twenty drachmas or so, to pay for the child's funeral...because I haven't a bean...'

And he showed him two silver earrings and a ring of his wife's.

'Of course you've got money,' said Master Argyros testily. 'You made loads of lime this year, so I've heard.'

'I even earned a bit yesterday,' said old Stergios, 'but I used it to pay off a debt...how was I to know?'

'Why don't you go back to the same people you paid off, and ask them to lend you some more?' observed Master Argyros, without touching the silver trinkets.

83

Even in tricky situations, old Stergios was always ready with an answer.

'The people I owed money to are grocers, they don't lend,' he replied. 'I had bought some things on credit there.'

'And what makes you think I lend out money, eh?' said Master Argyros.

Old Stergios said miserably:

'Please, Master Argyros... after all, I can't bury my child on credit...'

Master Argyros took the three silver objects in his hands and examined them at length.

'Who knows if they're even silver?' he said. 'You have to be a proper goldsmith to know... Anyway, I don't believe everything you've said, Stergios... You owed money and had to pay it back... it's possible. In this day and age, bless you... Business is bad, alright, there's a lot of poor people in the world... I don't know where the money is, you never see any around... And then, Lord love us, you go and drink and get drunk... You've got no feeling of respect for the money you earn... None comes my way, as God is my witness... I'll go and see, as I hope for mercy, if I have twenty drachmas to give you...'

He looked again at the three pieces of jewellery, weighed them in his hand, and said:

'These aren't even worth ten drachmas... Go and bring me something else.'

'I haven't got any more silver in the house.'

'Didn't your wife have any brooches?'

'No, she didn't.'

'No red silken dresses? No gold-threaded scarves? No gowns of satin or jackets of velvet?'

'I'll go and see.'

*　　*　　*

Old Stergios returned home, took whatever silk garments Thodoria possessed, and went back to Master Argyros, whereupon the old usurer counted out twenty drachmas and gave them to him.

He had returned to his house at dawn at the insistence of Yorgis Sefertzis, who had gone to the wine shop. The doctor had also been persuaded, since he would be going home anyway to sleep in the morning, to pass by the house of the old lime-burner. They arrived at the house, Yorgis Sefertzis in the lead, treading in the same tracks he had made in the snow on his way to the market-place, and holding a lantern. After him came the doctor, and lastly old Stergios, staggering and sliding in the snow, falling down and getting to his feet again.

They arrived when the child was at death's door, and were present when it breathed its last. The doctor had pencil and paper on him; he wrote out the 'burial certificate' or post-mortem report, handed it to old Stergios, and went off to bed. Thodoria beat her breast and wept...

*   *
*

In the evening, the little procession came out of the church: it consisted of a small coffin, like a cradle, carried by two men, the two parish priests, old Stergios, Thodoria, and four or five other women, who were neighbours or relatives.

At the door of the village shop opposite the church, a group of men were standing, who removed their hats on seeing the procession. They were the assistant harbour-master, the telegraphist, the secretary of the court, and two others. Aristidis Manganopoulos, recognizing the old lime-burner, asked:

'What's old Stergios doing there?'

'It's his child that died,' replied one of the locals.

'Really? And we were having such a good time at midnight last night... What a time to choose to die, with all this snow!'

[1891]

Translated by Liadain Sherrard

The American

A Christmas Story

T HAT EVENING DIMITRIS BERDES'S SHOP seemed like a ship caught in a storm, a ship sailing with a following wind, one side buffeted by waves, with the water breaking over the gunwale and spraying the unfortunate passengers, while the captain and his sailor, looking preoccupied, gave and took orders in an incomprehensible language, one forcefully guiding the tiller, the other playing out and reefing in the sails, or pulling an oar on the leeward side, both of them running from stem to stern, alarming the less seasoned passengers, who, sprayed by the spume, smelled and tasted the salt at first hand. It was Christmas Eve and each of the customers was anxious to get his shopping done. With the storm scudding across his face and calmness stowed in his heart, Mister Dimitris Berdes hurried to and fro, offering adulterated drinks to his customers, selling short weight to those who bought. He was delighted by the voices of the patrons, inspired by the chink of the coins that fell from above, like sparrows into a trap, into his securely locked drawer. The lad helping him, his cousin's fifteen-year-old nephew Christos, who barely managed to fill bottles from the barrel, weigh the butter short from the jar and empty honey out of a goatskin bag, an apron tied high around his chest, would let out a shrill 'Right away!' in eight different tones and pitches, an expression he had succeeded, over time, in abbreviating to 't'away', then to curtail to 'way' and finally to simplify to 'ay'.

In one corner of the shop, a group of five men sat drinking their mastic brandy before they separated and went home for supper. They were all local merchant ships' captains, waiting for the feast of the Epiphany, when the cross is thrown into the water,* to pass so that they could set sail. One of their number, Captain Yannis Imbriotis, had returned safely with his schooner that very evening and they were welcoming him back. Everyone took turns to toast the captain with a 'welcome home!', then Captain Yannis wanted to toast them himself with a 'safe landfall!' Then each of his friends wanted to order another round for a 'welcome home!' and again Captain Imbriotis responded with his 'safe landfall!' By now the men were in the midst of an animated conversation about the affairs of their profession, about lading, about slumps and lay days, loading and unloading cargo, shipwrecks and damaged vessels. Captain Yannis was telling the story of his last voyage at great length, and he said that because of the obstructive tactics of Turkish officialdom, he had been unwillingly forced to spend some days in Volos where he had called to unload some cargo.

'Ah, I didn't tell you about the traveller I took on in Volos?'

'You took on a passenger from Volos?' asked one of his friends.

'He didn't want to disembark; he stayed on board the schooner. I told him I'd put him up at my house, but he didn't want to.'

'And where's he headed for?'

'Here, for the time being. I asked him, but he didn't want to tell me.'

'What's he doing here?' — 'What sort of a fellow is he?' — 'What did he look like to you?' The sea captains' questions came thick and fast.

'He's a person who's shaved off his moustache and beard and left only some whiskers under his jaw and on his neck. He looked to me like an Englishman or an American, but not quite like a real Englishman or even a real American. The few words he spoke to me in Greek, he pronounced with a lot of effort and thought, not really like a foreigner, but as if he had known Greek at one time and forgotten it. Most of the time we communicated with what little Italian I know.'

'Did he tell you his name?'

'I put him down in our records as John Stothison, with an American passport.'

At that moment Captain Yannis, who was sitting with his back against the wall, facing the door, suddenly cried out:

'Ah! There he is!'

Everyone turned towards the door.

＊ ＊
＊

A tall, well-dressed man entered, about forty-five years of age, handsome, with an open face, clean-shaven except for the few whiskers beneath his jaw and along his neck, with a heavy gold chain on his chest from which hung a small talisman and some gold nuggets. It would have been difficult to guess what race or clime he belonged to. He seemed to have acquired a sort of veneer over his face, like a mask from some other region, a mask of good living and sophistication beneath which his true origins were concealed. He walked with faltering steps, glancing hesitantly at the surrounding faces and objects, as if he were trying to ascertain precisely where he was.

Although, as Captain Imbriotis had said, the stranger had declined, before sunset, to disembark at the town, as soon as night fell he asked the sailor keeping watch on the ship, who was not a local and having nowhere to go remained on board the schooner as a guard, to take him ashore. The sailor complied. The stranger left his luggage, consisting of three very large trunks, in the forward cabin. Coming ashore, he found himself in the waterfront market and looked to left and right as if he did not know where he was. There was no one out of doors because of the bitter cold. The mountains all around were snow-capped. It was 24th December, 187_. He looked into two or three small taverns and coffee shops, then inside two of those village stores that double as grocers' and ships' chandlers. But he appeared dissatisfied, as if he didn't recognize them, and continued on his way. He walked uphill to the small square in front of the church of the Three Hierarchs.* There he seemed to recognize the place. And even though he did not cross himself when he saw the church, he took off his hat in the darkness and put it on again, as if he had met an old friend and was greeting him. Then he looked to his left, saw the little wine shop and general store belonging to Berdes and approached it. He stood for a few moments looking inside. Finally he went in. Actually he had not seen Captain Imbriotis, who, though facing the door, was partly hidden by his drinking companions who had their backs to the door, and by another group standing and drinking at the counter at the front of which stood the bottles of liquor. If he had seen him, he would probably not have gone inside.

'There's the American,' repeated Captain Imbriotis, pointing out the man entering to his companions.

The four captains turned their eyes towards the newcomer and stared avidly at him.

'*Bueno pratigo, signore*,' Imbriotis cried out. 'You made up your mind, I see, to get off.'

'*Please, Captain*,' said one of the skippers in English. He was Captain Thymios Kourasanos, the owner of a large brig, who had made two ocean voyages as far as London and had learned eight or ten English phrases.

'*Thank you, sir*,' the stranger answered politely.

And he tossed a ten-lepta piece on the counter saying only one word to the lad: 'Rum!' Taking the glass in his hand, and so as not to appear to be systematically avoiding people, he approached the group and with some difficulty, making an effort to get his tongue around the words, he spoke in Greek.

'Thank you gentlemen; I no sit and *parler*. It's hard me to *parler* Greek.'

'What's he saying?' asked Captain Thymios Kourasanos, wrinkling his brows. 'He doesn't want to play with us?'

The stranger heard and hastened to correct the misunderstanding.

'Forgive me, sir,' he said. 'To *parler*, to make *conversazione*, how you say it?'

'He means, it's difficult to carry on a conversation in our language,' Captain Imbriotis said, understanding the problem.

'Ah yes! conversation,' said the stranger, 'I forgot the Greek word.'

'*An' whouer you com?*' said Kourasanos, in broken English.

'At this time I came here,' answered the American, 'afterwards, I don't know; I make other trips.'

Captain Kourasanos stared at him, not comprehending a word.

'Won't you sit down, *signore?*' said Imbriotis. 'Where better will you find?'

'I won't sit down. I'm going to make walk, to bring around, how you say it?'

'To go for a *spazio?*'

'Ah, yes! *Spazio,*' said the stranger. 'Yes, I see, if one doesn't speak Italian words, the other doesn't understand Greek.'

He nodded good-bye and turned towards the door. Following this conversation, the five captains continued sailing in a greater sea of ignorance than they had been in when they were enlightened by their colleague Imbriotis.

*　　*
*

Emerging from the wine shop, the stranger headed towards the Kolona, the place that took its name from the column that stood opposite the church of the Three Hierarchs. In the old days, they used to tie the moorings of boats wintering in the harbour to it. He kept looking around to left and right and finally fixed his gaze on a small house, which he stared at for a long time, as if he were trying to remember or recognize something. Finally he turned into a narrow lane that led through the neighbourhood and disappeared from sight.

If someone had followed him though, they would have seen that having walked on a few paces he turned uphill and came, four houses beyond the small house he had stared at so fixedly before, to an empty space between two houses, a space partly buried by the remains of two walls.

It appeared to be the rubble, the ruins of a house that had not long been torn down. Having glanced all around, perhaps to see if anyone was watching him, the stranger stepped timidly into the ruins where, in a corner between two walls, a blackened recess suggested there had once been a hearth. He entered bareheaded, and cap in hand, knelt and rested his head against the cold stone of that corner. He remained on his knees for a few minutes, then rose, wiped his eyes and slowly walked away.

Making his way back down the hill, he stood in the middle of the lane, not far from the house he had seemed to stare at earlier. He stood still, glancing all around to make sure no-one was watching him, and tried to catch some sound. What was it that he was listening to? Perhaps it was songs of the neighbourhood children, their voices mingling and drifting away in the air like the twittering of winter sparrows as they visited the houses singing Christmas carols. In one place these verses could be heard:

> *Christmas, the first birth, the year's first feast*
> *Come out, hear ye, learn that Christ is born*

and over there rang out:

> *My lady with your daughter*
> *My lady with your precious child*

and from elsewhere:

> *May you live long*
> *With hair as snowy as Olympus*
> *White as a turtle dove...*

Innocent voices, pure-toned, joyous, voices of childish delight and happiness.

Suddenly the stranger was obliged to step aside because two children, one carrying a lantern, had just descended a flight of steps and were coming in his direction. He took a few steps backwards, in the direction he had come from. The children passed right next to him but they did not even see him. They climbed up the steps of the very house the stranger had been staring at for such a long time. Seeing that, he made a movement, turning back again with lively interest. He stood straining his ears.

The children banged on the door.

'Shall we come and sing, Aunt?'

After a moment, footsteps could be heard from inside, the door opened and an old woman wearing a black headscarf leaned out. Speaking in a sad voice she said:

'No, my children. What would you sing to us? Do we have any-one? A good year to you, and go and sing somewhere else.'

She handed them a five-lepta piece and the children left, de-lighted to have earned five lepta without any more effort than climbing up and down the steps.

Hidden behind a corner, the stranger saw the lined face of the old woman and heard her embittered voice. Oddly, he let out a sigh of relief, and seemed to be pleased.

An idea came to him then, and without much reflection he proceeded to act on it. As soon as the door was closed and the old woman was out of sight, the children came down the stairs exchanging some words with each other.

'Hey, Glior', now we've got one sixty-five.'

'How much does that make each?' said the other, who was in charge of the cash.

'Eighty lepta each.'

'Aren't we goin' to share the old lady's fiver?'

'Yeah, we'll split it, Thanas', eighty for me and eighty for you.'

'Let's get some walnuts and share'em, Glior'.'

'An' if they give us five walnuts, how'll we share 'em?'

Suddenly the stranger appeared in front of the boys, held out his hand and showed them a five-drachma piece.

The children, who had never seen a man without a moustache and beard before, were startled and the one holding the lantern let out a small cry, while the other, with pockets jingling, turned and fled. Then Thanasis, suspecting that if Glioris went off, he might hide the next day and not share out the money, put his lantern on the ground and was about to start running in pursuit of the fugitive. Displaying presence of mind, the American contrived to show the boy the five-drachma piece in the light of the lantern he held in his hand and say:

'Wait! Take this dollar.'

Torn between two fears and two desires, the boy stood with trembling knees and frightened look, wondering what to do.

'Two words to tell me I want,' said the stranger. 'This house you went up, who lives?'

The boy didn't understand very well.

'What's that you're saying, Uncle?' he asked, beginning to take heart.

The stranger put the five-drachma piece in the boy's hand, and tried to explain more clearly.

'You went up now house; the old woman to door came. Who else with her lives this house?'

The child struggled to grasp his meaning. At all events after receiving the five-drachma piece, he had entirely lost his fear.

'Aunt Kyratso lives up there,' he said. 'She gave us a five-lepta piece. There's also another lady; I don't know what she's got to do with her.'

'Her daughter up with her, is it?'

'Must be her daughter, yes.'

'Her daughter married?'

'I don't know if she's married, but she doesn't seem to have a husband.'

'And how many years is her daughter?'

'I don't know how many years it's been, but it must be from when she was born till now.'

And taking his lantern, the boy ran off, clutching the five-drachma piece tightly in the palm of his hand, not wishing to entrust it to his pocket. He ran to find Glioris, to ask for his share. The stranger did not attempt to hinder him.

※　　※　　※

After this the American went off, heading for the waterfront market where two or three coffee shops were still lit up. He looked to see which one had the fewest customers and entered one where he saw a single man, the owner of the café. The old man, freshly shaven and his moustache twirled, with short full breeches, high boots and clean apron, seemed about to close up, but when he saw the American coming in, he looked at him, full of curiosity. The latter ordered a rum, throwing a ten-lepta piece on the counter. Seeing the tenner, Uncle Anagnostis wanted to give him five in change, but the man said 'No! No!' and so the owner poured him another rum, to make up the other five, as he thought, but the stranger threw down another ten-lepta piece on the table. 'He doesn't seem to know Greek,' thought Uncle Anagnostis, and to test him he launched into a conversation:

'A newcomer, are you?'

'I today came with Captain Yannis's schooner.'

'Captain Yannis Imbriotis's?'

'Yes. Can you yourself make punch?'

'Gladly,' said Uncle Anagnostis.

And trying to recall some ancient knowledge to memory, he endeavoured to make punch, but the rum would not catch fire and so he offered it as it was to the stranger. The latter made no complaint and threw a silver shilling down on the table.

Uncle Anagnostis took it.

'How much is this worth?'

'I no understand your money here,' said the stranger.

The old man opened his drawer, to see if he had enough coins to give him change, but he didn't find more than eighty lepta in ten-, five- and two-lepta pieces. Nevertheless his conscience didn't permit him to cheat his customer so he said:

'Haven't you a *svandziko*, sir?'

'I have money no more from England and America,' said the stranger.

'I haven't enough change, sir. Take your silver. I'd say this must be worth about one drachma thirty-five, one forty. Tomorrow you give me twenty lepta.'

'Keep the shilling. I don't want change.'

Uncle Anagnostis stood with mouth agape, staring intently at the stranger. But at that moment a group of three men came in and, standing in front of the counter, ordered a drink each. One of the three men, well in his cups, was singing in an abandoned voice:

Vasilo, you dazzling dame,
cradle me in your arms.

The second man, bare-chested and barefoot despite the cold, began to stare fixedly at the stranger.

'I've seen that fellow before somewhere,' he mumbled.

These three were the town porters and also the town criers, a merry trio of workmates who spent their time drinking away in the evenings whatever they had earned by day. With an abrupt change of rhythm and melody, the singer took up the song again:

Come out you bitch, come out and see,
the body you cause such misery.

'Here's to you, mates!' They clinked their glasses noisily. But the bare-chested, barefoot fellow never stopped staring intently at the stranger. The first one resumed his singing:

What have you put in your pistols?
Damn it, Vasilo, I said,
they're almost as heavy as lead!

At that moment heavy footsteps were heard above on a wooden staircase leading to the living quarters overhead. The stairs were closed in by boards, cutting off one corner of the coffee shop. By the upper part of the partition near the ceiling, a small door opened and a head with a white cap, white moustache and coarse features leaned out of the doorway.

'How many times have I told you, Anagnostis!' came a voice from the head appearing in the doorway, a voice that matched the coarse features. 'When are you going to come to your senses? You're ruining the peace of decent homebodies! Just think what day it is tomorrow, and we have to put up with you singing and shouting again! And what time is it now?'

It was half past eight. The singer of the porters' triumvirate took up the conversation, saying with mock solemnity:

'We're leaving right now, Captain Anastasis! We wouldn't dream of disturbing your peace and quiet!'

'Shut up, you fat-head!' Anastasis shouted.

'Right away, Captain Anastasis,' the café proprietor called out. 'I'm closing up. You see, I can't throw these people out.'

'Such honourable mugs!' Captain Anastasis guffawed from the doorway. 'Be sure you treat them with the ceremony they deserve!'

'Ah, we didn't insult you, Captain Anastasis. It's you who're insulting us,' said the porter. And in a low voice he murmured: 'You want the rent paid to the last penny, and you even know how to ask for it in advance, but if this poor fellow doesn't make a fiver, how's he going to pay you?'

'Quiet, all of you, he's in the right now. It's Christmas Eve, after all,' said the conscientious proprietor. 'It's other times he seems a hard man, bless him.'

In the meantime the head in the white cap had disappeared behind the door, and Uncle Anagnostis was preparing to close up. The three porters left arm-in-arm, singing. The stranger nodded goodbye and left just ahead of them, but the proprietor called him back and said:

'Where are you going to sleep tonight? Do you have a place to stay? Where are you staying? I'm sleeping here for the night. If you're going back to the schooner, that's fine, but if not, stay here if you like; it's warm.'

'I'm not sleep,' said the stranger. 'I'll go walk and then we'll see.'

'Whatever time you like. Just knock on the door and I'll get up and let you in. I have some covers for you too.'

*   *   *

This time the American headed for that neighbourhood by another smaller lane and saw the house that was the focus of his attention from the other side, the south-west. Opposite the little house, at the corner of a neighbouring cottage, there was a heap of wood and stones that had lain there for an unknown number of years like the rubble from a house that had been torn down or the remains of some ruin. The light from a small window shone on this side of the building. One shutter was closed, the other open, and if one moved higher up it was possible to see the interior of the house through the windowpane. Observing that the road was empty and not a shadow of a passer-by could be seen, the stranger climbed up on the pile of rubble, and with his heart pounding, peered into the house. Opposite the half-shuttered window was the hearth, where a slow fire was burning. A single log was casting sparks and high above it the lamp was lit in front of the holy icons. At the hearth sat a woman who seemed still youthful; she rested her head on her hand, pensive and sorrowful. Her lips and voice were whispering something, and the murmuring turned out to be the faint undertone of a song, sung in a soft voice, clear and virginal but at the same time faded. And these two lines clearly reached the stranger's ears:

Woe is me and misery,
alas for the sailor so far from me . . .

The stranger felt pain in his heart and a tear in his eye. He had a sudden urge to climb down from the pile of rubble and run into the house. To do what? He scarcely knew himself. He managed to restrain himself. At that very moment a faint sound could be heard, a creaking as if someone were climbing an inside staircase, as if a trapdoor were being shut. A second woman, old and bent, wearing a black scarf on her head, approached the hearth and, kneeling in front of it, threw some sticks on the fire. It was the same woman who had given the five-lepta piece to the children and sent them on their way.

'When are tha' goin' t' come to tha' senses I'd like to know, daughter? . . . Goin' t' weep a' the while? . . . Ach! what's on thy mind? Just hearken t' thee! . . . Cut off from other folks, we are . . .

Dost thou think thou be the only one? When they were still after thee while there was still time, after that good-for-nothin' fellow of yours went off to America, why didn't thou want any of them? Didn't I tell thee? Why don't tha' listen to thy mother? I told thee over and over again. Now thou'rt grown too old, whose fault it is? And dost thou think thou'rt the only one? There are some older than thee. There's Mahou's daughter Mygdalio, and Yorgina's girl, Krystallio — why thou'rt just a chicken compared to them!'

The stranger was all ears, and seemed, oddly enough, to understand what the old woman was saying, probably from intuition and awareness of the situation, or from the little Greek he appeared to know.

At that moment footsteps and the sound of voices could be heard from the corner of the street. Two men were approaching. The eavesdropper made haste to climb down from his vantage point and disappear. Reaching the end of the lane, he turned right and found himself once again in the small square in front of the church of the Three Hierarchs.

* *
*

The little wine shop where the present narrative began was still open. Dimitris Berdes did not scorn even small profits, nor did he turn down a single five- or even two-lepta piece. He called these 'small bait'. The others, the profits he made earlier in the evening, he called 'net hauls'. 'Whatever you haul in,' he would say, 'whether it's with a troll or a drag-net is good.' Berdes was taking good care of the bailiff and the local constables; he plied these guards or nightwatchmen with watered wine, and they permitted him to stay open until eleven o'clock, finding it certainly warmer to sit there than to walk around the town getting cold.

The wine shop owner was standing at that moment at the till, counting the ten-lepta pieces, the twenty-five-lepta pieces from the period of Otho's reign,[1] and the *svanzika*. The lad Christos, with his

[1] See note to p. 28.

apron tied nearly under his armpits, was asleep on his feet, his head nodding like a small row-boat rocked by a light southerly as it comes alongside a two-masted schooner resting at anchor. From time to time he was woken abruptly by the stamping of the proprietor's foot, and by the even louder sound of his voice repeating the orders of the customers. Then like a sleepwalker, he would move, serve drinks, take the coins, throw them mechanically into the till, come back and continue his sleeping.

Stamping their feet as they danced, shouting and whooping, the merry band of the three town porters, having been expelled from Uncle Anagnostis's shop, invaded the wine shop. One of the three, Stoyiannis Dobros, a Macedonian Serb by origin, was acting the bear and dancing, while the second, Pavlos Halkias, who had been singing earlier, had blackened his face and played the gypsy bear-owner. It may not have been Carnival time yet but since it would be Christmas Day tomorrow, after Christmas 'comes St Basil's Day', they say, and after St Basil's, Epiphany, and after Epiphany it's only a week or two until Carnival.* The third fellow, Vangelis Pahoumis, the leader of the gang, hairy-chested and barefoot, with his trousers rolled up, as usual, just under his knees (a result, perhaps, of his long habit of wading into the sea to unload boats) had not stopped thinking about the American. 'He keeps coming back into my mind,' he had said.

And lo and behold, a moment later the object of his meditations came in. He walked up to the counter, ordered a rum and threw a silver shilling down on the metal counter-top. Berdes picked it up.

'What's this worth?'

The American shrugged with indifference and said:

'I don't know local money.'

'That doesn't tally with our money, and it's no good here,' said the wine shop owner. 'If you like I can take it as one drachma.'

'*I don't care,*' muttered the American in English. Then he said it again in Greek.

Berdes gave him ninety-five lepta.

While this was going on, Vangelis Pahoumis did not leave off staring at the stranger. Suddenly he turned to the people gathered in the café and said in a loud voice:

'Hey, you fellows, do any of you remember Uncle Stathis Mothonios's son Yannis, the one who's been in America for the last twenty years?'

            *   *
               *

When he heard this name, the stranger started and turned involuntarily towards the speaker. Nevertheless, he restrained himself, tried to feign indifference, and went to sit in a corner of the shop. He lit a cigar and began to smoke.

Nobody answered the porter's question; its hidden allusion escaped them all. Vangelis went on:

'No wonder you don't remember! You're all younger than me except for Uncle Triandaphyllos, who's not from hereabouts, and I'm nearly forty now. I was about eighteen years old when Mothonios's son left for abroad; he must have been about twenty-five then. But it seems to me that I'd recognize him if I were to see him right now. Uncle Stathis and his wife, God rest them, both died of sadness over their Yannis. And their little house fell to wrack and ruin. All that's left of it now are two half-ruined walls up there near the church and a blackened hollow in the corner that used to be their fireplace once. Their son "shook the dust from his feet" too, as they say, never to return. But what a lot of folks disappear for ages and ages in America! Did you know he was engaged too?'

'Who was she?' asked the town bailiff, chief of the nightwatchmen, without much interest.

The stranger was listening with the greatest attention, but refrained from turning his eyes towards the speaker.

'She was Melachro, the daughter of Aunt Kyratso, Michailis's wife. After he'd left and two or three years went by, a lot of men came asking for her hand because she was a charming, good-looking girl, well-respected and gifted at handwork; she was the only embroideress in our village, and had prepared a lovely trousseau. But Melachro wouldn't have anyone, and so the years went by and she's become an old maid. And with all her sighs and sobs, she's grown thin and pale. Still, they say when a woman's built well, she doesn't age easily. She's still quite something, fellows. She must be over thirty-five and she looks twenty-five; I happened to see her one day when I was carrying a sack of flour to their house — the more you look at her the tastier she gets!'

'Come on, Vangelis, cut that out!' said the bailiff sternly. 'It's not right to talk about families and girls in taverns.'

'You're right, *Barba*-Triandaphyllos,' said the porter, 'but I didn't mean any harm.'

The expression of the American became joyful and a ray of happiness burst through that veneer, that seeming mask we referred to earlier, and lit up his face.

Barba-Triandaphyllos, together with the constable and the two nightwatchmen carrying their rifles, turned back and addressing the wine shop owner, said:

'Come on, hurry up Dimitris! Behave yourselves, you lads, enough of the singing and dancing! It's not Carnival. You know what day it is tomorrow? Close up quickly, Dimitris, so people can get some sleep. They'll be getting up at two in the morning to go to church. And the gentleman, I suppose he has some place to sleep?' he asked, indicating the American.

'Don't worry, *Barba*-Triandaphyllos,' said Vangelis. '*Barba*-Anagnostis told him he could sleep the night in his shop. In any case, there's no reason for you to worry about the gentleman,' he added, winking at the bailiff. 'If he wants a place to sleep, he's got plenty to choose from.'

'What's going on?' asked the bailiff, conspiratorially.

'He's from around here, a local,' Pahoumis whispered in his ear.

'How do you know?'

'Somehow or other I recognized him.'

'And who is he?'

'The fellow I was telling you about before. Uncle Stathis Moth-onios's son, Yannis. When you came to live here, he had already left. That's why you don't remember him. But I'd say you must have come in time to meet his father, *Barba*-Stathis.'

'I did meet him. Hurry up, Dimitris!' the bailiff said again in a loud voice and went out.

Vangelis's two fellow porters had stopped their song and dance and were preparing to leave. Suddenly, going over to the American, Vangelis said in a low voice:

'What'll you give me, Boss, if I go and tell the glad tidings?'

The stranger did not put his hand in his pocket. But between the thumb, index and middle finger of his right hand he found he was holding a British sovereign. He thrust it into Vangelis's palm with such eagerness and joy that he seemed to be the receiver and not the giver.

✲   ✲   ✲

When the neighbours of Michailis's wife, Aunt Kyratso, woke up after midnight to go to church where the bells were ringing loudly, how surprised they were to see the poor widow's house: there, where the children were not welcomed to sing the Christmas carols but were sent away with the phrases 'We have no-one' and 'Why should you sing to us?', all was now brightly lit, the shutters were all open, the windowpanes gleaming, the door opened and shut frequently, two lanterns were hanging out over the balcony, shadows flitted back and forth, joyful voices and happy sounds could be heard. What was going on? What was happening? It was not long before they found out. Those who didn't find out in the neighbourhood, found out in church. And those who didn't go to church, learned it from those who were returning home at dawn after the Divine Liturgy had ended.

The groom who had been abroad, the man who had been in foreign lands for twenty years, the one who had sent no message and left no trace for ten years, who had met not a single compatriot nor spoken any Greek for fifteen years, who had wandered in many parts of the New World, had worked as a contractor in the mines and as a foreman on the plantations, had now returned with some thousands of dollars to the place of his birth, where he had been reunited with his faithful fiancée, older now, but still in her prime.

The only thing he had learned about, fifteen years earlier, was the death of his parents. As for his fiancée, he had been almost convinced she must have married years ago; still, he held out a faint hope. Out of superstitious fear, the nearer he got to his native land the more hesitant he was to ask directly about his fiancée, and so he did not identify himself to any compatriots that he happened to meet when he arrived in Greece. He preferred to remain in ignorance about what had happened to his fiancée until the last moment, when he would disembark in his birthplace and pay a devout visit to the ruin that had once been his father's home.

* * *

Three days later, on the Sunday after Christmas, the wedding of Ioannis, son of Eustathios Mothonios, and Melachrini, daughter of Michailis Koumbourdzis, was celebrated with all joy and dignity.

After so many years, Aunt Kyratso wore her many-coloured 'Constantinopolitan' headscarf again for a few moments to kiss the wedding wreaths.* And on New Year's Eve she stood on the balcony calling to the groups of children passing by:

'Come, children, sing for us!'

[1891]

Translated by Gail Holst Warhaft

A Pilgrimage to the Kastro[*]

A Christmas Story

'DID YOU HEAR? Yannis Nyphiotis and Argyris, Mylono's son, are snowed in near the Kastro, up by Stivoto.' *Papa*-Frangoulis the Sakellarios[1] announced the news after blessing the family meal of beans and olives on the evening of 23rd December in the year of 186_.

Besides his wife, the *papadia*, those present included his two unmarried daughters, his twelve-year-old son and his neighbour Panagos the carpenter, a fifty-year-old *pater familias* who had come to the priest's house, as was his habit, for an evening chat and a *raki*. Aunt Malamo Kanalakaina was also there, a distant relative who had come to bring the offering loaf she had made for the liturgy,* a pious widow in her sixties, keen to attend all the religious services and help out in the churches and country chapels without expecting payment.

'We heard it too, Father,' answered their neighbour Panagos. 'That's what they said.'

'What do you mean "they said"?' It's for certain, I tell you,' insisted *Papa*-Frangoulis. 'God bless 'em! They'll never come to their senses. They went out in this weather to bring down wood from the rocky ground up above Kouroupi at Stivoto, where even the goats can't clamber. Serves them right!'

'People just don't think straight anymore, I'd say. They're so reckless nowadays,' added Aunt Malamo.

'Do you think they had anything with them?' asked the *papadia*.

'Who knows?' answered Aunt Malamo.

'Of course they would,' interjected Panagos the carpenter. 'They

---

[1] An honorary ecclesiastical office.

would've taken supplies. It's impossible any other way. They went up there with their sacks full. They'd've taken their rifles and nets for catching blackbirds. And a whole lot of salt for preserving the birds for Christmas.'

'But really, d'you think that they'll be spending their Christmas up at Stivoto?' asked the *papadia* incredulously and not without sympathy for the stranded men.

'Isn't there some way one could help them out?' murmured the priest, who appeared to be thinking it over to himself.

The priest was a man of about fifty-five with receding hair; he was tall, robust and most benevolent in appearance. As a young man he had been a sailor and still seemed to harbour hidden strengths. He was certainly brave and tireless.

'How could they be helped?' said Panagos the carpenter. 'There's no getting through by land. It's snowed and snowed and it's still coming down. Been years since we've had such a heavy winter. St Thanasis's been joined up with Kambia. You can't tell Mygdalia from Kouroupi.'

The names referred to by Panagos were of four mountain peaks, at some distance from each other. Then *Papa*-Frangoulis posed the question:

'And what about by sea, Master Panagos?'

'By sea, Father, the same and even worse. A mighty easterly gale, stormy sea, massive waves. And gaining strength all the time. Nothing but tempests. You can't even poke your nose out of the harbour down at Asproniso!'

'I know about the "Sofran", Panagos, but what about the "Stavet"?'

That was how the priest called the 'Sopra vento' and the 'Sotto vento', that is, the prevailing wind and the leeward wind — the northeaster and the southwester in particular.

'Well, as for the "Stavet", Father, I fears it'll turn into a nor'-wester.'

'In that case, we might as well lay down and give up the ghost! That's no way to speak, Panagos,' concluded the priest.

'Every man's got to look after his own business. Nobody's going to stick his head into the lion's mouth to save you.'

Papa-Frangoulis sighed, as if out of pity for the self-interest and pettiness of which Panagos was a living example.

'And what's going to happen to them anyway?' asked the carpenter, trying to soothe his conscience. 'They'll be holed up in some cave, with their tinder-box and plenty of firewood. If only my wife Panagaina'd have a fire like theirs burning in my hearth tonight. They'll have supplies for at least a week and it's not more than five days since the winter weather bore down on us.'

'If someone were to go now to celebrate the liturgy at Christ's church in the Kastro,' the priest went on, 'he would have twice the profit since he would bring them help too. Last year when the winter was milder we didn't go... this winter when it's bad...'

He stopped there in order for his words to take their effect. The good priest had the temperament of a person who spoke his mind in careful instalments. It will become clear later that he had already taken his decision and all this preliminary discussion was premeditated.

'So why doesn't Christ bring good weather, Father, if he wants people to go and celebrate his feast?' asked Master-Panagos impudently.

The priest cast him a side-long glance, and then responded judiciously:

'Ah, Panagos, my friend, I see that we don't really know what we are talking about, do we?... Who are we to understand these things!... What's generally true is one thing and what's true in a particular time and place, Panagos, is another... The heavy winter comes for the good, for the earth's fertility and even for our health. Christ has no need for people to go and celebrate the liturgy for him... but where there is a little good will, and one has a debt to pay, and maybe even if there is a risk involved, where it has to do with helping others, as in our case here, there God comes to our side, even in the case of bad weather and a thousand obstacles... there God keeps us company, easing the way, working a miracle even. What do you say, Panagos? And besides, why do you want

Christ to give us good weather, since in other years he did but out of indifference we didn't go to celebrate his feast?'

Everyone present listened in silence to this brief, improvised lesson by the priest. Aunt Malamo hastened to add:

'It's true, Father, it's not a good thing that, leaving Christ's church empty on the day of his birth without a liturgy being celebrated there for so many years... God'll be angry with us for that!'

'And didn't we make a vow last year at Christmastide, *papadia*?' the priest asked, turning suddenly in her direction.

The priest's wife looked at him as if she didn't understand.

'When Lambrakis was sick,' the priest continued, gesturing towards his twelve-year-old son. 'Remember the vow we made?'

She remained silent.

'You vowed that if he recovered we would take the next opportunity to celebrate the liturgy at Christ's church on the day of its feast.'

'I remember,' she said, nodding her head.

Out of both irony and fondness they called the priest's only son, the twelve-year-old Spyros, by the name Lambrakis ('the radiant one'), on account of the way in which his little face somehow glowed because of his great thinness and feebleness. He had indeed come close to dying last year at Christmastide. The *papadia* was already nearing her fifties and he had been born some time after her four girls who had survived — the first two of whom were married already — that is, after eight births (of which two were twins) and five deaths. She had vowed that if her son lived she would go this year to the church of the Nativity and celebrate a liturgy there.

She had had the vow in mind and had been reflecting upon it some days before, and from the moment the priest began speaking had been thinking of nothing else. But she could see that this year it would be terribly difficult — formidable, really — an unspeakable act of daring in the light of the severe winter weather, and she judged that Christ would be forgiving and grant them more time to keep their vow.

It was for this reason — since she recognized the priest's usual tactics, and his obstinacy — that she resolved within herself not to oppose him. And not only that but even more heroically — and many could hardly believe it — she was determined that wherever he decided to go, she would follow him.

The *papadia* was a most faint-hearted woman, but only when apart from the priest. When she was near him, she gained strength, her heart caught fire, and she became fearless. If he were to leave without her to go up to the Kastro, her heart would begin to tremble like a hunted bird. But if he took her along, it would be tranquil.

The elder daughter, twenty-year-old Mygdalio, caught the drift of the conversation at once. She was sitting by her mother's side, near the hearth, and she started bending her mother's ear with miserable complaints:

'Where are you going? Have you lost your senses?... In this weather! ... You're going to the Kastro! Ah! Poor me ... what'll happen to me?

The younger daughter, sixteen-year-old Vaso, also began to catch on and whispered:

'What's that?... They're going to the Kastro?... And you start weeping and wailing! Are you out of your mind? Be quiet, you! They'll take me with them... Will you take me, mummy?'

'Shush! Keep still!' snapped their mother.

'What's going on?' asked Aunt Malamo, hearing all the whispers over by the hearth.

'Nothing, Malamo,' replied the priest with a stern look. 'Don't worry about it!' Then he turned to his neighbour the carpenter and, coming up with a plausible way to get rid of him, asked: 'Panagos, would you be so good as to go and tell *Barba*-Stephanis Verkas to come over so I can speak with him?...'

Panagos the carpenter, a big man with a slight stoop, stood up to his full height and gave himself a shake.

'I'm on my way,' he replied. 'Anyway, I want to go and see if Panagaina's got anything ready for us to eat tonight.'

'Go and tell him first, and then go back home and eat.'

'Your blessing, Father.'

And bidding goodnight to the priest's wife, he went out.

* * *

'Well, I say, what's happening here?' asked Aunt Malamo once Panagos had left. 'So, Father, you're going to the Kastro?'

'We'll see what *Barba*-Stephanis Verkas has to say.'

'I for one'll come,' said Aunt Malamo, ' if you decide to go.'

'And me too,' the *papadia* joined in.

'You don't need to come too, *papadia*,' said the priest. 'It's enough for me to suffer... We shouldn't both be away from the house.'

'I made the vow,' she responded.

'But it's the same if I go.'

'But I'm a bundle of nerves unless I'm by your side, Father,' she confessed.

'And what about us, where will you leave us!' cried Mygdalio, with tears in her eyes.

'Keep quiet, you silly thing,' said Vaso. 'They'll take me with them — so you just hush!'

'Oh, right — you still think of yourself as a little girl, my pet. That's how they've taught you to be! You're not to blame,' retorted Mygdalio, venting her innermost jealousy of her sister's fortune, who as the younger daughter had not yet been 'hidden away', hung in a sort of social limbo as were girls of marriageable age, and so still enjoyed relative freedom.

Little Lambrakis had thrown his arms round his mother's neck.

'Will you take me too, mummy?' he whispered, hugging her tightly.

'Whatever do you mean, my darling! What are you saying, my child?' she answered, kissing her little son. 'If I go, it will be for your sake, my boy. And if I stay behind, it will also be for your sake, my little laddie, so that you don't catch a cold. As your father decides, my little one. Now go and say your prayers, kiss your father's hand and go to bed so you don't get a chill, my sweet.'

'Yes, you'll go! but then you won't!' cried Mygdalio, imitating her mother's manner.

'Quiet! We haven't decided anything yet and you're already up in arms,' said the priest. 'Let's see first what *Barba*-Stephanis has to tell us.'

Then he turned to his wife and asked:

'Has anyone at least brought bread for the liturgy?'

She cast a glance toward the few offering loaves, covered by a striped cloth, that had been brought to the priest's house by some women of the parish who were planning to take communion the day after tomorrow, on Christmas Eve. Aunt Malamo had noticed them earlier and had tried to uncover them with her eyes in order to discover how many there were.

'Have we got some rusks as well?' he then asked.

'There must be some from the feast of the Entry.[1] All during the Christmas fast we make bread from the *vlogoudia* and eat that,' his wife answered.

The *vlogoudia* were the small loaves of bread stamped with the sign of the cross that the women of the parish offered to the priests' families during the fast. But in the place of these little loaves, most parish women in more recent years preferred to offer plain flour, and for this reason the *papadia* said that they 'made bread from the *vlogoudia*'.

✻　✻
✻

Footsteps were heard in the hall. The door opened and in walked *Barba*-Stephanis Verkas, tall and sturdily built, nearly sixty years old, with a thick, grey moustache, tough, sunburnt skin, and wearing a broad hat and a dark blue woollen shirt with a red belt two spans wide. Behind him there appeared another figure standing beside the door. It was Panagos the carpenter, whose curiosity had been roused to find out what was wanted of *Barba*-Stephanis —

---

[1] This feast, which falls on 21st November, commemorates the presentation of the Virgin in the temple by her parents.

even though he had already bid them goodnight, saying that he was going home to have dinner — and so he had come back again to the priest's house.

'Captain Stephanis,' the priest greeted him, 'what do you say about this weather? Could one get to the Kastro by boat with the southwester blowing?'

'With a southwester?. . . by boat?. . . to the Kastro?. . .' was heard, as if the question was echoing back from the door. It was Master-Panagos the carpenter, his head protruding below the lintel, one side of his body squeezed against the door jamb.

But *Barba*-Stephanis, as soon as he heard the priest's query, and without a second's thought, shouted in his thick, rapid and muddled way of speaking:

'Bravo! Bravo! D'ya hear? D'ya hear? To the Kastro? With pleasure! Just got to have the appetite for it, Father, the appetite!'

'There's my man!' exclaimed the priest. 'That's the way to be, Stephanis! So what do you say, is it dangerous?'

'Dangerous? Nah, not on your life! On my head be it, Father. Only you might get cold, that's all. Is the *papadia* coming too? Lots of other folk coming too? The boat's large, you see, takes thirty, forty passengers, and all your provisions, all your bags, all your things. And, you see, the storm's on its way out now. Pretty soon we'll have fair weather, smooth sailing, calm. It's getting better all the time, it's got better now as we've been speaking!'

As if to contradict the old boatman, a sharp blast of the freezing north wind was heard blowing through the trees of the garden and against the wooden walls of the kitchen that was tucked in under the house's covered balcony, and the glass panes and windows groaned mournfully in reply.

'Ah, right! Did you hear that? It's got better!' exclaimed Master-Panagos triumphantly.

'You keep quiet, you don't know what yer talking about!' boomed Stephanis. 'You know how to hew the ribs of a boat and nail planks together. This is the tail force of the tempest, it's the death rattle of the storm. Tomorrow the weather'll let up, I tell you. I'm not saying that we won't still have a bit more snow, but with the sou'wester, I tell you, we'll be fine.'

'And if it turns into a north-westerly wind?' insisted the carpenter.

'And even if it doesn't turn into a nor'wester, from Kechrea on-wards, I tell you, it 'll be a bit rough,' replied Stephanis, rubbing his hands together. 'Those swells follow on the storm once it's died out, you see, the waves get bigger in the bay and the weather gets wilder. But that makes no difference to us. On my head be it — Stephanis takes it all upon himself!'

'Bravo, Stephanis, now you've made my decision for me. Have you had a *raki*? Have another,' said the priest.

'I've drunk five or six already, Father, with your blessing.'

'Have another to make it seven.'

Barba-Stephanis drank down a generous glassful from the small flask kept in the priest's front room that was always being emptied, but was never exhausted.

'Are you ready, are you all ready?' he then asked. 'Have you got your holy things and all your papers, Father, have you got them all together? Is there anything I can carry for you, so that we're all set?'

'From right now?' asked *Papa*-Frangoulis.

'From right now! What d'you say? We've got to be prepared, Father. I'll come at two o'clock to give you a shout and you all have got to be standing by. You read whatever you've got to read, Father, and at three we'll embark.'

'I'll be up from one o'clock,' said the priest, 'since I've got my alarm clock ... and anyway I'm my own alarm clock. But three is awfully early to be setting off, Stephanis. Wait for first light and then we'll set sail.'

'At three, at four, Father, so that the wind doesn't fall, so that we'll have a fair wind as far as Koukounaries, and the day in front of us. From there to Mandraki and Aselinos, we'll take it slowly by oar. From there to Kechrea and as far as St Helen's the sail will carry us gently along. And from St Helen's, if we can't make any progress...'

'Then what?'

'I'll get out where the water is knee-deep and get onto dry land so that I can tow you by the rope as far as St Saviour's.'

They all laughed heartily at the simple sailor's joke, but the priest, who also was afraid of the winds changing at that point, tried to console the company by saying:

'But I say that we'll be able to walk along the shore and uphill from there. However high the snow is piled up on the mountainsides, it will still be possible to walk along the seashore.

They all agreed that the old boatman would come round at three o'clock to get them going and that at four o'clock they would set off. *Papa*-Frangoulis arranged for the bread for the Liturgy — as many loaves as there were — to be put into sacks, along with some dried biscuits, and they packed two large crates with olives and fish roe. Two ten-litre flasks were filled with their own homemade wine. And they wrapped in paper two or three dried octopuses, and filled a small case with dried figs and raisins. The priest's two daughters, the one with her complaints and her whining, the other with her suppressed mirth and anticipation of joining in the adventure, boiled as many eggs as they had — as many as four dozen — and placed them at the bottom of a basket, which they then filled with two offering loaves wrapped in a linen cloth, together with candles and incense. In addition, *Papa*-Frangoulis had asked *Barba*-Stephanis to pass by the houses of two friends of his, sea captains who had their ships tied up in the harbour sheltering from the storms. The priest sent Stephanis there to request on his behalf that they send — if they had any — a little salted meat of the sort that they cook on long voyages. These generous men sent two large pieces — over six kilos all together.

The priest made all these provisions with careful foresight for the men who had been trapped on the mountain by the snowstorm, about whom the discussion began in the first place; but also for himself and the pilgrims who were to set out with him since there was a possibility that the weather would again flare up and trap them in the citadel — assuming they even reached the Kastro safe and sound.

Before going to bed, *Papa*-Frangoulis sent a message to the other parish priest, *Papa*-Alexis (who was anyway the priest on duty that week) telling him that he would not be there on Christmas Eve to co-celebrate in the parish church, because he had decided to go and celebrate, God willing, at the church dedicated to Christ's Nativity in the Kastro.

* * *

A handful of parish women — neighbours of the priest — had got wind of the plans that evening thanks to Panagos who, upon leaving the priest's house had told his wife all about it and she in turn had passed on the news to her neighbours. Aunt Malamo too had sent word to *Kyr*-Alexandris the chanter, urging him to recruit two or three men to join the feast and as many woman to accompany them as pilgrims.

When the time came to board, fifteen people had assembled. It seemed that after the initial shock over the idea, the resolve of the priest and the fearless *Barba*-Stephanis had given courage to the others. All the usual suspects were there — the men and women who took ineffable pleasure in going along, as often as possible, to religious festivals, especially those celebrated at country chapels. There was *Papa*-Frangoulis with the *papadia*, Vaso and Spyros, *Barba*-Stephanis with his seventeen-year-old son, a sailor himself, Aunt Malamo, *Kyr*-Alexandris the chanter, plus three other men and four other women who had joined the feast-loving company. At the last minute, a sixteenth pilgrim came aboard.

It was Vasilis, the son of Mylono and brother of Argyris who was one of the men snowed in up at the Kastro. He arrived at the quay with a bag full of food and other supplies for the journey. Seeing him there, the priest asked:

'How did you find out, Vasilis?'

'Master-Panagos the carpenter told me, Father.'

'When and where did you see him?'

'Round about ten o'clock he came to the tavern of Yannis

Boubounas. He'd already had some bread to eat and came in to drink a few glasses of wine with his cronies. He said that you'd decided to go to the Kastro and was grumbling about you on account of your foolhardiness. But I was thrilled, since I'm worried about my brother and want to come with you if you'll have me.'

'So be it — welcome!' answered the priest.

They set sail. Heading out south-west from the harbour, they set their course for the promontory of Kalamaki. The wind was favourable and the journey began with good omens. It was, of course, freezing cold, but they were all heavily dressed. The priest sat near the rudder wearing his fur-lined coat. His wife had her double-weight shawl, Aunt Malamo her heavy jacket and long tunic. *Barba*-Stephanis was wearing his oil-skin and his waxed hat with the strap fastened under his chin and the long flaps of the hat down over his ears; his son Spyros, known to everybody as Berkaki, with spots and pimples on his face, had the sleeves of his woollen shirt rolled up to his elbows.

Fortunately it was not snowing, but the wind was bone-chilling. The sky was clear, the north wind had fallen. The moon was in the first quarter and had set long before. The stars twinkled in the firmament, the Pleiades were at their zenith, the Milky Way encompassed the heavens. Pegasus and the Bear and the North Star shone brilliantly in the deep of the night sky. The sea rippled under the north wind. They could hear the roar of the waves crashing against the shore and their melancholic echo as they splashed against the prow of the large and well-built boat.

They rounded Kalamaki but the darkness still lingered. Day began to break as they were nearing the welcome embrace of Platania. They came to Strouflia, opposite the delightful, thickly-shaded pine forest known as Koukounaries. Only then the passengers began to see each other by the first dim light of day, as if they were setting eyes on one another for the first time. Pallid faces, blue lips, red noses and hands stiff as boards. Aunt Malamo had already fallen asleep twice, sitting by the stern with her black scarf pulled up over her face as far as her nose. She huddled there, bent over with her nose almost touching her knees. *Kyr*-Alexandris had nodded off briefly and was dreaming that he was still in his bed, lulled by the similarity between the boat's gentle rocking and that of a baby's cradle. The priest's son, Spyros, was making frequent prostrations and whatever blood he had in his body had rushed to his nose, which was anyway the only part of him visible. The *papadia* in her pious affection for him had decided that she ought to bring him along, since he was the reason for the vow in the first place. She had snatched him swiftly out of bed, given him a quick wash, and dressed him in double undershirts, two flannel vests, a thick woollen waistcoat, double jackets and overcoats, and wrapped round his neck two soft all-woollen scarves, striped and many-coloured, which hung down at both the front and back. She was now sitting in the stern, to the left of the priest and with Spyros on her left, and was feeling round somewhat absent-mindedly for her son's arms and chest, but could scarcely find anything to get a hold of beneath the thick clothing she had wrapped him in.

The priest, his cheerfulness unchecked, had been exchanging jokes and banter all the while with *Barba*-Stephanis. He turned to his wife occasionally to tease her:

'You know it's for that son of yours, Lambrakis, that we're going through all this.'

'Nothing's gone wrong yet, thank the good Lord,' replied the *papadia*, who was secretly terribly anxious about their daring undertaking. Fortunately, her husband's presence gave her strength.

'Tell me, *papadia*,' said *Barba*-Stephanis in his rough voice, wanting to share a joke with the priest's wife as well, 'why do they say "Lord have mercy, *papadia*, five the months and children two"?'

'Don't you know why, *Barba*-Stephanis?' she replied, not at all offended, 'well, take my example: eight births, ten children.'

'So that's to say that priests' wives are very fertile. Why's that?'

'Because priests aren't away from them for long periods of time,' answered Aunt Malamo.

'You're right on the mark again, Malamo,' the priest interjected. 'You and your cousin Alexandris (meaning the chanter) have got great minds.'

Papa-Frangoulis kept on joking with all his parishioners on board. To one woman he said: 'But that Thodoris (meaning her husband) does he make those children in his sleep?' And to another he remarked: 'There's not a single woman who doesn't want to get married! I have wed couples now for thirty years — more than two hundred of them — and not one woman has refused!'

But Papa-Frangoulis's main victim was Alexandris the chanter. All of a sudden he turned to him and asked: 'Tell me, Alexandris, what exactly does it mean in the Christmas hymn "Thou has raised up our horn"? What is this "horn"?'[1]

'For sure, that's the horn he blows to call the people to church, like we ring bells today,' answered Alexandris, unaware of any other meaning for the word.

'And what does "Babylon despoiled Zion the Queen"[2] mean?' the priest inquired again.

'Well, that means that Babylon let Queen Zion have whatever she wanted,' replied Alexandris, grasping neither the words' literal nor symbolic meanings.

And so the conversation tripped along while the boat was on the sheltered side of the island, the oars slowly plashing in the water. On the right hand they had the bays of Anagyros and Aselinos, and on the left hand side they had the open sea between Trikeri and Artemision. Papa-Frangoulis sat with his hand on the rudder while the others helped with the rowing. And even Kyr-Alexandris, though uninitiated in nautical matters, felt the need to row in order to stay warm. Aunt Malamo rowed for almost half an hour. Fortunately, even though they all were cold, and the chilling blasts blowing down from the snowy mountains froze their ears and

---

[1] Cosmas of Maïumas, canon for Christmas Matins, 3rd ode, 1st troparion.
[2] Ibid., 9th ode, 4th troparion.

necks, at least their feet were warm, the happy effect of their proximity to the sea. The sun had peeped out from the clouds for only a few minutes ('sun with teeth — a Christmas wreath!' cried out Lambrakis), whereas during the night the sky had cleared and the 'heavens were like a lantern'. In the daylight, however, the clouds gathered again and the north wind seemed to be giving way to the east wind, as if rain were threatening. But the sun did no more than peep out — and seemed to be looking to see which was the highest and closest peak among the snow-white mountains all around: was it Pelion or Othrys?[1] — only to hide again as quickly as possible. Then the clouds gathered once more, sparing it the effort.

The precise distance between the southern harbour and the northernmost tip of the island, which was their objective, was about ten nautical miles. The priest had begun to understand that it would be night-time before they reached the Kastro. It was already evening and they had not even made it to the beautiful, melancholic valley of Kechrea, with its olive-covered slopes, its thick oak forest which they called Aradia, and its stream, plane-trees and watermill. When they did reach Kechrea, the fate befell them which the gloomy Panagos had foretold, Stephanis had been aware of and *Papa*-Frangoulis had expected. Either due to a change in the northwester or because of off-shore winds, the waves started to swell in front of the little vessel and the boat, with its white sail, its jib and its yard, began bobbing on the waves like an Albanian Greek dancing a heroic dance, with his white skirt billowing in the air, his one arm bent at an angle to his waist and the other held high as he twisted and twirled his fingers. The women were growing fearful. Aunt Malamo asked the priest whether it wouldn't be a good idea to disembark and walk up to the church of the Virgin Mary at Kechrea and celebrate the Christmas Liturgy there. *Kyr*-Alexandris was seasick and huddled in a corner, and the other passengers became terribly anxious. Only two men were unafraid, *Barba*-Stephanis and *Papa*-Frangoulis.

[1] Mountains on the mainland.

One of the passengers suggested that they moor temporarily at Kechrea until the wind dropped. Stephanis and the priest communicated with each other in silent gestures. They were still over three miles from the Kastro. They needed to choose which of two approaches was likely to be more effective. Either they could furl the sails and carry on rowing, disregarding the unbearable discomfort of the women, shivering and miserable, drenched by the waves that were breaking against the boat and leaping into it. Or, they could disembark, and attempt to find some path that was not entirely snowed over and still passable on foot. Vasilis, son of Mylono, had brought two or three shovels and pickaxes with him foreseeing the need to open a path to reach his snow-bound brother. *Papa*-Frangoulis declared that since in any case it would soon be dark, it was worth trying the first option. Any further progress by sea would be to their profit, he argued, and they could later resort to the second course of action if need be.

After one last appearance, the sun was already slowly setting in the west. It was half past three in the afternoon. The sun sank lower and lower. And the little boat of *Barba*-Stephanis with its human cargo danced on the waves, rising up to the watery crests and then racing down into the waves' humid valleys, first nearly plunged into the depths, then almost smashed against the precipitous coast. All the while the priest was reciting to himself the whole of the Office of Supplication to the Theotokos, from 'Beset by many temptations' to 'Protectress of all', and *Barba*-Stephanis — distressed at being unable to let fly in the presence of the priest the guileless blasphemies that he was biting back and squelching within his breast — muttered under his breath: 'Fume away, go on, froth at the mouth, you devil of a tempest! Just burst, you Anti-Christ, you Turk! You and your old Mohamet!' And Aunt Malamo, crossing herself, said the 'Theotokos Parthene' hymn[1] and repeated, 'Come, dear Christ! Help us, dear Virgin Mother!' And the waves beat against the prow,

[1] The hymn known in the West as 'Ave Maria'.

smashed against the sides of the boat and rushed into the hold, striking the backs and arms of those on board. And the sun sank lower and lower. And the little boat was close to disappearing. And the abrupt, rocky coast appeared to be vying with the depths for this prize.

*   *   *

Finally it began to grow dark. Night fell just as they caught sight of the Kastro ahead of them, now only two miles off. Clouds which had gathered in the east deprived them of the comfort of moonlight. The wind, instead of falling, increased in strength, and grew even wilder. No further progress was possible. They could no longer see anything either in front or to the right, except for two dark, gloomy masses. Fortunately, *Barba*-Stephanis knew the area well.

'This here's a little harbour, Father, below Pryi,[1] just below St Anastasia, at Bostania.'

'Your memory's good, Stephanis?'

'Father, just like your Reverence knows the church words by heart, I can recognize blindfolded all the little harbours, the capes, the sandy beaches, the reefs, the jagged rocks and whirlpools.'

With enormous effort, trial and tribulation they managed to get near the harbour — soaked through, nearly drowned and half-frozen.

'There, over there, we can pull it up!'

There was a ledge of marble in the sea, a sort of natural jetty that was sometimes covered by the waves and sometimes exposed as the sea retreated; again hidden by the waters, then uncovered.

As they neared it, all at once they felt a delightful sense of relief as the rocking stopped and they entered the protected harbour.

'May every voyage be a fair one!' exclaimed *Kyr*-Alexandris as he crossed himself, finally freed from his sea-sickness and able to stand on his two feet again.

One by one, they leapt out onto firm ground, unloaded their

---

[1] The ancient ruin of Pyrgi.

supplies and unburdened the boat. In between the marble jetty and the steep coast was a narrow strip of sandy beach, just big enough for a fisherman to haul up his little boat, turn its side against the sand, and stretch himself out against its other side so that he could doze contemplating the stars.

'We should haul up the boat first, Father,' said *Barba*-Stephanis, 'and afterwards we men can load up everything and make a start at walking up slowly. The women can take whatever they can manage.'

'Now'd sure be the time to have my mule,' said Vasilis, 'I told you to take it on board, *Barba*-Stephanis, but you wouldn't have it.'

They hauled up the boat and lit the two lanterns they had brought with them. Vasilis took his shovels and pickaxes and set off on his own for a while to find a path where the snow was not so thick that they would have a difficult time getting through.

Not more than an hour's walk separated them from the Kastro, which loomed as an immense, dark mass high up to the north. But given the amount of snow on the path they could see that three hours might not suffice for them to reach their destination. They ate a few dried biscuits and olives while still standing, and had a swallow of *raki* or wine along with it.

Vasilis reappeared with the news that he had found the path, much obstructed by the snow, but that with serious effort — if two people led the way, clearing the snow as they went — there was hope that they could reach the Kastro ... by midnight at the earliest. They loaded themselves up with the supplies. *Kyr*-Alexandris took one lantern and one of the women took the other. Vasilis, *Barba*-Stephanis and his son, taking the shovels and pickaxes, led the way and started to clear the path of snow. The narrow footpath led uphill, first snaking its way to the cliffside, then descending again into a hollow beside the sea. They trod carefully, as if counting their steps. The moon had escaped from behind the clouds and was trying to shed its wan light over their path. Now and then they strayed from the path's course, only to find themselves suddenly at the top of a towering crag below which gaped the abyss. Slowly, knees trembling, they would retrace their steps, clutching onto rocks and bushes to steady themselves. They were meandering up the cliff like a small, lost herd of goats that two goatherds, lanterns in hand, were trying to round up and take back to their pens. Anyone who saw them from afar could take them for a writhing, serpentine monster, the two lanterns aglow at its head and tail.

Despite the snow-clearing, which was anyway far from thorough, they sometimes took a wrong step and found themselves up to their knees or even their thighs in snow. It was nearly midnight when they arrived below the bridge to the Kastro, half-drowned, frozen, salty from the sea, and white from the snow, their lips blue but their hearts afire.

✻   ✻
✻

There at the entrance, before crossing the bridge, they heard shouting from the Kastro's iron door:

'Who's there? Who's there?'

And the loud jangling of a rusty lock echoed down from the bridge, as if someone was trying to shut the iron gate from within. They also heard a click, as if the trigger of a rifle had been cocked.

'We're friends! We're friends! Compatriots!' answered *Barba*-Stephanis, 'But who are you?'

'Tell us your names!'

'We're . . . ,' *Barba*-Stephanis began, catching the priest's eye for his advice.

'Hey! That's my brother's voice!' exclaimed Vasilis. And then he bellowed: 'Argyris! It's me!'

'That's a relief. . . they spared us some explaining,' whispered the priest.

✻   ✻
✻

They climbed up to the Kastro where they found Argyris, the son of Mylono, and his companion Yannis Nyphiotis. In a few words they described how they had been snowed in at Stivoto, where they had spent two nights holed up in a cave, and how the day before yesterday — on the twenty-second of the month — two goatherds, Yialis Konizas and Yorgis Bandas, had come to their rescue, digging away a huge amount of snow to do so. These two were now also in the Kastro with all their flock.

This stronghold (which we have described elsewhere) was a gigantic rock planted beside the sea, an extension of the earth that reached out into the briny waters, as if the dry land were raising a fist to the sea in provocation; an amazing, sea-battered granite monolith over which owls and gulls fought for possession, disputing over where the proprietorship of the one begins and where the rights of the other ends. Much-favoured destination of the north wind and his neighbours Kaikias and Argestis,[1] whose wide playground stretches between Chalkidiki, the Thermaic Gulf, Mount Olympus and Pelion.

The island's inhabitants had been forced to shut themselves up on the isolated rocky summit, out of reach of pirates and marauders until, after 1821, they abandoned its remoteness when the present-day town was built on the island's southern side.

Until only a few years previously, a few houses inside the Kastro were still preserved with their roofs and floors intact. But recently the indifference of the local authorities, the indolence of the people that kept them from visiting the Kastro more often, and the unscrupulousness of those few who came to pilfer the place, either out of pure greed or because they needed building materials, had reduced it to a heap of ruins. Thenceforth, even the parish priests of the present-day town were neglectful and already for years had left the church dedicated to Christ's Nativity unused on the day of its annual feast.

The church of the Nativity was the Kastro's old cathedral. The little church, built one hundred years earlier, was still in decent condition and not terribly run-down. When *Papa*-Frangoulis and

---

[1] Kaikias, a north-easterly wind, and Argestis, a north-westerly.

his party finally set foot in the church, an indescribable warmth and sweetness flooded their hearts.

The priest whispered, '*I will come into thy house*',[1] choking back his emotion; Aunt Malamo, who had changed out of her drenched skirt and was now wearing another dry one and her good tunic, which had fortunately been well protected in a bundle under the boat's prow, tied together a large bunch of twigs to make a broom and began to sweep the church floor, while the other women busied themselves lighting the lamps with great care — including most of the candles in the two candelabra. And they built a great bonfire from dry wood and branches in the church courtyard where a long and narrow passage ran along the southern wall and was closed off by a still-upright wall of a neighbouring building. They filled the large brazier that was kept in the sanctuary with charcoal, placed it in the centre of the church and fed it with lavish amounts of incense. *And the Lord smelled a sweet savour.*[2]

The entire church was aglow and in the dome the Pantokrator shone down with majesty and grandeur.* The gilded and finely-carved icon screen glimmered, with its beautiful icons in the finest Byzantine style and the great icon of the Nativity, 'Where the Virgin sits imitating the cherubim',[3] in which the figures of the divine infant and immaculate Mother sparkle exquisitely and the angels, magi and shepherds appear life-like; one thinks that the gold actually shines, the frankincense wafts fragrantly and the myrrh sends forth its comfort — to the extent that if pictures could speak one would expect at any moment to hear 'Glory to God in the highest!'

At the centre of the church hung a great, many-armed brass candelabrum encircled by another in the shape of a crown, which was adorned with icons of the prophets and apostles. It was beneath this glimmering assemblage that in the old days the rite of holy matrimony for Christian couples was celebrated. And all round, the

[1] Psalm 5 : 7.   [2] Genesis 8 : 21.

[3] Andrew of Jerusalem, hymn from the Praises of Christmas Matins, 1st *troparion*.

figures of the martyrs, saints and confessors covered the walls, still, dispassionate in their bearing, the blessed inhabitants of Paradise, who focused their gaze straight ahead, as if they were clearly beholding the Holy Trinity. Only St Merkourios with his heavy helmet, his breastplate, greaves and shield, seems to look slightly sideways and strikes an active pose, there on the right side of the church, where he runs his spear through the sallow Apostate seated on his throne. Livid, the deranged tyrant, his eyes dull, his breast bloodied, vainly struggles to wrench the sharp blade from his chest; he belches forth his last blasphemies and with them, his sullied soul. Next to this horrendous scene is the sweet and most pleasing icon of St Kirykos, a three-year-old child held by the hand of his mother, St Ioulitta. Plying him with gifts and favours, the persecutor Alexander made every effort to lure the child and through him, his mother. But instead, the child called out to his mother and, murmuring the name of Christ, spat in the tyrant's face. Wild with anger, Alexander had the child flung down the marble staircase and shattered his tender head, created to bear a martyr's crown.*

In the apse of the sanctuary, high up, hovered the Virgin 'Wider than the Heavens', crowned by angels. Lower down, around the altar, stood in silent solemnity the sweet-smelling figures of the great Fathers of the Church, the Brother of the Lord, Basil, Chrysostom and John the Theologian, and they seemed on the brink of great gladness, as if about to hear once again the prayers and hymns of the Eucharist that they themselves had composed, inspired by the Holy Spirit.* All around them, both in the sanctuary and in the nave of the church were depicted with admirable skill the cycle of the twelve great feasts, the ranks of angels, the slaughter of the Innocents, the Righteous residing in the bosom of Abraham and the thief who confessed Christ on the cross.

*   *   *

When they reached the Kastro and entered the church of the Nativity, such a warmth infused their souls that even though they were exhausted and some of them were nearly overcome with sleep, the thrill of being alive and of having actually reached the goal of their journey, the temple of the Lord, simply put to flight all drowsiness and fatigue. The goatherds looked around for work that would give them an excuse to smoke, or even every now and then to stretch out and snatch a bit of sleep wrapped up in their overcoats by the fire. They had lit two torches outside, one behind the apse and the other in front of the church's north face. The temperature in the church was quite pleasant thanks to the fires both inside and outside its walls. The rugged goatherds who had rescued the two snowbound woodcutters had heaped together great bunches of dry wood and branches and taken refuge there with the few remaining goats and kids that had not yet succumbed to that year's heavy witer. Then the priest began matins and chanted the processional litany for the great feast, after which *Kyr*-Alexandris started the readings and those who were struggling against drowsiness dropped off to sleep propping themselves up in the wooden stalls that stood along the church's interior walls, lulled to sleep by the nasal monotony of his recitation. (Ah! What a pity that the magnificent hymns from King David's psalms have been demoted to the level of lullabies and skipped over as burdensome and tedious!) The good *Kyr*-Alexandris belonged to an inimitable, but unfortunately dwindling breed of chanters. He chanted terribly; but devoutly and with feeling. He hardly got a single verse right, either musically or grammatically. Sometimes he sang one and a half verses as one, other times he counted two and a half as four. But it is better to be unschooled than full of oneself...

But when the priest emerged to chant 'Come, Faithful, behold where Christ is born',[1] the figures of the saints on the walls seemed to delight; 'Let us follow whither the star leads' the priest continued and *Kyr*-Alexandris, filled with enthusiasm, took up the long rod and set the candelabrum swinging with all its candles alight.*

[1] First *kathisma*, Christmas Matins.

'The angels hymned there without ceasing' and the whole church trembled from the thunderous voice of *Papa*-Frangoulis, when he chanted with passion: 'Saying, "Glory to God in the highest", to the one who was born today in a cave . . .', and the painted angels that encircled the Pantokrator high up in the dome bent their ears to hear the familiar strains.

And then the priest recited the first prayers of the preparatory office before vesting himself and began to offer to God a sacrifice of praise.*

*   *   *

All of a sudden, shouts were heard outside the church. Some of the men dashed out to see what was the matter. Aunt Malamo stepped out too and *Kyr*-Alexandris, still wearing his reading glasses, looked towards the door on his left and his chanting trailed off. The priest shot him a piercing glance and nailed him to his place.

The source of the shouting was one of the goatherds and one of the woodcutters who happened to be sitting next to the torch situated east of the church and they were responding to cries they had heard coming up from the opposite direction, from the sea.

Midway between the Kastro and the rocky coast below Kouroupi was a protected harbour called Mikros Yialos. The cries rose up from the direction of the rough cliffs and hollows below Kouroupis's treacherous shore.

A long time passed before they understood what was going on. Nearly all the worshippers had left the church. Only the priest remained, undisturbed in the performance of his duties; he was already wearing the holy vestments and about to proceed to the oblation table — and there was also *Kyr*-Alexandris, kept in his place by the priest's glance.

They surmised, without being certain, that a ship coming from the open sea had dropped anchor down below Kouroupi. The moon had set and the torchlight did not reach far. They could dimly see, about a mile away, against the dark bulk of the sea-smitten cliffs, a moving shape that was even darker than the rock face. Reverberating across the stillness of the night, amplified by the echo effect, they could hear cries of anguish and turmoil, like the voices of men about to be tossed overboard, or of shipwrecked sailors.

The men rushed to throw into the flames as many branches they had to hand in order to increase the bonfire. It was the quickest way to bring help that they could think of.

Meanwhile, the boatman Stephanis, Bandas, Yannis Nymphiotis, Argyris and his brother took a torch each and the two lanterns and raced down to Mikros Yialos. Even in circumstances when the abrupt path down was not snowbound, they would have needed nearly half an hour to descend from the Kastro to the sea, but in present conditions — at night-time, as it was the third hour past midnight — one hour would not be enough for the descent. But one hour was sufficient for dozens of ships to succumb to the waves and hundreds of sailors to meet a watery death.

Nonetheless, these simple men took up their torches, rushed out through the gate and over the bridge and hurtled along the descent to the sea. They went out of spontaneous concern for their fellow man, impelled by some natural impulse, a sympathy of the flesh and blood for the flesh and blood of another, that all-absorbing feeling that stirs the heart after the initial shock and before the chilling breath of self-preservation and indifference manage to take hold of the spirit.

Those who remained above in the Kastro occupied themselves with feeding the flames, adding more and more dry branches to the bonfire.

∗ ∗ ∗

The priest deliberately took his time preparing the bread and wine, calling to mind that early morning all the names of the departed, not only those of his own kin and of his fellow pilgrims to the Kastro, but of all his parishioners as well — not only those names that had been written on paper and passed on to him, but also as many as he knew from memory. He knew by heart all the names of his flock in the town, both the quick and the dead.* He prayed too for the rescue of the ship that was in danger, whose dire straits he had already discerned without needing any explanation.

At long last the cries grew less frequent and ceased altogether. Calm returned. It was said that either mute disaster had swooped in on them, or that their difficulties had come to an end. Two more of the men grew anxious and went out, holding torches, as far as the church of St Kyriaki, beyond the wooden gate.

*　*　*

More time passed. The priest proceeded gradually to the liturgy, hoping that in the meantime the rest of his flock would appear. But the service went on and not a soul came into sight. Finally, at the moment of communion when the priest uttered 'with the fear of God', there first appeared the last to have gone out to survey the scene, then *Barba*-Stephanis entered, followed by three unknown men dressed as sailors and wearing waxed overcoats. Everyone returned just in time to kiss the icons and receive the *antidoron*.

As *Kyr*-Alexandris was reciting the '*I will bless the Lord*',[1] the men began recounting the events in low voices. The ship that had run aground was a schooner belonging to Captain Kostantis of Limnos, who was there in person. He himself, a middle-aged man, stout and with a full moustache, explained what had transpired:

Two days earlier he had been moored at Daphni, the southern harbour of Mount Athos, but the north wind was blowing up a tempest, the anchor chains had broken under the force of the wind and the ship and its crew had been swept all of a sudden ten miles out to sea. In vain he had tried with all his powers to approach Kophos, the well-known harbour of Sykia, Chalkidiki's middle peninsula, where one enters with difficulty and once inside cannot understand how it was possible to have sailed into it the first place.

[1] Psalm 34 : 1.

The bay looks like a landlocked lake without a visible mouth, which makes it all the safer. The schooner, its sails furled in after their vain efforts to reach a safe haven, was dragged by the great waves towards the islands, where on Christmas Eve the struggling sailors suddenly saw light, like a lighthouse guiding them, the torches that the rugged goatherds had lit in front of Christ's church. That torch appeared to them truly as a divine miracle, as if it were kept alight by those shepherds abiding in the fields, those who heard the 'Glory to God in the Highest'. Borne along (rather than really sailing), they made their approach to that spot, but then found themselves in danger of being smashed to bits on the rocks of Kouroupi. But fortunately, thanks to some artful handling, disaster was averted and the vessel was brought to rest in the shallow waters of the sandy beach where it was more safely moored than it had been with its two anchors that had stayed behind as hostages in the depths of Daphni's harbour.

✻ ✻ ✻

God's grace shone brilliantly that joyful day and the goatherds felt put on their honour to slaughter two tender kids, while the two woodcutters had brought from the mountain several dozen blackbirds. Captain Konstantis came up from the schooner, now safely moored as long as the south wind did not blow up from the mainland and drive it back into the sea, bringing with him two flasks of vintage wine, and a basket of eggs and a head of mature cheese from the Haimos mountains, as well as half a dozen hens and a small barrel of mackerel. They all ate and made merry, celebrating Christmas with uncommon splendour on that deserted crag. They slept that night amidst abundant fires, well-warmed by coverings and overcoats, as many as the pilgrims from the town had brought with them, as the goatherds kept at the Kastro and as the generous captain from Limnos had carried up from his vessel.

The next day, the wind dropped and the chill lost its bite, so that, taking advantage of the winter's retreat, they decided to set sail. *Barba*-Stephanis and his son, with two men to help, went back down to the small sandy beach below Bostania, where they launched the boat, boarded it and sailing round the Kastro under the prevailing wind brought it to the north-eastern side. With the help of *Barba*-Stephanis's sturdy vessel and the slight felucca of the Lemniot captain — with so many strong arms working together — it was not long before the schooner was afloat again, unharmed by its buffeting and having rested gently on the sand after its many labours. They bade farewell to the goatherds, some embarked on the schooner and others on the boat, sometimes towed, other times towing, both sailing and rowing, travelling north-eastward this time round, because it was briefer and easier. And in this way they made their happy return to the town.

[1892]

Translated by Elizabeth Key Fowden

CARNIVAL NIGHT

IF SPYROS VERGOUDIS wasn't a diligent student, and didn't perhaps know how he was going to pass his time during all the many days between the holidays and Carnival,* he was still able to find some occupation sitting at the window, watching and listening to the goings-on outside. There wasn't a street outside, there was a courtyard, very old, spacious and irregular, with high walls but of an unequal height surrounding one of the most venerable dwellings situated along the ascending edge of the ancient city, close to the Acropolis, high up, by the side of the Ayiotaphitiko.[1] The three tenants on the ground floor, *Kyra*-Katingo, known as Christaina, with her unmarried sister Froso; 'ma Vangeli, known as Lemonou, with her daughter Yorgaina, and Stamatoula Yemenitsa, with her adopted daughter Marousa, argued about everything at the drop of a hat and at least three times a week. Usually the inhabitant of the middle lodging, Lemonou, sometimes for the slightest of reasons and sometimes without any specific reason at all, picked a quarrel, one day with the one and the next with the other of her two neighbours. And on feast days, instead of finding plenty of scope for gossip in the form of other women passing by the courtyard, or women sitting quietly in their homes, they found it more convenient to quarrel among themselves. If by chance one of the three, the sister of the one or the daughter of the other, got dressed up, the other would stubbornly insist on wearing her everyday clothes so she would have a reason to gossip about the one who had put on her finery, saying 'she doesn't know how to

[1] A monastic dependency (*metochion*) of the Holy Sepulchre Brotherhood of Jerusalem still in existence today in Plaka, the older quarter of Athens below the Acropolis.

turn herself out', and then would add: 'Look at her! she's dressed up like a bride-to-be; can't she see how ghastly she looks!' On weekdays, sometimes two and sometimes all three of them did their washing and neither the whole wash-house nor all the space in the courtyard was room enough for them to spread out their sweet-smelling laundry. Frequently, 'ma Vangeli Lemonou, after reproaching her neighbours on her right and her left as good-for-nothings, clumsy, and slatternly, thus providing the 'fuel', would then suddenly calm right down and with an ironic smirk say that she had work to do, that she wasn't going to put herself out for them and she wasn't about to reply to their gibes. At other times, Stamatoula Yemenitsa would take the words of one and slander the other with them, and then standing off to one side at her ease would enjoy the ensuing quarrel. They quarrelled over every single thing: about a wash-tub turned over and left slightly askew in the wash-house, about a few drops of boiling water spilled on the ground, about traces of wood ash that had somehow got into the laundry-basket.[1] On one of those days, 'ma Vangeli got angry with Christaina Katingo because she boasted that she was being paid twenty lepta to starch shirts, and she called her 'a slut' and 'an idiot', while at other times Katingo raised her hand against Marousa, the adopted daughter of Stamatoula, who had just turned fourteen, calling her 'you bastard child!' because she saw her washing her hands next to the basket that held the laundered clothes. Thus did these three poor women spend their days in the spacious courtyard of that very old dwelling.

As for the evenings, Spyros Vergoudis was able to occupy himself, if he so desired, leaving his lamp unlit and remaining in his first floor room, by installing himself behind the east window in order to spy on those coming in, or by gluing his ear to the keyhole, listening to words, thuds and whispers. This was the main entrance to the dwelling, the official entrance, through which he also entered his

[1] Lye, which is water made alkaline by dissolving wood ashes in it, was used for the final rinse of the laundered clothes to remove all traces of soap.

humble room, and through which all the relatives, friends and acquaintances of those living in the building, numbering in their hundreds, entered. And if he wanted to he could switch to the further window in his room, the one facing south, and from there watch the other door, the back entrance, connected to the kitchen, where Mrs Zacharias, the mother of the family, usually spent her day, comfortably smoking cigarettes. This was a house where it was easily possible to play hide-and-seek and other children's games. Two people, the first pursued by the second, or indiscriminately hunting each other without it being clear who was the pursuer and who the fugitive, could go in and out of the two doors over and over again, day and night, without either one ever running into the other.

And if he returned again to the east window, or to his small door, to spy on the main entrance, he would hear, as night fell, the door banging every five or ten minutes. And then a light step would sound inside the house, there would be the rustling of a gown, and the door would open and the visitors would go in, and after that he would hear the 'good evenings' and greetings and reciprocal compliments, followed from time to time by kisses... between women, which the descendants of Eve exchanged in an exaggerated way, in keeping with our presumptuous and western-influenced European mores. I hasten to add, to reassure the reader, that the customs of the family in question remained strict indeed in regard to this phenomenon. But the household floated on the borderline of the indefinite and the uncertain, in that twilight between tradition and innovation, where the twilight could not last but would of necessity regress into gloom and become night. These were admittedly people of feeling, affable and generous. They were acquainted with half the city and if a day passed without them increasing the number of their acquaintances, at the very least by one, the two daughters would consider that day as lost.

Furthermore, these were the days of Carnival, and people were celebrating. As soon as night fell, the young man, living alone in his room, would hear voices, songs, and guitars strummed outside the courtyard. And if for a few moments the small entrance passage remained free of visitors and the rough young man ventured to come out onto the porch with its old stone stairs that connected the house to the courtyard wall, and stretched his neck to look over the courtyard gate, iron-barred like a prison door, into the street, he would see them there, in couples, in fours, and in sixes, standing with their guitars out in the night under the gate at the side of the ascending street, proclaiming *with stringed instruments and organs*[1] the eternal complaint of their cruel treatment at the hands of the two young ladies. Because all the young men in the neighbourhood, and more than a few from other neighbourhoods, were in love with these two sisters. Some were more in love with Melpo, and others more enamoured of Koula; most of them were in love with both. Many of them were acquainted with the house's inhabitants, but if at the time there was a small disagreement, or they were in disfavour, or if among the host of visitors there was no room for them, they took their guitars, their mandolins, their harmonicas, and through music sought to assuage the heart's pain.

That evening, the middle of Cheesefare week, there had been as always an increase of a certain degree in the number of acquaintances visiting the residence. Among others there came a young warrant officer, blond-headed and with a twirled moustache, who had been introduced by one of the third cousins of the family. Unfortunately, the two young daughters were not at home. Accompanied by two of their mother's nieces they had gone out to do some shopping in Hermes Street.[2] At the house were to be found only the old lady, smoking her cigarette in the kitchen, the maid, sweeping the two stairways and that part of the courtyard not under the jurisdiction of

---

[1] Psalm 150 : 4.

[2] One of the more elegant shopping streets of Athens, running from Syntagma Square towards the old part of the city.

the three washerwomen, and Mr Zacharias, the landlord, an eccentric old man, who lived on the small income from the two dwellings and his three shops, and of whom, if one happened to hear his eternal censorious mutterings and his reprimands, one would say, 'Now there's a strict father!' The household, however, was ruled by the old lady and her two daughters, and all the shouting of the old man was just so much sound and fury, meant only for the ear. The four sons of the family never gathered at the house. The third had already married, at eighteen, and without the permission of his parents, while the youngest had an arrangement with a family where he stayed, preferring to do his studying there rather than going to the high school for his second year; the first-born was an employee at a bank, supported by the family and spending his salary elsewhere, and the second-born son was a sergeant in the Infantry. And even the *koumbaros*,* a single man, who had installed himself in the house as if he owned it under the pretext that he had no family of his own, while in fact he had three bastard children with a poor woman he had deceived, the blackguard, was not there but at work during the warrant officer's visit. To his great displeasure, Mr Zacharias was obliged to receive the visit of this third cousin, and showed the young soldier in. The blond sword-bearer had already seen the two sisters at a store, where he had pointed them out to his friends, launching into a great deal of dubious praise. He liked the two young ladies very much. When he saw them again taking a stroll, the one walking with the other, he greeted them, explaining that they were cousins. The warrant officer told him: 'I've heard that they are very social, that they run an open house.' 'Do you want me to introduce you?' said the cousin. 'Would you like that? They would be delighted, because one of their brothers is a sergeant.' And the following day he took him to the house.

The warrant officer, expecting to see two blossoming figures before him and suddenly finding himself face to face with the gloomy visage and white beard of Mr Zacharias, became flustered and was unable to strike up a conversation. Nevertheless, the old man, feeling obliged to say something, indicated the broad expanse of the city and the olive groves that could be seen through the window from there and said:

'Here we have a truly beautiful *scene*, my dear warrant officer.'

'Indeed,' the warrant officer replied, muttering almost to himself, 'indeed, you have two beautiful *scenes*.'

Then for a few moments they were both silent.

'I've heard you have a son in the army,' the warrant officer said.

'Yes,' Mr Zacharias replied, wondering why he hadn't thought of mentioning him first. 'He didn't want to go against established *transmission*, so when he'd finished his obligatory service, he remained in the army. And now he's expecting a promotion! if he's lucky, given the way the army has degenerated with all these parties it's involved with! These politicians, these *lawmockers*, have destroyed the nation, a curse on them! They should all be burned at the stake! I'd be their executioner all right. In my time I knew *surgeons* and *cockerels* who, even to this *diurnal*, are *kernals* and *mayors*! How often I have *replented* of not going into the army during the time of King Otho! I'd be a colonel by now!'

'And I can see you at least have one talent, Uncle,' the third cousin said, hinting at the distortions in the old man's speech.

'Everyone says that,' the warrant officer replied with a smile. 'Of course, all those in their sixties would be colonels now and all those in their seventies lieutenant-generals. The only thing is, who would then work to pay the taxes, to pay for all these salaries?... Of course, the army,' the warrant officer went on, 'had, and still has, its good points, it goes without saying. Except that these good points,' he added philosophically, 'are the ones that seem bad, those the Greek has a difficult time getting used to, and that is why we see them all leaving the army and thinking of the day they get their discharge as a day of celebration. And that is why so few have the patience and the will to follow a military career.'

'And just what are these good points, may we ask?' Mr Zacharias said.

'These good points are a regular life, discipline, getting used to hardship, training, fatigue-duty, the harsh military life in general, bluntness...and sometimes a whack or two...the unwritten rules, which have more authority than the written ones.'

'And what are these *unridden* rules?' the master of the house asked.

'Unwritten rules mean that when, for example, a deserter is arrested...you beat the hell out of him...'

'Ah! is that so?' Mr Zacharias said, 'though the means *scream* to me barbarous, I am not, however, all that much *advere* to it. "A good thrashing is the heart of Paradise", as the saying goes.'

So saying he sighed, remembering, perhaps, his own four sons.

'And then,' the warrant officer went on, 'there are the other tormentors as well... Greek vermin, the hospital, the *needle* and the *marble*.[1] The disciplinary actions, eight days in the lock-up, fifteen days, the *monthlies*...'

'What monthlies!...soldiers don't get a monthly salary!' the old man exclaimed.

'Yes, the *monthlies*...does that seem strange to you, Mr Zacharias?'

'Uncle,' the third cousin said laughing, 'a *monthly* in the army means a month in the lock-up.'

'Ah!' went Mr Zacharias. 'Then it gets interest.'

At that moment steps were heard in the entrance passage. It was the two young ladies, returning from Hermes Street, accompanied by the two nieces. They breezed in, full of charm, dressed with a peculiar elegance and wearing hats of a bizarre shape bedecked with red feathers; Melpomeni was brown-haired, short, plump, and pale, with a romantic sentimental air, while Kyriakoula was ash-blond, tall, slender, overly-thin even, with lively sensual eyes, which were of an indeterminate colour and which seemed to have a thousand stories to tell. Crafty, temperamental, and ironic, she beguiled with

---

[1] Respectively, a preliminary rite of passage imposed on all new recruits in the army obliging them to rotate in place like a compass while standing at attention, and standing at attention by the hour.

her manner and disappointed with her words, encouraged with her glance but used her tongue like a sabre; she had dozens of potential lovers, to all she gave hope, and all were equally mocked. This then was the pampered Koula.

The introductions were made. The warrant officer was enchanted by the two young women and didn't know whom to fall in love with first. He left after half an hour, a hostage, having received an invitation to come over on one of the nights of this final week before Lent, as every evening there was a social gathering and dancing.

*　*　*

On the final evening of Cheesefare week in the year 188_ there was so much dancing at Mr Zacharias's the rotten worm-eaten floor of that venerable building was in danger of coming down on the heads of Christaina Katingo, 'ma Vangeli Lemonou and Stamatoula Yemenitsa, the only means by which these three would forever cease their daily quarrels.

The eastern door to the residence never stopped opening and closing. They arrived in couples and in groups, both men and women, in various impersonations and personas, others in a variety of masks. The door creaked as it opened, the floor groaned, the corridor echoed, the room buzzed from the multitude of guests. The two young women barely had time to run to the door every two or three minutes to greet the new arrivals, or to see off those who happened to be departing, return to the reception room, take care of those remaining, to go into the other rooms, and exchange conversation with their intimates. And the dancing would stop and then start up again every ten minutes. Koula danced as if she had wings on her feet; with a nod she would pick out her dancing partners, royally permitting them to ask her for a dance. Melpo accepted every invitation, tender-heartedly, not wanting to refuse anyone's request. And the courtyard and the stairway glistened and from every window came the sounds of music, as if the dwelling itself were a gigantic cymbal harmoniously echoing there on the elevated rim of the old town. And when by chance the sounds of the music stopped for a moment, there could be heard coming from outside the courtyard the melancholic serenades of the neighbourhood guitarists, all those who for some reason had not been received into the noisy and hospitable household. At that point, Koula would imperceptibly lift her liquid eye to some vacant spot, while Melpo was heard to whisper through her teeth: 'The poor things!'

Stretched out on his bed, Spyros Vergoudis was daydreaming. He was a penniless student, in his first year at the School of Philosophy, and as much as he wanted to go out into the world he didn't have the where-withal to do so.

It is true that the two young ladies had invited him to join in the evening's entertainment, but how could he respond to the invitation, shy and inexperienced in social niceties as he was, so poorly dressed, amidst all those strangers? Furthermore, for one of them, Koula, he nourished an unsullied feeling of true passionate love, and he was jealous; he couldn't stand to see her dancing with so many men... and not knowing even one European dance himself! He had eaten at seven and since the coffee-houses closed early on that evening, and he was troubled by a slight toothache, he had dragged himself back to his room by eight feeling aggrieved, like a stranger always does on days like that. But when he reached his room, his sorrow dissipated, and now, stretched out on the bed, he daydreamed and felt some consolation, thinking that he was without a doubt the most fortunate of men, because without being at any party, he was taking part in three or four at the same time. He listened to the indescribable noise issuing from the house, which alone was the equivalent of three or four celebrations, and, involuntarily, danced with his bed which was rocked as if lullabied by the songs, the music and the dancing. When in an interval between dances he heard the melancholy singing and the guitars out on the street, he forgot about all his problems and he asked himself: 'Don't they have anywhere to celebrate Carnival, those poor fellows?' Or then again he would think: 'Undoubtedly, they do have some place to spend Carnival, but prefer gazing up at the lighted windows.' Then he listened to the singing and dancing in two neighbouring houses. Imagine, he was sharing in all these festivities without even being present! And he said to himself again: 'There are no two ways about it, to truly appreciate music and dancing, one must remain a spectator from afar. Close at hand, all the noise deafens the ears and diminishes judgement. Suddenly he felt in his aching teeth something strange, like a kind of numbness, and remembering the fable, whispered: 'Sour grapes'.[1]

But lo and behold! he could hear right under his feet more noise and another celebration. They were dancing *syrtos* and *kalamatianos* and singing the 'Black Kerchief' and the 'Mill of my Aunt Kontylo'.

Directly under his feet, down in the ground floor apartment, lived Stamatoula Yemenitsa and her adopted daughter, Marouso. It appears that for the evening they had made a love pact, with Lemonou and Christaina, with Froso and Yorgaina, and her husband, and had decided to 'carnival' together. Now, after eating, they too had started to dance, one man and five women, with three small children. It was still early when Spyros came back from the restaurant where he had eaten, and he had just climbed up to his room and lit the lamp when he heard a light knock on his door. The entrance passage was still quiet, because the hordes of guests had not yet started to arrive. Spyros thought it was Mrs Zacharias, and that she would be repeating her invitation, the one her daughters had already made. He hurried over to open up. Surprisingly, it wasn't the old woman. It was Marousa, the adopted daughter of Stamatoula, a girl of fourteen, dark-skinned and pretty, with black eyes, a white scarf wrapped round her head, who two years ago, when he was still a student at the high school and living in a neighbouring room, left in one's mind the image of a small ugly girl, dingy and shrivelled, in truth a catch-penny icon stamped on tin, and now that icon had been re-burnished and become beautiful. It was the second or third time that day the girl had come up to his room. She

[1] *Aesop's Fables*, 33 (Halm).

had come the other two times to pick up his clothes to be washed or to bring back the clean laundry washed by the hands of her step-mother. And this time Spyros supposed that she had come to ask for his clothes again, and was ready to reply: 'Is your mother washing tomorrow, on Clean Monday?'* But the girl spoke first and said:

'Mr Spyros, my mother says, won't you make the effort and come down and share the feast with us, if you'd like, that is?'

Spyros hadn't been expecting this invitation and without think-ing replied.

'Thank you, my child, I've had my feast; my greetings to your mother.'

The girl repeated:

'And even if you have eaten, my mother said, you should make an effort later on, when we will be dancing.'

'Bravo! It would be a pleasure,' the young man said smiling. 'Who will be there?'

'There's my mother and me and Mrs Christaina and Froso and Mrs Vangeli and Mrs Yorgaina and Mr Yorgis and Kikos and Tas-sos and Antonakis, Mrs Yorgaina's children.'

'So many!' Spyros said astonished, 'Are you on good terms now with Mrs Christaina and Mrs Vangeli?'

'There's no problem...'

'So much the better. Send my greetings to your mother, it would be a great pleasure... but I have a toothache and will be going to bed early.'

He'd wanted to say yes but he said no. It hadn't seemed digni-fied to him to 'eat cheese' with his washerwoman, and in any case he would have had a bad conscience, because with so many women, and so many of them young, mingling would not have been without its dangers for him, and his intentions, had he accepted the invitation, could not have been completely innocent. He would have preferred to kiss the young girl then and there in secret, sent so imprudently by her stepmother, but he was neither daring enough, nor debauched enough, to do that.

He sent off the young girl unblemished and philosophically lay down on the hard school of his pallet. He was pleased because he had overcome temptation; he was now at peace, almost happy. And behold the three warring parties on the ground floor were now also at peace, and had come together to celebrate the last night of Cheese Week. It was good they had been so clever about it, Spyros thought, and chosen the residence of Stamatoula in which to have their party, right below his own room, so that if suddenly the upper floor collapsed from the weight of the dancers they had some hope of being saved there, unless the walls also caved in and then not a soul would be left alive. 'What beautiful, what ingenuous customs the Greek people have,' Spyros thought. 'Behold these three ill-starred families, which though they are at loggerheads throughout the year have decided to put it all aside on the last day of Carnival, to celebrate the night of Cheesefare Sunday together! For some (what do you expect?) life is an ongoing carnival, for others a long and sorrowful Lent. Fortunately, there is an end to it! At least for the latter may this night of Carnival be like an oasis in the desert!'* And he was a wayfarer wandering through the vanity of this world. For him life was an endless uphill trudge, a rough road and a long period of fasting. When would he reach the end? Perhaps he was being put to the test by the bogies of his imagination, but he saw an inauspicious future for himself; the only good thing was that he was able to philosophize in advance about how everything would turn out for him.

The gruff voice of an old man broke through his reveries, mixed in with the dancing going on beneath his feet in Stamatoula's apartment.

The voice was hoarse and the accent peculiar:

> *Oh, how the devil's monks*
> *can grind the pepper up!*

Despite that, Spyros recognized the voice. It was *Barba*-Antonis's, the husband of 'ma Vangeli, the one she threw out so long ago.

'Ah ha! Is *Barba*-Antonis back?' the young student wondered. He recalled that, quite a few months ago, when the old man was sick, 'ma Vangeli had said plaintively to one and all:

'What's a person going to do with the poor thing! He has that catarrh of his... and he lost his shoes... and needs his cigarette!'

But when he got a little better and didn't want to work, the old woman gave him her own slippers to wear and threw him out, saying: 'Let him find his own bread to eat!' But lo and behold, the old man was back again after all these months and working to stay alive, and had remembered at Carnival to come back to his old wife and show his love for her... and maybe even bring her a few coins.

The carnival couplet *Barba*-Antonis sang was immediately repeated by the sweet fresh voice of a young woman, which Spyros also recognized. It was the voice of Froso, the sister of *Kyra*-Christaina. He had some time ago fallen in love with the pale willowy girl, so poor and hard-working, and had loved her as today he loved Koula, with a purely platonic love. He had had so little to do with her that in the beginning he was even ignorant of her name. Two women's names were heard in that remote section on the ground floor. Froso and Katina, Katina and Froso. He thought Froso was *Kyra*-Christaina and Katina was her sister. 'I took Froso for Katingo,' as he himself later said. And in the verses that he wrote about her (because he wrote, alas! verses as well, which fortunately, he didn't publish) he named her, in good faith, Katina.

> *Tell me, poor Katina, what is it that you do*
> *that every eye looks only enviously at you*
> *and every voice speaks with so poisonous a hue?*
> *Ah! but of you, dear Katina, that should not be true...*
>
> *God forbid, that marriage be seen as an inauspicious choice!*
> *As, Katina, for all poor people it will ever be*
> *like your swarthy neighbours, who exercise their voice*
> *in endless chatter, all Athens buzzing like a bee.*

The misery you've gone through and the life you've borne
you've measured out with torment, paid with hate,
bent always down toward the earth, as if imploring
Fate to take compassion on you, improve your state.

Yesterday your grandma's friend stopped me on the street,
house-proud, though her mouth twisted as she spoke
such bitter, wicked things she said of you, my sweet.
Hail, Katina! even in old women, it's envy you invoke...

✻   ✻
✻

In the third stanza the girl's profession of helping her sister with the washing was alluded to. In the final verse, the old woman, about whom all these things are said, was perhaps even this Vangeli Lemonou herself. Worth noting is that the young woman had not married, but had become engaged some time before to the owner of a small tavern, who when informed she had no liquid assets abandoned her after having first gratuitously exposed her to the malicious gossip of censorious shrews. But Spyros, who from the beginning had considered the wedding to be certain and had written in his verses that the young woman 'was wed', was just as sorry about the dissolution of the match as he had been sorry in the beginning about the engagement itself because, in the meantime, he had ceased to be in love with her and had fallen in love with Koula in her stead, and though it was undisclosed if she was in love with anyone, it certainly wasn't with him... However, that night, the voice of the young woman, despite the satyric aspect of the song, moved him. And he wove in his imagination a completely romantic idyll of an impossible unrealizable cohabitation with the young washerwoman, who herself didn't appear to be devoid of tender feelings.

✻   ✻
✻

He was rudely awakened from this vision by angry voices, heard in the middle of a buzz of whispering which abruptly interrupted the singing and dancing in Mr Zacharias's living room. He clearly heard two words thundered out with indignation and passion, which rose above the din and produced a long silence: the words were 'ill-bred' and 'scoundrel'.

He pricked up his ears. But he couldn't hear anything else. After a few seconds the only thing he heard were the hasty footsteps of two or three people, heading down the south-facing stairway to the back entrance. He leapt up at once and ran to the window. But the people who had gone down the stairway had already turned the corner by the south wall, and after a few moments he heard only the bang of the opening and closing of the courtyard gate through which they had fled.

In the living room he could hear only talk, but could not make out a single word. He went back to his bed and lay down again. What could have happened? He wasn't all that curious and it didn't really concern him. Nevertheless, he made various conjectures about the cause of the disturbance, and with these conjectures he fell asleep because he had already been soothed enough with the songs and dances. Not even his mother had ever lulled him to sleep so sweetly when he was a child as those cries and effusions of emotion from the entire neighbourhood had done that evening.

Only many days later did he happen to learn from Stamatoula, his washerwoman, who knew everything, that 'that officer, the fellow with the blond moustache, got angry, while dancing, with someone wearing a mask... who was pestering a young lady... the cousin of the daughters, my dear fellow! the niece of *Kyra*-Zacharias, who had come to the dance along with her sibling ... and with another gentleman, whom they say will marry her... People get married, I'm telling you, they're not like we were. Otherwise, how would they have children and how would creation be fruitful and multiply?'

It is worth noting, in regard to Stamatoula, that it remained a mystery why she had separated from her husband. But she always liked to maintain that they had never married. She was thirty-five years old, tall, gaunt and bony. But she never admitted to being more than twenty-five. Stamatoula then went on:

'And then there was another man, who didn't want to take off his mask, who had taken liberties with her too, it seems, while dancing ... and then the officer, the one with the blond moustache, pulled out his sword and wanted to run him through with it, and called him a scoundrel... and the other one, who didn't want to take off his mask, slunk off, tail between his legs ... with two friends of his who had come with him... but the conduct of the officer with the blond moustache made quite an impression ... and made his name known to everyone. And so both of the woman's daughters fell in love with him ... and he couldn't make up his mind which one to take and which one to leave... But let me tell you, I think that by the time Easter rolls around Koula and the officer with the blond moustache will be getting married. People are getting married, I tell you!'

* * *

That evening, as Stamatoula was telling all that to Spyros, the young man dreamed that the tooth that had been aching so long ago fell out. And by Easter, when the marriage of Koula to the young officer was celebrated, his teeth no longer pained him at all.

[1892]

Translated by Philip Ramp

THE MONK

A SHORT STUDY

I

AS OFTEN AS THE DOOR of the tiny dwelling would open, from the west, opposite the entrance to the church, two young women, lean and pale, the one not entirely unattractive, the other well nigh ugly, would stoop to the opening, peering inquisitively at the goings-on in the roadway or at the passers-by — as do indigent girls when they have no work to do or when periodic inertness descends through the fantasy and the head down into their arms and torso. Then behind them would appear an older woman's form, ruddy and rounded, but as yet relatively unwrinkled. This could be none other than the mother of the two young damsels, and, in her prime, she would evidently have been much more attractive than her two daughters were today.

Thereupon, from opposite, one of the neighbours, the wife of *Kyr*-Kostas, enamoured as much as any of ill-speaking, would say:

'There go the priest-wives!'

And any stranger from another neighbourhood who chanced to pass that way would, on hearing these words, turn in puzzlement towards the middle-aged woman — standing in turn by the doorway of her house, spinning as she stood with a long distaff around which there coiled a fat clew of wool — unable to comprehend how three wives of priests could be found together in one place, especially in a city in which, imperceptibly and uncanonically, the institution of marriage for priests is tending towards abolition.* But *Kyra*-Kostaina, poker-faced and silent, would draw her lips together, sullen as a sphinx that, having uttered her enigma, would mercilessly leave her victims to torture themselves to find, if they could, the solution.

✻　　✻
✻

148

One evening, vespers having been sung as usual, Father[1] Samuel emerged from the church door, which he was accustomed to leave ajar for an hour after evening prayers in the hope that some one of the passers-by would enter to light a candle. Father Samuel was still young, under the age of forty. He had come from the Holy Mountain[2] to be treated for the ophthalmia from which he had been suffering, and, for reasons of temporary economic exigency, had attached himself to a parish church in Athens as sacristan. But, after his cure, the years passed by and he continued on in the position of sacristan, planning, certainly, to return as quickly as possible to the 'monastery of his repentance', but never taking the decision. He had gained the trust of the members of the Church Council who averred that they had never met a man more pious or with hands more unsullied. Indeed, Father Samuel enjoyed the respect of virtually the whole parish.* Only one parishioner, a neighbour living not far from the church, by the bend in the first street, tormented the poor monk, never leaving him in peace. This was *Kyr*-Yannis Manaftis, a man in his fifties, well-built, a former merchant, moderately well-off, married and the father of children. He was not without education and was a regular reader of ecclesiastical books. His one failing was that he concerned himself with other people's business. And if, on the street or by the church door, he chanced on Father Samuel — who always greeted him with a smile and a courteous bow as he was accustomed (the monk was of medium height, with auburn hair, an olive complexion and exceedingly affable) — *Kyr*-Yannis Manaftis, in place of any other greeting, would say to him:

'Wherefore hast thou come hither, O brother?'

Or:

'Is it perchance from some necessity or coercion?' or some such similar phrase. All these were taken *verbatim* from the questions

[1] The word 'Father' is used in Greek to address any man of the cloth, whether he be a monk or a priest.

[2] Mount Athos, an independent monastic community of twenty-two monasteries and many sketes and hermitages, situated on the Halkidiki peninsula in northern Greece.

and answers at the ceremony of monastic tonsure,* and were designed to remind the poor sacristan of his spiritual promises and obligations. Father Samuel would at times smile tolerantly, at times he would show his irritation and refuse to endure the goads, and at times he would conceal his distress and anger. *Kyr*-Yannis, for his part, however, never seemed to weary of repeating his taunts.

Now, on the evening of our present tale, *Kyr*-Yannis, as he was walking along, saw the monk and, nodding his head, addressed him saying:

'Take the scissors and give them to me.'

The allusion, once again, was to the Tonsure Service, or 'Office of the Angelic Habit', in which the priest, in order to demonstrate that the decision to enter the monastic life is taken freely and without any coercion, commands the novice to present the scissors with his own hands. Twice the priest returns the scissors to the table, and only after being given them for the third time does he perform the tonsure.

On this occasion the monk became more incensed than usual. One reason for this may have been that, because it was a Sunday evening in May, the small square in front of the church was not completely deserted. Perhaps Father Samuel was afraid others might hear and understand *Kyr*-Yannis's cryptic comments. Here and there children were playing and a little further off two or three youths were standing talking. *Kyra*-Kostaina, too, was sitting, without her distaff, facing the door of her house, opposite the church, and, a little further to the south, standing by the door of their little house, were those women whom she named 'the priest-wives'.

'Let me tell you this, *Kyr*-Yannis,' said the monk, seething with rage, 'there's a proverb that says: "The man with the beard has the comb to comb it."'

'That I know, Father Samuel,' replied *Kyr*-Yannis, 'but there's another one that goes: "It's the one who loves me dear who brings me many a tear."'

The monk hung his head and offered no reply. Now *Kyr*-Yannis, who was a kind man at heart, more in an attempt to offer comfort, added:

'Don't you remember what the divine Chrysostom[1] says? I'm sure your reverence knows much better than me — I've little enough education — I believe he says: "Better blows from friends than caresses from enemies."'

'I don't believe he says that anywhere,' declared the monk emphatically.

'Of course he does,' insisted *Kyr*-Yannis gently. 'I said I've little enough education, but I did get as far as the second class of elementary school, and in those days they weren't ashamed as they are nowadays to teach the words of the Holy Fathers. Our teachers got us to learn a passage from the Homily to Eutropios by heart, and, if you like,' continued *Kyr*-Yannis, 'I can still remember how it goes: "Have I not told you when you constantly chide me for telling the truth, that I love you more than the flatterers? Do I, who rebuke you, not care for you more than those who court favour. Have I not said that wounds from friends are more easily borne than kisses from enemies? If you had borne my wounds, their kisses would not have produced this death in you. My wounds work healing, their kisses harbour incurable disease." '[2]

'He was Chrysostom the Great, however,' interjected the monk.

'I know, and that's why I quote him and take off my hat to him and bow to the ground before him,' said *Kyr*-Yannis accompanying his words with actions and gestures. 'But whatever you think, I didn't mean you any ill in speaking to you and I promise you, since you are annoyed, that I won't say another word about this. We simple folk, you know, give more importance to words than things. Why let words bother you, and what harm do I do you if I beat the air with my tongue? Look at the reality. What does your conscience say? Is your conscience clear? If so, you've nothing to fear from

[1] The Church Father, St John Chrysostom (345 or 347–407).
[2] *In Eutropium*, Migne PG, 52, 391d.

words. Now forgive me, brother, and I'll never say anything to you again about these matters.'

' "Every little lamb needs be caught by its little hoof",' concluded the monk with another proverb.

Thereupon *Kyr*-Yannis turned westwards and set off in search of his debating and drinking friends with whom he shared a relish every evening before heading home for his meal.

No sooner had he turned his back than the matronly Tasou approached the monk. (She was the 55-year-old, ruddy-faced, as yet unwizened mother of the two young women whom *Kyra*-Kostaina entitled 'priest-wives'.) She bade him good-evening, entered the church, crossed herself and, taking up position next to the candle stall (for she willingly played the part of church officer), she turned to the monk who was standing by the door-post, and said to him:

'What was he saying to you, Samuel?'

'Who?'

'*Kyr*-Yannis Manaftis.'

'Oh, that stuff he's got into his head, don't you know?'

'And what's the meaning of those things he keeps saying to you?'

'What things?'

'Do you imagine I can get my tongue round the words to tell you? He says things like: "Why have you come here, O brother?" and "Will you endure all sorrows and tribtations?" and so on.'

'Everyone's free to say what they like, aren't they? Don't bother your head with it.'

'But why does he come and spill it all out at you?'

'He means, probably...,' said the monk, upset and blushing, '... that I should consider what I'm doing and serve the Church with zeal.'

'Why? Don't you serve better than anyone?'

'True enough... but isn't that what people are like? You can never please everyone.'

At that moment into the church stormed two boys from the neighbourhood, the one about fifteen, the other fourteen. They were unshod, ragged and unwashed and with smoke still emanating from

their nostrils. The one had just discarded his cigarette outside the
church, the other had left his alight on a marble block by the doorway, ready to pick up again when he came out. Both were in tumul-
tuous high spirits and as they slapped their feet noisily on the stone
slabs they shouted out to Samuel in their wonted local accent:

'Hey you monk! Get the font out for us...'

'Quick! quick!' said the other.

'What's up, boys?'

'We've got a baptism. Get all the stuff ready.'

'Get the censer and all the what-not,' added the other.

'Right away! right away!

These were the monk's two assistants who would carry the font
to the houses when there was a baptism. The same boys would
also deafen the parishioners on feast days and even on non-feast
days with their excessive and unending bell-ringing. They would
also often spend the night outdoors behind the walls of the church
where they would light a fire and occasionally attract younger and
more innocent boys to their much desired company.

Samuel went into the sanctuary and brought out the vestments,
the Prayer Book, the Holy Myrrh and the censer. He handed over
the font to the two urchins and followed behind them, making his
way to the house where the baptism was to take place. As he left,
he gave *Kyra*-Tasou instructions to lock the church. At the last
moment she whispered to him:

'Shall we see you this evening? The girls have something to tell you.'

The monk replied: 'I'll drop by,' and as he turned to go he saw
opposite him *Kyra*-Kostaina, her gaze transfixed on him, a gaze full
of suspicion and ill-will.

II

The drinking companions of *Kyr*-Yannis Manaftis were *Barba*-
Grigorakis, *Kyr*-Athanasis and *Yero*-Pantelakis, all of them elder
citizens of good cheer. On this evening they had all already gathered

in Kosaropoulos's general store. They had ordered a few anchovies and a dish of dried mackerel to accompany the yellow resinated wine they were drinking. Mastic liquor and all spirits they avoided systematically, but every evening each would usually take two or three glasses of wine before their meal. Good householders all, they would bewail the political situation and day-by-day debate matters political, religious, social and occasionally scientific. On this May evening the others were mixing water with their wine, but *Yero*-Pantelakis would hear nothing of it. Even in the heat of the dog-days he would take his wine neat.

Yero-Pantelakis accepted the truth of all proverbs, except for the couplet: 'In the month that has no "r", add water to your jar.' Indeed, he affirmed that he once knew a teacher so fond of his glass that in order to make the rhyme redundant he embarked on the major intellectual undertaking of introducing the letter 'r' into every month name. *Maio* (May) became *Mario*. Intruding an 'r' into *Ioulio* (July), however, proved more troublesome, so the audacious teacher transformed it simply into *Oenoulio*, 'a little wine'! This was as far as his oenological renaming enterprise ever reached.

When *Kyr*-Yannis arrived the evening discussion had already begun. That evening, as almost invariably on a Sunday when each of the convivial elders would contribute his impressions from the morning service, the topic was a religious one.

They did not all belong to the same parish. On Sunday morning each would attend church in his own parish, and in the evening when they came together they would find fault with the priests, the singers, the members of the Church Councils and above all with the bishops.

'Come on now, *Kyr*-Yannis, good to see you!' said *Barba*-Grigorakis. 'Haven't you got something to say?'

'What about?' asked *Kyr*-Yannis.

'Bring us, lad, a gill and another glass,' ordered *Kyr*-Athanasis.

Kyr-Yannis sat down at the table completing the foursome.

'Good health, gentlemen,' he said.

'We're having an argument here about our church affairs,' said

Barba-Grigorakis. 'You're more of a churchman than we are. My friend here Thanasakis is a real thick-head. He insists that monkery, the monastic habit as they call it, is nowhere to be found in the Gospel and if the Holy Synod would give them leave to marry, they'd marry each and every one of them.'

'And who'd marry the Holy Synod?' said *Yero*-Pantelakis.

'Irreverent, but true,' commented *Kyr*-Yannis. 'Of course, in that case the first to marry would have to be the bishops.'

'Do you get the point now, Thanasakis, old boy?' repeated Grigorakis in triumph. 'Do you see that you were headed off on a road to nowhere?'

'How can I get the point? I'm slow in the uptake,' replied *Kyr*-Athanasis, a trifle ruffled. 'It's true, I'm slow, but when I understand something, I understand it well and good, Grigorakis.'

Barba-Grigorakis chuckled quietly.

'Be patient, gentlemen, let's look at the matter. Would you like to give me a hearing?' said *Kyr*-Yannis.

'Of course,' said *Barba*-Grigorakis. 'I told you you were more of a churchman than any of us, and you've read a book or two.'

'But let's have a drink first,' suggested *Yero*-Pantelakis.

'Gladly.'

And they clinked their glasses.

Kyr-Yannis listened without protest to *Barba*-Grigorakis's compliment about his learning. It's true that he, if anyone, was aware of the attractions of false modesty. When he had affirmed to Father Samuel the sacristan a little earlier that he'd only got as far as the second class of elementary school he had not been telling the truth. He had attended secondary school and, moreover, being an avid reader, he had developed his ideas. Nor was he by nature without sound judgement.

'Come on, then, we're listening,' said Grigorakis.

'I'm not listening to anything,' said *Kyr*-Thanasis.

'Don't listen then, because you'll be none the wiser. Waiter! Bring some cotton wool to block his ears.'

'Wait a moment,' continued *Kyr*-Yannis, 'never mind what Grig-orakis says, *Kyr*-Thanasis. Your question, as I understand it, was whether in our days there should still be monks or not. Is that right?'

'Yes.'

'Well then, in a word. Do you think, gentlemen, that we should stay within the bounds of Orthodoxy or should we proceed into the realm of Protestantism?'

'God forbid,' said Grigorakis.

'What? Become Protestants?' said *Yero*-Pantelakis. 'Let's hear no worse!'

'That, I assure you, is where the matter leads. Shall I tell you what our Church says about marriage and celibacy or shall we simply recite our own opinions "*after the commandments and doctrines of men*",[1] "*deceiving, and being deceived*"?[2]

'What does our Church believe then?'

'If you wish for us to remain within the bounds of Orthodox doctrine, then listen. Imagine that I today am unmarried and decide to remain unmarried: I leave the city, climb to the peak of Mount Hymettos[3] where I own a piece of land and there I build a hut, wear black clothes of hair, sackcloth or rushes or whatever, and live cultivating the earth or living off wild herbs, and spend my time praying without coming into frequent contact with people. How does that trouble you?

'When it is demonstrated that I am interfering with you or with your wives or with your animals, then you have every right as state or as society to pass restrictive laws against me and to punish me severely. As long as I don't interfere with you, you may condemn me, you may jeer at me and you may disdain me as much as you like, but you cannot stop me.

'That's how the monastic life arose. Because, naturally, if I do it,

[1] Colossians 2 : 22; see also Matthew 15 : 9. [2] 2 Timothy 3 : 13.
[3] Mount Hymettos, one of the main mountains surrounding the Attic basin and overlooking Athens.

it's probable that someone else, and then someone else in turn will copy me. And thus gradually the monasteries grew up.'

'But the ancients, if I'm not mistaken, didn't they make marriage compulsory?' interrupted *Kyr*-Grigorakis.

'There may have been societies in antiquity with such laws of a social and family character. But these societies also had the Kaiadas and the Barathron, those pits where they cast down to their deaths all those who were seen as useless. But modern, Christian societies are founded on non-compulsion of the will, the absolute freedom of the individual. Just as there are individuals who are unable to marry (the sick, the disabled, the impotent and those unable to work), so there are also individuals who do not wish to marry. And freedom of will forbids us from forcing such persons to marry.

'The whole matter of marriage and celibacy is profound and one of the most difficult social questions. Let's not make barbarians of ourselves, desiring to compel people by force. Do you meet today many married people who are happy with their lot, or do you see marriage to be an easy matter as it should be, as our daily social bread, as a fundamental institution of society? Very far from it. Or are all unmarried persons today monastics?

'Let's first make marriage possible for those who wish to wed, and then we'll have time enough to compel those who don't. Let's open first the door for those who desire to enter, then we can think about pushing those who don't.

'So much for that. The man who will abolish monasticism, whether in the East or in the West, has not yet been born. Luther in north-west Europe wouldn't have dared do so if he hadn't been a monk himself and wanted to marry a nun...

'Something of this sort, *Kyr*-Thanasis, is what it seems Christ commands in the Gospel, and don't listen to the babbling of the Protestants. Christ said: *He that is able to receive it, let him receive it*[1] and declared that the most perfect life is not for everyone, but

---

[1] Matthew 19 : 12.

for those *to whom it is given*,[1] meaning purity and poverty, which form the basis of the monastic life.

'But you'll say monasticism has fallen now from its high ideals. And what hasn't fallen? All the institutions of old are good, and all have been corrupted by ignorance and evil.

'But however much monasticism has fallen, and however far it may fall in the future, never, and I repeat, never, do you have the right to prevent someone from remaining unmarried, from fleeing the world and from clothing himself in a cassock.

'The only right which the State has, in support of the Church, is to compel those monks who, forgetful of the sacred promises which they have given, leave their monasteries and return to the world, to compel them, I say, to return to their monasteries.'

'Amen. God rest your good father!' exclaimed Grigorakis.

'Right on the mark. Well said!' conjoined *Yero*-Pantelakis, 'But shouldn't we be pouring another drink now?'

'Let's have a drink.'

And they clinked their glasses.

'Look at us,' continued *Kyr*-Yannis, licking his lips, 'we sit here in our cups and we think we can solve all the important questions of the day.'

'But wine is good for getting ideas flowing,' objected *Kyr*-Pantelakis.

'It depends on the head it's poured into,' said *Kyr*-Grigorakis. 'Look at my friend here Thanasakis. What ideas would get flowing in there?'

'Say what you like, you really are insufferable,' said *Kyr*-Thanasis.

'I can see that I've sent your heads a-spinning,' continued *Kyr*-Yannis, 'but I still want to say a word or two especially about the state of monasteries in Greece, because that's where my conclusion about keeping monks in monasteries leads us. Many people have written a lot and said more about the monasteries in Greece and about their spiritual decline and moral weakness, but I

---

[1] Matthew 19 : 11.

believe that the prime reason for the decline of the monasteries is the scandalous interference of the State and of worldly people in monastic affairs. And the proof of this can be found in the fact that in Greek lands that are enslaved to Ottoman rule the condition of monasteries is relatively better. To cut a long story short, I tell you I believe that the State in co-operation with the Church would do well to amalgamate all the monasteries into forty or fifty — the largest and most important of the existing ones — where all the monks would be brought together. But the land of the others shouldn't be appropriated by the State in the sacrilegious manner of the Bavarian regency;* they should remain as daughter monasteries of the forty or fifty, with every care given to the upkeep of the churches; and any surplus income from the land should be deposited in a common Church fund to help indigent and sick priests and monks. In the forty or fifty main monasteries a strict cenobitic rule of true monastic life should, of course, be introduced.* First, women should be forbidden entrance to the monasteries, and no female should approach within an area a mile around. You will say, "whoever wants will find". That's beside the point. The monasteries should remain monasteries, even if the monk as an individual may sin. The monastery is the monk's castle, and then, at least, whoever wishes, can "keep to his castle". The main thing is to avoid the invasion of various women relatives and hangers-on into those consecrated places. Local dignitaries and officials with their wives should not be allowed to frequent the "reception rooms" seeking "hen pie". That's all. Also, the rule of prayer should be complete, following all the old *typika*, with the vigils and pre-dawn matins, with all the appointed verses and readings from the Psalter. And the monastic rule should be imposed on all the monks in the cenobia, with a common table for meals, strict observance of fasts and everything. That's my opinion, and I don't believe it's far off the mark.'

'I agree entirely,' said Grigorakis.

Yero-Pantelakis ordered another gill of wine, and when they had downed it, the four of them went out and left. Night had already fallen.

*   *   *

That night at about eleven o'clock, when the monk returned to his cell, he started to rinse his mouth with water aplenty. He felt a most peculiar sensation, like the taste and smell of earth, in his nostrils and on his lips. Strange! Is it true then what Moses says in Genesis: *And the Lord God formed man of the dust of the ground, and breathed into his nostrils the breath of life; and man became a living soul?*[1] Is the taste and smell of human flesh still the taste and smell of earth?

And yet Father Samuel had not yet neglected all his duties — his duties as sacristan at least. He was a faithful and honest servant of the Church — the members of the Church Council could vouch for that. As a man, too, he lived with every propriety, and even as a monk he had behaved well until that day, insofar as a monk can behave well when being tossed about on the waves of the world. On that evening he had gone to two homes where baptisms were to take place, because that was his duty. To weddings also he would go, bearing the Gospel book and the holy vestments. Every duty incumbent upon him as sacristan, as servant of the Church and of the priests, he would execute. In the church he was ever zealous in serving the priests, the Council members and the congregation. He would even carry out small tasks in the homes of the Council members. Eagerly he would attend to the pious women who came to the church with their hats, their feathers, their perfumes and their fans, often sweeping through their ranks, offering them seats, listening to their 'thank you's', and until now he had never sinned, unless through some involuntary contact on days when the church was especially crowded, such as during Holy Week and other feasts. The women, for their part, did not seem so innocent, so pure, so indifferent! Clearly, it never even crossed their minds that beneath the

---

[1] Genesis 2 : 7.

monk's cassock any fleshly desire could lie hidden. And most of them were not in the least displeased by the involuntary contact, and virtually all did nothing whatever to eschew proximity with men. In what way until now had the monk been guilty of any sin?

And was it as if he was the only monk? On weekdays, when no one from the parish came in to light a candle and kiss the icons, the whole church was like a monastery. On the right hand side in the choir stalls stood Father Arsenios and the Archimandrite Grigentios, while on the left stood the priest-in-charge Pavlinos and Father Antonios, all four sharing the priestly duties. The last of these had once been married, but was now a widower, and did not differ essentially from his three co-celebrants. There had formerly been a married priest, Father Yannis, but the Church Council had got rid of him because he was not to their liking, and in his place they appointed the priest-in-charge Pavlinos.

The four would stand in their choir stalls and the church would then assume the venerable aspect of a monastic *lavra*. As they stood they would glance from time to time towards the door, just in case some woman might enter to 'take a blessing', because the priest officiating at the service, if he happened to be responsible for the area of the parish in which the woman lived, was quite capable of interrupting vespers in order to make sure that he was the one to give her the blessing, fearful that the other three might 'steal' his parishioner. And after vespers, when they started arguing about the share-out of the candle money, accusing each other of greed and grubbing, then the church would become not so much like a monastic *lavra*, but (God, forgive me) a rowdy *havra*.[1] Another kind of noisy *havra* could be witnessed when they went to perform the service of Anointing of the Sick[2] in some home: prayers, litanies and Scripture readings would be gabbled by all four at the same time, as if they

---

[1] The Turkish word for synagogue and which also means a place with a lot of noise.
[2] The sacrament of the Anointing of the Sick, the *Euchelaion*, a lengthy service for the healing of the sick formerly celebrated by seven priests and latterly by four or less.

were in a hurry to finish with the sick person as quickly as possible.

And in what way was the poor monk to blame? He was, after all, simply the servant of the priests. And how were the priests to blame? They were simply the servants of the Parish Council. The members of the Council, known to some as the 'light-snuffers' because of their obsession with extinguishing the candles lit by the church-goers before they are half burnt, lorded it over the priests, the cantors and the sacristan. In order to be appointed to this office they would ingratiate themselves with those in powerful positions, as though it was a matter of their livelihood. The majority seek the position out of vanity and self-aggrandizement, but a number are filled with genuine zeal. Recently, the Parish Councils have introduced the fashion of celebrating two liturgies *à la franca* in even the smallest churches in Athens, as if liturgies could be treated as successive ovenloads of bread from a baker's oven or as so many ferry-boat departures (Lord, have mercy!).* In this way the Councils compel the priests to do violence to their consciences, making a mockery of the sacred rites, when, for lack of time, they celebrate the liturgy without the Midnight Office, without the Hours and virtually without matins. They have reached the point where they disdain the divinely inspired book of the sacred Psalmist, a heresy which, were they adorned with every virtue, would be sufficient alone to condemn them to perdition. The poor monk saw these things, and in conscience comparing himself with the priests, who — and this is the rub — bear the burden of souls, and he could not help regarding himself as a hundred times better.

And he was not wrong.

But what is to be said about the Chief Shepherds of the *peculiar people*,[1] those who shear the sheep of the Lord in the sheepfold which prefigures the Kingdom? They and they alone bear the greatest responsibility for the present decline. Are not they those who, 'for a small fee and a little glory', bartered away all independence and all

[1] Titus 2 : 14.

dignity to the civil authority? Are not they those who have confined their whole activity to display and ceremonial alone? And do they at least observe the outward forms with precision and good conscience? They hasten to memorial services on Sundays, giving in to the foolish vanity of ignorant and vulgar people, when it is well known that, in accordance with the canons, memorial services are held on Saturdays or else on weekdays.* They tolerate the mutilation of all the services, tacitly abolishing every *typikon* in the Church. Are not they those who append their signatures to encyclicals about ecclesiastical definitions and decrees, and then unashamedly are the first to contravene those encyclicals? Are not they those who have so often made written prohibition of any innovation in music, and then foolishly tolerate the histrionic parody which, in the worst possible taste, pollutes all the churches of the capital city. Are not they those who prohibit with encyclicals the celebration of marriages and baptisms in homes, then speed off in carriages to celebrate marriages and baptisms in domestic dwellings? Are not they those who acquiesce in the presence of a multitude of priest-monks as parish priests in the towns? Why then is marriage permitted to priests, if priest-monks were not destined for the monasteries where they have sworn solemn vows of purity and flight from the world? Are they, who are supposedly educated, not those who tolerate grotesque solecisms in the divine services, and are themselves not infrequently guilty of the same?* Are not they those who ordain as priests the most ignorant and sorry types, giving in to pressure from some friend or patron rather than giving obedience to God? Who can believe that they are above money and that the horrific charge of simony is untrue, when they see them on their death leaving large inheritances to their kin? And are not they, the Chief Shepherds of the peculiar people of the Lord, those who go round the villages and the monasteries on an annual fleecing tour, maintaining in equally weighted harmony, like two equipoise and not dissimilar scale-pans of a balance, the belly and the money-pouch? And with such principles, with such sentiments and such a way of life, how is it possible for them to guide aright the affairs of the Church in Greece? And is it not time for the Great Church of Christ in Constantinople to consider whether it might not be more expedient to withdraw from her juvenile sister in Greece the autocephalous status which was granted her only out of condescension and on certain conditions?*

All these thoughts, it is true, did not pass unaided through Father Samuel's head, but then, was there ever a writer who did not from time to time substitute his own cogitations for those of his hero? And with the reader's leave, we have here interpolated a number of our own personal ideas into the sentiments of the hapless monk. We hasten to add that with these thoughts we do not strike at the authority of the Church, but simply express our sorrow at the state of affairs.

*　*　*

And Samuel, having rinsed and re-rinsed his mouth, yet unable to be rid of that peculiar smell, fell into a kind of deep reverie: he saw before him his cenobion by the foothills of the majestic Mount Athos, which, when it knits its brows, brings down over its crown at times a white scarf and at times a black veil; from whose heights storms rage with myriad thunder claps and darkness of infinite nights; and on whose summit lightning never ceases to adorn with reddish hue the pre-eternal snow, an unbroken wall along which are steeled the sharpest darts of Phoebus, and where the perpetual hurling of lightning is like the blinking of the unsleeping eye of Divine Providence. And he beheld a spring dawn on which matins was being chanted in the wonted way in the *Katholikon* of the monastery, and all the brethren, more than a hundred, had gathered in the church and were standing motionless in their stalls, all wearing their monastic veils, some girded with the many crosses of the Great Schema.[1] Outside in the narthex he saw frescoed on the wall

---

[1] A fully ordained monk having reached the highest degree in his tonsure, that of the Great Schema (*Megaloschemos*), is vested with a special black sleeveless inner garment inscribed with red letters.

the icon of the monk crucified in imitation of Christ the Lord, and
the devils with their spears, their swords and their bows, all striking and piercing the monk, stretched out and sacrificed on his cross.
And at the same time he remembered the 'Hymn of Blessing' sung
at the funerals of monks and nuns: '. . . those who take up the cross
as a yoke and follow me in faith'. And then at once the whole of
the Funeral Service for Monastics came before his mind and he saw
the dead monk wrapped around and sewn up in his cassock, like a
babe in swaddling, the face covered and with red crosses embroidered on the chest and at the knees, and he remembered the verses
of the 118th Psalm: O *how sweet are thy words unto my taste; yea,
sweeter than honey to my mouth! Therefore I love thy commandments above gold; yea, above fine gold. So shall I keep thy law continually; for ever and ever.*[1] And he recalled the 'Hymns of Ascent':[2]
'Blessed is life for those who, winged with divine love, dwell in the
desert'. And then he entered the *Katholikon* and he saw all the
brethren standing motionless all around. By the Holy Doors stood
a young man of twenty, with flaxen hair and efflorescent mentum,
his head uncovered and his feet unshod, his nakedness covered with
shirt and drawers. With his arms crossed across his chest and his
head bowed down in an attitude of penitence and humility, he
stood facing the icon of Christ, the Lord and Master. The sanctuary
doors opened, and out came the celebrating priest newly vested in
his full hieratic robes — with the embroidered Seraphim on the
smooth white silk stole and his chasuble all broidered with inter-
twining crosses. His head was uncovered and his black monastic
veil and hat hung over his shoulder. With hands tucked beneath his
chasuble, the priest was holding in the folds of that garment the
Holy Gospel Book and stood on the steps running beneath the
icon-screen. And from across on the right-hand side of the singers

---

[1] In the King James version, Psalm 119 : 103, 127, 44.

[2] The 'Hymns of Ascent' (*Anavathmoi*): a series of short hymns designed to be interpolated between verses from the Psalms of Ascent (Psalms 119–33). They are sung
at matins on Sundays and feast days.

came the abbot — the sponsor of the young man who was about to receive the monastic tonsure — to stand by his side during the ceremony. Then the first choir began to sing: 'Hasten to open unto me Thy fatherly embraces; in prodigality I have wasted my life.' And then the questions and answers began, those of which *Kyr*-Yannis Manaftis had irreverently reminded Samuel earlier in the day, 'Wherefore hast thou come hither, O brother?' etc. 'Wilt thou remain in thy monastery and in spiritual struggle until thy last breath?' asked the priest, and the novice seeking tonsure replied, 'Yes, with the help of God, honoured Father.'

And again with greater severity the priest continued, urging the novice to more mature reflection: 'Consider Whom thou art approaching, to Whom thou art joining thyself and also whom thou art abjuring.' And the novice confirmed that he was not coming 'out of any necessity or coercion but of his own free will'. Thereafter the threefold handing over of the scissors was played out, whereupon the priest cut crosswise hairs from the neophyte's head. And then he began to hand to him one by one the tokens and garments of the monastic habit, saying with each item given: 'Our brother (*name*) receives the cassock, the belt, the analavos, the sandals, etc.' Now the former novice, standing half-naked before the icon of Christ, put on, in the presence of all, the symbols of the monastic habit. And the man hitherto called Spyridon received the new name of 'Samuel'.[1]

After this, when the Holy Eucharist had been celebrated and the neophyte had received the Divine Mysteries, the abbot commanded the cook to prepare fried sweetmeats and ordered the monk in charge of the wine cellar to fetch up a bottle of spirits as solace for the brothers. Since this was the monk's only wedding feast and only earthly joy, the whole brotherhood rejoiced with him as they congratulated their newly tonsured brother: 'May he remain steadfast and may his life be pleasing to God and men.'

---

[1] A tonsured monk receives a new monastic name, keeping only the first letter as a remnant of his worldly name.

Poor Samuel recalled all this, and it was poor Samuel himself who had been through it all. And yet this evening he had just returned from the tiny dwelling where there lived those girls whom their neighbour *Kyra*-Kostaina called 'the priest-wives'. He had entered therein at about nine o'clock after returning from the houses to which he had accompanied the priests for the baptisms. And there in the little house he found the two pale girls, the one, anaemic, somewhat rickety and rather ugly, and the other, lean but rather attractive. There was also their mother, middle-aged and more, but still ruddy and not over-wizened. The monk had voluntarily established these relations a year before. They were poor women who worked as domestic servants in other houses and they willingly offered their help with the cleaning and preparation of the church. The poor sacristan would slip them something from his miserable wage and from the money given to him as a tip for his services. Naturally, the monk could not escape converse with them.

III

The women were not at all deterred by the aspect of the monastic habit and scaled two at a time the steps of audacity. It was evident that they had been brought up in the capital city of Greece where (glory be to God) prejudices and 'rusty old ideas' did not prevail. Gradually they began to insinuate themselves even into the small cell where the monk lived. After all, their barely wrinkled and ruddy-faced mother was always at their side. Then they started to complain that he had never even once crossed the threshold of their home for a cup of coffee, and accused him of being too proud to accept their hospitality and such like. Finally, in order to relieve himself of their ever more burdensome insistence, the monk went to visit them, but fully determined not to go again. Then, because the complaints increased, he went a second time and a third time, and after two months he had reached the point where he was visiting the house twice a day. The two young women appeared to harbour entirely sisterly sentiments towards him, nor did they evidence the slightest distrust or suspicion. The poor monk suffered much, he was vexed and he was tempted. Nevertheless, he stood his ground; he did not fall. Until the Sunday evening on which our present narrative begins, he had not fallen in any way. Tonight, when he had stayed for more than two hours in the little house, it was only the second or third time he had made a nocturnal visit. Until now he had guarded against it — most especially since it was during the hours before midnight that he was required to be in his cell. The parishioners were very numerous, and if someone on their deathbed needed to receive Holy Communion, or if an infant in mortal danger needed to be baptized, or if a woman in childbed suddenly gave birth and needed a prayer, or if some other such occasion arose, it would be to the sacristan that the parishioners would run to open the church and call the priest. And what if they did not find him in his cell?

On this night, after the monk had conversed much with the girls and not a little with the old woman, the two sisters confided to him that their neighbour *Kyra*-Kostaina was ever suspicious of them, gossiping against them mightily, and even presumed to speak ill of him, the monk — all of which, they said, was on account of her jealously on seeing their innocent relationship. Their innocent relationship! The monk, of course, believed this in all good conscience, and the girls believed no differently. What, after all, had been their sin? Had they not behaved with propriety? And yet the cheeks of the none-too-wrinkled old dame were ruddier than usual that evening, and behold the reason why: After having invited the monk, telling him mysteriously that the girls had 'something' to tell him (which 'something' was concerning their neighbour *Kyra*-Kostaina), she took heed to purchase a little resinated wine to offer her guest. She herself had drunk a glass and a half (which was why her cheeks had taken on the colour of a hot mullet and her wrinkles had diminished even more in number), the monk had taken two glasses and the girls half a glass each. On that evening the monk heard what the two sisters were telling him more with his eyes than with his ears. He gazed at the lips from which the words came forth; he stared at them as though he wished to sup in the words and lick the lips from which they flowed. It seemed to him that those words had another ineffable meaning beyond the meaning of the words expressed. He responded mechanically with commonplaces and monosyllables. By the lamplight the two sisters appeared almost beautiful. The pale yellow, sun-like, honeyed hue of the one sister, the attractive one, shone radiantly. Both of the girls had become more animated and excited on account of the company and the light infusion of wine. Then the various movements of the facial muscles, the smiles, the laughs, the postures, the gestures, and on top of this the careless atmosphere of the domestic surroundings, all conspired to make them appear somehow different, unrecognizable. Elpiniki had her forearms bared to the elbows and was wearing a thin white tunic, while Katina, the attractive sister, happened to be missing the top button from her white breast band and her blouse was collarless, and from thence her neck and the uppermost part of her breasts were revealed naked.

The old dame in all this had noticed that Father Samuel had been aroused by the close contact and conversation with the two girls, and a sense of indeterminate foreboding arose in her. Her girls weren't that sort, no indeed. She was simply *redeeming the time*,[1] deriving some small profit from her friendship with the monk. In ample measure she had been sympathetically and generously disposed towards him, as indeed many women often are charitably disposed, with chastity if not selflessness, towards footloose bachelors who have neither home nor family in Athens and who live a colourless life in a single cold room for which they pay a rent of fifteen or twenty drachmas simply to avoid sleeping out of doors in the winter. But single 'laymen', 'civvies' as old Tasou would call them, do not merit pity so much because most of them have the

---

[1] Ephesians 5 : 16.

whole market-place as a family and the great outdoors as a home. They spend their days in coffee shops, wine bars and other places less reputable. For the monk, however, all such delights and entertainments were forbidden. He was obliged to play the stay-at-home or to run at the beck and call of the priests. For this reason the ruddy-cheeked, past-her-prime matron felt genuinely sorry for him; her heart had gone out to him as she said. It had never crossed her mind that Father Samuel could throw everything to the wind, grab one of her daughters and abscond with her by night, taking her to wife by marriage or without marriage, with a priest's blessing or without a priest's blessing. Other mothers perhaps were capable of reconciling such an act with their consciences. But she, even though she was without education and even though she lacked any clear and potent religious sensibility, living as she did in the midst of the social and ecclesiastical wretchedness which presses in on us from every side, nonetheless she could never swallow it. In no way would she accept to appear 'excommunicated' in the eyes of the world. She knew a woman from another part of the town whose daughter had married a monk. (Lord save us and have mercy!) After her consent to the unlawful wedding, that woman seemed changed, as if she had changed personality and was no longer herself. She appeared to her in very truth as an 'excommunicated' soul. A public laughing stock! Had she no shame? Her eyes flashed with a wildness, her ashen face seemed swollen and her jaw twisted, as if she had been struck by some evil spirit. Father Samuel, who would never leave off his monkish tales, had told her about a sometime 'brother' of his who had been a deacon in one the monasteries on the Holy Mountain. This man had later left Mount Athos and come to Athens where suddenly one morning Father Samuel saw him with his beard shaved off and sporting a Frankish suit and hat. Anyone else might easily have failed to recognize him, but Father Samuel knew him well: 'What's happened to you, Father Symeon? What's come over you, brother?' 'What can one do? It's embarrassing to go around in the city in a cassock!' 'Didn't you think to go back to your

monastery as you said?' 'Each *hath one that judgeth him ...*'.[1]
Three days later he learned that this Symeon had married. Father
Samuel was puzzled how a priest could have been found to marry
him and wondered whether such a priest would have acted know-
ingly or unknowingly. But just to add good measure he learned that
the marriage had not been conducted in accordance with the rites
of the Eastern Church. One of the so-called Evangelicals, grazing
on the scarred and wounded body of the East, had conducted the
marriage. The former monk had attached himself to some club by
Hadrian's Arch[2] and lived licking the bones they threw to him.
Father Samuel crossed himself repeatedly with both hands. The evil
spirit that had gone out of this man had gone and found *seven other spirits more wicked than himself*[3] and had come back to dwell
permanently in his heart. Spare us, O Lord!

The old woman was recalling those things she'd heard from the
monk when he rose up to go off to sleep, and she, without taking
the lamp, escorted him to the door. The two daughters stayed in the
house at the back of the second room where the conversation had
taken place. There in the darkness, the old woman came up as close
as she could to the monk and, flushed as she was with the resinated wine, started to whisper something in his ear. The words were
disjointed and the monk comprehended only the perilous phrase:
'...you've wasted your youth away!' Now why did this middle-
aged woman with ruddy cheeks come so close to the monk and
why did she say this to him? Perhaps... was it to shield her daughters whom she wished honourable and blameless? But the shield
was alive with flesh and blood. When the monk, with a sense of
melancholy and loneliness, bade her good night, old Tasou involuntarily took his hand and squeezed it. And the breath of the
rotund matron burned on his cheek... And a lock of her hair

[1] John 12 : 48.

[2] A Roman monument in Athens built by Hadrian as the gate leading to the new
section of the city constructed during his reign.

[3] Luke 11 : 26.

which had escaped from beneath her headscarf brushed on his forehead. This was all. And when the monk went off to his cell next to the church, there lingered on his face for a long time the sense of the light touching of flesh and he smelled the smell of earth as from a grave dug open for the translation of bones. *For dust thou art, and unto dust shalt thou return.*[1] And instinctively he began to rinse his mouth, his face and his hands. *And God formed man of the dust of the ground.*[2]

Hell and torment here and Hell and torment there! The unsleeping worm and eternal fire! Gehenna! Wailing and gnashing of teeth!

After his first vision of remembrances from his life in the monastery — of the crimson and dark-blue window panes of the Byzantine church, of the dark apses, of the melancholy saints pictured on the walls, of the blue-black smoke rising from the censer, of the gold-embroidered drapings, of the icons with their smoke-tinted silver and gold 'shirts',[3] of the silver and gold-chased reliquaries, of the domed firmament blushing red in the light filtering in through the windows, of the mysterious grey-twilight, of the rosy dawn, of the sparrows chirping in the foliage of gigantic cypress trees, of the exquisite nature and of the climate, and of the unending forests of chestnut trees — there returned to his fantasy the two young damsels with their sallow complexions, with their white careless attire, with their plaits dangling at their necks, with their lean arms and delicate hands with knuckly fingers, with their white throats, with their damp eyes with the dark circles all around, with their innocent and tender looks. They returned and wished violently to take possession of his heart. But how strange! The old woman, so zealous to defend their virtue as a living shield, suddenly became

[1] Genesis 3 : 19.   [2] Genesis 2 : 7.

[3] The 'shirt', *hypokamison*, a silver or gold covering placed over an old icon, leaving the face and sometimes the hands exposed, and two-dimensionally molded to follow the lineaments of the holy figures portrayed. The 'shirts' were put on icons, partly to protect them, and partly as a sign of devotion.

for the poor monk an asp and a basilisk, towering upright terrifyingly, raising her head, curling round and round, hissing and seeking to bite him on the mouth ... which breathed the odour of earth and of the light-touching of flesh.

And on either side of her the two maidens became blurred and indistinct and, dissolving in smoke, they assumed a dream-like existence, entirely transformed. And shortly small wings appeared to sprout from their shoulders, their arms vanished, their throats became thinner and longer, their faces sharpened to a point, becoming reptilian snouts, and they were transformed into threatening dragons. And between them the old woman again changed shape. She opened her mouth like a cavernous well; the members of her body were obliterated and she became all mouth, a mouth gaping and ready to ingest. She was the gate of Hell and they were the two dragons guarding ever vigilantly lest any of the sinners should escape from Gehenna.

The monk quaked in dread on his pallet; he awoke trembling, but then again was overtaken by torpor and heavy sleep. And he beheld the mystical ladder on which monks ascend upwards, to watchful prayer, to contemplation, to Paradise. And he saw in the air the dark forms of the demons which impede the monks from reaching there. He beheld his own soul struggling and slipping, unable to ascend and in danger of being hurled down into the old woman's mouth. And he saw above him at intervals the dread points of reckoning, with the pairs of scales and the gigantic books held open by compassionate angels and the demons frenziedly dragging the tongues of the balances downwards. And he saw a great number of monks falling headlong from various steps of the ladder which stretched to the skies. And he pitied those hapless souls as, with trembling knees and strengthless arms, he tried desperately to hold fast to the bottom rungs. But suddenly, hovering in the air beside him, a black demon, with the characteristics of one of the two girls etched on its face, grabbed him furiously by the hem of his cassock and with all its might dragged him, dragged him relentlessly to fling him down. His trembling hands were just at the point of losing their grip on the upward leading rung of the ladder when he awoke suddenly with a nervous shudder.*

'Hell and torment here, and Hell and torment there,' breathed the monk as he made the sign of the cross.

. . . .

The next day before midday Samuel made his way to the offices of the Archdiocese where he tarried for about half an hour. Then, having lunched, in the afternoon he visited one after the other the homes of the Council members and of the priests. Thereafter he secretly summoned a neighbour who owned a cart and who had finished work early. He spoke a few brief words to him which the cartman listened to with astonishment.

'And why forever at a time like that, Father?' he asked him,

'I don't want anyone to see me,' answered Samuel. 'And please, not a word to anyone.'

'Don't the Council members know anything of this?' asked the man again.

'Don't worry, I've spoken to them.'

'And why do you need to worry about other people, whether they'll see you or not?' insisted the cart owner.

'I don't need to worry about other people, I need to worry about myself. That's for sure.'

The man didn't seem convinced.

'Look then, go away and ask *Kyr*-Yannis Rigitsas who's on the Council and he'll confirm it for you. But please, don't say a word to anyone else until tomorrow.'

The man with the cart set off, indicating with a nod of his head that he would go and ask and that he would keep the secret.

A few moments later old *Kyra*-Tasou appeared, the nightmarish spectre of yestreen.

'How come we didn't see you today, Samuel?' she addressed him.

'Well, I've been busy here and there,' answered the monk coldly.

'Where did you go?'

'Oh, I went down to the Archdiocese office and various other places.'

'Where else were you?'

'I'll tell you some other time,' said the monk looking elsewhere.

'Oh, so I see you've got secrets, Samuel!' said the ruddy goodwife.

'What secrets would I have, blessed woman? But never mind. We'll talk about this some other time.'

At that moment the carter returned. He nodded to the monk from a distance, indicating that he'd been to *Kyr*-Yannis Rigitsas and that his suspicions had been laid to rest.

'They told me you've handed over and that you're free now,' he announced.

'Shoosht!' signed the monk as he raised his finger to his lips.

The old woman heard the man's words and as soon as he'd gone she started to interrogate the monk.

'What have you handed over, Samuel? What was that about? And why are you free now?'

'Oh, it's nothing, good woman,' answered the monk. 'Just that I hand over ... I hand over the church candle accounts to the Council members every month.'

'You seem different today,' said the reddened old dame suspiciously. 'I hope you've not taken it into your head to leave us, Samuel?'

'Leave you? Not at all,' said the monk emphatically.

'Now look here, don't let us be losing you, because we've got used to you, Samuel my boy, and we'd really be put out, you know.'

'Well, you never know, I may go at some point ... I've said that to you often enough ... but no one leaves lightly, you know.'

'Because we've really felt for you and you've felt for us,' added the woman.

'It's quite true,' said Samuel. 'You've been very good. But a monk can't escape returning to his monastery some day.'

'You can do that once you're old and grey.'

'I'll do it when it's the will of God.'

The old woman fell silent for a few moments and then she said:

'What a fine time we had last night! The girls were thrilled with your company... When will you visit us again, Samuel?'

'Oh, some evening or other...the time will come.'

And the old woman, seeing that *Kyra*-Kostaina, distaff in hand, was spying on them from opposite, made off in haste.

*　*　*

Late that night, just before midnight, there was a banging on the door of the small cell.

'Father Samuel!'

Answer came there none.

'Samuel! Father Samuel!'

Still there was no sign that the invocation had been heard from within. Nor was any light to be seen at the window.

'The monk's sleeping like the dead tonight,' soliloquized the man who was hammering on the door. 'Had a glass too many at the Founders' Feast, I reckon.'[1]

He raised the lantern he was holding towards the window of the cell, and his face was lit up: a man of middle age, stoutish and with a well-trimmed beard. It was none other than *Kyr*-Yannis Manaftis. He continued to beat noisily on the door and rattle on the windowpane of the ground floor chamber, muttering through his teeth:

'Wherefore hast thou come hither, O brother?' and then starting to shout loudly again.

The result of *Kyr*-Yannis's banging and shouting was for a window of a neighbouring house to creak slightly and open and for a

---

[1] [Papadiamandis's footnote] The phrase denotes drunkeness. Its origins go back to the monastic custom relating to the feast day of the monastery; the brethren being usually busy with serving the numerous pilgrims have no time on that festive day to sit at the table, and on the following day, when official intercessions for the repose of the souls of the Founders and benefactors of the Monastery are offered, they find the time to partake of the Feast.

head to appear through the opening. *Kyr*-Yannis heard the light
squeaking noise, turned around, and discerned in the darkness the
emergent visage.

'What's happened to the monk?' he asked. 'Has he perhaps gone
off somewhere?'

'What do you want him for?' asked a woman's voice.

It was *Kyra*-Kostaina, without distaff, who, having gone to sleep
at eight o'clock was now fully rested, and having got up, had come
to the window to see and hear.

'My mother-in-law's in a bad way,' replied *Kyr*-Yannis. 'We need
to bring her Holy Communion. But I don't know where the monk
can be.'

'He'll be over at the priest-wives,' came *Kyra*-Kostaina's pat response.

'What priest-wives?' asked *Kyr*-Yannis in feigned puzzlement.

Kyra-Kostaina did not give a straight reply, but after a short
pause she continued:

'Who knows? Perhaps the priest-wives have got him tucked
away in case anyone else gets their hands on him.'

'What priest-wives? I don't understand what you're going on
about, dear lady,' said *Kyr*-Yannis, who, on the contrary, had understood all too well from the very beginning, because he was not
entirely innocent of the relationship to which the woman from the
window was alluding.

'He'll be stashed away, I tell you,' insisted *Kyra*-Kostaina. 'Knock
there and you'll see,' she said, pointing to old Tasou's door.

'I can't go knocking on other people's doors,' said *Kyr*-Yannis.

'Don't worry about offending her!' said Kostaina. 'Think up
some excuse. Say that because you couldn't find the monk you
thought he must have gone off to some country chapel and that you
wanted to ask if perhaps he'd left the key with her since she's always in and out of the church.'

Kyr-Yannis marvelled at the woman's plan. Nevertheless, he hesitated to put it into action.

'I'll go rather and knock at the door of Father Pavlinos who lives nearby,' he said with sudden inspiration. 'I believe he's the priest on duty, and perhaps he's got the key himself if the monk's away. At any rate he'll know.'

And he did as he said. Father Pavlinos was indeed the priest on duty and was found to have the key normally kept by the sacristan. The priest got out of bed and went and administered Holy Communion to the dying woman. *Kyr*-Yannis was embarrassed to ask the priest how most unusually the key came to be in his keeping that evening and what had become of the monk. Not until the morning did he learn along with the whole neighbourhood that the monk had departed that evening, abandoning his position as church officer.

✣   ✣   ✣

At ten o'clock at night the man with the cart had arrived outside the cell. As soon as night had fallen, Father Samuel had prepared all his meagre belongings, and having loaded them onto the cart, he climbed on himself. They set off for Piraeus. The whole neighbourhood was asleep, and no one saw them, except for a few street urchins who assumed that the monk was on his way to some country chapel or other.

He had not succumbed to the pressure from the Council members to stay on for a few days longer until a successor could be found. He was in a hurry to leave in case he might change his mind the next day. In the morning he had requested a church pass from the Archdiocese. The Council members were greatly sorrowed by his departure.

He boarded the first steamer for Thessaloniki, and with a sense of relief, which came as a surprise even to himself, he returned to Athos and to the monastery of his repentance.

[1892]

Translated by John Raffan

At Saint Anastasa's

FIVE MEN CAME DOWN TO PRYI, one July Sunday in the year 1875, and of those five, three were antiquarians carrying field glasses. Of these three, the first pronounced that the ruins there belonged to a pagan temple, the second maintained that they were the remnants of a Christian church (if not a Roman bath house), and the third insisted that they had been just an old mansion, perhaps a Venetian castle. To butress his opinion he invoked the name itself, Pryi, which he thought came from Pyrgi (castle) by metathesis. This opinion was embraced unreservedly by the village primary school teacher, who was another member of the party and whose skill in etymology was generally acknowledged. '*Aïnte* (come on!) is from the classical *age dē*', or so he would maintain; '*arē* (used to address the local women) is from the ancient *aristē* (the best); and *vre* is from *móre* (O fool!) by successive deformations (*mōré – m're – mvre – bre – vre*).' And he would thunder on indignantly against anyone who dared suggest a Turkish origin for these words, it being so easy, he insisted, to find, in every case, a Greek root.

Here is how it had all come about. The mayor of the little town, who had entered on a second term of office the year before, had taken it upon himself to invite the three antiquarians for a good meal up at the church of the Prophet Elijah,[1] and with them certain othēer friends of his. The party made the long ascent at dawn on donkey back. Though only several hundred metres high, it seemed to the good islanders as tall as Mount Kissavos. They got to St Elijah's at sunrise, cooled off in the welcome shade of the imposing

---

[1] Churches dedicated to the Prophet Elijah are invariably situated on hill- or mountain-tops.

plane-trees, and drank from the copious spring whence crystalline waters gushed forth and spread into the enchanting valley below. While the others reclined under the plane-trees and watched the lamb longingly as it browned on the spit, looking forward to enjoying soon an appetizer of tasty *kokoretsi*, our five comrades remounted their donkeys and headed for Pryi. They ascended to the highest part of the mountain, and thence made their way down to the right, past the spot known as Manolis's Sorb. After an hour's journey they reached Pryi. There they turned left and westward, making their way along a shady lane under interlocked oaks and elms, until they reached the ancient ruin.

The party's fifth member, who accompanied the three antiquarians and the teacher, possessed — to all appearances — the best mount, a tall, healthy, broad-boned donkey, its grey coat slightly tinged with red. And yet, far from running on ahead, it was lagging behind the other four. It seemed not even to notice the blows its rider administered to its rear, first with his stick, then with the rope attached to its reins. Either it had not properly digested its hay or straw, or it was just determined to irritate its rider in any way it could. The more he struck it, the more indolent it became. Several times he tried to get it going by digging his shoes into its belly. But all in vain. It was a wonder he did not lose sight altogether of the other four, who were by now well ahead of him, along with the muleteers two had brought with them. These watched the last rider's predicament with indifference, and he, for his part, was not going to call for their help. Eventually he too made it to the place where stood the ruined remains.

The three wise men expressed their conjectures with regard to the ruin's function and date of construction, and deplored the authorities' failure to have the place excavated. Then the visit was over, and the little party set off to return and meet the remaining members of the rustic excursion. The trio of antiquaries and the teacher had long since reached St Elijah's, consumed their *kokoretsi* and two glasses of *masticha*, and were onto the *splinantero*. It was an hour before noon, but the fifth member of the party, trailing far behind, had yet to appear. Another hour passed by, and they had sent the pair of muleteers back to look for him, when suddenly they saw him riding triumphantly on his donkey, which was now charging ahead like a steam engine. Nor, as everyone was expecting, did he appear from a westerly direction, but on the contrary from the east, in other words as if he were coming from the town.

Nothing is stranger than the simple truth. Everyone was convinced he had done it deliberately, to cause a stir. But in fact, what had happened was this. The perfectly robust donkey, divining, it seems, its rider's weak point, had overdone it this time, all the more as the return journey was uphill. It progressed at the speed of a tortoise. The four scholars had gone on so far ahead, that the fifth member of the party was out of both sight and hearing of them. It did not take him long to realize that he had lost the road, and that either he or his donkey had gone too far east, into a deep ravine, a damp place full of shady trees between two high peaks. Then he recognized where he was. It was the spot known as the Cold Well. Seeing no point any longer in beating the donkey's numbed flanks, since the beast did not respond, he went on foot. Clutching the reins in his left hand and in his right the stick, he tried to see if he could get the donkey to move forward by driving him from behind. Then, absent-mindedly, without thinking, he goaded the donkey in the hind quarters under the saddle, exactly in the kidneys, with the sharp stick. In a flash the donkey lurched forward at such speed, that the youth came to his senses with a start, almost losing his grip on the reins. But now he had found his donkey's weak spot. Remounting, he began to goad it mercilessly, and the donkey ran furiously ahead. His rider knew the road now, took a right turn, and in a few minutes galloped up to St Elijah's from the east, just exactly at the moment that Dimitris Michoyannis was artistically carving the roast, while under the giant trees was being laid a table fragrant with ferns and plane leaves.

Dimitris Michoyannis's skills were not confined to roasting on the spit or slicing the meat. He was also an accomplished teller of tales about the life of the shepherds and goatherds around Pryi, in the environs of which he had himself grown up.

*   *   *

Yannis Koutris, tall, fortyish, with a beardless face already starting to wrinkle like an old woman's, had conceived that year (to be precise, almost two months ago) a daring Easter scheme. The shepherds from Kalyvia, who made up a whole neighbourhood on their own, were in the habit of attending church at St George's of K'stodoulitsa.* The goatherds from Kambia, Mygdalia and Kouroupi went to the liturgy at St Charalambos's. As for the luckless shepherds of Kechrea, St Constantine's, St Athanasius's, Bostania and other places, they were scattered 'like the rabbit's offspring'. Yannis Koutris — he was also known as Yannis the Crone[1] — was extremely jealous of his second cousin Yannis Ladikas, who was churchwarden at St George's of K'stodoulitsa, as well as for all the country chapels that had special festivals for their patron saints. He would grab from the candle stands the half-burned candles, gathering them together into big bundles and putting them out by stamping on them on the flagstones of the church floor with his heavy shepherd's wooden shoes. He pretended they were in danger of flaring up, if he let them burn all the way down.* He would also circulate a special offertory plate round all the festival congregations, collecting money 'to repair the churches'. 'God forgive us for thinking such a thing, but isn't it possible that his hands were not entirely clean?' All this behaviour stirred feelings of envy in Yannis Koutris. They began to hatch from the first week of Lent

---

[1] [Papadiamantis's note] *Koútris* (that is, *késphos* = 'big head') is what we call in our dialect the unbaptized male child; the female is known as *kossoú*. *Drákos* and *drakoúla* are the names we use for baptized babies when they have been through some difficult or alarming and unpleasant illness, such as convulsions or epilepsy; this appellation acts as a talisman and amulet against the evil eye. In the text, *koútris* = 'beardless'.

when the idea came to him, and matured during the forty-day fast. His plan was to detach from St Charalambos's congregation Yorgis Trygologos and his family, the Michaloyannises both father and son, and the four Mavrodimos brothers with their wives and children, and to entice them to Pryi where he had his own flock. Along with the three or four other goatherds in that area, he would then invite a priest so that they could celebrate their own Easter.

* * *

Despite the etymological prowess to which we made allusion at the beginning of our tale, the teacher had oddly enough forgotten one thing, to wit, that in the mouth of the people the ruin was called St Anastasia's. The remaining section of wall faced eastwards and curved outwards, and the most natural interpretation was that it belonged to the apse of the sanctuary of a Byzantine church. Admittedly it was made of large white marble blocks, rectangular and carefully finished; and otherwise it rather resembled the remains of Pelasgian walls. Only this section remained standing, to the height of a man. No other remnants of the building were visible, and its plan, size and purpose were hard to divine. Nevertheless it was known as St Anastasia's.

On the inner side of this fragment of wall, there was no sign of an altar. There was no plaster, far less a fresco or other distinctive feature. But from this spot the smoke of incense had perhaps, some eight or ten centuries earlier, been sent up to the throne of the Christian God; and possibly there had been offered, on an altar no longer extant, the spiritual and spotless sacrifice *after the order of Melchisedek,*[1] that priest of the Almighty who, according to Holy Scripture, *brought forth bread and wine.*[2]

Its name was St Anastasia's. Once upon a time it had perhaps been a temple of Kore from Hades or Hecate the Venomous (Pharmakis); and the Christians, natural heirs of dying paganism, had

[1] Hebrews 5 : 6.   [2] Genesis 14 : 18.

baptized it and made it, out of a spirit of contrariness, into a church of the Pharmakolytria ('She who cures'), or else of the Romaia ('the Roman Woman'), deriving the name straightforwardly from the building. And Father Angelis, whom Yannis Koutris had asked to come and celebrate for them on Easter Day, had no idea to which of the two Anastasias the church had originally been dedicated. For there are two saints of that name, the Romaia and the Pharmakolytria.

Seeing neither altar nor lamps nor icons, and knowing nothing of outdoor liturgies (something so daring, it would have seemed to him like a return to idolatry), he sought with naive sophistry to persuade those rude goatherds that it would be better for them to celebrate their liturgy at nearby St Anna's. 'After all,' he pointed out, 'St Anna is already half a St Anastasia.' But crafty, beardless Yannis Koutris replied that 'they didn't want half a resurrection [*anastasi*], but the whole thing'.

In the eyes of the goatherds, St Anastasia was the Resurrection itself. And it was hardly to be expected that they would be more erudite in these matters than that venerable priest who, when asked some years ago which is the greater, St Kyriaki [Sunday] or the Transfiguration, answered without blinking that 'St Kyriaki is greater, for she is celebrated every week, while the Transfiguration comes only once a year'. And are not many, even today, under the illusion that the renowned church of the Wisdom of God (Hagia Sophia) is dedicated to the martyr St Sophia whose feast is commemorated on 17th September?*

*   *   *

Not only did Yannis the Crone want to celebrate the Resurrection apart, with his fellow shepherds in his own pastures; he also desired that the Resurrection service be held not just in any church, but specifically at St Anastasia's. Since it had been a church in times past, and given that the place had been consecrated for the worship of Christ, what possible reason could there be for not holding a liturgy there? In vain Father Angelis exhausted his little learning and his innate common sense, trying to persuade him that he was asking for something unreasonable. The goatherd remained unpersuaded.

'How, my dear fellow, can I possibly celebrate the liturgy without a roof?' the priest asked him. 'Have you ever seen a liturgy under the stars?'

'But isn't the Resurrection service always sung under the stars?' countered the shepherd. 'Other people have perfectly good churches with slate roofs or tiles, and still they go outside the church, as you well know, for the Resurrection service. Its true we don't have a church. But why can't we — don't you understand? — have our Resurrection out of doors, but in a place that was a church once upon a time, so they tell us?'*

For a moment the priest just looked at him helplessly, then his eyes lit up, as if he had had an idea, and he said:

'They hold the Resurrection service outside the church, yes. But the liturgy?... How are we going to have the liturgy?'*

'In the ruins, since the altar was there originally.'

'But there isn't a proper consecrated altar.'

'In the old days, when they built it, you know — wasn't it *conservated*?'

'*The Rudder*[1] says that when a church is desecrated, it shouldn't be used for the liturgy, unless its been rebuilt and reconsecrated.'

Perhaps in the end Father Angelis would have persuaded him to move to St Anna's, which was not far away, and was after all 'his neighbour', just as the goatherd boasted that St Anastasia 'was his neighbour'. But the good priest was not himself so sure that he could get away with celebrating the liturgy at St Anna's. The little church still had its roof. The sanctuary, which was a curved recess in the thickness of the wall, and the oblation recess on one side of the sanctuary, were covered with a foot or so of earth and stones that had fallen from the roof of the apse. The icon screen in front of the sanctuary was still in position, though bereft of its icons. The

---

[1] *To Pedalion*, the standard commentary on the canons of the Church Councils.

two windows in the north and the south wall were without glass, and the wind played in and out of them. The chapel resembled a toothless old woman, her eyes mere sockets, the merry voices of children now but a buzzing in her ears, harshly mocking her feebleness. There was not even a single lamp lit by the vow of some pious woman, nor a candlestand to shed consoling light on the few blackened, disfigured saints who could be discerned on the walls. The chapel had been dedicated to the Nativity of the Mother of God, but it was usually called the Panayitsa,[1] or by some St Anna's. Still, Father Angelis was doubtful whether it was lawful to celebrate the liturgy there, even with icons borrowed from elsewhere and lamps hung in front of them in any way that seemed best.

Eventually he devised a compromise, and announced it to Yannis Koutris.

'Very well then, we'll hold the Resurrection service at St Anastasia's, but straight afterwards you'll all gather up your stuff, and we'll go down with Paschal candles lit to the Panayia Doman,* and I'll celebrate the liturgy for you there.'

'The Panayia Doman?... But it's a long way off!'

'Oh, come on... It'll take us half an hour.'

'Forgive me, Father, but it's over an hour.'

'More like three-quarters of an hour, no more. And anyway the whole night is ours. We've more than enough time to get there.'

Yannis Koutris gave in. Anyway, he had little choice.

The priest began the service in the open air, wearing a black stole. He started by reading the night vigil office and the canon 'On the wave of the sea', but all without intonation. Then he lit incense in the thurible, he censed all those present, and having pronounced the dismissal to conclude the office, he put off the black stole and put on another one of violet silk, with a white cope — all these he produced from the saddle bag in which he had stored the holy

---

[1] Panayitsa, the diminutive of Panayia, the popular appellation of the Mother of God, meaning the All-Holy.

vessels. Next he lit the Paschal candle, turned towards the people, and began to sing in a musical voice 'Come, receive the light', and after that 'Thy Resurrection, O Christ our Saviour'.

Everyone now lit their candles. The priest read the Resurrection Gospel, and after having glorified the Holy Trinity, he then began with thunderous voice to chant 'Christ is risen from the dead' antiphonally with his twelve-year-old son, who had come along on the outing to assist him. That was a beautiful and charming sight there in the impressive marble ruin, made all the more resplendent in the dancing light of fifty candles stirred by the breath of the nocturnal wind. It was a sight at once lambent and sombre, bright yet mysterious, amidst the giant oaks that proudly lifted up their mighty boughs to make tall crowns, their rustling leaves scintillating like flakes of gold in the torchlight gleam. And in the shadows and murky spaces amidst the branches, one might imagine unseen spirits lurking and waiting, that had existed of yore, fine-limbed Dryads and slender Orestiads holding sway over the dense oak forests, and today metamorphosed into nocturnal spirits, afraid to emerge into the light of the paschal candles.* For a time they had taken heart at the Christian God's desertion of his fine marble sanctuary, but now with wonder they beheld the rekindling of the Easter torches and smelt the fragrance of the Christians' incense, there in the depths of the oak wood.

❊   ❊
❊

While the priest intoned the litany, and prayed for the stability of the Churches, the abundance of the fruits of the earth and so forth, behind the immense trunk of the thousand-year-old oak — which three men linking hands could barely embrace — was heard the following brief dialogue between three or four goatherds, the first of whom, Yannis Koutris, had an answer ready for the enquiries of all the others:

'So we're setting off straight away?'

'Right away.'

'And we'll do it all in one go?'

'Of course, friend.'

'To the Panayia Doman?'

'Yes, that's what the priest said.'

'Through the gorge?'

'What are we waiting for?'

'We're off, friend.'

But this conversation was interrupted by the voice of the priest, who had now removed his vestments. He shouted out to his flock:

'Is everyone ready? Let's go!'

Two of the goatherds hurriedly loaded the holy vessels, along with the shepherdesses' baskets brimful of festal provisions, on to five or six donkeys, while the priest mounted the seventh. The others went on foot. Some held lighted candles in their left hand, and tried with their right to protect the flame from the land breeze that was blowing. The others lit small lanterns of the sort goatherds find so useful when shutting their animals up for the night or milking them. They all set off together, descending in a northerly direction, then turning eastwards across rough country that no feet but theirs could bear, treading lightly in the shepherds' wooden shoes that sheathed their nimble feet, goading their donkeys to run along, or even dragging them to keep them on the track, placing themselves on the left-hand side in order to support the burdened beasts on the abrupter parts of the road. Two or three of them, in their capes, brought up the rear, driving the goats on with whistlings and incomprehensible monosyllables, while their little kids charmingly bounced along next to their mothers, bleating inquisitively, to which interrogation the she-goats could return but a vague response, having themselves no way of explaining this unwonted night march. The moon had come up before midnight, and her slightly reddish disk emerged now and then behind the crowns of tall trees, only to hide again behind the mountains, as the party wended its tortuous way. The bushes too bent and shook wherever the procession passed, and the insects stirred early from their sleep. Flies dashed

merrily round the candle flames, gently buzzing, singeing their fragile wings or destroying with a terminal explosion their ephemeral
existence as they touched the fire. The birds of the night fled in fear
from rush to arbutus, from the dry-stone walls to the trees, adding
the gentle rustling of their wings to the delicate, harmonious exha-
lation of the morning breeze. The wild clematis with its snowy-white
flowers, glistening fragrantly on the fences, white-robed myrrh-
bearer revelling at the Resurrection, together with the ivy and the
honeysuckle, tresses of Spring who shakes her sweet-smelling locks
across the fields: all these shed a still keener perfume into the night
air. As the moon rose up, the silvery dusting of stars grew paler in
the vault of heaven. The nightingale could be heard warbling deep
in the forest's heart, while the owl, unable to compete with his melodious sister, left off for a time from his mournful song.

✳   ✳
✳

Following the floor of the gorge, they had by now descended the
greater part of its length, and before them in the distance they beheld the sea, a blue expanse faintly silvered by moonbeams. After a
while they heard a heavy splashing sound as of a torrent descending with a crash from the rocks, a constant, loud, monotonous rum-
bling. It was the stream of the Panayia Doman, which in times past
drove twenty watermills, while scores of acres of terraced gardens
were nourished by its refreshing stream. Just opposite, by the
seashore, reared up the Kastro, an ancient fortress that once was a
dwelling-place of men, before it became a nest for owls and a haunt
of gulls. On the perennial stream of the Panayia Doman depended,
in those olden times, the area's flourishing vegetable gardens and in
general all its vegetation.

It was already about two hours after midnight, when Father
Angelis and his goatherds arrived at the Panayia Doman. The little
chapel stood amidst a copse of enormous trees, which framed it pic-
turesquely and tenderly shaded it under spreading branches. It was
an undistinguished little church, but at least it was kept up and in

suitable condition for a liturgy. It was one of the few chapels that had survived intact from olden times. There had been numerous others in the general neighbourhood, not far off fifty of them on the lower slopes where the valley broadened out into a little plain washed on both sides by the sea. Most of them were now ruins. The Panayia Doman was a straight copy of the church of the Life-Receiving Spring in Constantinople.[1] Crowned as it were by the evergreen diadem of its immense trees, it still stood upright, and seemed to say to its humbled siblings that the weariness of centuries had brought to their knees: 'Be of good cheer, I will stand for all of you!'

The ordinary folk had long felt a pious impulse to make up for the many temples and altars it had once possessed, by multiplying country chapels in every vale and on every mountain. They forgot the old gods, but substituted their new saints. This impulse prevailed over the stricter and more canonical view, according to which Christians were not permitted to build country churches. Monks and ascetics who adhered precisely to the letter of the law refused to celebrate the liturgy in these country churches.* But the heart tends to prevail over the head, and so the common people, hard-working, ground down, poverty-stricken, burdened with peasant chores and scattered in hamlets and villages, lacking as they did the funds to build large and resplendent churches, instead built numerous less pretentious ones. And the Saviour, more accommodating than his official interpreters on earth, 'mindful of the human predicament', as St Gregory the Theologian put it, and recalling the widow's offering, accepted the pious tithe of the poor, just as he had accepted her two mites.[2]

❊   ❊
❊

In the twinkling of an eye the chapel was illuminated, and the shepherdesses lit innumerable candles in the two stands appointed for

---

[1] The Church of the Holy Virgin of Pigi just outside the walls of Constantinople, famous for its holy spring.

[2] See Mark 12 : 42, 43; Luke 21 : 2, 3.

that purpose. They lit a fire too in a sheltered spot just outside the door, and setting up a large cauldron, started to prepare the soup. Two of them, newly-weds, wore their red dresses, their jackets with embroidered lower sleeves, and their white headscarves. And the priest recited the prayers that are said in secret before the liturgy, then put on all his vestments, while his son, his co-celebrant, chanted the canon. As for Yannis Koutris, he had realized his dream of presiding as churchwarden. He supervised the lighting and extinguishing of the candles, stamping on them now and then with his shepherd's wooden shoes, copying his cousin Yannis Ladikas. He stood to the right at the choir stall, presiding with such a serious air that one would have thought him a cantor, though oddly silent.

Just at that moment his twelve-year-old daughter Koumbo entered the chapel, having previously been standing just outside by the door, supervising the boiling cauldron. She whispered in his ear:

'Father, there are people coming.'

'Who are they?' asked Koutris, taken by surprise.

'Dimitrakis the son of K'tsina is coming, and his wife As'minio, and Yannis the son of Kostalo, and *Barba*-Yorgis... '

'Which *Barba*-Yorgis?'

'Yorgis the son of Panayotis.'

This name fell as a thunderbolt on Yannis Koutris's ear.

'Yorgis the son of Panayotis!' he repeated mechanically. And then he asked his daughter (as if she could have known!):

'What, didn't they have their Resurrection at St Charalambos's?'

He just could not understand how Yorgis the son of Panayotis had found his way over here. He presided at St Charalambos's, and nobody disputed his right to do so. What then had happened to prevent him going to his own church? Had he lost his position there?

Why had he, Yannis Koutris, made such an effort to hold a separate Resurrection this year with his neighbours in his own territory? Precisely in order to free himself from the burdensome spectacle of his second cousin Yannis Ladikas at St George's of K'stodoulitsa, or that of Yorgis, Panayotis's son, at St Charalambos's, where respectively they presided and discharged the duties of churchwarden, each in his own territory, lighting and extinguishing the candles, whispering ostentatiously in the priest's ear at the north door of the sanctuary, free to take round the offertory plate to the refrain, 'Oil for the church, good Christians!', and in general being boss of everything both inside and outside the church. Now that he had managed to have the Resurrection service sung in the open air at St Anastasa's, to coax away so many shepherds from other pastures, and to bring them down all the way from St Anastasa's to the Panayia Doman in the middle of the night, with their wives, their children, their flocks, and their kids bleating heartrendingly round the she-goats, was he to be condemned once more to take second place to Yorgis son of Panayotis, just because he was older and thought that gave him rights? What rights?

Let him produce his papers and have them read out! True enough, neither of them could read, but Father Angelis was there, thank God, and he could read them... That was his job, after all, reading... But no! Why should he give in to someone else? He'd act as if he'd not seen him. He would look straight ahead, at the altar, and he wouldn't look westwards even for one moment, but he would follow the liturgy reverently. He was in the right after all, it was his territory... But at that moment Yannis Koutris froze, his heart skipped a beat. He was not in his own territory! On the contrary, he had crossed the boundary, he had moved into somebody else's territory... Oh that Father Angelis, who had insisted so much on not celebrating the liturgy at St Anastasa's... There, beyond the faintest shadow of doubt, Koutris was on his own ground. But here, at the Panayia Doman, he was — precisely — in the territory of St Charalambos, in the jurisdiction of Yorgis the son of Panayotis!

What was to be done? You see, that Yorgis son of Panayotis was not just anybody. He was a strong man, and the goatherds and shepherds were under his spell. And now here he was, already entering the chapel. He was a tall, robust, handsome man, with a well-drawn face and regular features. He was some sixty years old, but his thick black head of hair had only just begun to show a few traces of grey here and there. He had taken part in the island's first insurrection at the beginning of the century, in 1808. He had spoken with Stathas, he had offered *kokoretsi* with his very own hands to Vlachavas, he had served under Nikotsaras.[1] His whole bearing, his appearance, manner and movements, even now after forty years, at the moment he entered the little church, seemed like a translation into flesh and bones, or as it were a concrete realization, of the old distich:

> *On Skiathos and on Skopelos no Ottoman has trodden,*
> *For Nikotsaras keeps watch there, and Stathas has his hideout.*

Koutris sensed that he was entering, and discerned his presence there in the little church. For all his resolve not to look at him, he turned his head involuntarily, and their eyes met. As soon as Yorgis son of Panayotis had reverenced the icons, he came and stood behind Koutris, who could no longer pretend that he had not noticed him. In any case Yorgis gave him no time to think. Bending down, he spoke in his ear, with a sly smile:

'Y've took from me territry Yorgi Tryouloou, y've took the Michouyannises, father 'n son, y've took all four Mavrod'moses, 'n now 'er's just a few 'f us left at St Charalambos. The priest for St Charalambos's away, yer know — 'a's gone to Koutskia, to the villerges. The priest from the Panaya, down in 't town, didn't want to come 'cause there're so few of us, not worth 'is while, yer see. T' other priest, the one from the Three Hierarchs, St John's,* is busy with 'is parish, 'cause Father Angili, 'oo 'elped 'im, yer took away. We nearly had no church at all, Easter 'n all, 'cause we didn't know which church yer goin' to for Resurrection. So 'a said, 'a'll go back to Kichria, mayhap 'a'll find 'em in s'm chapel or other. Just when 'a was goin' past Douman 'a was lookin' over at 't Kastro, y' know, 'n case 'a sore light s'm'where — 'a thought praps they'd gon' to one 'f the little old churches in 't Kastro for Resurrection. But 'a

---

[1] All well-known heroes of the Greek War of Independence, which began in 1821.

never thought you'd come t' Douman, right in my territry!'

From this explanation Yannis Koutris gathered, a little too late, that despite all his plans and everything he had done, the further he tried to escape from Yorgis, Panayotis's son, and his precedence, the closer he had been drawn to both him and his territory. For it is not enough, just to run away. One needs, as well, not to be pursued, or at least to have some idea where one is going.

He had no choice but to concede him the place of honour; in any case he took it, even before Koutris conceded it.

*   *   *

The liturgy ended just as day was breaking, and the purplish hue of the eastern sky was seeping into the blue of the sea spread out below it. The moon grew pale, and one by one the few remaining stars, trembling in the sky, were extinguished. Dawn broke, and touched with an exquisite reddish tint mountains, vales and woodlands. Throwing off its mysterious nocturnal veil, the position of the Panayia Doman stood now revealed in all its magical beauty. To the right were visible the high cliffs of the mountainside, cut by tree-filled gorges, descending to the abrupt coast around Kouroupi. To the left hills, valleys and forests composed a picturesque and varied view. Exactly in front the bare, wild rock of the Kastro exuded majesty, with the pair of rocky islets in front of it, and beyond, the boundless sea glittering in the first rays of the rising sun. On the far northern horizon, Chalkidiki could be discerned with its three peninsulas, and emerging above it, like a step on some titanic lightning-struck ladder leading up to Heaven, the greyish cone of Athos, its peak in the clouds. To the west was Pelion with its countless valleys and glorious vegetation, and beyond it the peak of Kissavos, like a head stuck on to an alien body. And the stream of the Panayia Doman no longer surged and loudly bubbled in its rocky bed as before, but instead greeted the break of day with a gentle murmuring, flowing gently over moss and water crowfoot. Daytime's many familiar sounds were now to be heard all around.

At last the sun's first ray appeared, and out of the sea sprang forth a brilliant, fiery shaft from this most glorious luminary. At the same moment was heard a mighty and impressive voice, the eagle's piercing screech greeting the rising sun from its nest high on the mountain's inaccessible, untrodden precipices. Then a second voice was raised in greeting, the cry of the hawk in a ravine high on dizzying Mount Kouroupi. A third voice, the stuttering of the partridge and the turtle dove half way up the valley, intensified the chorus that greeted the resplendent daytime star. Last to greet the sun's appearance with its song was the sweet swallow, who this year too had rediscovered her nest untouched in the holy dwelling-places, in the house of the Lord, and also in the huts of the peasants, and likewise in the houses of the good burghers. Dim twitterings might also be heard from the little sparrows in their bushes. One of them, its faltering song barely to be heard, had resolutely perched its delicate feet on a branch, while another flew around it singing of its love, paused for a moment on the branch, then threw itself upon the object of its affections, kissing it, begging it, imploring it and then breaking once more into song.

Now the goat kids too, feeling the warmth of the day upon them, started to bound around, happily rolling in the grass, gambolling about their mothers, nuzzling at the teat — nor did they have any thought that the slaughterer's blade too was glinting in the rising sun...

*　*　*

Tall trees, their branches adorned with cocoons and hairy tassels of leaves, were swaying in the morning breeze above the clear waters of the stream as it whispered down into the valley. The shepherds had all gathered under them with their wives and children, and were contentedly sitting around on a thick carpet of ferns and leaves. They had begun to cut up the lambs and kids that smelt so deliciously on the spit. They ate with relish, and Father Angelis blessed (as was proper) the capacious wine-flask of fresh leather with its red strap, whence emanated incomprehensible gurgling and hissing sounds. Then he passed it to the leader of the group, who was sitting on his right hand, Yorgis the son of Panayotis. The latter got up and addressed the gathering at length:

'Chris' ris'n, me friends! True 'e's Lord! 'e lives an' rules! — Cheers! Good 'ealth! An' a prosp'rous yar! Be of good 'eart! May'd we all 'ave a 'ealthy ol' age! Many 'app' returns! 'ere's to meetin' up next yar too, in goodn' 'ealth! 'ave a goodn' year! Many 'app' returns! A blessin' on yer cloth, father!'

Then he turned to Koutris:

'Yannis, yer alwus welcom'!'

Perhaps this was an allusion to the foregoing events. But Koutris was quick off the mark:

'And you are welcome too, *Barba*-Yorgis!'

Father Angelis could not suppress a laugh, and the others followed suit. Yorgis passed the flask to Koutris who was seated opposite him, and he made a brief response and drank. By the time the flask had gone round three times there was a general feeling of brotherliness, and Yannis no longer felt any antipathy toward Yorgis. The latter, who was given to reminiscing about the war after a good meal, began to tell the gathering about the heroic death of Nikotsaras.

'There were three ships off Kassandra, carrying Nikotsaras's men and Stathas's. Stathas's ship was completely black. Its sides were black, the rigging was black, the sails were black. He'd made a vow not to have anything white, until he made a triumphal entry to Thessaloniki. There wasn't a breath of wind all day, the three ships couldn't go forward, and they couldn't go back either, to their anchorage. But the Turkish fleet managed to catch the current, and the current took them here and there, and eventually it brought them up alongside. Still, the two captains were very courageous. They were real heroes. I don't think there were any others like them — I knew them well. Captain Stathas gave me an amber mouthpiece for my pipe, so that I'd remember him now and then. As for

Captain Nikotsaras, once when I served him *kokoretsi* I'd made with my own hands, he liked it so much that for many months afterwards, whenever he saw me he'd say: "What's there to eat, friend Yorgis, haven't you got some *kokoretsi*?" "If you've got the appetite, Captain," I'd reply, "do you want me to make you some?" On three separate occasions I killed three sheep, just so I could make him *kokoretsi*. Later, they went off against Kassandra. Their other comrades — there were lots of boats, with seven leaders of war bands — they weren't with them. They'd agreed to go afterwards and find them. So the day the fleet with the Turkish force caught up with them, there were just Nikotsaras and Stathas. The Turks fired three cannon shots, there were volleys of musketry, then the cannon got down to serious work. Nikotsaras's ship and the Turkish frigate tangled their rigging, like two women neighbours who fall out and get into a fight and start pulling each other's hair. Nikotsaras managed to break the Turk's grappling irons with an axe and cut his bowsprit. That way he saved his boat from the jaws of destruction. But at the last moment, when our side was on the point of winning, and the Greek band was roaring abuse of the Turks' religion, Nikotsaras was hit. The shot buried itself deep in his belly, and gave him a serious wound. Eh, the true hero is a hero in death as well. "The dogs have got me," he exclaimed, and gritted his teeth. With his hands he grasped his guts, that were spilling out of his belly; by the skin of his teeth he held on to his soul, which was departing from his mouth. These were the words he managed to get out: "Comrades! Take hold of me and sit me up there on the ropes. Prop me against the mast ... so that the dogs don't realise they've killed me and take courage ... so our men don't hear about it and lose heart." They did as they were told, and propped him half dead against the mast ... and the Turks, seeing him from a distance, were struck with terror and cried out: "Tsaras reis! Tsaras reis!" Captain Tsaras! Captain Tsaras! Our men on the other ships didn't understand what had happened. They went on fighting heroically, and put the Turkish fleet to flight. And when it had disappeared from sight, then they heard the news, and came back to our island, to bury Nikotsaras, who had died holding his intestines in his hands so that they didn't spill out, and his soul by the skin of his teeth so that it wouldn't abandon him. They came and buried him, down at Lechouni by the sandy beach, and they sang him this song:

> ...*The man who terrorized the Turks and filled their hearts*
> *with panic,*
> *They went and buried him in the gorge down by Lechouni's*
> *seashore.*'

This, then, was roughly what he related, as he had heard it himself (but with much mutation of vowels and contraction of syllables). With a deep sigh, *Barba*-Yorgis brought his tale to an end. The goatherds listened to him admiringly, and Father Angelis, following with intense interest, felt a tear trickle down his cheek.

*　　*　　*

As if to console *Barba*-Yorgis, whom he no longer resented for thwarting his ambition, Yannis Koutris loosed his donkey, which was grazing peacefully in the meadow, and began to show off some of his tricks. His fifteen-year-old son Thodoris, in order as it were to provide some musical accompaniment to his father's performance, took up his flute and began to pipe a simple, unmodulated tune. Meanwhile, Yannis Koutris had mounted his donkey, having substituted a saddlecloth for its saddle. Advancing slowly, with mock seriousness, he put the animal through its paces, imitating and parodying the movements of cavalry horses. At one moment Yannis was kneeling on the saddlecloth, at another he was lying on the donkey's back. Then he would hang on to its mane with one leg over its back and the other dragging along on the ground, and next he would slide under the donkey's belly. Or else you saw him disappear from his head to his knees between the animal's four legs, and you were sure he would fall off and be trodden under foot; but suddenly, in the twinkling of an eye, he was up on the donkey's back again. At this sort of mock warfare, Yannis Koutris was an expert. It was more than enough to keep the whole company guffawing happily for a long time.

* * *

Eventually Yannis Koutris left his donkey alone, and *Barba*-Yorgis, by way of thanking the mimic and bringing the symposium to an end, offered the day's last toast specially to him. It had a somewhat muffled sound, as if emanating from the bottom of the flask, which began now to gurgle and hiss again.

'And may'n we met agin, all bein' well, nex' yar!'

Yannis Koutris replied:

'You'll be welcome, *Barba*-Yorgis!'

[1892]

Translated by Garth Fowden

AROUND THE LAGOON

REMINISCENCES TO A FRIEND

WHEN AFTER SEVEN YEARS you returned to this beautiful place, so dear to your memory, it wasn't February and there were no more narcissi to sweeten the air with their intoxicating scent. But neither was Polymnia there, that narcissus in human form who had once intoxicated your childish fancy with the mere rustle of her white dress woven from linen and silk. Nor did good Parrisis's melon-patch still survive as a green border that had once framed the calm lagoon whose waters reflected the serene blue of the sky, nor even Loukas Thanasoulas's hut, washed by the ripples near the mouth of the lagoon, where no fisherman ventured within range, since, even while Loukas slept, his carbine kept vigil at his side, and you would hear in the dead of night a sudden shot that boded no good for any impudent fellow who tried to approach. If rumours were true, this carbine was the alarm-clock for the lagoon's tenant fisherman, warning him with a mysterious tap on his right shoulder of the stealthy approach of a boat from the harbour at night. For the terms of his contract stated that all the crabs and grey mullet that approached the lagoon belonged to the lagoon, whereas those that ventured outside it did not belong to the harbour, thus applying to the full the maxim, 'all that is mine is mine, and all that is thine is mine'.[1]

In those days *Barba*-Yorgos Kopsidakis, God rest his soul, used to bring his few ewes and lambs down to pasture there, and he never tired of telling everybody about all the visions he had seen: saints, angels, demons, the state of the souls of the dead, even the Last Judgement —

---

[1] A humorous variation on John 17 : 10.

all these he had seen. Once he was even proved spectacularly right
when he persuaded the townsfolk, including the mayor and corpora-
tion, that it was necessary to rebuild St George's from the foundations
up, prophesying that when they dug down the Saint would come and
assist them. And indeed, as the mattock disembowelled the earth with
a dull thud, growing ever blunter as it struck stones and pebbles, it
revealed twin tombs containing yellowed skeletons buried there as a
result of who knows what plague during the course of the preceding
centuries, and among the commingled bones and soil they found a hundred Venetian florins. Some saw this as a miracle, others were amazed
at the coincidence, but the visible result was that the chapel was built
rather splendidly. It was in this chapel, when it was still old and narrow and cramped, that you used to shut yourself when you wanted to
invoke the Saint's aid to soothe the early pangs of your heart. No one
could have accused you of irreverence, since you didn't ask the Saint
for earthly happiness but for consolation for your sorrows. Meanwhile
you were floating in a false sense of security, convinced that nobody
else could see you but God and the Saint. Yet that young lad who
looked after the sheep of *Barba*-Yorgos Kopsidakis, God rest his soul,
even though he wasn't endowed with the gift of prophecy and visions
like his master, when he caught sight of you from the hill as you went
into the chapel and closed the door behind you, used to race down in
his little clogs, stepping as lightly as mist slipping over the grass, and,
holding his breath, silently approach the small glass window half
covered in whitewash and oil from the icon lamps as a result of the
excessive piety of devout women, and watch your prayers and prostrations without being seen, and listen to your whispers and sighs
without being heard. How many years have passed since then!

✻　　✻
✻

The lagoon was separated from the sea by a broad strip of sandy soil
full of pumice, one part of which was the town's boatyard and the
other Parrisis's melon-patch. At its westernmost corner, from where
the harbour began to stretch out, this strip narrowed to Argyris

Barbapanayotis's windmill, which, with its ceaselessly turning triangular sails, seemed to be challenging the boats anchored in the harbour, saying, 'There, I'm sailing on land!' How many times were you obliged to remove your shoes and socks and wade in, rolling your trousers up to the knee and obstinately insisting on crossing the stream when the frequent floods made the marshes one with the sea! Why didn't you abandon your walk and return to the town? Because you seemed to enjoy seeing something in this landscape, even though she who had given it life had long since disappeared. Then again, you preferred to take the roundabout northern route on the far side of the lagoon, crossing the whole of Kivouli with its fields and vineyards. There you walked on lush grass, not always certain that there was firm ground underneath, and you would sink into the marsh up to your ankles, but you thought yourself fortunate because you always imagined you were running to pick narcissi for her. And when, your shoes muddy and your socks soaked through, you finally reached *Barba*-Konstandis Mitzelos's white cottage and you greeted him from afar as he hoed his broad beans with a 'Good evening, *Barba*-Konstandis!', and he replied in his affable manner, 'Well, hello, my boy!', you loved to imagine yourself as *Barba*-Konstandis, and Polymnia as Aunt Siniora, forty years younger, and you imagined how happy you would be if it were possible to live together with your beloved in that white cottage (whose rather excessive whiteness was due to Aunt Siniora's incessant whitewashing), and how delightfully romantic it would be if you spent your days with your beloved in the midst of that fragrant and luxuriant garden, with its pomegranates, its rose-bushes, its almond-trees and lilacs, with all those exquisite trees and flowers (which, however, were due to *Barba*-Konstandis's assiduous labours), at the edge of the beautiful lagoon, where there was one sky above and another seemingly below, and poplars and cypresses extended their tall tips upwards, while other poplars and cypresses hung topsy-turvy. And when myriads of stars adorned the night, shining in the firmament, as many myriads twinkled down in the depths. Reeds shaken by the wind reared their fragile stems two fathoms above the surface, and mosses and chaste-trees and asphodels lived on the mercy of the lagoon and on the slime of the marsh, inclining their low heads towards the water as if bowing in gratitude. Opposite rose the grassy banks of the harbour, presenting their green slopes to the sun like the full breasts of a maiden offering life and vigour to the whole of creation. Trees adorned the undulating sandy margins of the shore, while other trees planted in the sea — the masts with their sails — embellished the waters of the harbour.

In the distance, towards the north, appeared the two rows of hills that rose on either side of the plain which, though extensive, could be easily taken in at one glance. The eastern hills were high, closer to the spectator, crowned by the hut of *Barba*-Yorgos Kopsidakis, God rest his soul, where more than once you celebrated May Day as a child, with milk, and lamb on the spit, and garlands of flowers, when your maternal grandfather, *Barba*-Alexandros Karoniaris, God rest his soul, was alive, who loved to celebrate May Day in grand style, entertaining not only all his sons, his daughters and his grandchildren, but his godchildren and his *koumbari* and even the daughters of his share-croppers, with whom, at the early age of seven, you were not slow to fall in love, imagining yourself running after them to the little coves where they washed the sheets and hiding with them in caves invaded by the sea that foamed with the north wind's breath, and daydreaming of the delight within their elegant white bodices, their cherry-red silk jabots, their well-turned, blue-veined forearms in their long embroidered sleeves. Precocious dreams of impetuous youth, like an almond-tree blossoming in January!

The other range of hills, to the west, was Platana, more distant from the spectator, lying supine but sloping slightly upwards towards the peaks at whose foot stood the fine tower of Metochi, with the beautiful chapel of St John the Theologian. You could see all this, like the perfect painting of a true master, beyond the lagoon, from *Barba*-Konstandis Mitzelos's little white house or from the boatyard which was visible on this side of the lagoon.

✻   ✻
✻

On the whole of the long, broad beach that stretched between the lagoon and the harbour there was as much sawdust as there was sand, no pebble without a chip of wood lying next to it. How many forests had been transformed here from time immemorial into tall-masted vessels, with thousands of fathoms of ropes and sails, and how many of those vessels must now be sleeping eternally in the depths of the Mediterranean or the Black Sea! That day two such skeletons could be seen lying on their sides in the shallows opposite the boatyard, with blackened, worm-eaten timbers and rusted nails, while their gaping ribs, stripped of their planking, through which the sea ebbed and flowed freely, seemed to be smiling sorrowfully, with lipless teeth, out of pity at the spectacle of such frenzied human industry and inventiveness. How many human hands that had once worked feverishly here now lay withered in the depths of the earth, how many heads containing enough brains, in the words of an old sailor, 'to tar a whole ship', had nourished the insatiable monsters of the deep! Yet that same old seaman, known for his bitter sarcasm, had recently lost his own boat and his two sons in a storm near Cape Malea, and now, in his old age, with the assistance of his third son but bereft of his chief helpers, was struggling to build a larger one. Thus are human affairs dominated by habit and material necessity! Perhaps for him this new boat was a source, if not of satisfaction, at least of consolation for his old age. In this way the old sea-dog would continue to live his last days until the hour came when the sea, that greatest of monsters, which he had persistently challenged, would arise and spurn him from her bosom to the skies, as Byron puts it, sending him shivering and howling 'to his Gods', and dashing him again to earth: 'There let him lay'![1]

They went on incessantly building boats, and their skill came closer to perfection, and trade increased. Anyone who wanted to build a boat would have found an eager adviser in the late Cap-

---

[1] Byron, *Childe Harold's Pilgrimage*, Canto IV, stanza CLXXX, quoted in English in the text.

tain Dimitris Kassandrianos, with his long pipe with its amber mouthpiece, who had seen and heard many things in his life. He spent his old age watching the boat-building, coming every evening with his pipe, his long tobacco-pouch hanging from his thick woollen breeches, to take pride in the hopes and labours of others and to console himself for having been persuaded to relinquish the command of his boat to his sons, who maintained that he was too old. 'When you cross yourselves before cutting the timber, boys, look carefully to see how many days old the moon is. And when you begin to build, with God's help, check to see where the star is. Take care not to build a boat or launch it at the solstice.'* In his lisping voice he would give valuable instructions to the captain, and even to the master builder, concerning all matters that contributed to the successful construction as well as to the launching and sailing of the boat. If anyone refused to listen to him, so much the worse for them! Certain innovators among the ships' captains had tried ignoring him, and they had suffered cruelly.

✻   ✻   ✻

At that time, you remember, there were three large craft being built next to one another under the supervision of the same master shipbuilder. What a wonderful man he was! How was he able to cope with all three ships, running from one to another with his cubit measuring-stick in his hand, his plumb line, and his adze hanging from his neck with its handle across his chest? And what an army of men laboured under his command: the captain, his assistants, the sawyers, the hewers, the carpenters, and the caulkers! The gypsy blacksmiths were there too, having erected a makeshift hut behind each ship. With their furnace full of charcoal, their bellows, anvils, sledgehammers and other smaller hammers, they were forging great bolts. What a fearful din! The blows of the sledgehammer drowned out the rhythmical rasping of the saw, the knocking of the adze overpowered the thumping of the wooden mallet with which the caulker was banging in the oakum, while all the other sounds were dominated by the resounding bang of the huge sledgehammer with which the thick iron bolts and wooden pegs were being driven into the curved sides of the colossal hull. One tall, strapping man with a straight back, his breeches hitched up under his groin with a broad red sash, had ingeniously climbed way up on to the gunwale, and his shadow was immensely elongated in the last rays of the setting sun, the legs falling on the melon-plants growing on this side of the lagoon, the torso faintly undulating on the surface of the water, and the head outlined magnificently beyond the lagoon, at the foot of the mountain towards the east. This was the driller, whose task was to bore holes in the timbers. A huge basket lined with pitch, lying between two great unhewn timbers beneath the stern, was full of drill-bits of various sizes, some three dozen of them, of which the smallest was about two spans in length, while the biggest, bulky and heavy, was almost the same height as its owner. At that very moment this wonderful man was handling one of the largest drills and, leaning over the gunwale and hanging in mid-air like a tightrope-walker, was drilling a deep vertical hole in the side of the hull. How he did it was incomprehensible!

* * *

Meanwhile the sun had hidden behind the peak of the high rocky mountain, and the driller's shadow was expunged from the surface of the water and the sand of the beach. The builders, along with the many evening strollers who had come to offer visual support to the workers in their toil and occasionally to delay them with their untimely questions, stepped over the beams, ribs and unhewn timbers strewn all over the boatyard, and gathered in a confused swarm around the captain's hut, which was full of cleats and other bits of wood, baskets of tools, clothes and bed-covers, to drink *tsipouro* poured from a great demijohn, everyone using the same glass. The huge ship's dog, tied by a sturdy chain outside the hut behind the stern of the great ship, let out the occasional muffled threatening growl, as if he alone could distinguish the buzz of the drones from

the buzz of the workers, and seemed ready to pounce if only someone would untie him. But Captain Yorgakis, who looked quite
cultivated, with his long, hooked, fair mustachios, his sunburned
complexion and his short stature, restrained the dog's impetuous-
ness with curt shouts of, 'Back, Tsourmos! Down, Tsourmos!' Tsourmos reluctantly obeyed, expressing his frustration with prolonged
barking. The spirit-glass began circulating, and all the builders and
strollers proposed the customary toasts: 'Good luck! May her nails
be golden, Captain! Good sailing!' A certain curious fellow with
coarse, ugly features and a thick moustache planted like a thorny
burnet between his cheeks and reaching right up to his eyes, half-
sailor, half-workman and half-stevedore — this was Alexandros
Charavlos, the same man who, one night, while steering a large ship
during a long voyage in the Black Sea, when asked by the captain as
he paced up and down the deck between stern and bows, 'What's the
matter with you, Alexandros? Why are you sighing?', replied, 'Captain, I'm wondering how we're going to pay all those millions the
country owes!' — this Alexandros Charavlos, who was more than a
little simple and had been hired the previous day to help with the
building of the ship, when his turn came to drink to its good fortune,
by a clumsy slip of the tongue, uttered the last toast as 'Good failing, Captain!' The others chortled, but the fair-moustached captain
frowned, while Tsourmos reared up on his hind legs and let out a
fearsome bark. The captain's brother, Dimitris Tsimbidas, raised his
hand to seize Alexandros Charavlos by the scruff of his neck and
give him a few hefty cuffs. However, Captain Yorgakis prevented
him, despite the fact that he had to make an effort to restrain himself too, since no sailor, even those relatively educated, is free of
superstitious fears. How can one not be superstitious when he is
struggling with that greatest of monsters, wrestling with the unknown, never certain whether tomorrow he will be sailing or
sinking? The captain confined himself to shouting angrily:

'Hold your tongue, Charavlos, you idiot, or I'll grab the hawser
and...'

It was with great difficulty that he prevented his brother from thrashing him.

✳   ✳
✳

There, behind the bushy hedgerow, between the fields, the vineyards and the shore, where not infrequently the sea would trespass in an attempt to appropriate half a garden or an orchard of figs, apples and pears, while passers-by made the other half of the same garden or orchard into a road (and who could the happy owners complain to?), in the evening, around dusk, as the ship-builders, loaded with their baskets of tools, were returning to the little town, you would often hear a conversation between two or three carpenters counting the days until the first Sunday that would be followed by three or four feast days in succession (those of the Apostles Peter and Paul, the Twelve Apostles, Sts Cosmas and Damian, and the Deposition of the Holy Robe of the Virgin Mary)[1] and joyfully anticipating the pleasure with which they would shortly sail across, crammed into two heavy cargo boats, the work of their own hands, for a four-day holiday on the eastern island over yonder,[2] which kept all her children, wherever in the world they might be, tied to her with an invisible emotional thread of longing and nostalgia; you would often hear, I say, a conversation such as the following:

'There, we're getting close, Dadis.'

'We've still got a long way to go, Befanis.'

'What do you mean, Dadis? Monday's gone, Tuesday, Wednesday, that's one, Thursday, Friday, that's two, Saturday, God willing, we're there.'

And 'thus does a long road become short', but not according to Sophocles.[3]

But it wasn't always evening when you walked to that sandy beach with its shallow waters, and you didn't always see groups of

[1] These festivals fall on four successive days between 29th June and 2nd July.

[2] The island of Skopelos.

[3] Cf. Sophocles, Antigone, 232 ('thus does a short road become long').

men returning from the boatyard, nor groups of poor women, their thin shoulders laden with sacks of wood-chips. It was morning, and the winter had not passed, and the big ships had not yet been put on the stocks. In the boatyard just one lugger and two small dinghies were under construction. The only people working there were master shipbuilder Yorgos Vangelakis, God rest his soul, with his red cap, which was neither a fez nor a beret nor a brimmed hat, but partook of all of these, with his tar-lined canvas shoes and his smock many-coloured from all its patches, and Panayou's son Yannis, with his tall, upright cap, his long pleated breeches, his white vest and his big basket. The sun had only just risen, dissipating the white mist that rose from the sea towards the verdant shore, and the water rippled in the light breeze. That morning even the north wind seemed to find itself in a playful mood, softly caressing the sea. The nip in the air was not displeasing to the farmer riding his donkey out to his field, nor to the ploughman shouting orders to his oxen: 'Whoa, Honey! Gee-up, Blackeye!', and caressing with his gaze the large saucepan of beans, well cooked in abundant fragrant olive oil and with plenty of red pepper, which his trained eye had espied coming along behind the hedge, gradually approaching, well covered so that the food would not get cold, crowning the large basket on the shoulders of the dutiful housewife, almost sailing like a boat, since he could not see the hands that steadied it or the feet that walked beneath it. A few more moments would go by, and Honey and Blackeye, temporarily released from the yoke, would graze blissfully by the thick, gnarled roots of the olives, while the ploughman and his boy would sit down enviably under the blessed foliage as close as possible to the saucepan.

But you, friend, took no notice of these trivial things, but envied far more the little ten-year-old boys hitching their trousers up to their thighs, stuffing their shoes into their pockets and wading knee-deep into the water. You would suddenly see one of them bending down to catch a small octopus in his hand, bite it behind the head, struggle to detach the suckers from his wrist, run to the sand and give it a generous beating on the first large stone he found, a remnant of an orchard's dry-stone wall washed away by the waves, or of a now ruined jetty. Your loving mother not only forbade you to run barefoot like other children, but demanded that you wear socks as well. What bonds of pedagogical servitude! Fortunately you had your friend Christodoulis near you, who, while he was the same age as you, was more fortunate in that he was always barefoot and never wore socks. What an obliging child! All day he would run from beach to beach, gathering enough rock snails, limpets and other shellfish for two, enough crabs for three, and enough octopuses for four. One portion of these he used as bait when he went fishing with his rod from early evening till nightfall, while another he shared fraternally with you. That morning, shortly before you both arrived at Barbapanayotis's mill, which stood guard over the neutral territory between sea and land by the western mouth of the lagoon, your friend Christodoulis wasn't very far out, since at that point the sea bottom shelved down rather steeply, and as soon as he saw that Polymnia had approached you and started talking to you, he hastened to come out of the water to listen to what she was saying.

What a slenderly built figure was concealed by that dark dress woven from linen and silk, how harmoniously delineated was her face, with her downy white complexion and her red cheeks, her honey-gold neck and her slightly swelling bosom! How soft were those hands, how melodiously the sound of her divine voice vibrated in your ears! Her blond plaited hair, slightly unkempt as though she had hurried her toilet so as to get out and enjoy the delights of a walk along the beach in the sea-breeze, was blown by the north wind's breath, and her eyes, like feathered arrows with their long lashes, shot sweetly piercing glances into your heart. Do you remember what you felt at that moment, and how, scarcely fourteen years old, you had already fallen in love? Polymnia had spoken to you! Polymnia was calling you by name! What childish intoxication, effortlessly induced by such a small draught! You felt as though you couldn't take any more. And yet there was a simple explanation. Her twelve-year-old brother knew your name and had told Polymnia who you were. As for her, it hadn't occurred to her that she would be shooting arrows into your heart if she addressed you, since all she wanted was to ask you a favour. Meanwhile Christodoulis was running up to you, hurriedly rolling down his trousers, as if to share the burden of your happiness.

Polymnia's melodious voice said:

'Do you know where the narcissus grows? Could you pick me some?'

You remained open-mouthed. But fortunately Christodoulis had arrived.

'Why certainly, Miss Polymnia, I know where they are. We'll go and pick some now.'

'I shall be much obliged to you,' said Polymnia to us both.

Christodoulis ran off, light-footed, one trouser-leg still rolled up to the knee and the other down to his ankle, without shoes, the skin of his feet tanned by the brine and puckered from long immersion in the water. You ran after him, sluggish and panting, but, by the time you reached the shore of the lagoon, stepping into the slippery mud, sliding amongst the glasswort and the bulrushes, Christodoulis had already picked a whole bunch of those early, intoxicatingly fragrant flowers that Polymnia had asked for, running between the clumps of grass that lovingly shaded those humble but beautiful blooms, so tender and delicate, with their white petals and their yellow trumpets, which seemed to regret that they grew on the earth and were so lowly. Christodoulis picked them pitilessly, in twos and threes, mixed with grass, and bundled them in the crook of his arm as he dashed from reed-bed to reed-bed, looking at the rushes and sighing because he had not fished as many perch and red mullet as there were rushes, and had not used the latter to string the former in bunches.

By the time you had managed to find a few narcissi to pick, Christodoulis had already gathered a whole sheaf and was running back towards the windmill where Polymnia stood waiting with her brother. You arrived at the same time, bringing her a little bunch, small enough to be held between forefinger and thumb, and her 'thank you' to you was, as expected, more lukewarm than her 'thank you' to your friend. But you were nonetheless gratified, satisfied with little, overcome by a complacent torpor, that resembled the tender flower that Polymnia had sought from you but had received from your friend.

*　　*　　*

From then on Christodoulis began to decrease, then discontinued, the share he had formerly given you of his shellfish, crabs and gobies, and you soon found out that he was giving them to Polymnia's brother Nikos. In vain did you accompany him, as always, walking along the road as he waded in up to his thighs, and occasionally shouting to him:

'Hey, Christodoulis! Haven't you caught an octopus yet?'

He would put the crabs and octopuses in the bulge of his wet shirt, knowing the knack of killing them with bites and amputations, and showed you only the limpets, saying that he would go fishing in the afternoon with his rod. And when in the evening you looked out for him on the quayside near the market and you actually saw a goby wriggling on the end of his hook, he would pretend that he was going to use it for bait to catch some bigger fish. That's how friends are lost!

Many mornings slipped by after that morning in late February. The whole of March went by, then Easter came, and April, and Polymnia never went out for a walk again along the seashore to the boatyard. In vain did you run to the beach regularly every morning and evening. You later learned that Polymnia had fallen ill at the beginning of spring, and around May, on the advice of the doctors, she had gone on a journey for a change of air with her aunt, who received a state pension as the widow of a commander in the Royal Hellenic Navy. Three large ships had been on the stocks since early March, and you had never ceased to run to the boatyard every day, often stopping for hours near the windmill, sitting on the masts that had once belonged to a schooner but were now lying on the ground, recalling that on this very spot Polymnia had stood some months before, when she had asked you to gather narcissi for her; but Polymnia was far away.

It was not until about the middle of August that the third and largest of the boats being built was completed, and you went to the boatyard with a large crowd to see the launch of the great ship. It was an impressive spectacle, as they say nowadays. The town was almost completely deserted, and the strip of land between the lagoon and the harbour was thronged with people. Beyond the ship the sun was already high, and the rough, hardened sailors and workmen were completing the tarring of the keel, driving the last nails into the slipway or digging underneath the base of the stocks so that they would be ready to fall away. On the near side of the ship, where the shade was gradually diminishing, in addition to the men helping with the launch stood the spectators, including quite a number of women who had come to enjoy themselves. How your pulse quickened when, among them, you recognized, under a red parasol, the beautiful figure of Polymnia! She had returned from her journey without your knowing. Christodoulis, who had gone out to the steamship in a dinghy, had seen her, but hadn't told you. Yet, in the depths of your being, you felt a secret and inexpressible sense of happiness when you saw her again!

In the meantime the tarring had been completed, the struts had all been nailed in place, and the slipway, with its great unhewn timbers well greased, had already been laid down. The master shipbuilder made the customary sign of the cross on the rudder three times with the sledgehammer, and dealt the first blow to get the huge ship moving. The supports all fell away in a trice. The captain's wife, a beautiful, dark-haired, slightly-built woman who, as she was still young, had put on her full bridal costume for the occasion, with her ethereal white silk kerchief, her bonnet with its gold-embroidered pot of flowers and sprays, her velvet dress with its sleeves, woven with gold thread, slightly rolled up, her gold-embroidered crimson silk jabot, her belt with its silver gilded studs, her silk skirt with its gold hem three spans wide, holding a silver-plated tray in her left hand, walked all round the ship, showering sugared almonds and rice on the bow, the stern, the keel and the sides of the vessel with her right hand. The sailors, the builders and many of the spectators, like grapes on a vine or lead weights on a drag-net, grasped the hoist and began to pull the thick cable, all of them nodding towards the sea and repeating in rhythm the command, 'Heave away! Heave ho!' However, either because the ground on which the ship had been built did not slope down enough, or because of some imperfection in the hauling mechanism, the ship groaned and groaned, but did not budge. A few moments passed, and the haulers redoubled their efforts. The huge bulk moved a little, about two spans, but the hoist broke under the strain, the cable and the two pulleys hung useless near the stern, those of the men who were on the west side of the ship fell on the sand towards the sea, while the others remained holding the cable on the lagoon side. There was much groaning and guffawing from those who had fallen, some of whom had suffered slight bruises on their right arms or ribs, and the sunburnt captain, bathed in sweat and generally in a pitiful state, was horribly upset, while Captain Dimitris Kassandrianos, who, with his pipe with its amber mouthpiece, his coarse woollen breeches, and his knee-high boots which he liked to wear all the year round, had come to preside at the launch and since early morning had not stopped giving orders and advice, on seeing the accident, sighed and shouted in his lisping way:

'Pfui! It's nothing but a nest of worms and ants!'

In the meantime the hoist had been spliced, and a new effort was made. But a few moments later the hoist broke in a different place. A new one was brought, while the captain, too preoccupied to mop the sweat from his brow, could not but remember the unintentional curse, 'Good failing!' If he had seen Alexandros Charavlos in front of him this time, he would certainly have given him a good flailing. Captain Dimitris, with his pipe, standing next to the gypsy's hut below the stern, repeated:

'Pfui! It's nothing but a nest of worms and ants!'

The two priests — former sailors — who had thrown their stoles over their right shoulders and leapt lightly on to the deck and performed the blessing, came over to the gunwale to see what was happening, because, the makeshift ladder having by now collapsed, they were about to be left on board the ship, unable either to disembark before it slipped into the sea or to get down into the dinghy with their holy icons. Meanwhile a crowd of small fry — children of eight and nine — ran up and down the deck in an attempt to launch the ship.

Finally, after many efforts and by the application of many remedial measures, the great ship, like a proud bride, gradually slipped into the sea. There were great whoops of joy from women repeatedly crossing themselves, children leaping about, and men running behind the stern as though trying to intimidate the ship and force it to slide into the water. Tsourmos, the big ship's dog, who was also running about as much as the extreme tension of his chain would allow, barked frenziedly to send off the ship on which within the day he would embark. While everyone else was running towards the sea behind the ship as it slid down the slipway, one man suddenly turned round, holding his sledgehammer, and ran in the other direction, away from the sea, as if to hide in the captain's hut, which had been used as a storehouse and sleeping-quarters by the night-watchman. The man who was running was the master shipbuilder, and he was running for no other reason than to avoid sharing the captain's dunking, which some people were seeking, according to custom, to extend to him too. For at that moment a great cry arose above the multifarious other noises:

'Into the sea with the captain!'

The cry came from many mouths at the same time. Captain Yorgakis, giving in to the crowd's demands, threw off his light shoes and ran on tiptoe along the slipway behind the stern, and the moment the stern at last slid free of the slipway and the ship, proudly flying the blue-and-white Greek flag from a pole topped by a red cross, received its first baptism, he threw himself, fully clothed, headlong into the sea, first sinking and then immediately re-emerging at the surface, and after swimming around the ship two or three times, returned to the shallow water, stood on the sandy bottom, came out on to dry land and to the accompaniment of whoops of excitement from the crowd ran to the hut, where in a trice he changed out of his wet coarse woollens into his Sunday best.

You were present at all this, my friend, yet you saw scarcely anything of it. Your heart, your fancy, your eyes were riveted on the girl who wore a linen and silk summer dress and was shaded by a red parasol. It was only the shouts of the crowd when the ship slipped into the sea and the captain had plunged into the water after it that aroused you from your deep meditations. But once you had awoken you saw something else, alas, which many of the bystanders did not notice. Running excitedly behind the captain with a shriek of delight and triumph, a young lad of just fifteen years old threw himself into the sea. It was Christodoulis, your childhood friend. What could have driven him to do this? Did he hope that by offering up this willing sacrifice to parsimonious Fate he would one day be fortunate enough to become a captain himself? Or was it simply that he wanted Polymnia to see him? It was neither of these things. Christodoulis had arrived rather late at the boatyard, when the plank serving as a gangway had been removed and the supports had been dug away. He felt an indomitable desire to climb on to the ship. But what could he do? Two or three times he tried to grab hold of one or other of the supports, even though they stood so precariously, and climb boldly up to the gunwale of the ship. Each time either the master shipbuilder or one of the carpenters saw him and vigorously prevented him. Then what could he do? Since he had not been lucky enough to board the ship in time, he consoled himself by plunging into the sea and following in its wake. Nevertheless, you felt a bitter pang of jealousy. You were cut to the quick by this childish exploit. Poor Christodoulis! What had come over him? He didn't even come out on to the beach to change; besides, he wouldn't have found any clothes there. Instead, he swam behind the ship as it floated further and further away, his shirt and trousers billowing above the surface of the sea like a dinghy's sails; then, getting into a small boat, he signalled to the boys triumphantly shouting on board the ship to throw some clothes down to him. A small cabin-boy took pity on him and threw him a shirt and trousers of his own, and Christodoulis, having changed, came close to the side of the tall, unballasted ship, grabbed hold of a rope and hauled himself triumphantly on to the deck.

The crowd at the boatyard was still congregating round the captain's hut, where his magnificently adorned wife was eagerly and graciously handing round sweets and drinks. But you had a bitter taste on your palate, as though your bile had risen into your mouth. Polymnia, whom you had seen smiling at your young friend's escapade and whispering, 'What a strange boy that Christodoulis is!', returned to town, and you followed her at a distance.

*   *
*

This wasn't the only time that Christodoulis threw himself into the water fully clothed in front of Polymnia or for her sake. A few days later, one Sunday at the end of August, Parrisis, the melon-farmer, sunburnt, cheerful and light-hearted, the long tassel of his fez hanging down to his shoulder, and Loukas, the lagoon's tenant fisherman, tall, long-legged, his flaxen moustache projecting beyond his ears and his complexion the colour of boiled lobster, had sat down for a drink, as they very frequently did, at the edge of the lagoon under a cool trellis outside their hut. The sun was sinking, and for an hour, each taking his turn, they had already exchanged many fraternal kisses with the wine-flask, which held four okas and had recently been brought from town full of *moschato*. Their faithful friend Argyris, the joint-owner of the windmill, had just visited them and entertained them with his pranks, giving Loukas a cigarette containing gunpowder, which made a slight explosion that singed his reddish moustache when he lit it, after which he said quite calmly,

'*Zarar yok!*'[1] Argyris had given Parrisis a broken set of bagpipes, urging him to play a tune, but, much as he exerted himself with his puffing, the instrument refused to let out a sound. Finally Argyris said, 'You're no good for anything, the pair of you, it's a crying shame!' So saying, he walked off with feigned displeasure. The two friends remained there alone and continued to drain the flask slowly and methodically. They had grilled half a dozen grey mullet and no small number of crabs on the charcoal, and the *moschato* was going down a treat. They reminisced, telling each other of their sufferings, of which there was no end. Indeed Parrisis, rising above the level of the prosaic, was moved to sing fanciful songs, such as:

> *They try to prune me, but I won't be pruned...*

Each of them kept saying to the other, 'D'you remember that, chum? D'you remember that?' When one is with one's best friend in a lovely spot in the countryside, one forgets everything with the help of a flask of *moschato*, and the two men little suspected that someone could see them — besides, they couldn't have cared less. But half a mile away, behind the reeds on the far bank, your childhood friend Christodoulis had been lurking unobserved for two hours. What was he after? In all probability the cunning lad was biding his time until Parrisis and Loukas left the shore for a moment, so that he could plunge into the lagoon and steal an eel or some grey mullet and a few crabs. But he had waited in vain, and, having espied the wine-flask and hoping that the two friends would be too merry to notice, he had already decided to carry out the escapade in front of their eyes. But at that moment an unexpected incident attracted his attention.

The sun was setting when a woman accompanied by a boy approached the hut, outside which the two topers were sitting. She was wearing a white dress and holding a red parasol, and Christodoulis, despite the distance, recognized her immediately. It was

[1] Turkish, meaning 'no harm done'.

Polymnia with her brother Nikos. The two men stood up immediately, and Christodoulis, lurking in the reeds, understood from their gestures and their bows that they were welcoming her courteously and seeing to her every bidding. A few moments passed, and he saw Polymnia jump into a small felucca, a craft with a flat bottom and no keel, which was moored at the edge of the lagoon not far from the hut and which Loukas used for catching eels and grey mullet in the lagoon. Behind the young woman, her little brother, untying the mooring-rope, stepped into the craft and, grasping the pole, began to thrust it into the bottom of the shallow lagoon. Christodoulis concluded rightly that Polymnia must have conceived a fancy to go punting on the lake for once in her life, and Loukas, being in a good mood, had given her permission.

The small craft moved away towards the middle of the lagoon, while the two men sat down again and occupied themselves with the task of emptying the flask. Christodoulis, hidden in the reeds, watched in admiration, as you would have done, the charming scene of the young woman and her brother, who continued to thrust the pole into the bottom with all his might. Polymnia seemed radiant with joy. She was delighted and captivated by this excursion, like a three-year-old girl with her toys, while her brother seemed to be as happy as those seven-year-old boys who, leaving school with their satchels slung over their shoulders, find inexpressible delight in running to the beach and the marshes to sail neat little toy boats made by the more skilful among them. Christodoulis forgot the eels, the crabs and the grey mullet that he was planning to steal, entranced at the sight of the two young people gliding across the lagoon. But he could not fail to notice Nikos's ineptitude at pushing the pole in smoothly and regularly, and, lurking in the reeds, your childhood friend sighed and said, 'Oh, if only it was me!'

*　　*　　*

Suddenly, while Nikos was punting in his clumsy way, the craft got caught in a clump of tall waterweed that almost reached the surface. He tried and tried to push with his pole, but the more he tried, the more the punt became entangled; now the pole didn't reach the bottom, and finally it too got caught in the luxuriant black weeds; Nikos struggled in vain to extricate it, but the more he pulled, the more the pole slipped out of his hands, until it finally fell from his weak fingers, half of it caught under the surface, the other half floating above. Polymnia, getting up gingerly, leant over the side where Nikos was standing to see where the pole had gone, and the punt lurched over, almost capsizing. Realizing the danger and not wishing to take an unintentional bath amongst the water-weed, Polymnia sat down again quickly near the stern and, raising herself slightly, waved her white handkerchief towards the two topers at the little hut, shouting:

'Hey, Uncle Loukas!'

But by the time Loukas had noticed and decided to come to their aid (which would have been difficult, since the bottom of the lagoon was muddy, and anyone who waded into the water would sink knee-deep into the slime, while the shallowness of the water would not have permitted a large man like himself to swim), it would have got dark without anything being achieved. Fortunately, however, Christodoulis, your childhood friend, lurking in the reeds, was far nearer the punt. Without a moment's hesitation and dressed in his shirt and trousers, which was all he ever wore, he unexpectedly and amazingly leapt out of the reeds like the last descendant of an ancient lake-dwelling water deity, unknown and of uncertain birth, forgotten for nineteen centuries, inhabiting the reeds and escaping the attention of the Christian world, and, throwing himself into the lagoon, began swimming. With ten strokes, his belly sometimes scraping the slimy bottom, he reached the place where the punt had got caught, sprang up to the right side of the boat and, with a strength incommensurate with his age, raised it slightly, freeing it from the tall weeds. Then he disentangled the pole and said to Nikos:

'Look, this is how you punt!'

So saying, he demonstrated how it should be done, then threw the pole to Nikos. Taking the punt by the stern, he pushed it away from the waterweed and the shallows, while Polymnia watched him with a smile and, in involuntary admiration, whispered:

'What a strange boy!'

He swam beside them towards the hut, where the two topers were standing in amazement, wondering what was happening. Loukas, mistaking the lagoon for the sea, said:

'A dolphin must have come up to the boat.'

'As long as it's not a shark that'll eat all your mullet, friend,' said Parrisis.

✻   ✻
✻

Christodoulis returned to his reeds, where *Barba*-Konstandis Mitzelos, of eternal memory, had witnessed the incident from his white cottage nearby; calling the young lad, who had taken his clothes off and was trying to dry them on a rock that was still burning from the heat of the sun that had just set, he gave him some clothes to put on. And *Barba*-Yorgos Kopsidakis, God rest his soul, who happened to be nearby with his few ewes, gave him a blessing and assured him he would receive 'a great reward',[1] not suspecting that Christodoulis was the illicit fruit of the loins of a forgotten deity. And Loukas, learning about this little incident from Polymnia and holding up the flask containing a few drops of *moschato*, shouted across to the opposite bank:

'Your health, Christodoulis!'

✻   ✻
✻

Why should one lose the affection of one's friends? It's not as if Polymnia was destined for you or for him. Silly child! She was older than either of you. But how is one to grow to manhood without falling in love and being disappointed at least ten times?

---

[1] See Matthew 5 : 12 and Luke 6 : 23.

Is Polymnia dead or married now? I don't know, and neither perhaps do you. And Christodoulis? He became a renowned sailor, but for years now you haven't heard anything about him. Perhaps he went to America, like so many others. And you? Like me, you waste your time philosophizing, and do nothing.*

[1892]

Translated by Peter Mackridge

FEY FOLK

THAT EVENING, half an hour before the sun went down behind the mountain, Agallos Manouil Agallou had set out to go all the way back to the Arvanitis's, to Manolis's Sorb... no, to Aradias, in the Kechrea ravine. The watermill was not so very near... no, nor was it so very far, being less than two hours on foot. But he had dawdled on the way, who knows for what reason. Perhaps he'd been reflecting on his happy, delightful and enviable position of some years before, when he was a handsome and very eligible young man, with endearing eyes and a large red fez, with a long tassle, that he wore cocked to one side. And he had been comparing this with his present state: a wife who had lost all her freshness and comeliness and who sat and waited for you at the watermill with two children, one of which told fairytales to the other. Naturally, this present situation more than pleased him, but the former seemed exceedingly more desirable and he would willingly have agreed to begin all over again. Just imagine, eight years of being betrothed, and to two girls, first to the one then to the other, sometimes to both at the same time. If ever in the whole world there was an eligible young man who lived well, it was him. And old 'ma Agallaina, God rest her saintly bones wherever they may be, was more than content. Come Christmas time, there was the special Christmas loaf from the one girl and another loaf from the other. Fried honey dumplings from the first, turnovers from the second. Then eight days later, on New Year's Day, St Basil's cake from the one and St Basil's cake from the other.* Come Easter again, syrup cake from the one, *baklava* the other. Come the feast day of St Agathonikos, *baklava* from Smaragdo, *baklava* from Afendra. And still more syrup cake from Bonoraina, wonderful cook she was, and even more *baklava*. And each time the syrup cake would be bigger in size and the *baklava* twice as thick. But the first girl was unable to get the better of the second. The poor girl was an orphan, all alone in the world: there was no one to look out for her, no one to speak well of her to the in-laws. The other had a more-than-large family, and her brothers, with their lugger, brought her fancy gifts of all kinds. And they put up her dowry and an extra dowry to boot. This is why it was she who won out in the end.

*   *   *

As soon as it grew dark, Afendra lit the lamp, closed her door and, after washing some fresh greens, placed them in a small copper pot, poured water inside, threw some dry wood on the fire and lifted the pot on to the trivet; then she began to blow on the fire. Her two children, seated on the rush matting, were playing: Lenio with her doll, Manolis with his toy boat. The former, a five-year-old, was trying to tell a fairytale to the latter, a four-year-old, who was listening and gaping. She always began with verses:

> *Man's calf for a mother,*
> *A bush for a midwife,*
> *an eagle took me . . .*

This was about all she knew. But this was enough for Manolis.
   Lenio begged her mother to say the rest:
   'How does it go, mummy?'
   And Afendra continued:

> *An eagle took me,*
> *Lifted me atop a tree.*

'Afterwards, afterwards?' asked Lenio.
   'Aterward?' repeated Manolis.
   And, in a few words, Afendra related how the maiden born out of a man's calf and with a bush for midwife was loved by a king

and then, through the wiles of her mother-in-law, was left by him and condemned to a life tending geese.

And bending over, Afendra blew on the fire, stopping only to say to her children:

'Your father's on his way... he'll be here any time now. Be good children... and he'll have a treat for you... Roasted chickpeas and almonds.'

'Chipeas and amons!' repeated Manolis, his mouth open wide.

The time passed, however, and Agallos was nowhere to be seen. Afendra wasn't concerned, she knew that her husband was a 'slow-coach'. He was like a bride who takes an age to make herself beautiful and, like a bride, walked with a proud air. Ah... a bride! She too had once been a bride ...she remembered it still. How could she forget? For eight long years, her mother-in-law had had her dancing to her every tune, and not only her, but the whole of her family as well. Agallos had been a most eligible young man. Eight years, sixteen trays of *baklava*, twenty-four tins of syrup cakes, over forty chickens and pies. And who's to begrudge all that? Yet, so much stubbornness and sulking. Sometimes, he'd break off with the one girl, sometimes with the other. At first, he'd exchanged engagement rings with the other girl. Then they'd fallen out and he'd 'pledged his troth' to her. Afterwards, he'd made up again with the other and gone back on his promise to her. Later, he returned the ring to Smaragdo and got back together again with Afendra. And he was a comely young man, long life to him, and they both loved him. Then again, he was indeed most comely, thought Afendra, fair-skinned, blue-eyed and ruddy-faced. He was even more comely than Afendra herself, who was scrawny, pale and thin. Finally, after he'd taken one last stroll in the direction of Smaragdo's and no one had set eyes on him for a week, the two brothers, who'd arrived with their lugger on the Saturday, got round him, took out the licence and married him to Afendra that Sunday evening.

Her kin only just had time to dress the bride. Such finery, such a rich dowry. She herself had embroidered the sun and moon on the sleeves of her scarlet silk chemise. And on her bonnet she had embroidered a large pot with flowers and branches, while on her bodice she had embroidered a variety of sprays. She also had a lovely petticoat made from precious Russian brocade. And the gold-embroidered flounce of her skirt was three inches wide.

Her mother-in-law had only just been persuaded at the last minute to give her blessing, having hitherto been adamant, saying that she felt sorry for the other girl, that she pitied her, orphan that she was. Eventually, she donned her best attire and came, wearing her widow's black scarf, keeping the 'fancy' coloured Constantinopolitan scarf to wear only when she would kiss the wedding wreaths.* Her sister-in-law had come too and stood there beside the *templa*, a banked-up pile of bed-furnishings, a living bank herself, tall, broad, unmoving, adorned like a bride. For it doesn't do for the *templa* to be missing from the room where a marriage ceremony is being performed. Mattresses and blankets and rugs carefully folded, pillows and sheets piled orderly and neatly against the wall in one corner of the room, covered by a silk sheet and crowned with two silk-covered bolsters: such is the *templa*.*

Once the best man had arrived with the fiddlers, then the guests came, followed by the priests, and the ceremony began. The rings were exchanged, then the wedding wreaths, the wonderful blessings were read out and the wedding hymn 'Rejoice Isaiah' sung. In keeping with the custom, the newlyweds walked three times in a circle and were showered with rice and sugared almonds. Finally, reaching out his hard and bony hand, Father Nikolas took hold of an eight-year-old boy who had both his father and mother, shoved him between the newlyweds and, separating their joined hands with the boy's head, loudly wished them 'may all your children be male'.

Next, taking up the large tray, the groom himself offered sweetmeats to the priests, the best man and the guests, while the bride, standing erect between the *templa* and her sister-in-law, looked on in pride, and it required the bridesmaids, all decked out and standing in attendance, to gently rock her head from behind to make her nod in response to the plethora of wishes from the guests: 'Long life to you both! May you be blessed with sons!', while her lips barely moved to say thank you and her voice was inaudible.

In the meantime, *Barba*-Ghioulis, the cook hired for all the weddings, had lit two large fires in the front yard of the house. On one he placed a huge cauldron used for distilling *raki*, into which he cut up an eight-month-old lamb and began browning it to make the Persian pilaf customarily served at weddings, while over the other fire, once the charcoal was ready, he set two spits side by side with two more slaughtered lambs.

Leaning over the two fires, he turned the spit with his one hand and in the other he held the huge ladle with which he stirred and browned the meat and onions. Ol' Sigourantsas, a self-invited assistant, also came to turn the other spit. As soon as the meat began to brown, as soon as the pot roast began to emit a mouth-watering aroma, Ghioulis, taking out the knife from his wide, yellow sash, began cutting generous morsels from the two roasts and, using the ladle, scooped out some big pieces from the pot roast. He gulped down three pieces, as an appetizer, so he said, and gave one to ol' Sigourantsas to satisfy his craving, and on seeing two or three 'hangers-on', whom the old-timers called 'recorders' and who apparently keep a precise register with the exact dates of births, marriages and saints' name-days, he began to drive them away with reproaches and threats, rather like a house-cat that, discovering all its tigerish nature and bristling its fur and snarling threateningly, suddenly scratches at the eyes of the good-natured raiding dog as it instinctively approaches.

On hearing Ghioulis's gruff voice from above as he was driving away the pestering cadgers, one of the guests (who had himself just previously turned them out of the house, after having treated them several times to *baklava* together with mastic and rum), stuck his head out of the window and saw Ghioulis, who was a professed enemy of *baklava* and all confectionery, generously slicing into the loin of the roasting lamb with his broad knife. Whereupon, the guest not only did not reprove him, but feeling his own appetite whetted, secretly took hold of one of the many jugs filled with wine that the guests had brought, and quietly coming down into the yard offered it to Ghioulis, who gulped down a goodly measure and gratefully cutting off a large morsel offered it to the discreet fellow. After two or three reciprocal courtesies of this kind, the jug was half-empty.

The two roasts were eventually cooked and the pilaf too. Then, Ghioulis removed the huge cauldron from the fire and also put the two spits to one side. And after he'd stirred and stirred the rice and swallowed two or three spoonfuls to try it, he began emptying the rice into deep serving dishes, and carving the two roasts into large pieces, continuing as he did so to taste it all, not once but twice. But it was time to take the brimming dishes up into the house and the guests arranged themselves in long lines along the length and breadth of the large room and ate and made merry in honour of the newlyweds.

Then the various jugs and bottles began to go round in different directions through the ranks of the revellers. *Barba*-Konstandis Xesouros, the bride's uncle, holding in his left hand a large ten-litre demijohn which he rested on his knee and in his right a small fifty-dram glass, poured the wine for the guests, courteously pouring one glass for the first person on his right, then modestly drinking one himself, then pouring one for the person on his left, and having one himself so as to drink the health of both, or offering a glass to the second person on his right, and downing one himself to return the good wishes, and so on and so forth. There was great merriment and the floor almost gave way beneath the dancing. The festivities lasted a whole week. It was a wedding, said Afendra, that would long be remembered in the village.

✻   ✻
✻

It had been dark for over an hour, and the flickering lamp lit the sparse room separated off inside the mill, and the fire glowed comfortingly in the corner, and the fresh wild cabbage, which Afendra had cut with her own hand, gathering it with not a little toil from the ravine's snow-covered slopes, from among the rocks and bushes surrounding the ramshackle watermill beside the old plane-trees, had now boiled.

But Agallos hadn't arrived and Lenio was still reciting the fairy-tale to her brother. She'd already repeated the first verses of the song at least ten times, verses summarizing the words of the beautiful girl's bizarre adventure in the fairytale, and still she hadn't learned them. She'd now come to the final verses.

> *An old woman tricked me,*
> *in the king's arms.*

And she called for help to her mother, who completed the song as follows:

> *in the king's arms;*
> *the king with his mother,*
> *while I tend the geese.*

And before learning them herself, Lenio took it upon her to teach the verses to Manolis who, spluttering, repeated them:

> *An ol' woman ticked me*
> *in the kling's arms.*

Suddenly, a loud banging was heard. Someone was outside knocking on the door, which Afendra had bolted from the inside as she was accustomed to doing when she was alone at the watermill with her children. In delight, Afendra leapt up, took the lamp, descended the four wooden steps which led down from the room to the mill floor, and went to open the main door. The children ran behind her, jumping up and down.

Before she had even opened the door, Afendra heard a woman's enquiring voice outside:

'What have you locked yourselves in for? My, my, it's not night yet.'

It wasn't Agallos. Afendra recognized the voice: it was her mother.

The old woman came in carrying a basket on her arm, with her black outer-skirt laid under the handle of the basket, wearing only her old faded dress, her woollen stockings with holes in the toes and heels and without shoes. The children immediately rushed towards the basket, and looked to see what was concealed inside beneath the folded outer-skirt, hoping that their granny had brought a treat for them from the village, but all they found was the aged woman's old clogs, which she always carried in the basket, preferring to walk barefoot so that her feet might be free but also in order to preserve her clogs.

Seeing her mother entering instead of her husband, Afendra supposed that the latter must have stayed behind to spend the night in the village, as he sometimes did, and so she wasn't too surprised. But when they got up to the room, ol' Synodia, seeing that Agallos wasn't there, asked:

'Where's your husband?'

Afendra stared at her in bewilderment.

'Didn't you leave him in the village?'

'No; he set off an hour before me.'

'To come here?'

'Yes, here.'

'And why hasn't he arrived then?'

'Why hasn't he arrived?'

'Where is he?'

'Where is he, indeed!'

The two women were overcome with great anxiety. Afendra wrung her hands in distress.

'Whatever can have befallen him?'

'Where can he be?'

'Why didn't you come together since you were going to come yourself?' asked Afendra, complainingly.

'I wasn't sure. I had things to do. I was in two minds about whether to come. You go on, I told him, before night falls, and I'll see. I'm used to walking in the ravines at night.'

And, indeed, they were all accustomed to trudging at night through the hills and dales. The two mothers-in-law, 'ma Synodia and Agallos's mother, may she rest in peace, had two watermills in the Kechrea ravine. The mill belonging to Agallos's family had been in disuse for some time and was deserted now. But the mill belonging to Synodia, widowed of late, was still in operation. And because he was used to having a mill, Agallos demanded the mill as part of his dowry, and 'ma Synodia was forced to let him have it. Both families, parents and forebears, had been partly brought up in the village, where they had cottages, and partly in the Kechrea ravine, where they had their mills. Women and men, sons and daughters, were not afraid of walking in the wood at night.

They were regarded as rather 'fey' folk, though they weren't afraid of spirits. It's true that they themselves often recounted how they'd seen sprites and the like, but they spoke with a courteous tongue about ghosts. They were neither harassed nor harmed by them. They were on good terms with them. Agallos often recounted how he'd seen fairies with his own eyes, how they'd spoken to him and how he'd made sure not to answer them, aware that they had the power to 'rob him of his speech'. Then again, when he was still a boy at his father's mill, his fairy godmother had appeared to him and had given him a florin with her own hand. He was certain of it, and still had the florin and showed it, so that no one might think he was a fraud or that he didn't believe it himself. On the contrary, he believed it with all his being.

Yet compared with 'ma Synodia, there was no one who knew more when it came to sprites and the like. From birth, she'd been on the friendliest of terms with the fairies. She knew the sprites, the blackamoors with their long pipes, the Lamias and the hobgoblins that would be coming then at Christmastide. The house spirit never does any harm. Sometimes it appears as a peaceful lamb, sometimes as a broody hen with its chickens. Fairies like to come out during daylight, when it's warm, and dance in the midday sun.

Don't let them trick you and make you open your mouth to

speak to them, because they'll take away your speech and you'll remain dumb. The blackamoor with his long pipe and the Turkish she-devil with her veil come out at night and sit around the springs in the ravines. The hobgoblins like to scare people, to hide inside chimneys and play nasty pranks. Apart from this, they're harmless. Only the vampire is evil, Lord preserve us. Yet it seeks only its own kin.*

*   *
*

'Ma Synodia was certain that her son-in-law couldn't have come to any harm from the hobgoblins, who would only just now be on their way there as it was Christmas Eve. Besides, Agallos was a Saturday-child, and it's well-known that whoever has this good fortune is not subject to the wiles of spirits.* Nevertheless, she couldn't understand why her son-in-law was so late, as he'd set off from the village an hour before her, and she'd come by the same path that they always took.

'The one we always come by, dear child,' she said to her daughter. 'Where could he have got to? What can have happened?'

'Could he have been drinking and fallen somewhere because of the snow?'

'He didn't seem at all drunk, dear child; and what snow are you talking of? The path's clear all the way... just a bit of trodden snow here and there... the only place where there's any snow to talk of is up on the heights. And when have you ever seen real snow? You should have seen it in my old granddad's days, when I was a little girl, as high as two men the snow was, three men... It blocked the door so we couldn't get out, right up to the lintel, two yards deep it was. While we were clearing the snow from in front of the door, and we were at it with spades and shovels for two hours, the roof that was creaking under the snow suddenly fell, crack! and flattened us.'

The two children, who had lost their jollity and were now almost in tears, involuntarily raised their eyes to the ceiling that the old woman had pointed to while recounting her story.

'Mummy! What's granny saying?' shouted Lenio, bursting into tears. 'Daddy's been flattened by the snow...and the roof is going to fall and flatten us too!'

'Hush, hush! Don't cry child,' Afendra cried out. 'Granny was just talking...don't be afraid...daddy will be along any moment and he's sure to have some sweets for you...'

'Hush, darling Lenio,' said the old woman. 'I've come on purpose to get you up early in the morning, to take you to St Elijah's, so you can receive communion, my dear little girl...'

'And me, and me!' cried Manolis.

'And you too, young lad...'

'Is there going to be a service tomorrow at St Elijah's?' Afendra asked, momentarily forgetting her worry.

'Yes there is...and at long last; it's about time you had a little incense over you... Get ready, young lady, get your things on quickly and let's be off... Your husband must have turned off along the way and gone to some cottage to find a friend...perhaps he went to buy some *mizithra* cheese or fresh cream for tomorrow... Don't worry... Wherever he is, he'll turn up.'

So, indeed, on learning that Father Konstandis Brikolas would come up the hill in the morning to celebrate the liturgy at the country church of the Prophet Elijah at the request of some shepherds and farmers, the old woman had decided to go to the Kechrea ravine rather than spend Christmas in the village and persuade her daughter and grandchildren to get up early in the morning and go up to the church, which was situated halfway along the path, on a level clearing close to the top of the hill, an hour from the village and an hour from Kechrea, in order to attend the service and take communion, so that she might make humans of them, as she said, as they'd been down in the ravine for months without going to church.

It was very rare for a priest to come and celebrate the liturgy in the tiny church at Kechrea, which was an old, ruined monastery, annexed as a dependency of the cenobitic Monastery of the Annunciation, and if a priest did come, Agallos, Afendra and their two children, dwelling as they did in the ravine and having the stumbling gait of river-crabs, would be unlikely to hear of it so as to go and attend the service. Since Agallos had sold his family house in the village and had been permanently living at the mill, he went to church only once a year, on 23rd August, on the ninth day after the Dormition of the Holy Virgin when the tiny church in Kechrea celebrated its feast day.*

*   *   *

Finally, ol' Synodia put her hand deep inside her dress and took it out full of almonds and hazelnuts, which she divided between the two children. She unfolded her new, black outer-skirt in which to their great surprise there was a small sweet-smelling Christmas cake wrapped in a cloth that she handed to her daughter, saying: 'Compliments of the season!'

Afendra emptied some of the greens on to a plate and sat the two children down to eat, certain that if they ate, they'd go straight to sleep and thus 'they wouldn't be a nuisance and they'd be able to wake up early the next morning'.

After eating the almonds that his granny had given him and then swallowing a couple of mouthfuls of greens, Manolis was the first to shut his eyes and fall asleep in his chair. His mother laid him down beside the hearth on a woollen rug and covered him with one end of the quilt. She made the sign of the cross three times over his head and left him to sleep.

Lenio didn't want to go to bed, saying that she wanted to wait up for her father, who had promised to bring her a pretty trinket from the village. But 'ma Synodia put her on her knee, covered her with her old dress to keep her warm and rocked her so much that she made her sleepy. Before long, she'd fallen asleep, and her mother, lifting her from the old woman's lap, cradling her in her arms and lulling her with 'coo...coo...', laid her next to Manolis.

Agallos had still not arrived and the two women, who were becoming increasingly anxious as the night progressed, now free of any annoyance from the children, discussed what should be done. The old woman said that if, God forbid, her son-in-law had fallen anywhere on the way, she would have seen him as she had come by the same path that they always took. Except, she was forced to admit, somewhat belatedly, when she'd reached Kechrea, she hadn't passed by the little monastery of the Holy Virgin.

'Why?' her daughter asked.

'I passed lower down, by the olive grove.'

A little north of the Holy Virgin's of Kechrea was one of Synodia's olive groves. Before arriving at the Holy Virgin's, she had turned off and gone to have a look at the olive grove, even though night had fallen. She was afraid that the snowfall of five days previously might have broken some of the olive trees' branches and she went there to see for herself, even though it was night. On arriving there, she saw that no damage had been done by the snow and, now content, she returned to the path lower down by way of the ravine, and arrived at the mill without passing by the Holy Virgin's of Kechrea.

'So, let's go there and take a look,' suggested Afendra hesitantly, who apparently with this in mind had hurried to put the children to bed.

'It wouldn't be wise for you to come,' said Synodia. The children will wake up and see that they're alone; they won't know what to do and they'll be scared out of their wits.'

'What can we do?' asked Afendra.

'I'll go and look on my own in case he's fallen anywhere... He might have gone inside the church to light a candle before the icons.'

'How can you go off all alone again?'

'I'll take the oil cruse to light the lamps in the Holy Virgin's... I've brought candles with me from the village... Don't worry!'

'Where can that man have got to! I'll go crazy. I'm almost at my wits' end!' cried Afendra, straining even more, as women do, through their spontaneous but uncontrolled emotions, her already strained nerves.

At that same moment, they heard the sound of a high-pitched voice in song:

Twee, twee, my peacock, twee, twee!
Come here, come here to my knee...

'Oh, it's Peacock!' said ol' Synodia. 'Hold on, we'll call him.'

And without waiting for her daughter to speak, ol' Synodia went down to the ground floor, opened the front door of the mill and began shouting loudly:

'Peacock! Hey, Peacock!'

*   *   *

The singer, astride his donkey, was passing by the mill, on the other side of the ravine, travelling along a path leading from the Aradias wood to the Kechrea seashore.

He wasn't visible among the trees in the darkness. But they could hear the donkey's clopping, the switch hitting against its rump and the cry of its rider, 'Gee up, get on there!', which he directed at the beast whenever he left off from his favourite song, which had given him his nick-name, the one 'ma Synodia had used to call out to him.

He was apprenticed to a landowner who lived in the town, and he tended his master's cattle below St Eleni's, where the latter had extensive pastures and a small country house. He must have been delayed in town for some reason, so it seemed, and he was returning late to the cottage, which was not a rare occurrence.

'Peacock! Hey, Peacock!'

'What is it, 'ma Synodia?' replied the young farmhand, recognizing her voice.

'Are you coming directly from the village, or not?'

'From the village, by way of St Yannakis's, Synodaris, Vromovryssi, Philippeika, the Mamou gully, Vigles, Stamelou, Petralono...'

'Have you passed by all those places, Peacock?'

'All of them and still more...'

'Have you seen my son-in-law, Agallos, anywhere?'

'Your son-in-law, Agallos?... Why, hasn't he arrived? He'll have bumped into his fairy godmother again... Perhaps she came to him in a dream and got him to go and find some *groschen*, and told him to go at night-time so no one would see him ... Or he'll have bumped into some spirits on the way and got into conversation with them and forgot the time...'

'Enough of the twaddle, because we're sick with worry, lad... Don't make light of it... Who knows what's happened to him... Do me a favour, dear Peacock, will you come up with me, as far as the Holy Virgin's, to see if we can find him anywhere?'

'Let's go, what have we to lose?' said the young lad, willingly.

And turning his beast towards the stream's channel, he came to a place where he knew that the stream narrowed to only two spans in width and spurred on his donkey, which had halted, not wanting to step into the water and cross the stream, and so he arrived in front of the mill.

Having been persuaded to stay with her children in the mill, Afendra lit a small lamp and put the bottle of oil and three candles in a basket. This time, 'ma Synodia wore her black outer-skirt, put on her clogs and, taking hold of the basket and the lamp, followed Peacock, who had dismounted, tied his donkey to a tree and had set off on foot.

*   *   *

Peacock walked ahead in silence because, on seeing the woman's worry regarding her husband's fate, he had felt sorrow and respect and had of his own accord ceased his merry song.

'Ma Synodia followed behind, walking slowly along the wet narrow path, where not long before the snow had been trodden down and had hardened, forming a thin layer as far as the low vale in the west which lay next to the sea. Instinctively, she looked to left and right, through the branches that formed a cool green border along the uphill path, with an inner fear, afraid of suddenly seeing the body of her son-in-law lying between a clump of gorse and an arbutus bush. For she was extremely worried and had no idea what might have happened to the ne'er-do-well. Every so often, a shower of snow would break away from the branch of a tall bush with a crack and a thud, coolly caressing the eyes and brows of the two nocturnal wayfarers. Coming from the left through the branches and bushes, a last weak gust of the North Wind, visiting in those lower regions his virgin sister, the snow, turned the infinitely varied patterns that she had so majestically spread over the boughs of the trees into crystal. It was not without reason that Proteus, that figure from ancient mythology, was so called. In an allegorical way, the creative mind of that most gifted of all peoples wished to show that one primary seed, embedded in the world by the Creator and procreating in infinite combinations, would produce such an infinite variety of individual types and forms that no two leaves are alike, as that truest of sayings goes.

To the right, on the other side of the ravine, began the Aradias Wood, consisting of thousand-year-old oaks climbing all the way up the mountain to its highest point at St Constantine's, and the mountain, tall and sheer, appeared like a vast ivy-covered wall. Snow shone here and there on the face of the dark forest, a white mystery, silent, responding in the language of the stars to the Pleiades above, to the North Star, to the Bear and the entire galaxy. And through the gusts of the North Wind, which blew through the leaves of the age-old trees, the forest — magnificent, haunted, unsullied, unravaged by fire and, as was said, inflicting harm on any woodcutter who dared to raise an irreverent axe against it — related in a language incomprehensible to all how many eras and ages it had lived through, and how many generations of men it had seen, one after the other, but without the later ones learning from the experience of the earlier and becoming wiser. And the frosty wind of the forest, chill, icy, plaintive, rippling through trees and crevices, reached across to the other milder side and transmitted its chill to the shoulders and backs of the two nocturnal wayfarers.

They had already reached the first high ground, from where the olive groves began to spread out to the left of them. Suddenly Peacock, perhaps because he felt cold and wished to get warm, perhaps trying to comfort 'ma Synodia, who he could see was downcast and worried about her son-in-law, started up once again singing his favourite song:

Twee, twee, my peacock, twee, twee!
Come here, come here to my knee...

'Ma Synodia, who had remained for a few moments staring at the east slope, cut him short:

'Over there,' she said to him, 'what's that?'

She pointed to the dome of the little church of the Holy Virgin of Kechrea, which rose above the walls of the church and the little monastery and became visible behind the trees in a sudden flash of light. Behind the monastery's west wall, which was lower, plain and without cells, sparks rose into the sky, lighting the dome and the western side of the church's roof, as if there was a fire burning in the church grounds.

'Ma Synodia crossed herself and let out a sigh:

'Holy Mother of God!'

'What can it be?' said Peacock, obliged to cut short his song for a second time.

'Didn't you pass by the church earlier, on your way here?'

'No!'

'Me neither. Shall we go and see?'

'Let's go!'

* * *

Afendra waited at the watermill, huddled up by the hearth and beside the sleeping children. There was no longer any sound of fairy-tales or songs in the silent mill; her mother wasn't present to comfort her by way of her cheerful and vigorous old age, and those reminiscences of her wedding, momentarily recalled, had gone, not wishing to implant themselves in a grieving spirit and a sad home. The only sounds to be heard and her sole company were the breathing of the sleeping children and the crackling of the fire occasionally emitted by the glowing logs, and her gaze remained intentionally fixed on the lamp burning before the icon of the Three Holy Figures that she had received as her dowry, depicting Christ in the middle, standing erect, blessing with his right hand and holding a book in his left, with his gentle expression, his beauteous form, his slightly parted fair beard, his blue raiment and red seamless robe. To Christ's right was the Holy Mother of God, to his left St John the Baptist, both bowing with arms crossed at either side of the Lord. And next to the icon, hanging from a nail and wrapped in a piece of white veil, were the two wedding wreaths. Ah, yes, the recollections from the wedding were still coming, but unpleasant ones and in another guise.

For more than once since then her mother had told her that she was afraid of the spells that might be cast on her by the other, her rival, the orphan girl unjustly passed over. It wasn't the spirits that she was afraid of, even though she was said to be fey, or rather she was so called precisely because of this, because, whatever she saw, she was never afraid. But when it came to spells, this was another matter. First of all, she was afraid lest her rival 'fill her with girls', a goal that is achieved through certain incantations made while the prayers for the betrothal are being read, immediately before the main wedding ceremony. Her fear increased initially when her daughter's first-born was a girl, but eased when her second was a son. 'The spells didn't work,' she said. Next, seeing that her 'ne'er-do-well' son-in-law was not doing very well in his business affairs, that he'd been forced to sell his family house and become a country bumpkin, she declared 'you're not going to prosper, daughter'. It was only to be expected. It's no small matter, stealing away the orphan girl's good fortune to get married yourself. But then again what are you to do? How else can you live? Life's like that; it's war. To attain perfection, to put the other before yourself...it's like deciding not to live in this world. It's like going and drowning yourself. Just thinking about it clouds your wits. It's enough to send you out into the wilderness.

Yet was this then the greatest evil, which sometimes happening unavoidably brings implacable hatred between two families? There were others far worse. The smaller the village, the bigger the evil. Hatred ran amok and in so doing prevailed between families and individuals. It ran through all the arteries and through all the veins of a small community. The sacred law of Christ was transgressed, evil was always returned for evil, multiple evil for good, never good for evil. An insurmountable wall separated the two parties, the two factions. You'd think they lived together in order to hate each other, that fate made them residents of that same township in order to quarrel with each other. Every leading man in his time, whether it was the mayor or local deputy or whatever he was called, implemented in full the popular saying: 'first take care of your own'. He was the protector of his family, his kin, his friends, his party, not the protector of the township. And in addition to this basic division, there were hundreds of other sub-divisions. The one neighbourhood declared war on the other neighbourhood; each family on the other families; each individual on the other individuals. The one neighbour didn't so much as say good morning to the other, let alone a kind word. Each rejoiced at seeing the other's misfortune. When it was a question of some inheritance, the relatives argued as to who would get the most. They would rather go to court, be sold as slaves in Barbary, than see their relative get more than them. For a quarter of an acre of land, they were quite capable of getting into all sorts of disputes, of driving themselves to death with 'temporary measures', 'legal proceedings', 'appeals' and 'counter-appeals'. If some unfortunate olive-tree happened to have one of its branches hanging slightly over the adjacent field, the neighbour would rush with his spade in the night to re-dig the borders and shift the boundary ditch. The next day, the astonished olive-tree would wake to find itself in the neighbour's grove. It had changed owner during the night.

Whole battles were fought for a newly-grafted tree in an olive grove, for three vines of a vineyard, for half a stretch of wheat field. And the olive-trees had for seven long years ceased to bear fruit, as if deeming the heads of these sinners unworthy to be anointed with their oil; and the vines, prematurely turning pale, did not provide ripe wine-bearing bunches, refusing to delight the hearts of unworthy people with their ambrosial juice; and the golden wheat of the earth prematurely bowed its withered head to its mother, desiring to quickly return to her bosom, not wishing to nourish the bellies of irreverent people.

Such were the wars that the men waged against each other, and such were their spoils. But were the women any less belligerent?

The mother didn't want her daughter's good, the mother-in-law deeply hated her daughter-in-law. The daughter-in-law didn't so much as say good morning to her sister-in-law.

For the sake of an unguarded word, for the slightest backbiting, which found many gossips willing to convey what had been said, usually enlarged out of all proportion, to the person concerned, they were quite capable of not speaking to each other for the rest of their lives. 'Wouldn't lay my bones in the same grave as yours!' was the battle cry in the women's ranks. One night, 'ma Synodia had had a terrifying dream, which would have been a true vision if she hadn't had it previously in her mind. She was dozing lightly one evening, mumbling to herself these very words hurled at her that same day by a female relative and enemy of hers, 'Wouldn't lay my bones in the same grave as yours!' She fell asleep and recalled the cemetery, the ossuary in the town's old graveyard, close to which she often passed as she returned in the evening from the fields, and in which she saw the white and yellowed bones of the dead all mixed up, all lying together, without it being possible to discern with the eye which were the bones of old friends and which were those of enemies. While she was dozing, she dreamt that she was passing by the cemetery and heard a terrible din made by hard objects clashing together. She looked up and saw the bones of the dead standing on end, moving, shaking and striking each other. Ulna clashed with ulna, forearm with forearm, fibula with fibula, rib with rib, backbone with backbone. Two bare skulls that had been discarded there, perhaps because they were unworthy to be respectfully exhumed after three years and given a memorial service,* were pulverized by the hail of blows that they received from the furious tibias. On seeing this strange spectacle, 'ma Synodia attempted to cross herself and whispered: '*Kyrie eleison!*' Who wouldn't be shocked, even though asleep? Imagine seeing the bones in the cemetery come alive, rise up and begin striking each other and making such a fearful noise![1] In the end, while still terrified at the sight and wondering what would happen, she heard a loud crack and an even bigger din and saw one of the walls of the cemetery, the north one, which was higher than the others, suddenly collapse inwards, falling on all the bones and shattering them. 'Ma Synodia gleefully thought 'serves them right!' and woke up.

She wanted to relate this vision, that she'd had only a few days previously, to her confessor, but she hadn't found the time to go on Christmas Eve. She hoped she'd have time the next morning at St Elijah's, where she intended to go to confess and unburden her conscience. But coming to the mill, she found that her son-in-law was missing and she simply couldn't account for his strange delay. Now she'd left her daughter waiting with her sleeping children in the mill and together with Peacock, sent by a beneficent providence to help her, 'was sailing' through the night, albeit on land, above the ravine towards the Holy Virgin's. And Afendra too, reflecting in her solitude, seated opposite the lovely icon of the Three Holy Figures, felt the need to unburden her conscience. Prior to her marriage, she had lent an ear to old wives' tales about spells and potions for ensnaring a groom and, for a while, she had hoped through powders and philtres to steal the heart of her fiancé from the orphan girl, her rival, and win it for herself. And for seven long years she'd resolved

---

[1] [Papadiamandis's note] The author is not claiming the creation of this device, presented here purely for didactical reasons, since it may have originated from the unconscious recollection of previous readings.

a hundred times to do it but not once had she found the courage to confess this sin.

It was already after midnight, deep into the night, and from that profound silence, from those barely audible noises, so faint that it was impossible to tell whether they were the product of hearing or imagination, that vague and mysterious and inexplicable enchantment, Afendra, though not at all sleepy, felt that the hour was late. A long December night, *endless night*. Suddenly she heard the first cockcrow. The cock, who with seven hens, was housed in a small coop behind the millstone and the flour chute, like a pasha with his harem, had sensed the hour and let out his usual cry. Afendra, who had already begun to doze, without having lain down, suddenly awoke.

'The cock's crowing,' she murmured, 'it's past midnight...what can have happened to my mother?'

Her mother's delay bode no good. Yet, paradoxically, her hopes were raised and she was certain that no evil had befallen them.

She got up and poked the fire. Taking hold of the lamp, she went downstairs to get some dry wood and, coming back, threw it on the fire. Then she crossed herself three times before the holy icon and said the 'Our Father' and 'The Creed', the only prayers she knew.

At that same moment, the sound of a man's footsteps was heard outside. There was a banging on her door. It was Peacock's voice. She rushed to let him in.

✳   ✳   ✳

Dawdling like a bride, Agallos slowly descended the hillside before arriving at Kechrea, and though it was already dark he persisted in his memories of those happy years when he was a prized catch, envied and sought after, and had enjoyed himself for eight whole years betrothed to two girls, first dallying with the one and then with the other. But when he arrived before the old monastery of the Holy Virgin of Kechrea, he turned leftwards to face the church and make the sign of the cross and, through the open gate of the church grounds, saw a bright light inside the church. Some pious woman must have remembered to light the Holy Virgin's lamps on the eve of her immaculate Childbirth and must have overdone it with the oil and wicks, turning the lamps into brands. But at the same time, he heard voices and whispering inside the church, like the readings or quiet chanting of monks in prayer. Who could it be? The monastery had been in disuse since the time of the Regency; the church had remained deserted.

Agallos may have been fey, but he was also a Saturday-child and was not afraid. He walked up to the monastery gate, entered the enclosure, walked across the grounds and went into the church. The lamps were lit in front of the icons on the screen, but were burning with a normal flame and not like fire-brands. But there were also two large candles burning in the candelabrum together with five or six smaller ones. This was the source of the bright light.

To the right in the apse, a middle-aged monk wearing the long veiled headdress of an archimandrite, was chanting the hymn, 'Lord, I called upon Thee'. It was daybreak on Monday and vespers hadn't been sung that morning nor had the Liturgy of St Basil the Great been celebrated on the previous evening.* To the left, another monk was responding antiphonically to the first. Two or three other monks or novices, wearing cassocks though without the headdresses, were standing on the west side of the church in the stalls. From within the sanctuary at that moment, wearing a stole, a chasuble and holding a censor, emerged a venerable elder, a hieromonk, tall, bony, hoary, bearded and with pale, lean and almost transparent features. Who were they all? It was the first time Agallos had ever set eyes on them.

The venerable presbyter first censed the icons, then the cantor on the right, then the one on the left, next the three monks or novices and, last of all, Agallos. Agallos bowed in the direction of the censor and seeing the lean and transparent features of the venerable priest was convinced that he'd gone, while still alive, to Paradise. There was no other way he could explain this vision.

Not one of the five monks turned to look at the newcomer. Only the last one, the youngest of those wearing robes, who wasn't wearing a headdress but was holding his folded black cap under his arm, turned the side of his head with his mane of hair and, without looking, the corner of his eye to Agallos. So Agallos plucked up the courage to go over to him and ask:

'Who are you all?'

The novice gestured by way of reply that it wasn't a time for explanations, but the venerable priest, who had returned to the sanctuary and seemingly having the gift of foresight, turned to the novice and by way of a nod gave him his permission to provide their brother with an explanation.

*　*　*

When Agallos had satisfied his curiosity, he made up his mind to leave and go down to the mill and bring his wife and children all together up to the church of the Holy Virgin, because the strange monks were going to keep an all-night vigil and celebrate the liturgy towards daybreak. But as he was about to leave, he thought again to himself: 'I'll stay a bit longer' and then 'a bit longer' and it was already approaching midnight without him having felt at all tired. For he found the sweetness and decorum of the chanting most pleasing.

Finally, just before midnight, when they had begun reading the Synaxarion of the day[1] and just as Agallos had turned to go outside to warm himself a little next to the blazing fire and was thinking of his wife's anxiety, as he was sure that his mother-in-law would have already arrived from the village and told Afendra of his departure from the town, he suddenly saw his mother-in-law and Peacock before him.

Agallos didn't allow ol' Synodia's fey nature to begin to work. He called to her to come outside the church and told her who these monks were.

---

[1] The Synaxarion, which is read during matins, relates the main events of the lives of the saints commemorated on that day and, on major feasts, the main events of that feast.

It was decided that Peacock, who in any case had left his donkey tied up outside the mill, should be sent to give a simple message to Afendra telling her that in two hours' time her husband and mother would come down to wake the two children and bring them and their mother to the Holy Virgin's to attend the liturgy.

*   *   *

Afendra rushed and opened the door.

'Are you alone? Where's my mother?'

'At the Holy Virgin's.'

'The Holy Virgin's? And Agallos?'

'Agallos too. They're attending the vigil.'

'Vigil?'

'Yes, an all-night vigil.'

'Who's celebrating it?'

'Some newly-arrived monks.'

'Monks?'

'Yes, men in cassocks.'

'Are they from the monastery?'

'No, they're from elsewhere. They've just arrived. They're staying at St Thanasis's.'

'St Thanasis's?'

'Yes. That's all I know. They said you should get some sleep and before long Agallos will come with 'ma Synodia to wake you, to get the children and take you to receive communion. Good night and may tomorrow bring you good fortune.'

*   *   *

Afendra only just managed to steal a nap before there was a knocking on the door of the watermill. It was Agallos and 'ma Synodia.

Afendra woke the children, washed them, clothed them, combed their hair, adorned herself with whatever she had to hand in the mill and, taking the lamp, the five of them set out for the Holy Virgin's.

The six monks were indeed newly-arrived. They had come from

one of the Cycladic isles, where they had lived as ascetics for many years. They had arrived just a few weeks previously and most of the inhabitants still didn't know about them.* It was the first time that Agallos had seen them, which is why he'd taken them for a strange vision. On arriving, they had begun to build cells to live in, temporarily housing themselves in a village hut.

Since there was no church in those parts, they had come down to celebrate Christmas at Kechrea, an hour's walk away.

Some called them heretics, others again respected them as being most virtuous men. It was commonly said that they had in part embraced the doctrines of a religious teacher which had been denounced by the Holy Synod. The truth was that it was this teacher who had followed the old customs of a very archaic monastic community, to which these ascetics belonged. Thus they coincided in part in their doctrines. There are many, however, who believe that, since the majority of people thirst for religious instruction and those responsible and competent do little to meet this need by drawing on pure and orthodox sources rather than foreign and distorted ones, it was only to be expected that many pious and well-intentioned people would be misled, in good faith, on hearing the Christian doctrine, albeit adulterated, wherever this is preached, because when the springs and fountains grow cloudy, with those in authority concealing the clear spring waters, men and beasts, dying of thirst, will prefer to drink from the cloudy stream, finding some slight hope of deliverance in this, rather than die of thirst; *O Lord, thou preservest man and beast. How excellent is thy loving kindness, O God!*[1]

*   *   *

'Ma Synodia confessed to Father Ezekiel (as the abbot of the brotherhood was called) and he counselled her that if the orphan girl, who had been passed over as a result of her daughter's marriage, was still unmarried, she must, in order to find forgiveness, do everything

[1] Psalm 36 : 6–7.

in her power to get her settled; if, however, the girl had married or died meanwhile, then she would have to perform other forms of good works, as well as attending the Forty Liturgies,* preferably at her parish church.

Since Synodia informed him that the girl was still unmarried, the first directive was imposed on her.

Afendra, who at last found the courage to confess her sin of spellbinding, was required for her penance to abstain from receiving Holy Communion for a long period and, in addition, to fast and pray. She was advised to light a large candle to St Anastasia, the maker of healing unguents.

The two children received Holy Communion, and the family returned together to their mill as the sun was rising.

[1892]

Translated by David Connolly

SHIPWRECKS' WRECKAGE

A PRODIGIOUS WAVE, more frantic than the others, swelled to a head not far from the shore, furious and seething, breaking with a terrible rushing torrent against the rock, leaving behind its feebler fellows, taking up this contest as if it bore a personal grudge against the light craft, pitiable cork, carrying within it, in unison with the natural levity of the wood, the three-headed human lightsomeness of the seafarers. A most bitterly strong easterly wind had begun to blow up since the afternoon, whistling madly over sea and land, gripping and entwining the waves from hard by, intruding whirlpools and eddies into the sea, an infinite battleground for a merciless war in which the enemy's base and direction of attack were hard to distinguish.

The horizon had already darkened over before the sun went down, and a leaden sky, sullen and lightless, hung above a wildly raving sea, silent above clamour and immobile above commotion, like the vault of a dusky mosque over a floor of dancing dervishes. Then little by little night descended, confusing and concealing with its measureless black the disorder of creation, hiding stars above and land and sea beneath. Three stars flickered above to the north, now hidden over, now shining forth, ready to precipitate themselves to a grave in Poseidon's boundless domain, and another two shone to the south, dwindling and ready to go out, like the lamps of a poor peasant's hut in a year of dearth. And the waves, heaving, dancing and raving, broke with childish willfulness against the rock, defeated but not despondent, proud as if conscious of their superior strength and prescient of final victory. And one monstrous wave, swollen, lucifer-ic, cracking, massed, as if the demon of hate had entered and was concealed within it, presenting the image of a watery beast, bearing froth in place of white teeth, took hold of the small craft as if in a gigantic grasp, by the stern and by the prow, by the keel and by the two sides, and raising it up, threw it against the rock, where with a terrible rushing noise and splintering crack, the weak husk was smashed, to fall again in pieces on the numerous small waves into which the one great wave was instantly dissolved, and which received their portion of the prey with fawning clamour.

The shoreline was not at all precipitous. The sea shore as far as one could discern it in that star- and moonless, Erebus-dark night would have been sweet and laughter-loving under the rays of the autumn sun before the easterly Euros wind began to blow, inspiring its fury into the waves. There was one solitary high rock extending its roots down into the sea where instantly the water deepened. And for this reason it seemed that the wave, or the demon concealed within it, had deliberately chosen that rock, which stood alone between two sandy beaches, in order to crush on its back the light vessel. When, by divine licence, the evil spirit chastises the virtuous among men, though enraged and furious, it yet proceeds to its work with fear and involuntary reverence. But when some of his friends are handed over to the power of Satan, often the very ones through whom he has recently been torturing and tyrannizing other friends of his, or indeed his foes, with a fierce malevolence he executes his work, which consists in destroying and murdering his own well-wishers. The three men sailing in the small *tserniki* were assuredly no saints nor by nature malefactors. They were sinners succumbing in surfeit to the usual faults common to all mankind, and perhaps also to a little smuggling and a spice of nautical skulduggery.

Such being the case, the devil had not, it seems, received any great licence to inflict bodily harm on the men. One of the three, at the moment of violent collision, had struck his elbow and right side against the rock and, overcome by the sharp pain, sank into the sea, but he quickly recovered and rose up swimming on the wave which seemed surprised at the destruction it had wrought and, pacified, churned more calmly around the wreckage, like a wild beast licking the blood of its own mangled victim. The two others, who had not drowned, but were swimming with strong strokes on the wave, grabbed him and, carrying him along, set him down on the sand which shone white in the darkness, not far from the ill-omened rock.

* * *

Starting from this sea beach, there stretched inland a broad swathe of densely wooded pine forest garlanding that fold of the deserted shoreline. On one side and on the other two black low promontaries could be discerned, shortened in the darkness of the night, forfeiting half their height. Out in front of this sprawled the great expanse of the sea which seemed suddenly stilled, reverting with a muted roar to calm, and inspired that sense of melancholy self-consolation which makes the restless womenfolk of seaside hamlets, who an hour before were running through the night collecting bunches of candles, encircling seven times the little chapels with forty-fathom lengths of wax taper, and ringing by themselves the bells to wake up the early-bedded priest to sing prayers of supplication and shouting out at the same time, 'Holy Virgin, to the sea! Holy Virgin, to the sea!', one hour later, when the wind, as I say, has stilled and the storm died down, it makes them whisper softly, comforting one another with that Greek plasticity of speech and compound of Christian and pagan sentiment: 'If any have drowned, they've repentance found!'

The three men recovered on the sand from their numbness, crawling up to where the surging and ebbing waves could no longer bathe their legs in brine. Soaked through, shivering and trembling, they felt a great sensation of drowsiness. The eldest of the three, the owner and captain of the shattered vessel, spoke about seeking out some cotter's dwelling to find fire and shelter and he comforted his son saying, 'If health is ours, we'll make another and bigger *tserni-ki.*' But his son did not seem so distressed about the boat as about a fine new sail of white cloth which he had stitched with his own hands not many days before, and he seemed ready to dive back into the sea in the hope of finding the sail. He also groaned about the little felucca which he himself had painted very daintily and carefully in black and white a few days before. A sudden strong gust of wind had torn it away from them before they managed to take it aboard the vessel the moment the wind blew them away from Kyra Panayia.[1] They had come to anchor by the shore of a harbourless uninhabited islet to take aboard cheeses, but the strong south-easterly wind suddenly swept them out with only half the cargo loaded, cutting the chain of the anchor and whisking the little boat away. The third man, who was the merchant, the one who had hit his arm and ribs against the rock, did not feel pain so much from his injury but lamented as he remembered the one and a half dozen skin-clad cheeses which he had been carrying on the boat, and he conjured them with oaths to remain where they were until the morning so that they could see whether there was not any way of locating on the sea bed some of the eighteen skins which, as he said, had cost him more than two thousand drachmas. But the young sailor reproached him saying that he was not in his right mind to insist after such a great misfortune that they should search at the bottom of the sea for the cheeses (since the *tserniki*, after all, was worth a good deal more than the cheeses and, moreover, had the two of them not come to his rescue he might not have escaped with his life from the wreckage of the ship and the rock). Besides, the cheeses, being salty in any case, would, after their immersion in seawater, have become quite inedible.

Thus the young man abandoned his idea of looking for the sail and the old captain repeated more insistently that it was time for them to see if they could locate some human soul to help them or at least find a place to shelter from the wind. The two leaders got to their feet, with the third man following behind of necessity, and after a tiring search, having ascertained that the two promontaries

---

[1] A small isle in the Sporades, the group of islands east of the Greek mainland to which Skiathos belongs, near to the island of Alonysos.

were impassable and precipitous, they discovered, at the limit of the sand, some trampled tree roots projecting like veins in the ground at the edge of the forest where a small threshing-floor was evident, and from there a footpath began to cut its way through the trees. The youngest of the three, leading the way, set out on this footpath, first turning round and holding out his hand to the old man who was supporting his colleague on his left arm. And thus, scarcely making out what lay before them, and colliding from time to time against withered tree stumps or stones, they proceeded for a few minutes into the wood. They walked with the faint hope that some-where nearby there would be, if not a peasant's hut, at least a shepherd's fold, and that they would find some soul sympathetic to their distress. From time to time the young man shouted with his harsh voice which was capable of repelling rather than attracting any assistance: 'Hey, isn't there anybody there?' They were mis-erable, they were cold and they were suffering terribly in their wrung-out but still wet clothes, and the narrow, invisible footpath, which was doubly shrouded in gloom from the darkness of the night and of the forest, was not a thoroughfare on which they could try to warm up and revive by making swift progress.

* * *

After walking for a few minutes, traversing the wooded belt of land, they arrived not far from the edge of the little forest where the trees began gradually to thin out. There they then saw a feeble light, flickering on the slope of the hill opposite them to the north-west. 'Glory to God!' exclaimed the old man, while the merchant re-membered the skin-clad cheeses and groaned, and the young man, mindful of that white sail of new American cloth which he had sewn with his own hands five days before, chewed his words and swallowed down his mutterings.

The light, signalling a cotter's habitation, seemed not far away, perhaps half a mile. It was necessary for them to walk, if they, ship-wrecked mariners, were to reach that weak landward beacon. Deep was the darkness. Before them there stretched out a wide flat plain which appeared black, monotonous and treeless in the dark. One would have taken it for a sandy expanse some ten times the width of that sandy beach they had left by the shore half an hour earlier had it not been dull, lightless and unshining. It appeared more like a plateau blackened by a recent brush fire, a sandy plain where the grass had burnt and blackened the dust, without leaving ash from burnt trees, or where violent rain had blackened the ash and had assimilated the earth with the traces of the fire.

The old man, who, although he did not want to admit it, was more pained about his *tserniki* than the merchant was about his cheeses, and possibly was suffering from his recurrent rheumatism in the legs, was making heavy work of the walk and stumbled frequently at the obstacles along the route. For this reason his son was obliged to leave his position at the head of the march and to follow second in line holding his father by the left arm to guide and support his steps, while with his other hand he held the right arm of the merchant who followed behind. The old man, walking in front, unable to make out what lay before him, took a stride forward and, before his son had a chance to examine and recognize the terrain, he set foot on the blackened expanse before ascertaining well what it was. Down with him he dragged his son, who was compelled to take two steps forward to keep hold of his father, and the youth in turn carried the merchant forward to the precarious footfall.

A triple *splash!* was heard all of a sudden. The three had stepped into the water. The watery element was apparently exercising a fatal attraction on them that evening, it was chasing at their heels and was claiming them as its own. The three sank up to their knees in the mud and up to the groin in the water. The old man was brought down prone, the youth knelt beside him trying to grasp him by the waist, and the merchant fell on his side.

Here was a lake which extended on the far side of the forest and of whose existence the shipwrecked men were ignorant. It was of a considerable size and its slimy bed was the feeding-ground for no small number of eels and nesting place for side-limping crabs. The population of shellfish was beyond number. Their shells, for the most part empty and exuding disodour, constituted here and there the uppermost layer of the lake bed, beneath which lay an unfathomed depth of mud in which the three castaways enmired as they fell, the first bent face down on the bottom, the second kneeling in the shallows and the third lying on his side.

'Down into the drink again!' muttered the old man as his son, choking his oaths and curses, lifted him with great effort to his feet again.

'This time I had a soft landing at least,' said the merchant, hinting at his abrupt encounter with the rock, the pain of which had made him forget till now his skin-clad cheeses.

'A drenched and dripping man has no fear of the rain. Let's hope we suffer nothing worse. Glory be!' repeated the old sailor stoically.

At the same time, while they were with difficulty disengaging themselves from the slime and wringing out their clothes, the dry crack of a cocked trigger was heard nearby.

The youth turned round and faintly discerned to his left behind the trees the outline of a low cottage which they had not noticed previously, and nor was it possible for them to have noticed it, since, being hidden behind a dense clump of trees, it was not visible from the path along which they had come.

The cottage stood by the very edge of the lake almost lapped by the water. In front of the cottage the young man at the same time recognized a dark shadowy shape bending in the direction of the water.

The young sailor did not believe that it was a ghost or indeed a grazing beast of any sort. And from the suspicious silence which the shadow kept after the short crack which had been heard it appeared that it was not a wild animal.

The boy understood at once and shouted out quickly:

'Don't shoot! We're friends.'

The shadow made a movement as if drawing something away and then a rough voice was heard:

'Who are you? What do you want?'

'Our ship went down,' answered the captain's son. 'We're sea-drowned.'

After a few moments the voice said:

'Come over here.'

The man lit a torch and illuminated the path for the three castaways.

'And I reckoned you wanted to poach my eels,' he said.

'We fell into the water because we couldn't see,' said the young sailor. 'We didn't realize it was a lake.'

*   *   *

Beneath three mutually embracing trees stood the peasant's hut, supported on stakes and roofed over with plane leaves. Its occupant was the assistant and representative of the lake's tenant farmer. The master was away, he told them. He had left that evening, having lit the lamp of the little house opposite where the light could be seen shining from the window, and he had not left him the key. So, unfortunately, he could not offer them hospitality in the master's house.

The steward was a young peasant of very short build, a former herdsman, boastful and talkative. He did not have sufficient clothes to lend the three men, but he gave to the one a vest, to the other a shirt and to the third a shepherd's cloak. In the forecourt of his hut, on the swept and glistening ground, he lit a fire and the three men, sitting around it in a circle, attempted to dry out their wet garments.

In the meantime they related to the peasant how they had come to suffer shipwreck. He heard their tale, interjecting comments more frequently than giving attention to what was being said.

When finally he heard how, after their blind and dark passage through the wood, they fell into the water of the lake, he cried out in horror:

'You fell into the lake? I'm surprised that the eye of the lake didn't swallow you up!'

The three men, in spite of all the suffering and misfortune that had befallen them, still found the capacity to be astonished, and they remained looking at the peasant with an expression of insatiable curiosity.

'The eye of the lake!' exclaimed the merchant.

'The eye of the lake, of course,' repeated the peasant. 'It lies deep in the lake ... and if anything falls in, whether man or object, there is no escape ... The eye of the lake drags it down and sucks it away, and the eye of the lake carries it out to the omphalos of the sea. Time and again in the past our grandfathers saw with their own eyes that something that had been sucked away by the eye of the lake was suddenly found in the sea, far out, between the two islands over there. Did you see the two islands that are out there opposite us, about three miles out into the sea? ... Between them is the omphalos of the sea. My own great grandfather, God rest his soul, had a goat that went down to lick salt at the lake once and fell in and drowned ... He searched to find the carcass so that the fish wouldn't eat it and overgrow, but he didn't find it, neither in the scum nor on the bottom. The next day fishermen found it between the two islands out there ... The eye of the lake had sucked it in and the omphalos of the sea had vomited it up out there ... My other great grandfather, my mother's grandfather, lost his crook one day when he went down to wash. It was dry and light and it floated out of his reach. By the time he had taken off his boots to step in the water the crook was far away, and my great grandfather, may God forgive him, would have sunk forever if he'd gone any further into the mud. If it had been me, of course, I would have jumped in and swum to catch the crook, because no one can better me at swimming. But you see, people in those days didn't know how to swim. They were afraid to get in the sea. And if it ever happened to me what happened to you I would get away by swimming, not like you lot who fell overboard.'

'But we got away by swimming too,' said the youngest of the castaways with a laugh.

'Yes, you escaped. I don't say,' repeated the peasant undeterred, 'but if it had been me ... by swimming ... I would have saved the boat too ... Never mind, what was I telling you? Ah, yes, about my

great grandfather who lost his crook. On the Sunday when he went
to the village to shop he sees an old boatman holding a crook. My
great grandfather had put a marking on his crook and he recognized
it. It was his. He asks him where he found it. The boatman replies
that he found it out between the two islands. My grandfather didn't
say anything to him, but he realized that eye of the lake had sucked
it away and the omphalos of the sea had thrown it up ... And then
there was my grandfather's godfather old Konstantis Koumaris. One
day he found an old twisted, black sea-wood with the nail holes full
of rust that the lake had thrown up in the shallows and which was
floating just beneath the surface. Now how could a twisted piece of
wood like that find its way to the lake? A boat, like your own (if you
don't mind me mentioning the subject), if it sank it would sink in the
sea not in the lake. So as it seems the omphalos of the sea had sucked
it down and sent it to the eye of the lake, and the eye of the lake spat
it up ... Truly,' added the peasant, sensing the need to take his
breath, 'whereabouts did you sink, you three?'

The old man replied indicating with a wave of his hand.

'In the cove down there.'

The peasant stopped as if looking for ways to be persuaded himself by persuading others; then he continued with a faint flash of cu-
pidity crossing his eye:

'And did you have any cargo on board the boat?'

The merchant, rubbed sore by the question, was swift to reply
with a deep groan:

'Eighteen skins of cheese I had on board, and they all went
down.'

'Eighteen skins of cheese!' repeated the herdsman in a tone of
well-grounded suspicion. 'Undoubtedly the omphalos of the sea will
have swallowed them.'

'Can't the eye of the lake vomit at least some of them back?'
asked the youngest of the castaways with an involuntary smile, giving voice to the merchant's hope.

'Not possible,' said the peasant; 'the omphalos of the sea can't send so many pieces back to the eye of the lake; if the eye had swallowed them one at a time the omphalos could have brought them back.'

The merchant appeared eager but reluctant to ask something. Finally, making up his mind, he turned to the peasant and asked:

'And do you yourself know in what part of the lake this eye is to be found?'

'Of course I know!' answered the peasant with conviction. 'Of course I do, but no man can approach anywhere near that place. The eye would without fail suck him away; and it could drag him in even from far away if he's not careful. We know it and when we're looking for eels in the mud we're careful and never go near that place at all.'

The merchant lowered his head in dejection.

The young sailor commented that the place where the ship had sunk was miles away from 'the two islands' where the steward was saying that 'the omphalos of the sea' was located. The peasant replied:

'Yes, it's far away... but that's beside the point... the omphalos of the sea pulls things even from a distance if any ship with a cargo goes down...'*

*　*　*

The next day, having guided the three castaways into the little town, the lake steward installed himself in a wine shop and, after downing three mastic liqueurs, began to tell his tale within earshot of a large audience:

'What an incredible thing happened back there at Kanapitsa!... Eighteen skins of cheese, the cargo of a boat that went down yesterday... The omphalos of the sea swallowed them down and the eye of the lake spat them up... We'll be eating fat eels this year, boys... Next week, as soon as I get permission from the master, I'll start fishing them out... They fell on those cheeses, I tell you, and did those devilish eels eat!... Not half... They devoured even half the skins... they filled them with holes like a seive... Not a single skin was spared... Eighteen skins of cheese!'

'Eighteen skins!' repeated one of the audience in amazement.

'Eighteen skins, that's right! The eye of the lake threw them up... The eels and the mullet certainly made merry!'

The wine-seller, as if by prior agreement, brought out a mouse-eaten scrap of cheese-skin, and displayed it as proof to the assembled company.

'Look! if anyone doesn't believe,' he said. 'Only this scrap escaped from a whole skin!'

'It's true,' confirmed the lake steward, taking the piece of leather in his hand. 'I had to cut off the eel's head with my knife to get it out of its teeth. Look you can still see its bite marks.'

And he showed the traces of rodents' teeth.

'So it's worth our while to take a walk over there for cheese or for eels,' threatened one of the company.

'*Varda bene!* you'd be wasting your time. The master's there today,' said the steward.

'And the master doesn't joke,' chimed in the wine-seller... 'He'd think nothing of filling you with shot and then he'd say he took you for wild ducks and made a mistake.'

✻　✻　✻

It was a fine autumn day.

From early in the morning the merchant was on his feet seeking out a boatman who knew something about diving in order to get him to agree to undertake the search for the cheese-skins. But the first to whom he addressed himself demanded half the cheese-skins for his trouble, the second asked for three hundred drachmas in cash, and the third requested seven of the eighteen cheese-skins and then came down to five. Finally he agreed with a fourth ferrier for three cheese-skins.

But by the time he set out it was already afternoon.

In the morning, however, the first boatman whom he had approached, *Barba*-Yannis Xiniotis, having failed to reach agreement with the merchant, decided to raise the cheese-skins on his own account. So, arming himself with his hook, he set sail for Kanapitsa and after a search he eventually found and fished up thirteen of the eighteen cheese-skins.

Barba-Yannis, satisfied that he had not wasted his day, was making ready to get away by another route in order to ferry home undetected the thirteen cheese-skins. But that very moment *Barba*-Apostolis Chrysoheris arrived with his boat and demanded a share of the booty. *Barba*-Yannis was obliged to give him four of the thirteen cheese-skins.

Before *Barba*-Apostolis had left, *Yero*-Manolis Apantos hove alongside and demanded his share too. *Barba*-Yannis had no choice but to give him four of the nine cheese-skins.

No sooner had *Yero*-Manolis departed but *Mastro*-Konstantis Kalafatis appeared on the scene. He had borrowed a boat and had come out in search of his share. *Barba*-Yannis Xiniotis was ready to agree to give him two of the remaining five and to keep three at least for himself for his trouble. But *Mastro*-Konstantis would have none of it, shouting and saying that it was unfair because he had given four to each of the others and that he was going off to report on him. *Barba*-Yannis was forced to give him the four, keeping one for himself.

When in the late afternoon Dimitrios Ftelios, the ferrier whom the merchant had engaged, finally arrived with his vessel, the four boatmen had long since disappeared. Dimitrios Ftelios, after scratching over the sea bed for a long time with his hook, scoop and harpoon, eventually succeeded in discovering three of the sunken cheese-skins, exactly the number required to secure his agreed payment. The others had perhaps been swept away by the sea and were not found.

And this was eloquently conducive to widespread belief in the rumour which the lake steward had been spreading since the morning — namely, that the eighteen cheese-skins had been swallowed by the omphalos of the sea, that the eye of the lake had vomited them up, and that the eels had devoured them.

[1893]

Translated by John Raffan

EASTER CHANTER

I F THE HERO OF THIS TALE were the writer himself, then its title would have to be understood in a metaphorical or allegorical sense. For the fact is that by the grace of divine Providence and the fraternal benevolence of my distinguished friend from the village, *Kyr*-Yannis Pendeliotou, I am privileged almost every year without fail, during these resplendent days, to chant alongside him as, glasses in hand and following his beloved Constantinopolitan style, he draws out the musical phrases and cadences to infinity. We are in the little country church of the village of T., where the incense drifts in blue fragrant wreaths and forms a fleeting surround for the rayed haloes and solemn faces of the saints, and where the village girls, in their embroidered aprons and white sleeveless jackets, come bearing armfuls of roses and violets and sheaves of rosemary and proceed to heap mountains of flowers on the humble *Epitaphios*, which needs no further embellishment. Into the church comes a whole squad of impromptu chanters, each of them holding a leaflet with the text of the Good Friday burial service, and who feel duty-bound to chant the Praises* in ear-splitting discord, managing in the process to demolish, with their comical blunders, even the few words in the leaflets which are printed correctly.

Without being a principal in this impromptu choir, I must confess that, even though I try to chant somewhat tolerably alongside my willing and honourable friend, I am nevertheless much inferior to him, which is why, craving the reader's indulgence, I started by invoking the title's metaphorical meaning; for just as these days see the emergence, in all the churches, of large numbers of hitherto unknown, instant experts in Easter chant, so the present writer, who for the rest of the time is silent, twice a year, at Christmas and Easter, reveals himself to be an occasional short-story writer on contract. The situation has started to become somewhat tedious, and many have wondered at it, while others have even condemned it. 'There are quite enough fads and foreign fashions about as it is. We are not English, nor are we Americans. Don't you go pestering us as well. What makes you assume that the public is going to be charmed by your recollections or moved by your feelings? You've done it once or twice, but enough is enough; from now on you can keep quiet. Can't you see that you have exhausted your perennial subject, and that you are being forced each year to produce what is merely a variation on it?'

First and foremost, we would do well to distinguish what really is a foreign fashion from what may be, in the nature of things, common to all nations. For example, is it a foreign fashion for magazines to come out on Saturdays and Sundays? Is it a foreign fashion for the political newspapers to print material of a more literary kind on Sundays? Is it, in short, a foreign fashion to retreat on holidays from the hustle and bustle of the world, and from the perusal of political articles, and to feel the need to read something of a kinder nature, more pleasing, more devotional? — Yes, but at times of festival you can still publish stories or accounts without making any references at all to Christmas or Easter.'

This, then, is the reason for their dissatisfaction; and how naïvely they express it — or reveal it. To be a guest in princely style in the palace of a great lord, and not drink a toast to the head of the house! To enjoy 'hospitality at the board of the eternal Masters'[1] and not give thanks to the host! But in the stories that I, the undersigned, have published from time to time at Christmas or Easter, I was in truth inspired by my recollections and feelings, which attracted and moved me personally — and perhaps a few select readers of them. That these latter exist is attested by the fact

[1] Cosmas of Maïuma, canon for Holy Thursday, 9th ode.

that the two leading newspapers of the capital, as well as its one and only magazine, are happy to include the stories written about these days of festival. Furthermore, you will almost never find me forcing a situation or a plot in order to excite the reader's curiosity. Whenever I speak about people living abroad, who return after a long absence or send letters containing material solace to their families, it is all based on reality; for as all dwellers on the coast and in seafaring places are well aware, it is the case that before festival periods in particular, many of those who are abroad, and who normally appear unfeeling and thick-skinned, suddenly remember their families, and either return home, or, if pride forbids them to come back in respectable fashion, it is not unusual for them to send consolation to their old mothers and sisters. Sometimes I speak about social and family customs relating to the festival periods, and elsewhere the slight plot turns on some more modern and corrupt custom. What is so extraordinary about all this?

But most of the stories I write about times of festival have to do *a priori* (if I may use the Latin expression) with the matter in hand, that is to say, they are mainly religious. — What talent, pray, or power or originality can there be in someone's taking the trouble to describe in detail how a village priest went to celebrate the liturgy in a country chapel for a little community of peasants or shepherds, who and how many took part in the festival, and what their customs were like? In the opinion of the critics, such an undertaking would be thoroughly contemptible and degrading. For someone to write about an old man murdering his wife on Christmas Day itself — with neither the reader nor the writer having the slightest clue as to why he murdered her — is, in some people's opinion, superior and admirable. With a crime like this being committed on the actual holy day, the subject is exhausted, and henceforth no Christmas or Easter stories must be allowed to be published.

'No religion, for God's sake! The Greek Nation is not Byzantine — have you understood that? The Greeks of today are the direct descendants of the ancient Greeks. Then they became civilized and progressive, like other nations. What is poetical about writing that Christ "accepts the worship of the poor",[1] and that the humble priest "offered up to God a sacrifice of praise"?[2] Or to describe the interior of a chapel, with its drowsy oil-lamps and the shadowy forms of saints everywhere? We don't understand these things. We want a story which is all poetry, not the prose of everyday reality. And how do you dare to write, in relation to Julian the Apostate, pinned to the wall by St Merkourios's spear, the following blasphemous phrase: "Livid, the deranged tyrant ..."?[3] Some years ago, when another, more eminent writer published a drama of historical fancy, he prefaced it with a truly contemptible prologue, in which he grossly insulted the religion of his fathers — but no mention was made of anyone's being scandalized, because the thing was then in vogue. 'But for you, yourself, to dare to use such disrespectful language about Julian the so-called Apostate — why, such insolence goes beyond the limit.' Yet what this wise critic has not understood is that the phrase was objective, to use one of their own terms; that is to say, it was a rendering in words of the colours used by the painter; and neither has he understood that any discussion of the writer's own opinions (who does not deny, however, that he agrees with the views of the Byzantine wall-painter) is entirely superfluous.

We will conclude this preamble with the following brief statement: the nation of today, unfortunately, has not progressed as much as they say it has. The Greek nation, at any rate the enslaved portion of it, is still lagging behind, and the free portion cannot run far enough ahead without the whole rupturing, as it has already, alas, ruptured. He who runs ahead must wait for the one coming up behind, if indeed he wishes to run at all; the free man must help or relieve the prisoner. As time goes on, the free nation becomes

[1] Paraphrased from Papadiamandis's earlier short story, 'At Saint Anastasa's'; see p. 190 above.

[2] Quoted from Papadiamandis's 'A Christmas Pilgrimage to the Kastro'; see p. 127 above.

[3] Ibid., see p. 125 above.

ever more incapable, alas, of giving a helping hand to that portion of it which is in slavery. An Englishman or a German or a Frenchman is able to be cosmopolitan or anarchic or atheist or anything he likes. He has done his patriotic duty, he has built up a great country. Now, thanks to the luxury of his freedom, he can give rein to unbelief and pessimism. But for the Greek of today, sorry figure that he is, to want to act the cosmopolitan or the atheist, is like a dwarf standing on tiptoe and striving to emulate a giant. The enslaved portion of the Greek nation, and the liberated also, has and will always have need of its religion.

For my part, as long as I live and breathe and am of sound mind, I will never cease, especially during these resplendent days, to praise and adore Christ, to depict nature lovingly, and to represent with affection those customs which are authentically Greek. *If I forget thee, O Jerusalem, let my right hand forget her cunning; If I do not remember thee, let my tongue cleave to the roof of my mouth.*[1]

✳   ✳   ✳

However, the hero of this story is Mr Konstantos Z'marohaftis, third deputy in the municipality of Litis, of the village of A., who promised, as he had an easy habit of promising (and it was perhaps this very quality in him which was responsible for his success in politics; for whereas at every election the other deputies vied with each other for the first place, he, without any ostentation or standing people drinks, was invariably elected third deputy, there being no fourth contender) — he promised, as I was saying, to go and help Father Dianelos the Protekdikos[2] celebrate the liturgy out of the village, at the chapel of St John the Baptist. The chapel was three hours away from town, and Father Dianelos the Protekdikos had gone there on the morning of Holy Saturday, having received Mr Konstantos's promise that he would get there towards evening

---

[1] Psalm 137 : 5–6.

[2] An ecclesiastical office dealing with matters of canonical law.

to do the chanting and concelebrate the Resurrection. The priest had no other assistant; his youngest son was preparing this year to sit the examinations for the Teacher Training College and was unable to come for Easter, and his other son, who was at sea, was continually absent on voyages. Of daughters, one thing which the region (and indeed the married clergy) produced in plenty, he had been left an abundance by his deceased wife: five of them, praise God, and they kept on and on growing, bless them; they were so close to each other in age that no sooner had one grown than the next had grown too; and as they grew they seemed, particularly the three middle ones, to be about the same age as well as the same height; and Father Dianelos, now a hieromonk of necessity,* was not even free to escape to a monastery.

He had made the three-hour journey from the little town to the chapel in the morning after the liturgy, followed by his two younger daughters, girls of ten and twelve, and by a group of seven or eight women, all church stalwarts, and preceded by his donkey, which was laden with the saddlebags containing the priest's holy vessels and vestments. The sun was high when they entered Doctor's Vineyard, arriving next at Vourlidia, from where they panted up the hill to Matarona's Pine, which in those days still existed and gladdened travellers with the comfort of its shade on the hilltop, before some unscrupulous barbarian, with the tacit consent or complicity of those whom the most unfortunate people in the world keep electing to be their rulers and protectors, ruthlessly felled the beautiful tree and deprived the landscape of its outstanding ornament.

From there they went on to Petralono and Stamelos's Spring, took the uphill road to Kanakis's Spring, and passing through Klinias they descended to the Chairimona stream and reached the north coast of the island, high on which there stood, lowly yet dignified, overlooking the sea and hearing the beat of the waves against the shore, silently narrating five harrowing centuries of blood and martyrdom, the holy chapel dedicated to the Beheading of St John the Baptist.

They came to the church enclosure and unloaded the donkey. The women, red-faced and heated from the walk, chattering and laughing continually, shook out their perfectly dust-free skirts, and over their short travelling dresses they put on their long pleated gowns. The priest let down the side of his grey robe that he had tucked under his belt and put his black cassock on over it. They all went into the chapel and reverenced the icons.

Some of the women gathered dry sticks and lit a fire on which to make coffee for the priest, while the others cut bundles of twigs from the scented shrubs, terebinth and ilex and sage, tied them up with twine to make rough brooms, and proceeded to sweep the church floor and the porch with quick even strokes; the priest fashioned a broom out of bay and myrtle and rosemary and himself swept out the sanctuary and all around the altar. He grumbled and complained without ceasing about the fatuity, as he termed it, of the shepherds and goatherds who had asked him to celebrate the Resurrection service for them in the hills, and not one of whom had yet shown up; they sometimes came close to committing sacrilege by bringing their animals into the church, probably in rainy weather, as could be seen from the various traces of their invasion which they hadn't even bothered to clear away. Inside the sanctuary, as he bent to his sweeping, he could be heard from time to time muttering and sighing:

'O dear, dear... O Lord, *thou preservest man and beast*.'[1]

'No one's broken their leg, have they?' shouted Aunt Syraino from outside in response to the priest's sighs — she was the one who really took the lead on these occasions of country liturgies and feast days.

'*Man and beast*,' murmured the priest again.

It was already midday, and the priest with his little flock sat down to eat under the sacred olive-tree outside the church, next to the ancient stone-built tomb which according to some was a water cistern, and according to others a grave or an ossuary. Aunt Mathino, whom some held to be a godly old soul, while others said her

---

[1] Psalm 37 : 6.

piety was fake, a woman of upright life, looked towards the monument and said with a sigh:

'We're eating, girls; I wonder if the poor souls have something to eat too!'

'Do the dead eat, Aunt Mathino?' said Aglao, the priest's twelve-year-old daughter.

'Dead people eat *kollyva*, I know that,' added Kalliopo, her ten-year-old sister, 'and that's why, when they bring us *kollyva* at home, we give it all to the poor and to the children in our district, so that our poor mummy has something to eat in the other world.'

'Kalliopo, hush!' said the priest, trying to hide his feelings.

Twelve years and more ago, Father Dianelos had a friend who was a Greek teacher, a God-fearing man, but with a weakness for classical Greek names. He had become the priest's *koumbaros* and had baptized his two youngest daughters, giving them names out of the classics; but since these names had fallen on neutral ground, they had become neuter, as was only to be expected.[1]

'Why, the girl's right, you know, Father,' called Aunt Mathino, remembering her own dead: she had buried a husband and four children, and was left with two married daughters on whom she relied for support in this world. 'The girl's right. Father Theophilos, the abbot of the Monastery of the Blessed Virgin of the Annunciation, God rest his soul, said the same to us, about a man who was squashed under a water-winch, and everyone thought he was dead, and his wife did the three-day and nine-day memorials for him, and an Angel of the Lord used to take the plate with the *kollyva*, with the cross on it made out of raisins and pomegranate seeds, and bring it to the man who was squashed and he ate it for I don't know how many days, and he breathed through a hole in the earth, I think, until in the end he wasn't dead, and they raised the winch and freed him, isn't that true, Father?'

---

[1] The ancient and grammatically correct form of the girls' names ae Aglaïa (the youngest of the three Graces) and Calliope (the muse of epic song). In the popular idiom of Skiathos, feminine names ending in -e or in -a are often rendered in the more intimate neuter diminutive form, thus Aglao and Kalliopo.

'It's true, my good woman,' answered the priest, 'but well . . . it's true for those who believe it.'

'And what if they don't believe it?'

'They'll go to Hell, I know that,' said Kalliopo.

'But if it's true, Father, why didn't the Angel of the Lord just lift up the winch to let the man out?' said Annoudha, one of the women.

'Because the point was not to demonstrate God's power, which is proved by countless miracles,' answered the priest, 'but simply to show the power of memorials and of the offerings made for the dead, and that nothing that a person sacrifices, nothing that he offers up to God or to the poor, no good deed, no virtue, no patience, no tribulation, no tear, nothing is wasted. They all fall on fertile ground, like the grain of wheat, as the Lord said, which if it fall into the ground and die (like *kollyva*, and like the dead) it bringeth forth much fruit.[1] *They that sow in tears shall reap in joy.*[2]

'Is that what it says in the Gospel?'

'It says it in the Psalms, but it comes to the same thing, because the Psalms are also the word of God and are inspired by the Holy Spirit. And when we bury a dead person who has lived a virtuous life in Christ, it's as though we're planting a grain of wheat in the ground . . . and the Lord will raise him up on the last day, as he himself graciously promised us.

'*He that believeth in me, though he were dead, yet shall he live . . . and I will raise him up at the last day.*'[3]

'Amen!' said Aunt Mathino, and her tears in memory of her husband and four children quickly evaporated, like drops of rain after a summer shower in a long-dried-up river bed.

✽   ✽
✽

In the evening there appeared in the distance, descending the ridge, the hut-dwellers, wives of the goat- and sheep-herders of the district.

---

[1] See John 12 : 24. [2] Psalm 126 : 5.
[3] John 11 : 25; 6 : 44 and 54.

They came bearing huge baskets filled with flowers, tall candles, tapers, jars of oil, loaves of bread and small bottles of wine for consecration, or leading donkeys whose saddles were spread with rugs and cloths, laden with bags and panniers holding flasks of wine, fresh or cured cheeses, and dyed red eggs. Then there appeared, with strange whistles, two or three goatherds with their flocks, which they were driving along the steep cliff above the sea. The he-goats leapt from rock to rock, from hummock to hummock, from gully to gully, while the kids skipped prettily after their mothers bleating, happy in the new, for them, enjoyment of this unknown thing called life, and the sun shone on their grey or dappled or black-and-white coats; while the goatherds, tall, strong and rough, with matted hair and sunburned faces, ran backwards and forwards with their long crooks, as tall as themselves and curved at the end, chiding the unruly and skittish herd with many-toned whistles.

Last to arrive were the shepherds, without their lambs which they had left behind in the folds, apart from the two they had slaughtered and were carrying. They were all well turned out and dressed in their best, with clean tunics, short breeches and high stockings, broad red or yellow sashes, shaved, and their white or brown mustaches were curled.

Daylight was fading quickly and the sun set behind one of the ridges of the Pelion range opposite, having worn for five minutes a crown of azure and gold-purple clouds, himself aware of the light and glory he gave out; and for ten more minutes after he had set, the rays of his crown continued gold and purple and azure, bathing the mountain in violet light. Night then came softly down on the sides of the mountain, spreading over all things its deep ineffable mystery, and the living sounds and whispers of nature awoke on the mountain tops, in the undergrowth, in the dells, and the brow of the mountain steamed and gave off dampness, and the eyelid of the hill was lowered, enclosing 'as one' mountain, vale and river. And *Barba*-Konstantos Z'marohaftis, third deputy of the village of A. in the Litis municipality, was nowhere to be seen.

The priest was uneasy, and it was feared that they would end up without having a Resurrection liturgy. For obviously he could not celebrate without an assistant. A liturgy cannot be celebrated without at least one chanter or reader. The shepherds and goatherds were all, of course, illiterate, but a lot of them, poor souls, were also unchurched.

'Now what are we to do? Look how people promise you they'll do something and then leave you in the lurch! *O Lord, thou preservest man and beast!*'

He still had hope, however, that *Barba*-Konstantos would come. He was always slow, he knew. But at the moment the night was still dark and only the stars were shining. The moon would rise a little later, and then there was a chance that he might come.

Two hours went by and the moon, some way from the full, rose from the dark mountain above them, ascending slowly into the firmament, and the ranks of the stars were infinitely reduced and almost all of them grew dim at her passing. Another hour went by. *Barba*-Konstantos did not appear.

The priest began to get angry.

'How dishonest of him! the idiot . . . Lord I have sinned! "Man and beasts".'

He wanted to send one of the herdsmen to the town, to look for someone and bring him back to help celebrate the liturgy. But the shepherds and goatherds were all stretched out snoring among the lentisk and arbutus, wrapped in their capes, glad that the spring had returned and that the damp earth was less chilly. Their wives were also lying down, sleeping less audibly behind the apse of the chapel, wrapped in the covers and rugs which they had brought spread over the saddles of the donkeys. The women who had come from the village were also dozing, leaning against their baskets outside the inner door of the church, in the shelter of the portico within the wooden railing. Only the priest was anxious and sleepless.

'I know most of the words by heart, Father,' said Aunt Mathino in an attempt to cheer him up. 'I can say them in the ear of old Philippis, who's a good Christian man, and he can manage somehow.'

273

'I see the time has come to make a chanter of you, Mathino!' laughed the priest.

'I shan't be a chanter, just the prompter. It'll only be us by ourselves, there's no one with education here who'll laugh at us. Your holiness can give old Philippis the tone, and I can tell him all the words I remember. If I could read what it says on the page, I don't think it would be sinful to do the chanting myself.'

Meanwhile it was nearing midnight, and there was no hope now that *Barba*-Konstantos, the third deputy, would come. The priest did not decide to wake up one of the shepherds and send him to the village, as he had thought of doing earlier, because he reckoned that there were so few hours to go before daylight that by the time the messenger reached the village, looked for and found a chanter, persuaded him to come, and got back with him to St John's, the day would be fully two hours old... and the Resurrection was supposed to happen at midnight or slightly later.

Father Dianelos got to his feet with a sigh, went into the church, and bowed before the altar steps. Old Mathino and Aunt Syraino, the leader on these occasions, at once ran up behind him. The two women started to trim the wicks, pour oil into the icon lamps, and cross themselves fervently. An inexpressible joy and sweetness welled up within them: it was Resurrection, the Resurrection! The face of Christ the Lord, to the right of the Royal Doors, shone with divine light. To the left, the face of the Lady Mother of God, holding her Holy Infant, was bright with unspeakable bliss. The countenance of the Holy Baptist, with one curl of hair quivering upwards as if it had remained on end at the touch of the brutish executioner, who severed the venerated head of the greatest man ever born of woman, radiated a mystical joy at the side of Him upon whose hallowed head he had been permitted to lay his hands in consecration.[1] The beloved disciple, too, was there still, rejoicing in

[1] A reference to the hymn chanted on the Feast of Epiphany: 'Your hand which has touched the immaculate head of the Lord . . .'.

the Resurrection, although lines of care furrowed his high forehead, caused by the foreknowledge that a shameless church robber would shortly seize him from his setting and carry him off to Athens to place him, not in a church and a place of sacrifice and a sanctuary, not in a place for oblations, but in a Museum. Almighty God! a Museum, as if Christian worship had ceased to be practised in this country, as if its vessels belonged to a buried past, objects of curiosity!... Have pity on them, Lord!

*　*　*

Finally there was no hope left that *Barba*-Konstantos would come, and they were obliged to chant the service with the means at their disposal. Shaking off their drowsiness, the village women entered the church one by one. The countrywomen, the shepherds' wives, were soon awake, while Father Dianelos came out and, picking up a piece of old planking and a bit of wood like a hammer, he improvised a *semandron*; for alas, it was long since there had been a bell with which to waken the centuries-old dead and to stir the dust of the long-deceased inhabitants of the town that had once been there. On this *semandron* the priest began to beat, first in trochaics (*ton Adam, ton Adam, ton Adam*), and then in iambics (*to talandon, to talandon*),* raising the midnight echoes. On hearing the repeated sound the herdsmen leapt to their feet, threw off their capes, washed their faces and hands and hastened into the church, holding their candles. The priest commenced the service, chanting the vigil service and all of the canticle 'On the wave of the sea', censed the church, said the dismissal prayer, and then, donning stole and chasuble, he lit a tall candle, and holding it in his hand he came to the sanctuary doors and in a loud voice began to chant the invitation to 'come forth and receive the light'. The herdsmen lit their candles, as did the women, and they all left the church to stand in the forecourt, carrying the icon of the Resurrection and the Gospel and censer, and chanting 'Thy Resurrection O Christ the Saviour...'. Then the holy icon and the Gospel were placed on the ledge that did duty for a stand, and on which the women had spread a long cloth of woven silk. The priest slowly read out the passage from the Gospel according to St Mark beginning *And when the Sabbath was past*...,[1] and then, having censed and sung 'Glory to the Holy Consubstantial, Life-giving, and undivided Trinity...', he began full-voiced to chant the '*Christos Anesti*'.* When he had sung it through three times, and two of the herdsmen had sung it once or twice — not because they were more literate than the others, but because their accent was less broad and they were able to 'get their tongues round it' — Aunt Mathino plucked up courage and sang it through once, and so did Aunt Syraino, while Kalliopo and Aglao and Annoudha and some of the other women stifled their giggles with the palms of their hands, which they held before their mouths like self-imposed muzzles.

In conclusion the priest sang it through once more, and said the supplication for peace. Then, taking up the icon and the Gospel, he went into the church, followed by the congregation. He chanted the first two *troparia* of the first ode, went into the sanctuary, came out to say the preparatory prayers for the liturgy, and went back inside to begin putting on his holy vestments. The chanting, of necessity, had stopped. Aunt Mathino went up to old Philippis, the head shepherd, and tried to prompt him to continue.

'Come on, chant, old Philippis, the "Let us purify our senses".'[2]

But old Philippis couldn't get his tongue round it; so Aunt Mathino began very quietly:

'Let us purify our senses and we shall behold Christ, radiant with the light ineffable of the Resurrection...' Truth to tell, her pronunciation of the words was all her own.

'We've done that bit, woman,' called the priest from inside the sanctuary. 'Now comes "Come, let us drink a new drink".'

'Of course, that's right,' said Aunt Mathino; and began again with her own version of the *troparion*.

---

[1] Mark 16 : 1.
[2] St John of Damascus, canon for Easter Sunday, 1st ode, 1st *troparion*.

But the priest, who was still vesting, realized that he would either have to postpone the offertory, or break off the service. This could, if necessary, be dispensed with altogether, but he didn't see how they were going to manage the liturgy.

As he put on each garment he whispered the prescribed words:*

' "My soul shall rejoice in the Lord, for he hath clothed me in the garments of salvation, he hath covered me with the robe of gladness, as a bridegroom who decks himself with a crown and as a bride adorns herself with jewels, so he hath adorned me." '[1]

He then chanted the *troparia* of the canticle:

' "Now are all things filled with light; heaven, and earth, and the places under the earth..." .'[2]

Next he put on the stole, murmuring as he did so:

' "Blessed be God, who pours forth his grace upon his priests, as ointment upon the head, which runneth down upon the beard..." .'[3]

And again he chanted:

' "Yesterday, O Christ, was I buried with thee, and today I rise again with thy rising..." .'[4]

Putting on the girdle, he said:

' "Blessed be God, who girdeth me with strength, and maketh my way sinless." '[5]

Fastening one of the cuffs, he recited:

' "Thy right hand, O Lord, is magnified in strength..." .'[6]

Here he stopped to chant the *katavasia*, 'Come, let us drink a new drink, not one miraculously brought forth from a barren rock...'.

When, however, he had clothed himself in all his vestments, he came out and continued the service by chanting the entire canon himself, and was about to go on to the Praises and the exchange of

---

[1] See Isaish 61 : 10.

[2] St John of Damascus, canon for Easter Sunday, 3rd ode, 1st *troparion*.

[3] See Psalm 133 : 2.

[4] St John of Damascus, canon for Easter Sunday, 3rd ode, 2nd *troparion*.

[5] See Psalm 18 : 32.   [6] See Exodus 15 : 6.

the kiss of love,* when one of the goatherds, who had gone outside to see to his flock, came back into the church and reported that someone was calling for help down in the streambed of the Chairimona, someone so far down that he couldn't see him but only hear his voice.

The priest turned round.

'What's going on?'

'I don't know what it could be,' said the goatherd, 'there's shouting down there, someone shouting "where are you, where are you". Should I take a candle and go and see?'

'Yes, go.'

Two or three more young shepherds and goatherds immediately picked up their candles and ran outside.

*　　*　　*

Having spent the whole of Holy Saturday wandering around, Mr Konstantos Z'marohaftis, third deputy etc., finally decided, about two hours before sunset, to go to Livadia, outside town, where his donkey was tethered, in order to untie it, put his little bag on its back, and set out for the church of St John the Baptist, as he had promised Father Dianelos he would. But it was only then that he realized that he had forgotten to 'change' it, that is, to take it to a different grazing, and the unfortunate donkey did not seem as if it had eaten enough when its master came to untie it. Judging from the way it twitched its ears forward, the beast appeared to be hoping that it was finally going to be taken to another grazing place, but *Barba*-Konstantos led it to his house, tied a little bag containing food on its back, spread a threadbare old rug across its saddle, and got on himself, sitting sideways.

He made the sign of the cross and set out. But it did not take him long to realize that the animal, on account of its age and the inadequate amount of food it had eaten, was not very fit for the long journey and would probably wear out its rider. When he got to Upper St John's, not far from town, he got down and decided to lead his donkey on foot. But still the animal did not make good progress, for all the strokes it received on its hindquarters from a slender cane. He resolved finally to part company with it, as it would be more of a burden than a help to him, and to tether it somewhere and leave it to graze. He looked for a suitable spot to tie it up, but there was no good grazing at Upper St John's. He went back down to Lower St John's, but as he couldn't find any good grass there either, he went further in the direction of the place called Deserted Village, and there finally he tied the animal up to the root of a tree, in a fallow field beside a fence. He himself shouldered the bag and the rug, slung a small pruning-hook behind him at his belt, and holding his slender cane, he started off on foot. All these activities had delayed him by a good hour.

'Now,' he said to himself, 'it's time for me to get going, so I won't be out in the dark (though I will in fact be out in the dark), unless I don't go at all; but I mustn't do that, because I gave my word to the priest.' Having said this, he acted on it. Off he set, taking the shortest way, in spite of his sixty years, in spite of his status and character as a municipal official, his short stature, his pale, thin, worn face, and in spite of his unexceptionable, if old and faded, breeches and fez. He came from a family of landed farmers, and all his land was mortgaged: one of those simple souls who are the easy prey and profitable victims of the voracious, calculating knavery of yesterday's shopkeepers, small businessmen and moneylenders, the *nouveaux riches* of today, who ply their trade in towns and villages.

Barba-Konstantos climbed up Vigles and reached K'fandoni's Shack, then descended to the stream bordering Lehouni, where Demos Vlachos's watermill is, and from there he began to ascend the little hill of St Charalambos.

The sun had set when he got to the top, opposite the steep rocky mountain with the small crumbling monastery. Father Azarias the Syncellus,[1] abbot of this isolated monastic community, whose spiritual flock consisted of one ancient ninety-year-old nun and a useless

---

[1] An ecclesiastical office exercised by a priest who assists a bishop.

old lay brother, a widower cast up by life's shipwreck, had come out of the monastery entrance and was watching as the last rays of the sun gilded, for a few more moments, the tops of the mountains eastwards across from him, when he saw *Barba*-Konstantos appearing from behind the last hedge, which lined the way on both sides.

'Well, well, what in the world... It's been ages, Mr Konstantos!'

'Your blessing, Father!' And *Barba*-Konstantos, having looked in the direction of the church of St Charalambos and crossed himself three times, began, panting, to explain how Father Dianelos the Protekdikos had been asked by the shepherds and goatherds to celebrate the Resurrection liturgy at St John the Baptist's, how the priest had asked him, Konstantos, to come and help him, how Father Dianelos had been at St John's since morning without anyone to help him celebrate, how he, Konstantos, had been late in starting out because of his donkey, which couldn't walk all that way, and which every so often needed a fresh grazing patch (and that year God hadn't sent enough rain to ensure ample pasturage at Livadia), and finally, how Mr Konstantos had found himself obliged to decide to go on foot to St John's so as not to let the priest down, since he had given his promise to go and help.

'But it's getting dark now, it will be dark,' said the Hierarch of Charalambos. 'How will you ever get there? It's an hour and a half's walk from here, and the moon won't be up for three hours yet. It'll be black as pitch.'

'What ought I to do?' said *Barba*-Konstantos, who began immediately to waver and hesitate.

'Black as pitch,' repeated Father Azarias, 'the moon doesn't rise for three hours. How will you get there all on your own? The path is difficult, there may be robbers about... you might fall down a cliff and hurt yourself up.'

'What do you advise me to do, Father Abbot?' said *Barba*-Konstantos the deputy, scared.

✻　　✻
✻

Father Azarias thought for a minute, but his face did not express what he was thinking. He may have been saying to himself: 'What am I about, telling him things and scaring him? He doesn't need any second invitation, he was just looking for a good reason to hang around — and have the Resurrection here.'

Aloud he said:

'I don't know what to say, really. You people, you make promises and then you can't even set out in time to go where you've promised to go, and someone else has to wait around, stranded. If something's going to be hard for you to manage you should think about it first, use your judgement, don't make promises. What got into you, a respectable man, to go running round the mountainside, to have Easter at St John's? You could have come here, to St Charalambos's, couldn't you? It's too bad... You could have made yourself useful here, we could have chanted the Resurrection service, you would have attended the liturgy, and there's plenty of fresh cheese afterwards... As it is, I'm stuck with that idle good-for-nothing lay brother Gabriel, and that old bag-of-bones Evpraxia, her blessing be on us. Hardly a soul! The shepherds of course, bless them, come here when the weather is good to pay us a visit — except that this year Father Dianelos has taken most of them to St John's, barring one or two...'

Father Azarias, meanwhile, was assailed by the temptation to keep Mr Konstantos at St Charalambos's, and to leave Father Dianelos without an assistant, in order to pay him back for taking away most of the shepherds who made up his congregation. But his conscience reproached him, and he continued, speaking more emphatically:

'Whatever you decide to do now, you've made a mess of things; but the best thing would be for you to go on. You made a promise, and it's very wrong to leave the priest on his own without an assistant, this day of all days.'

Barba-Konstantos gazed fixedly at the blue and red glass of the sanctuary window, which seemed to draw him like a magnet, while he mentally compared the relative comfort he would enjoy at St Charalambos's, where he would have a warm cell with a good fire and coffee to drink before the Resurrection service, and milk and eggs after the liturgy, and two warm, relaxing sleeps, one before and one after the service, with the wild hillside, the rocks, the lentisk and arbutus scrub at St John the Baptist's, where there was only the open air or an inadequate shelter, and too much dew too early in the day.

'Don't hang around,' repeated Father Azarias. 'Get going or it'll be dark, and the moon won't rise till late.'

'It's dark already,' said *Barba*-Konstantos firmly. 'It's better if I stay here and rest for an hour, until the moon comes up.'

'And then?'

'Then I'll set off by moonlight.'

'But are you sure you'll go?'

'I'll go.'

'Do you know how to get there?'

'That doesn't matter... I may not have been for years, but I remember the way. And if one of my friends comes along, who lives in these parts...'

'Well?'

'I'll ask him to go part of the way with me,' said *Barba*-Konstantos.

'So you don't know how to get there?'

'No, it's not that, but...'

'You're afraid of ghosts, are you?' laughed the priest.

'God forbid — I'm not afraid of anything with God's protection, but it's always better to have company.'

'So be it — I can't turn you out, go into the cell and have a rest, and when the moon rises you can start.'

'Your blessing, Father.'

Barba-Konstantos went into the cell and lay down on the low rug-strewn settle, his feet towards the fireplace, where the embers of a fire were still glowing. He covered himself with a blanket he had brought with him, and in a few minutes he was asleep. Night had already fallen.

*   *   *

The cell in which *Barba*-Konstantos found himself was one of two which the abbot kept in operation, and it was used as a waiting room, a kitchen and a makeshift guest-room. No sooner had the old deputy gone to sleep than the lay brother, Gabriel, came in, wearing a white fez-shaped cap and a faded cotton sash, without a cassock, holding a lantern in his left hand and in his right some sticks for kindling.

'Not another guest!' he grumbled on seeing *Barba*-Konstantos lying there asleep. 'Why do they all have to end up coming here...! Bless us, Fathers.'

He hung up the lantern at the side of the hearth, knelt down, and began to build up the fire, continuing to mutter:

'Where's he sprung from, then! Good luck to them all, I say. Keep washing the glasses so the wine'll keep flowing. Long live the abstainers! Bless us, Fathers.'

He bent down to the hearth and began to blow through a bellows made out of a reed. Then he repeated:

' "Father Abbot, you gave the monks their tasks..." '

He chanted this in the fourth tone, then went on in a normal voice:

'Where that abbot of mine gets them all from, I don't know! Hurry up, Gabriel. Coffees, Gabriel. And it's not as if they ever bring anything either, not even oblation loaves, oh no, they come empty-handed. "You have given the cellarer keys",' (he chanted this, then went on normally): 'now stop it, old Gabriel. As if you were abbot, stop it!'

At that moment *Barba*-Konstantos stirred, half-woke and turned over.

'Hope it'll do him good,' grumbled Father Gabriel. 'The fellow must've been sleepy when he got here. What I'd like to know is, don't people down in the village ever sleep, don't they have houses and bedrooms? Two hours' walk to get here, just to sleep? That's right! Bless us, Fathers.'

He then chanted:

' "He gives scant quantity of wine..." '

But *Barba*-Konstantos, although he had turned over, was unable to go back to sleep; he raised himself on his elbow, turned to look at the monk and asked:

'What's the time, Father?'

'Time? it's night-time...when the stars come out...'

'Isn't the moon up yet?'

'What good's the moon to you, man? The moon won't make you rich.'

'I'm waiting for the moon to rise so I can go, that's why I'm asking,' said *Barba*-Konstantos peaceably.

'Go? go where, in God's name?'

'Haven't any of the people who live round here arrived?'

'I'd thank them to stay away,' said Gabriel. 'They bring one oblation bread and gobble a whole chicken; or they bring a little bit of communion wine and polish off a good gallon...'

∗   ∗
∗

At that moment the voice of the abbot was heard at the door of the cell.

'Ah, so you're awake, mister deputy,' Father Azarias was saying, 'and there was I thinking that Gabriel was talking to himself as usual. It's nice that he's actually talking to a person.'

'H'mm...h'mm...,' Gabriel stifled his mutterings, then added in a whisper: 'Bless us, Fathers!'

'I didn't sleep at all, Father Abbot,' replied *Barba*-Konstantos, who genuinely couldn't remember whether he had slept or not.

'So you didn't hear Gabriel talking to himself?'

'No, I didn't... I suppose I might have slept for as long as it takes to say the Creed.'

'I'm waiting for the shepherds, they'll be here any minute,' said the priest. 'When they come, I'll tell one of them myself to go along with you.'

'Your blessing, Father,' said *Barba*-Konstantos, who heartily wished he didn't have to go anywhere.

'Until they come,' repeated Father Azarias, 'since I go along with the old order of the Church and read from the Acts on Good Saturday evening,[1] let's have a coffee and then, if you would like to, you could come to the church and we'll do the readings together.'

'With pleasure,' said *Barba*-Konstantos.

'Why can't I read the Acts,' grumbled Gabriel, who always got jealous if an extra assistant or chanter came to the little church.

'Gabriel, you'll make more mistakes than there are words in the text. Just make us two good coffees, *idiorrhythmic*[2] ones mind, and bring them to us through there. Come along, Mr Konstantos, let's go into the other cell.'

Barba-Konstantos got up, took his stick, his bag and his rug, and went through to Father Azarias's cell.

*   *   *

The three young herders, holding their candles low in their left hand and shielding the flame from the night breeze with their right, while the moon, sailing high in the sky, was hidden behind clouds, ran in front, and the herder who had reported the news brought up the rear. They went down as far as the stream without hearing any cries, and they began to suspect that the first goatherd had got jumpy and had heard voices which did not exist. He, however, protested that he had not been mistaken, and that he had distinctly heard a voice saying: 'Where are you? where are you?'

---

[1] [Papadiamandis's note] According to the old *typikon*, the Acts of the Apostles are read in the Holy Monasteries on the evening of Holy Saturday before the vigil and the Pashcal Matins.

[2] [Papadiamandis's note] Idiorrhythmic monasteries are monasteries which are not cenobia, that is, they do not follow the ancient cenobitic order. [See also endnote to p. 159.]

Probably in order to reassure himself as well as to convince the others, he started to shout: 'Hey! we're here! Who is it?'

A faint voice answered, but they couldn't make out the words.

Having gone a few steps further, the shepherds called again: 'Hey! who are you? where are you?'

The voice answered more clearly:

'I'm here! come over here ...' And the voice was stifled by a moan.

'Someone must have fallen down into the streambed and hurt himself,' said one of the shepherds, thinking aloud.

And indeed, when they heard the plashing of the water as the little stream flowed alternately over rock and sand at the bottom of its gully, and approached the base of a rock, they saw the body of a man lying beside the murmuring stream which wound its way towards the sea.

It was Mr Konstantos himself, the third deputy.

They shifted him. He was not badly hurt, but he had fallen onto his left side off a rock about the height of a man.

Around ten o'clock European time,* when the moon had risen, he had set off from St Charalambos's, not so much because he wished to as because Father Azarias, an obliging and willing friend when it came to packing off troublesome visitors, had spoken to one of the villagers who had arrived at the monastery and insisted that he accompany *Barba*-Konstantos, who was setting out to go, as he had promised, to St John's.

The villager, with an eagerness less pronounced than Father Azarias's but greater nevertheless than that of *Barba*-Konstantos, accompanied the deputy a considerable part of the way, as far as Kambia, to the summit of the hill he would have to descend in order to get to the little church of the Baptist; and there, having pointed out the exact way he should take, he wished him a good Resurrection and left him on his own.

Barba-Konstantos started by going a good way along the main path, which was clearly visible in the moonlight. His sole company were the bushes to the right and left of the path, the trees which assumed strange forms or cast shadows in which the eye frequently discerned phantoms and the motionless figures of men, the rocks which, as he neared the northern coast, increased in number and took the place of the trees, the faint chirping of a few birds hidden in the thickets, the sound of the breeze in the branches and the treetops, and the mysterious rustling of leaves caused by unknown night creatures or little currents of air, lowly existences hidden in the dark and the loneliness.

But when he arrived at a place where the way divided into two little paths, one going eastwards and the other in a north-westerly direction, he couldn't decide which path to take. Even when a man is native to a place, if he only goes on a relatively long excursion as an exception, say once every two or three years, he always hesitates at the small places, especially when the landscape is rather wild and he himself does not own any fields thereabouts. The paths alter from one year to the next; often the old ways are ploughed up and cultivated and are no longer trodden, owing to the greed of the small peasant farmer, who encloses half an acre or so more land along with his own by placing the fence a couple of yards further out. Occasionally the opposite happens: the uncontested olive grove belonging to a well-known owner is walked over and becomes a public footpath for the convenience of the passers-by. At other times the herdsmen and their goats open new pathways, or they may abandon some old and well-worn footpath and leave it to be cultivated.

After hesitating for a long time, *Barba*-Konstantos finally decided in favour of the north-west fork, and descended rapidly to the Chairimona stream. But it's impossible to walk along it, unless you are a boy of twelve looking for crabs during the day. Mr Konstantos was sixty, it was night, and he was not looking for crabs. The stream which rises from the Chairimona source joins the stream of Panayia Doman further down and becomes a river which descends steeply to the sea, its bed a series of rocks and small waterfalls. At some point, when the moon above him had gone behind a cloud, unable to see where he was going, he stumbled, slipped off a rock and fell, landing with his head and side on the sand and his feet in the water. He was slightly hurt and he was in pain, more probably from the jolt and from fright than from the injury. Fortunately, he had seen shortly beforehand, from higher up on a large overhanging rock, the light from the little church, where the Resurrection office had been chanted in its entirety, and had realized that he was not far from St John's. Dizzy from the fall, he started calling with what strength remained to him: 'Where are you? where are you?'; and this was the call that had come to the ears of the first goatherd, when he had gone outside the church for a moment to see to his goats.

*   *   *

Kyr-Konstantos staggered to his feet, followed the goatherds, reached the chapel just as the priest had begun the ritual of the Paschal kiss, bowed to the icons and took his place in the choir stall. He chanted throughout the liturgy, notwithstanding his fall and the pain he was feeling.

Outside, under the light of the moon, to the right of the church, a good fire was blazing, and *Barba*-Dimitris Kamboyannis, the shepherd who came from near the little town, had already spitted a lamb and was roasting it. Sitting next to him with his back against the church wall, ready to give him a hand, was a little fellow from town called Yannis Boukosis; how and when he came to be there nobody knew. *Barba*-Dimitris Kamboyannis — yellow sash, shaved beard, curled moustachios — had left his knife in its sheath lying between the fire and the wall, and for some time now Yannis Boukosis had been casting alternate glances at the knife and the roast that was colouring over the fire. Opposite, at the root of a lentisk shrub, stood a large eight-litre flask. To judge from the way it had been propped against a branch of the shrub it was full of wine, a mixture of muscat and red. The reddening roast smoked and sizzled over the fire, the flask, like a mother hen summoning her chicks under her wings, seemed to be summoning the shepherds to revel in its fumes, ready to cluck and fluff up at the touch of a hand, at the merest approach of lips to its cork.

Two villagers were standing a few paces away from the roasting lamb, the flask and the lentisk shrub, engaged in animated conversation. They were using the occasion to argue about a one-acre field which they had been fighting over for years.

Facing them to the south, on the stony slope, lying between five rocks, three paths and a cliff, was the disputed field. One of the villagers was gesturing in that direction, and asserting that the boundary of his field was precisely marked by the third rock on the right.

'I inherited it from my granddad,' he was saying; 'ask Yannis Psarodimenas, who's been our neighbour for thirty years now.'

'The boundary is in the centre between the second and third rocks, where there's a dip in the ground,' maintained the other villager. 'You can still see where the old border ditch used to be.'

'It's marked by that great big rock,' objected the other, 'so why should I go looking for an old ditch as a boundary?'

Barba-Dimitris Kamboyannis started turning the spit with its roast more absent-mindedly, his attention increasingly absorbed by the two villagers and their dispute.

Yannis Boukosis slowly picked up the knife, drew it from its sheath, dextrously sliced off a piece from the side of the animal, which had practically stopped rotating, and wolfed it down voraciously.

Barba-Dimitris didn't even notice the theft of the meat or the little fellow's greed. He continued to watch the disputants.

'It's down clearly in the title-deeds,' the first one was saying. 'I took it to Father Lefteris, who can read the old writing, and he read it over to me lots of times.'

'Don't talk to me about title-deeds,' returned the second. 'If you want you can go to *Barba*-Anagnostis Ayelastos and he'll fix you up with as many fake title-deeds as you like.'

All of Dimitris Kamboyannis's attention was focused on the argument between the two peasants. Yannis Boukosis took up the knife again, which he had left out of its sheath, cut a second and bigger piece off the half-roasted lamb, and swallowed it down in one.

The dispute between the two villagers continued, and Kamboyannis followed it with undiminished attention. Boukosis, who understood the secret language of the flask with which it called its friends to it as the mother hen calls her chicks, took one step with his right leg at a right angle, then a second step with his left knee on the ground, got down on all fours, approached the lentisk shrub, and taking up the big flask filled with wine he put it to his lips and took a long swig without stopping to breathe.

Then, being by nature reasonable and realizing that if he made a third attempt on the roast he might finally be caught in the act, he returned to his place by the church wall, a little further away from the fire, sat down, and, having well and truly broken his fast, yet managed to look as innocent as if he hadn't.

* * *

After the priest had come out, the last to leave the church when the liturgy was over, and the table had been spread in the church porch (dawn was just beginning to break), Dimitris Kamboyannis started to cut up the roast. He noticed that there was a piece missing from its flank, but pretended not to understand, and turning to Yannis Boukosis he said:

'Look...now that's odd...! Funny that this lamb should be born mutilated, isn't it, Yannis, my boy?'

He continued calmly to cut up the roast, then said again:

'There's been a lot of very odd signs and wonders over the last years... Fancy me bringing along a lamb mutilated from birth and not noticing. Oh well, God be praised.'

Yannis Boukosis said not a word. But at the last minute, when the roast was being placed on the table, *Barba*-Dimitris skilfully concealed the two pitchers of water which were still full, and produced two empty ones for the table, saying that unfortunately he had forgotten to send for water to the Chairimona spring, and so someone would have to go now.

'The lot falls to you, Yannis my boy,' he said, turning to Boukosis. 'Off you go and fill the two pitchers — you'll have the priest's blessing, and we'll wait for you, we won't start to eat. Take a lighted candle with you to see where you're going, and walk steadily and carefully — don't break the pitchers, like in the song, and make us go without water.'

Yannis Boukosis would have liked to refuse, but he didn't dare. He shouldered the two pitchers and set off for the Chairimona spring, which was about two miles distant and which trickled as slowly as tears from exhausted eyes. It would take him a good hour to go, fill the pitchers and come back.

As soon as he had left, *Barba*-Dimitris Kamboyannis brought out the two full pitchers, and since the priest didn't understand what was going on, he explained:

'I had water, but I wanted to punish the rascal ... Fancy him bringing me bad luck, this day of all days, cutting bits off the roast while I was roasting it, and me not noticing a thing!'

       *   *

        *

When Yannis Boukosis returned from the Chairimona spring with the two pitchers, day had broken, the roast had been devoured, and only the discreet charity of Aunt Mathino, the woman of suspect piety, and Aunt Syraino, always in the front line at feasts and festivals, had set aside a few pieces of lamb for the famished man to eat in celebration of Easter Day.

[1893]

Translated by Liadain Sherrard

THE LADY'S HOUSE

THERE WAS NO BUSIER STREET in the entire village. It was impossible not to pass along it if you were making your way to the upper parish or going down to the lower one. A steep stone-flagged road all the way up from Stamatrizaina's house to the church of the Virgin, known as the Salonikia.* A thousand steps, puffing and blowing at each step. You would get out of breath on the way up, you would slip and slide on the way down.

No sooner had you set off down the flagged roadway, leaving behind Kapsospyros's store, Kaftanis's house, and Old Pagouris's dilapidated cottage with its walled yard, you would find yourself in front of the house of Hatzi-Pantelis, its courtyard fence perched on the edge of the cliff. A vast precipice gaped below, sheer and dizzying, dotted here and there by a few creeping shrubs which in the darkness of that night appeared like villains groping and clambering their way up, or like hobgoblins lying in wait for the right moment to break into the houses down through the chimneys.* The splashing of waves could be heard faintly at the foot of the cliff, and the north wind, the omnipotent, snow-capped king of winter, which had been blowing tirelessly from the day before yesterday, yet calm that evening, rolled some last remaining waves towards the small southerly harbour.

On the other side of the road, to the left as you went up, next to Old Pagouris's cottage and facing the house of Hatzi-Pantelis, rose a half-finished building. Only the four walls of the ground floor had been built, the timbers of the upper store stood bare and gaping, the roof was falling in, and the plaster was grey and crumbling. In short, desolation, wind and rain had turned it into rack and ruin.

292

The children, as many as went down from one school at noon or went up from the other in the evening, eager to dump their books at home, grab a piece of bread from the pantry and run at full tilt to play by the shore, would shower it with stones. In this way they would take revenge by day for all the terror it caused them at night whenever they happened to pass by. The priests, when they returned as one body on the eve of Epiphany from the house of the mayor, with their crosses and sprays of basil, blessing homes, roads, and stores, and driving away the hobgoblins, forgot to sprinkle even a drop of holy water also on this unfortunate, abandoned house,* which had given no joy to its owner, who had built it, and had not been blessed to delight in its mistress. It was to be expected, then, that such a house should end up as the dwelling-place of ghosts, possibly the refuge of vampires, perhaps even the den and haunt of the tyrants of that hour, the hobgoblins.

✳   ✳   ✳

It had not been blessed to delight in its mistress. Captain Yiannakos Syrmais, a gallant man of sentiment, a *bon vivant* if ever there was one among his contemporaries, had once fallen in love with Lady Annika at Stavrodromi.[1] She was pretty and tall and had golden hair, a fair complexion, the finest features, and when she looked at you it touched a chord in your heart. The Captain got engaged in Constantinople and sailed back to his native island, where he gave instructions to have that pretty little house built, with an unusually elegant design by the standards of the small town. He had intended on his first voyage to bring furniture from Venice with which to deck the newly-constructed house and make it worthy of the refined Lady whom he planned to fetch from Constantinople. But the house was fated not to be completed, and the Lady was fated not to come. Eight months after their engagement, she died of consumption at Stavrodromi, and the house remained unfinished, desolate and joyless, on the

---

[1] The neighbourhood Stavrodromi (meaning crossroads), also known as Pera, was in the European quarter of Istanbul.

uphill stone-flagged road by the steep cliff. Like an invisible inscription on the façade of the crumbling edifice, its name 'The Lady's House' remained as an elusive and tragic irony concerning its fate.

> *Oh, graves of Ferik-köy and cypress trees above,*
> *I'm full of longing and weep, for I lost my love.*

✻   ✻   ✻

That evening, Christmas Eve of the year 185_, two children were walking briskly down the flag-stoned slope. Their feet, unaccustomed to the wooden shoes that they had put on perhaps specially for that night, were plopping loudly on the stones. Both had light canes. One of them held a lantern in his other hand. It was about seven o' clock, on a starry and chilly night. An ice-cold wind was furiously blowing from the snowy mountains, making the tightly closed windows and the securely latched and bolted doors groan under its keen breath. The two children were arguing, like two true friends.

'But I saw him give you a twenty-five-lepta piece, Angelis,' said the one.

'No, I swear,' said the other, 'he gave me a fiver; here it is.' And he pointed to the five-lepta coin between his fingers.

'No,' insisted the first one, who was holding the lantern. 'I saw it, I did, it was a twenty-fiver. You can't fool me.'

'No, honest to God, Nassos, it was a fiver, I'm telling you.'

'Let me search you!'

'You'll drop the lantern.'

At once Nassos put the lantern on the ground and was getting ready to search Angelis. Since they didn't trust each other (they were ten years old), they had agreed that as soon as they came out of each house where they had sung the Christmas carols, they would divide up the profit fiver by fiver straight away, so that neither of them would be banker during their joint venture. But this last time Nassos did suspect Angelis.

In the heat of their quarrel, they failed to notice that they had already reached the narrow lane that led to the upper quarter, and that they were now beside the Lady's house, from where ghosts emerged. This is where they had stopped and Nassos had started searching Angelis.

While his friend was searching the pockets of his trousers, Angelis remained indifferent, but as soon as Nassos's hand began to grope up towards his chest, he grabbed his waistcoat on the left side and squeezed it with all his might, preventing the hand of his friend from reaching up there.

'You won't let me search you?'

'Let go of me! I haven't got anything.'

'You're a liar!'

Angelis raised a threatening hand. 'You're a liar and a thief!'

There was the sound of a light smack, and at the same time the voice of a strange being, with dark complexion and disheveled hair and odd rags for clothes, rang out:

'What are you two fighting about?'

The two children let out a strangled cry in unison and attempted to flee, leaving the lantern on the ground. But the strange being kicked over the lantern, which was extinguished at once, and with his two hands grabbed the trembling children by their arms.

'Who's got the cash-box?'

The children were trying to wriggle free.

'Don't be frightened, I'm not going to eat you. Just give me your money, so you won't argue and come to grief. A good thing I saved you from that.'

He searched the two children's pockets, dragging them at the same time towards the ground floor doorway of the crumbling house, from which this strange being had to all appearances emerged. There he immobilized Nassos behind the door, barricading the opening with his own body, and searched Angelis at his ease. He found fifteen- or twenty-five- and ten-lepta coins in the child's pockets. Afterwards he searched Nassos and found about the same amount in his pockets too. Then he sent the two children off.

'Away you go now, and don't be frightened. And don't get into a fight next time.'

* * *

Yannis Paloukas didn't have the where-withal to get drunk and celebrate Christmas that year. More often than not he was out of work, carrying out odd jobs from time to time, now lugging jars of water to various houses, now assisting those tending the vegetable gardens, threshing or working at the oil-presses, sometimes helping the fishermen to haul the endlessly long draught-net on to the wide sandy shore. But it had not been enough that year. What was he to do? How could he provide for such a feast day? What scheme had he come up with?

The Lady's House, which the children of the little town feared and the priests failed to bless when, crosses in hand, they were going down from the upper quarter, was a suitable spot to hide in and pass oneself off as a hobgoblin. The time of year called for it, indeed it was because of the time of year that Paloukas would do it. All the children from the lower parish, that is to say two thirds of the village children, would walk by there on their return from the upper parish, when their pockets would be filled with coins enough. Paloukas didn't think twice.

He took an old iron frying-pan, blackened his whole face with its soot — making Carnival-time come two months earlier just for him — and donned some old rags that he had somehow obtained. As soon as night came, he took off and as quietly as possible unnailed the ancient boards that crosswise formed a makeshift barrier to the ground floor of the Lady's deserted house, and sneaked in. An hour later, the first pair of carolling children, Nassos and Angelis, walked down the stone-flagged road. We've already seen how conveniently things turned out for Paloukas, and how in fact he managed to play the peacemaker between the quarrelling children.

After Nassos and Angelis, feeling that the ground was being taken from under their feet, took flight, more children came by, and then some more. Paloukas would hear in the distance the clatter of their footsteps, their cheerful voices, and would whisper:

'Here's another pair coming.'

The last pair that came by consisted of Stamos and Argyris, two well-behaved boys. They weren't quarrelling, but were planning out loud what they would do with the money that they had collected that evening.

'Let's also have an adze made.'

'Let's cut down a poplar.'

'Let's buy some linden wood to build a ship.'

'Let's cut wood for the keel and the ribs out of Albanis's pine-tree.'

'You'll be the carpenter, I'll be the master-builder.'

'Hey!'

Suddenly a voice was heard.

'Greetings to our master craftsmen!'

Paloukas had charged for the third or fourth time out of his den. Stamos and Argyris let out a choked scream and tried to flee, but Paloukas applied his well-tried method and robbed them.

'Is there another pair?' he asked then.

The children stared at him with glassy eyes, petrified with terror. But Stamos, who was a sharp twelve-year-old, had in the meantime realized that he was not facing a ghost. His fear abated somewhat, and he conveyed some courage to Argyris too.

The strange man repeated his unintelligible question:

'Is there another pair?'

'What "pair"?' Stamos managed to stammer.

'Are there more children coming down from the upper neighbourhood?'

'I don't know,' said Stamos.

This time around, Paloukas had neglected to put out the lantern, because his experience so far had convinced him that the children would not realize who he was. But giving him a hard look, Stamos was turning over in his mind that it was someone he knew and was not far off from recognizing him.

'Come on, tell me, is there another pair?' insisted Paloukas.

'We don't know,' Stamos repeated.

In the end, Paloukas let the children go.

*　*　*

After ten minutes had gone by, an abundant battery of stones start-ed beating on the roof, the timberwork and beams of the upper floor of the deserted house. Many stones falling between the beams and others passing through the doorway thudded on the ground inside. An army of children had started out from the forecourt of the Three Hierarchs church, some three or four hundred paces away, and they were carrying out a fierce assault on the hobgoblin's hide-out.

The first of the robbed children, Nassos and Angelis, having ar-rived out of breath at the small square in front of the church and no longer having anything to quarrel about, had been reconciled. After the friendliest conversation and with one accord, they rea-soned that the strange being that had taken their money, since it took away neither their voices nor their minds, could not have been a ghost or a vampire, and further, since it had not tried to devour them, it could not have been a hobgoblin either. What else could it have been then? It must, surely, have been a man.

It was not before long that the second pair of children arrived, then the third and the fourth. All the similarly afflicted children did not waste much time in reaching a consensus. Finally Stamos who along with Argyris joined them last, put a motion to carry out a tac-tical nocturnal assault on the house, which they all voted to do.

At that very moment, Paloukas was hesitating. He had already decided to withdraw, since he had amassed enough booty, as much as was needed to get drunk all through Christmas and the after-feast the next day, extending even to St Stephen's the day after that. He was about to depart when the first thick hailstorm of stones fell.

'Here's a pair!' shouted Stamos vengefully.

'Here's a pair!' repeated the children in chorus.

Had Paloukas decided to leave five seconds earlier, he would already have been out of range. Alas, now it was too late. He determined to grab a plank and, using it both as a sword and a shield, to execute a sortie directly through the enemy ranks. But a second, even fiercer, hail of stones forced him to retreat with two wounds on his shin and arm.

'Here's another pair!' shouted Stamos relentlessly.

'Here's another pair!' howled the children.

Paloukas clung to the innermost corner of the ground floor, his back against the wall, crouching under a ceiling beam that ran close to the stonework. But even there a large stone ricocheted off the wall and hit him with diminished force on the shoulder.

'Look at that unlucky rebound!' Paloukas muttered with an unwitting smile.

Fortunately for him, the enemy did not resolve to come up to the ground floor doorway. A remnant of fear still persisted, it seems, in the depths of their boyish boldness. Finally, as the battle was prolonged, Paloukas, after prudent reflection, decided to climb up the wall — he knew where the holes left from the scaffolding and timberwork of the construction were — stepping from hole to hole. He managed it swiftly, and after he reached the first floor, invisible to the enemy behind a vestige of some wattling, he decisively jumped over to the other side into the courtyard of Old Pagouris's. It was only twice his height, not more, for the ground inside the courtyard was two or three feet higher. Paloukas fell heavily, hurt his knee, toppled over, rose up, checked his limbs to make sure he hadn't fractured any bones, then took flight, running towards the opposite side of the courtyard which he knew was enclosed only by a low fence and offered access to the courtyard of a neighbouring house.

The thud of his fall resounded beyond the wall of the courtyard. Stamos shouted 'Charge!', and trying the bolt of the courtyard gate found it was unlocked. He stormed in first, followed by the rest of the children.

Paloukas's cry was accompanied, besides the thud of his fall, by an additional sound, the clinking of metal, as coins dropped from

his pocket. He did not turn back to pick them up. Angelis, one of
the children, had heard the metallic jingle quite clearly, and had listened very intently for the exact spot to where the coins had rolled.
Then while the rest of the children pursued the fleeing Paloukas,
hurling stones and yelling: 'Here's another pair! Here's another
pair!', he bent and groping around started to collect the coins by
the handful.

*　*　*

The creak of a window being opened sounded from Old Pagouris's
small cottage. On hearing the incomprehensible assault that had
taken place inside his courtyard that night, Pagouris had opened his
window and was asking, startledly:

'What is it? What's going on? Who's there? Who are you? Hey,
don't you hear?'

In the meantime, Angelis had already picked up as many coins
as he could find and retreated through the southern gate, while beyond the northern fence the other children in vain were pursuing
the now invisible Paloukas, repeating again and again:

'Here's another pair! Here's another pair!'

[1893]

Translated by Pavlos Sfyroeras and Maria Hatjigeorgiou

ENDNOTES

HANDMAIDEN

4   Bread ovens were fired by burning branches of wood in them, and before the bread was put in the oven, the ashes had to be raked to one side and the floor of the oven cleaned with a wet cloth. The fairy tale of the Forty Dragons relates how their mother, a giant with enormous breasts, used them to swab the oven floor. Tales of giantesses with such huge breasts that they could be flipped over their shoulders are common. Some of them, such as the one relating the exploits of 'Monovyza', derive from ancient memories of the single-breasted Amazons.

7   Graios (or Graigos, as it is more commonly known) is the north-easterly not the north-westerly wind, but the original Greek text is being followed in the translation.

8   The halcyon, a bird identified with the kingfisher, was fabled in ancient times to breed in a nest on the sea at about the time of the winter solstice and magically calm the waves while the eggs were being incubated — hence halcyon days.

THE GLEANER

16   The Forty Liturgies (*Sarandalítourgo*) take place during Advent, the forty days preceding Christmas, when the priest celebrates a liturgy every day in which he commemorates the names of the deceased. It is to be distinguished from the Forty Days (*Sarandaímero*), the memorial service for the dead, which is sung on the fortieth day after his or her falling asleep in the Lord.

16 It is interesting to note that the money lender in this story bears a name charged with monetary meaning, for Margaritis means 'pearl'. This character must be seen as a counterpart to Master Argyros Sirmatenios, the pawnbroker in 'Civilization in the Village' (see pp. 81–2), who is described as tall and pale, an embodiment of the coldness of 'silver', which is the meaning of his first name; his surname, Sirmatenios, describes a garment made of silver or golden thread, from *sírma*, a metal thread. Both these loansharks (Argyros is lending at the usurious rate of eighty per cent) display a passion for snuff, the cheapest of indulgences.

A VILLAGE EASTER

21 There are four fasting periods during the liturgical year which begins on 1st September: Advent, preceding Christmas, which lasts forty days; Great Lent, preceding Easter, which lasts six weeks; the Fast of the Holy Apostles, beginning on the moveable feast of All Saints and ending on 29th June; and the Fast of the Dormition of the Holy Theotokos, from 1st to 15th August. These fasts reflect the ascetical practices of the Orthodox Church implying a restraint from the utilitarian exploitation of the natural world and its God-given resources through abstention, on the material level, from animal foods — meat, eggs and dairy products — and also from fish, wine and oil on other days, coupled with spiritual preparation and contemplation, prayer and confession of sins.

23 On the eve of Easter Sunday the faithful congregate at church for the celebration of the service of the Resurrection which commences with a short vigil service, the *Pannychís*, and the chanting of the canon 'On the wave of the sea'. When the canon is completed all the lamps and candles in the church are extinguished and silence reigns. Then the Royal Doors to the sanctuary are opened from within and the priest emerges, clad in white robes and holding in his left hand the Gospel and in his right the burning paschal candle, chanting the words, 'Come, and receive the light from the inextinguishable light, and glorify Christ who has risen from the dead.' The faithful rush to ignite their candles from the light offered by the priest, then all

file outside, following the priest, for the reading of the Resurrection Gospel and the continuation of matins.

27 In normal Orthodox liturgical practice, the priest first partakes of communion at the altar, and then turns to the faithful and calls them to come and receive the Holy Gifts, which he dispenses to each from the chalice with a spoon. At the end of the liturgy the priest carries the liturgical vessels to the oblation table and there consumes from the chalice whatever is remaining of the Holy Gifts and recites the concluding prayers of thanksgiving.

27 On Easter Sunday, the vespers of the Second Resurrection, so called because the Resurrection gospel is read again in several languages to reflect its universal message, is celebrated. It is also known as the Vespers of Love because the kiss of love is exchanged between brethren amidst joyous exclamations of 'Christ is risen!' In Papadiamandis's time it was sung earlier than a normal vesperal service, at around noon, to allow the Easter day festivities to continue uninterrupted. This service is especially attended by children wearing bright garments and holding their decorated Easter candles.

28 At a baptism it is the godparent who represents the Church and brings the child within its fold, which also includes everything within the natural world. This reality is epitomized by the godparent's offerings of oil (the 'oil of gladness') with which he or she anoints the child during the sacrament of baptism, the cross, the pristine white clothes in which the child will be dressed after the sacrament, and the offerings of bread and wine for the subsequent liturgy when the child will receive its first communion. Traditionally, the godparent will also be the best man (*koumbáros*) or woman (*koumbára*) at their godchild's wedding when they will crown the couple with wreaths. In ancient Greece the victors of athletic competitions received crowns of victory, wreaths made of olive branches; in a Christian context the martyrs, athletes fighting for the faith, received their crowns of martyrdom from God. The crowns received by the married couple were traditionally made from the grapevine, recalling the blood

of Christ, an understanding reinforced by the fact the couple drink
from a cup of wine — the cup of salvation — immediately after
their crowning.

29 The correct rendering of the 'Christ is risen' (*Christós Anésti*) *tropárion* is:

> *Christ is risen from the dead*
> *trampling down death by death*
> *and upon those in the tombs*
> *bestowing life.*

29 A hymn sung in the service of Supplication to the Theotokos; the
full *tropárion* is:

> *Dumb are the lips of the impious*
> *who are not venerating your holy icon, the* Hodegétria,
> *the one painted by the Apostle Luke,*
> *the most venerable.*

The *Hodegétria*, meaning the one who leads the way, was a famous
icon at Constantinople attributed to the Apostle Luke. It subsequently became a 'type' much copied, especially in Russia.

29 The *kléphtiko* dance takes its name from the 'klephts', or robbers,
the legendary marauding bands of resistance fighters who were active during the Ottoman domination of Greece, living in the mountains and plundering village communities. The *syrtó* and the *kamára*
are traditional cyclical dances that commemorate events which
have marked the life of the community. The week following Easter
Sunday, called *Diakainísimos* — 'Renewal' or 'Bright Week' — a festive week marking the eighth day of the new Creation, the new life
that Christ brought into the fallen world by His Resurrection, is celebrated with daily liturgies in the chapels scattered throughout the
countryside followed by communal feasting, singing and dancing.

BLACK SCARF ROCK

33 This boundless, magnificent garden formed by the deep furrows of
the waves, bordered by the caves and rocks of the sea, its surface
mirroring the dome of heaven, is no ordinary garden. Just as

Yannios's garden-plot, softly caressed by the sea-breezes which crease it into seductive, innumerable lines, as on the forehead of some king's lovely bride displaying a capricious temper, so the liquid garden of the sea, the unpredictable sea, displays a childish temper and obstinacy, at times furious and at other times seductive. The sea *is* the garden, and Yannios's donkey, plunging 'its feet among the cool petals which waved and rustled around its hooves', is no ordinary donkey but a little boat: when he tethers it to a post, he is actually securing it in some spot of the harbour, and when he untethers it he is taking it into the sea in order to harvest his 'vegetables', 'cauliflowers and melons', 'the fruits of his labour', *fruits de mer*, as the gastronomically-informed French would have it.

Homer is invoked from the beginning of the story with his comparison of the waves of the sea with the waves of undulating wheat in an unharvested field. Elsewhere Homer has compared the foamy waves of the sea with a flock of little white sheep. Although not of the same etymology, the affinity between *skáros*, the sleeping quarters for a flock of sheep, and *skarí*, the name usually given to a large boat, evokes in modern Greek a common homophonic derivation between terms referring to the worlds of both land and sea. A similar analogy can be seen between *skáfos* (skiff) and *skafí* (wash-tub), confirming this ancient association where the lines between the two elements are blurred. This correspondence can also be seen in Homer's 'wine-dark sea' (*oinops pontos*), and in the representations on Attic vases of Dionysos sailing on a boat whose mast is a grape-covered vine seemingly growing out of the ship's hull. The land enters into the sea and the sea into the land. Papadiamandis takes this correspondence one step further by turning the sea *into* the land. In a horizontal sense, the expanse of the sea is the garden and in a vertical sense the dome of heaven is mirrored in the sea; the sun at the end of its laborious course plunges through this dome to rest at the bottom of the sea, and the moon grows ever more radiant over it and the distant light of the Pleiades sparkle in its unexplored depths.

This is an ancient, primeval garden that dates 'from the beginning, from the creation of the world', and contrary to the assertion of Bacon according to whom nature is an open book in which everyone can read the history of creation, this primeval Homeric garden is 'an open book written in hieroglyphic characters' that 'you cannot read . . . unless you are a seer'. The antiquity of the garden is further emphasized by the hieroglyphic characters in which it is described as well as the cryptic sayings of Homer, who is then conjured again because those 'hieroglyphs', literally 'sacred engravings', are compared with the ' "emblems of sorrow", the cracked lines engraved on the naked skulls of the dead, of which it is said that although they indicate the fate of the dead person, you cannot read them unless you are a seer . . . and anyhow it is too late then, since the dead man's life is over.' Unless this passage is read in an eschatological way it is totally devoid of meaning. How can anyone read the engravings on the skull while the person is alive? The engravings, like the hieroglyphic characters, have no useful purpose since they reveal the fate of the dead person *post mortem*, when nothing can be done about their life. It is the same with the scriptural garden. Death cannot be read in the garden of Eden which is full of life. But in the fallen garden, which is marked by death, the remnants of this once living garden can be read eschatologically, for the emblems of sorrow are there for all to see and interpret.

Yannios's hardships have revealed to him the meaning of exile from the living garden; the garden that he finds in the sea is but a vestige of the original garden of life; it is a garden that is harvested with toil, with the sweat of one's brow, that yields its once living fruits as dead 'vegetables' — all the sea-urchins, oysters, octopuses — as a reminder that in the fallen garden it is necessary to consume dead matter in order to live. And it is this garden which is rife with the 'emblems of sorrow' for the seer who knows how to decipher their meaning, one which is inhabited and epitomized by the solitary, sorrowful figure of a woman, her head covered with the black scarf of mourning, whose body is coated with weeds and scales as if with a coat of skin (see Genesis 3 : 21), the 'oyster-covered bride with shells for eyes', who becomes unmarried Yannios's 'unbedded' companion, the once living garden that will threaten to engulf the life of a drowning child and spew it out as dead matter. It is for all these reasons that the book, albeit open, retains its eschatological meaning hidden within its sacred engravings, and must be read as signs of the Kingdom of God, of our exile from this Kingdom which will be given back to us. For the unfortunate Yannios, who has suffered so much in this exile from the lost garden, the meaning of the earthly garden has already been revealed as in 'a book written in shining capital letters, clear, intelligible...'.

36 St Mary of Egypt, who lived in the fifth century, in her youth led a dissolute life but after an encounter with the living God, when trying to enter the church of the Holy Sepulchre in Jerusalem, she repented and fled to the desert where she lived for forty years in complete isolation. She received holy communion, shortly before her death, after being discovered by St Zossimas.

39 The fact that Papadiamandis associates the 'Great Idea', which had promoted the unification of all Greeks living under Turkish rule, with the intention of recovering the lands lost to the Ottomans during the previous centuries and re-establishing the centre of the political, religious and cultural life of modern Greece in the old capital of medieval Hellenism, Constantinople, with the theme of the ancient, primeval garden is extremely revealing of his reading of contemporary political events. As early as 1891, the year that this story was written, thirty years before the Asia Minor disaster that was the eventual catastrophic consequence of this tragic ideology, Papadiamandis had foreseen its utopian nature. He is weaving here, in the fabric of the theme of this bankrupt dream condemned to extinction, the loss of the two boats of Yannios, which bear the symbolic names of *Golden Horn* and *Saint Sophia*, the political and religious symbols of the messianic revival of Byzantine Hellenism. What is interesting to note is that the two boats have been lost in the garden and they are relics of Yannios's past, when he was living under the spell of the powerful illusions generated by great ideas, and before he realized the true nature of the garden, that is, before beginning to read the book intelligibly and clearly. If one sees in them two distinct 'emblems of sorrow' of contemporary Hellenism, written on the skull of its once living but now dead organism, the introduction of this theme of the 'Great Idea' acquires a singular

meaning for Yannios, who also knows how to read the engravings on the skull of an unrecoverable form of Hellenism, that of its revival by the shores of the Bosphorus.

These symbolic names and the eschatological ideas that they evoke, ideas which it was believed would find their justification when the liturgy held in St Sophia that was interrupted at the fall of Constantinople would be concluded and the city would again become Christian, are now associated with the theme of exile and the garden. They are indicative of Papadiamandis's grasp of the political realities of modern Greece. He transposes them into an eschatological reality, deprived as they are of any meaningful political context for the present times, because he does not share in the common conviction that the liturgy will be completed in this world.

POOR SAINT

48   This story recreates some of the principal characteristics which we find in the new Martyrologies, the first of which was compiled by St Nicodemos the Hagiorite under the title of *Néon Martyrológion*, and published in Venice in 1799. These are lives of recent saints recording from various popular sources the incidents which have led to their martyrdom at the hands of heterodox oppressors. As the story unfolds we get a glimpse how the new *Synaxária* (collections of the lives of saints) came into being as documents reflecting the collective memory of these events, put into writing by someone who assembled the different elements of the story from various narrators, and also from the church services that were composed in the martyrs' honour. Due to the particular circumstances of their martyrdom, the memory of a number of saints was dimly preserved in the consciousness of the country folk and there was no liturgy of the type known as *asmatikí akolouthía*, referring to the office of a feast, composed to honour their memory. This gave rise to the popular saying '*Phtochós ághios litourgía den échei*', meaning 'there is no liturgy offered for a poor saint'. 'Poor' must not be understood in this instance in the sense of material poverty: there can be neither rich nor poor, wealthy or pauper saints. In Greek,

'poor' and 'poverty' are frequently interpreted in an euphemistic as well as in a spiritual sense, and both terms are understood as virtues denoting dignity and a way of being marked by an un-compromised moral stand with regard to fair play, honesty, and respect towards others. In the case of the well-known St Nicholas, the Church commemorates him in a hymn with the following words: '...having obtained through his humility the highest things and through his poverty all things rich...'. It is very prob-able that Papadiamandis drew his inspiration for his story from the popular saying and then proceeded to provide a *synaxári*, a *vita sancti*, for the unknown saint, thus contributing in his own way to the preservation of his memory by rehabilitating him in the local *martyrológion*; the author is not simply offering us a histor-ical tale but also an example of the way in which the *Synaxária* were composed. For similarities in this genre, see Norman Russell, 'Neomartyrs of the Greek Calendar', *Sobornost*, 5/1 (1983), pp. 36–62.

48 Since antiquity the main settlements on islands were built on moun-tain-tops as such places could be best defended from attack by pirates. Following the Greek War of Independence and the subse-quent creation of the modern Greek state, many of these tradition-al settlements were abandoned and people built their new homes round coastal harbours to facilitate communication and commerce. These older settlements usually bore the name of Kastro, Palaio-kastro, Kastelli, Chora and Palaiochora.

51 The year 1872, when Papadiamandis says that the tale of the Poor Saint was related to him, was the year that he visited Mount Athos. The second edition of St Nicodemos's collection of the lives of the new martyrs was published in 1856, and one may safely conclude that the genre was then thriving on the Holy Mountain both in its oral and written forms.

52 Mr Anagnostis is always designated as a *kollígas* in the text, from the Latin *collega* meaning associate; in this form of partnership Mr Anag-nostis provides the land on which the poor shepherd grazes his goats.

CIVILIZATION IN THE VILLAGE

67 The icon stand (*iconostási*) is composed of a few icons, set on a shelf or in a small glass-fronted cupboard or simply hanging from the wall, usually of saints honoured by the household whose names are borne by the members of that family and which, in a similar way to the icons, are passed on from one generation to the next. It is set up in the corner of a room, usually in the east corner (the same orientation as the sanctuary of a church), and an oil-lamp (*kandíli*) that is kept burning at all times, lit from the light brought home from the resurrectional liturgy of Easter, is hung or placed before it. The wedding wreaths or crowns (see endnote to p. 28 above) are also placed on the iconostási; most usually they are removed when the second of the couple die, to be interred with the dead person.

67 The period from Christmas to the feast of Epiphany (*Theophánia*), which celebrates the baptism of Christ (see also the endnote to p. 86 below), that is, from 25th December to 6th January, is referred to as the *Dodekaímeron* — the Twelve Days of Christmas. Except for the strict fast held on the eve of Epiphany, it is a period of merry-making following the solemn forty days of fasting that mark Advent (see endnote to p. 21 above). The other major feast day between Christ's birth and baptism is that of 1st January, which commemorates two events: the first and most ancient in the liturgical calendar is the circumcision of Christ, which, according to Jewish custom, took place on the eighth day after a child's birth; and the second is the feast of St Basil, Archbishop of Caesaria in Cappadocia, when traditionally the exchange of gifts between Orthodox takes place in memory of his generosity and philanthropy toward his flock. The merriment continues with the feast of St John the Baptist on 7th January, and in some regions it goes on until the feast of Candlemas on 2nd February, a period punctuated with the major feasts of St Antony and St Athanasius celebrated on 17th and 18th January.

81 See second endnote to p. 16 above.

86 The feast of Epiphany, on 6th January, which now in the West marks the manifestation of Christ to the Gentiles, in the Orthodox tradition celebrates the baptism of Christ and is known as the *Theophánia* because at that event the three persons of the Trinity — Father, Son and Holy Spirit — were revealed and consecrated the water in which God Himself was immersed. On the feast day immediately after the liturgy Orthodox Christians go to a source of water, be it river, fountain, lake, sea, into which, as a sign of the divine presence in nature, the officiating priest throws a cross and young men plunge into the water to retrieve it. The feast is also known in Greece as *Ta Phóta*, the Feast of Lights

88 The Three Hierarchs is the main church of the port of Skiathos and is where Papadiamandis's father served as a priest. As a young boy Papadiamandis helped his father in the church as a server. The three hierarchs are St Basil the Great, St John Chrysostom and St Gregory the Theologian.

99 See second endnote to p. 67 above and endnote to p. 132 below.

103 See endnote to p. 28 above.

104 See endnote to p. 48 above.

104 The offering loaf, *prósphoron*, is given by the faithful to be consecrated and broken at the oblation table and used in the liturgy as the bread that will become the body of Christ. The bread that is not used for the holy communion is blessed and distributed to the faithful at the end of the liturgy as *antídoron* (meaning 'in lieu of a gift').

124 The dome of the church symbolizes the heavens, from the centre of which, in frescoed churches, the figure of Christ, the Pantokrator, the Almighty, King of Heaven (in contrast to the Autokrator, king of the earth, the word used in Byzantium for Emperor), looks down upon His creation.

125 According to Christian legend, the Emperor Julian the Apostate, who tried to re-establish paganism in the Christian Empire, was slain by St Merkourios. This wall-painting in the church of the Nativity in the Kastro is one of the rare representations of the legend; another one is an icon in the church of St Nicholas of Gourna, in Verroia in northern Greece. (See Dimitris D. Triandaphyllopoulos, 'Pelidnós o paráphron týrannos': Archaiologiká ston Papadiamándi ['Livid, the deranged tyrant': Archaeology in Papadiamandis] (Athens: Nefeli, 1996), pp. 87–113, for a detailed study of the fresco and its provenance.) Papadiamandis's graphic description of the Emperor's appearance in the fresco provoked negative comments following the story's publication which he refers to at the beginning of his 'Easter Chanter' (see p. 266).

St Kirykos and his mother St Ioulitta are much beloved saints who were martyred under Diocletian; Alexander was the Roman governor of Tarsos. Their memory is celebrated on 15th July.

125 The appellation Platytéra, 'Wider than the Heavens', frequently found in hymnology, refers to the Virgin Mary containing in her womb Him whom the heavens cannot contain. The wall-painting of the Platytéra is usually positioned above the apse of the sanctuary and forms an architectural link between the dome and the arch behind the altar that descends to the ground, thus affirming her unique role as the bridge between heaven and earth. Below the Platytéra are depicted the figures of the Fathers of the Church who have composed liturgical texts and which in turn shows the continuity between the texts recited during the liturgy and the presence of the Fathers who have written them.

126 Most usually it is in matins, during the chanting of Psalm 136, known as the Polyéleos because each verse ends with the word éleos ('mercy'), that the lit candelabrum hanging beneath the dome of the church is set into movement, creating in the darkness a vivid impression that the figures of the saints painted on the walls are moving.

127 At the beginning of matins the priest lamvánei kairón, that is, 'takes time', standing in turn in front of the icons of Christ, the Mother of God, and the saints depicted on the iconostasis, silently reciting the

designated prayers and hymns for each. The expression 'taking time' derives from the deacon's petition to the priest, spoken immediately before the deacon vests himself, that 'it is time to do the Lord's work', *kairós tou poiésai to Kyrío*.

129 Further on in matins the priest prepares the oblation by cutting a portion of the offered bread and arranging it on the paten that later, together with the chalice containing the wine, will be carried during the Great Entrance through the church to the altar table for consecration. The names of the faithful who have brought these offerings of bread and wine, together with the names of those for whom they are offered, are recited by the priest and slivers of the bread representing each name commemorated are placed on the paten alongside the special piece of bread, the 'Lamb', that will be consecrated as the Body of Christ. Additionally, a triangular portion of bread commemorating the Virgin Mary together with nine small portions representing the orders of archangels, prophets and saints are placed on the paten, as well as further particles representing all the names whom the priest sees fit to commemorate, both living and dead. All these portions of bread on the paten contain the totality of the Church and are co-mingled with the wine in the chalice, which has been constituted into the blood of Christ, and together form the living Body of Christ.

CARNIVAL NIGHT

132 The carnival period comprises the two weeks immediately preceding the beginning of Great Lent. The first week is known as Meatfare Week when the emphasis is on the eating of meat (except on Wednesday and Friday); it culminates on *Tsiknopémpti*, the Thursday of that week, which takes its name from the smell of roasting meat and which is celebrated with much gusto. The second week is known as Cheesefare Week in which the eating of fish, dairy products and eggs is allowed and during which carnival celebrations continue. Its equivalent in the western tradition is Shrove Tuesday, when pancakes are traditionally eaten prior to the beginning of

Lent on Ash Wednesday, the following day. In the eastern tradition Great Lent begins on Clean Monday, and contrary to the sober mourning character of Ash Wednesday, it is a festive day on which one refrains completely from work and people congregate in the countryside and fly kites and partake of their first Lenten meal which is accompanied by special unleavened bread, *lagána*, especially baked for this day. 'Clean' is to be taken in a metaphorical sense.

For the protracted period of holidays, see the second endnote to p. 67 above.

136 In Greek society the ties between *koumbároi* (plural) are held in high esteem and considered sacred since they are sanctioned by either the sacrament of baptism or marriage. In a liturgical context, the koumbáros represents the entire ecclesiastical community and it is this community in his person that introduces the child to the Church. Traditionally, the man or woman who acts as the *koumbáros* at the wedding will also be expected to be the godparent of the couple's first child.

THE MONK

148 In the Orthodox Church men who are called to the priesthood and who wish to serve the needs of those living in the world must marry before their ordination, and only those who would take monastic vows remain celibate. At the time of Papadiamandis, parishes began to be served by tonsured hieromonks (a monk who has been ordained to the priesthood) and archimandrites (a title normally conferred on the abbot of a monastery), which Papadiamandis viewed as a newfangled practice destroying the ethos of the ecclesiastical community and of parish life. He believed that the life of a parish priest must not be distinguished from the lives of his parishioners, that he should be a married man with children facing the same challenges, obligations and difficulties faced by his flock. An archimandrite, who ideally should remain in the monastery of 'his repentance', that is, of his initial calling, is, according to Papadiamandis, ill-equipped to respond to the needs of his parishioners who do not

share his eremitical way of life. With the increase of this practice Papadiamandis saw the risk of a western-type clericalism finding its way into the Orthodox Church which would by necessity imply a consequent problem of secularization (laicization). In Orthodoxy it had never been an issue since the life of the clergy was indistinguishable from the life of the laity. Papadiamandis revisits this theme in one of his essays entitled 'City Priests and Village Priests'. This tendency, noticed at its early stages by Papadiamandis, has become an all too common occurrence in the Orthodox Church today.

149   The character of Father Samuel is modelled on a real person, Nikolaos Aghiotis (1849–91), a son of the Skiathiot captain Dianelos, with whom Papadiamandis had been acquainted since his schooldays. His friend abandoned his career on the sea and was tonsured a monk on Mount Athos taking the monastic name of Niphon. He went to Athens for medical reasons and there he served as sacristan in the church of Aghioi Anargyroi (the two sibling 'un-mercenary' physician saints). Papadiamandis writes about him to his father from Athens, probably at the latter's request enquiring after him, in the following terms: 'Niphon is still here and he says that he will go to the Holy Mountain. He tried to accomplish something here but did not bring it to a conclusion. He did not misbehave while here at all and do not pay any attention to hearsay. He may be drinking a little but his overall behaviour is sober.' (A. Papadiamandis: *Allilographía* [*Correspondence*], edited by N. D. Triandaphyllopoulos (Athens: Domos Publications, 1992), p. 127.)

150   A similar scene of monastic tonsure is described by Papadiamandis in a draft of his first novel, *Gyftopoúla* [*Gypsy-girl*] (1884), which shows that the ritual of tonsure had preoccupied him eight years earlier (see A. Papadiamandis: *To Lávaron* [*The Banner*], edited by Photis Dimitrakopoulos (Athens: Kastaniotis, 1989), pp. 48–50). He most probably witnessed the ritual during his sojourn on Mount Athos in 1872.

159   During the reign of Otho (1853–62), the State, seeing the great influence monasteries exerted on all aspects of Greek life and wishing

to curb it, decreed that all monasteries with less than five monks should be demolished, as a result of which hundreds of establishments disappeared.

159 According to St Basil's monastic rules, laid down in the fourth century, there were two types of monastic establishments: the anchorite's skete where monks led a hermit's way of life, joining together with monks from the surrounding area for Sunday worship at the Kyriakón, the main church of the monastic compound, and the communal establishments, designated as coenobitic, where monks held everything in common. In Papadiamandis's time there was some deviation from these rules and a hybrid skete-like autonomous way of life had been introduced into some of the old coenobitic monasteries where although the monks were living in a communal establishment they did not share in all its liturgical or practical aspects, such as the chanting of the Hours, keeping of vigils and eating at a common table. These monasteries were known as idiorrhythmic.

162 In Orthodoxy, the undivided unity of the Body of Christ and the eucharistic community of which the Church is the living image is reflected in the fact that the Divine Liturgy can be celebrated only once a day in each church; correspondingly a priest can only celebrate one liturgy on any given day. The Orthodox do not subscribe to the western Christian practice which allows for more than one altar in the same church and permits the celebration of more than one Mass on these altars on the same day by the same priest.

163 Canonically, memorial services cannot be sung on Sundays, the Day of the Resurrection of the Lord, and it is Saturday that has been especially designated for offering prayers for the dead. The novel practice of holding memorial services on Sunday had been introduced even on Mount Athos, giving rise in the late eighteenth century to the great Kollyvades controversy, which took its name from *kóllyva*, the boiled wheat offered in memory of the dead during the service. The controversy pitted the traditionalist factions, identified with those opposing Sunday memorial services, against the innovators who had no qualms about performing them on Sundays. As a

consequence, it was the Kollyvades, who in their effort to return to a more authentic form of Orthodoxy promoting frequent communion, introducing the laity to the Jesus Prayer and other forms of traditional worship in strict observance of the *typikón*, represented the reforming spirit in the Orthodox Church. Of particular note here is that some of these traditionalist groups had been persecuted and fled from Mount Athos, settling in the neighbouring islands, and it is well known, and attested by Papadiamandis himself, that such a group had established itself in Skiathos and was responsible for shaping the Orthodox ethos and introducing reforms in worship in his native island. In fact, all the concerns voiced by the author in this section regarding both liturgical and social reforms can be traced to the principal ideas of the Kollyvades. These concerns, identified as crucial by Papadiamandis, still plague the Orthodox Church today.

163 At this point, Papadiamandis supplies a footnote citing specific solecisms committed by the bishops. Since the note deals with Greek syntactical deviations from correct usage it is virtually untranslatable and has not been included.

164 The Church of Greece broke from the fold of the Ecumenical Patriarchate in 1833 after the creation of the modern Greek state. In accordance with a view expressed mainly by the Bavarian triumvirate advising King Otho and a faction of like-minded clerics led by Theoklitos Pharmakidis, the Greek Church declared its autocephaly on the grounds that it could not belong to a Patriarchate that was tributary to a Muslim power. Although the decision to break appeared logical and was decided in a matter of hours at a Church Council convened under the pressure of the State, all clerics did not agree with this decision and there was considerable opposition at the time led by such influential figures as Constantinos Economos.

174 The 'Ladder of Ascent' to the spiritual life of St John Climacos, where each step of the ladder represents a virtue accomplished, is a common iconographic theme in wall-paintings, portraying in graphic visual terms the fate of those who fail in their spiritual aspirations.

AT SAINT ANASTASA'S

182 According to A. D. Alexiou, *Skiáthos: I architectonikí ton meta-vyzantinón naón* [*Skiathos: The architecture of post-Byzantine churches*] (Thessaloniki, 1996), the correct name is St George Christodoulitsas or Christodoulitsa's, this being a family name attested in documents from the late eighteenth century onward. [Translator's note.]

182 The unburnt portion of the candles, which in Papadiamandis's day were made of bees' wax, were, for reasons of economy, melted down again and made into new candles.

184 All these references to Anastasis (meaning resurrection) and the name Anastasia, and Kyriaki, the name given to the Lord's Day, Sunday (from the word *Kýrios*, meaning Lord) and the actual martyr who bears the name of Kyriaki as a testimony of her allegiance to the Lord, are a cause of great confusion in the minds of the country-folk. The Sunday liturgy is the commemoration of the Lord's resurrection, which further complicates the issue. The importance of these derivatives from *Kýrios* can also be seen in the name given to the main church of monastic sketes which is called the *Kyriakón*, the Church of the Lord. The same confusion is perpetuated with the name given to the Church of the Wisdom of the Word of God (*I tou Theoú Lógou Sophía*) and the actual martyr Sophia whose three daughters, Faith, Hope and Charity, represent the theological virtues, that is, the attributes of the Wisdom of God.

185 The matins of the Resurrection begins late on Saturday evening so the gospel of the Resurrection may be read on Easter morning as close to midnight as possible. The shepherd refers to that part of matins when the congregation moves outside the church for the proclamation of the Resurrection, permeating all the natural world with the life of the risen Christ. The church remains empty and dark, symbolizing the empty tomb, until everyone returns with their lit candles for the celebration of the liturgy bringing in this new life which will be consummated in the Eucharist.

186 Alexiou, *Skiáthos*, op. cit., gives Panayía Domán (Doumán) / Zoodó-
chos Pigí. The name Domán is taken from the spring/stream. [Transla-
tor's note.]

187 Dryads (and 'Hamadryads') are nymphs living in giant oak-trees (Ovid,
Metamorphoses, viii, 738) deriving their name from the word for oak,
drys, a derivation which led some scholars to attribute the same etymology to the word Druid because of their cult of the oak-tree. Oaks
have been considered sacred since time immemorial, thus the sacred
oak of Zeus at Dodona, an image that is combined in Papadiamandis's
mind with the oak-tree at Mamre where Abraham encountered God
in the form of three persons to whom he gave hospitality (Genesis
18 : 1–15). The sacredness of the tree was a frequent theme in his writings and can best be seen in his story 'Under the Royal Oak' (1901).

190 Country-folk tended to see the groves and vales as populated by pagan natural divinities, such as the nymphs, dryads, nereids, Lamiae,
and in order to appease them built churches in these places. Even
churches built on top of mountains dedicated to the Prophet Elias
(Elijah) are reminiscent of the ancient cult of Apollo Helios whose
temples were also built in high places; in the popular mind the
chariot of the Prophet Elias was similar to the chariot of Phoebus
Helios. See also the first endnote to p. 232 below.

193 See G. A. Rigas, *Skiáthou laïkós politismós* [*The popular culture of
Skiathos*], vol. 4 (Thessaloniki, 1970) p. 387: 'Skiathos possesses
two parish churches, dedicated respectively to the Three Hierarchs
and the Theotokos. The former is called the 'lower church', that is
to say, the church belonging to the lower parish. More commonly,
people call it St John's, perhaps because they prefer, among the
names of the three dedicatees, that of John, which is more familiar
and popular.' [Translator's note.]

AROUND THE LAGOON

205 According to Rigas, op. cit. (vol. 4, p. 279), the launching of a ship
should be avoided at the solstice. Sailors believed that with every
new moon a star is born which in the first two days of its existence

disappears into the depths of the earth and reappears on the third day. On the day the hull of a new ship is to be built care must be taken to align the stern of the ship with the new-born star after its reappearance.

222 This seems to be an ironic reference to an already humorous passage in Plato, *Symposium*, 173a, in which Apollodorus tells Glaucon that before he began keeping daily company with Socrates, 'what with running about aimlessly and thinking that I was doing something, I was the most wretched man alive, just as you are now, thinking that one should do anything rather than philosophize.' [Translator's note.]

FEY FOLK

223 The Christmas loaf, called *Christópsomo*, is a special round decorated loaf, taking a prominent place on the Christmas festive table. St Basil's cake, *Vassilópitta*, is a sweet pie offered in honour of St Basil on New Year's Eve, in which is hidden a small silver coin representing St Basil's generosity towards the poor. At midnight the whole family congregates and welcomes in the New Year by cutting this cake and offering pieces in turn to Christ, the Virgin Mary, St Basil, and the stranger, and then to all the members of the family according to their seniority. The person who gets the coin is considered especially fortunate for he has received the blessings of the saint.

For the feast days of the Twelve Days of Christmas, see second endnote to p. 67 above.

226 Concerning wedding wreaths, see endnote to p. 28 above.

226 This particularity of Skiathiot domestic life is also attested by Rigas, op. cit. (vol. 4, p. 13), and is referred to again by Papadiamandis in his 'The Little House in Livadi', 'A Heros' Eros', and, extensively, in his novella *The Murderess*.

232 Hobgoblins (*kallikántzari*), fairies (*neráïdes*), vampires (*vrikólakes*), Lamias (*Lámies*), and the blackamoor (*o arápis*) are all magnificent spirit demons surviving from the remote pagan past, each having his

or her domain within the natural world, inhabiting trees, vales, copses, groves, emerging from waters, hiding in lairs, congregating in the noon-day sun. Papadiamandis very frequently places them in their natural habitat, wishing to express in this way the sway these spirits hold over the popular imagination. One has only to bring to mind the story about a vampire that Byron had been told in Greece and which he related to his personal physician, John Polidori, who subsequently made it fa-mous in his extremely popular tale, *The Vampyre*, to understand the hold these stories had and often still have on the Greek people.

232   According to popular belief, the child born on Saturday is espe-cially lucky since on that day all Creation was completed and God rested from his works. According to the same belief this is also the day when the invisible phantoms and the various spirits are at rest.

234   The period of celebration of all major feasts in the Orthodox Church lasts for nine days during which the memory of the feast is kept by referring to the feast with special hymns and intonations in the daily services. On the ninth day the feast is given back to God and is referred to as the *Apódosis*. The days are counted from the actual day of the feast.

243   It is common in many parts of Greece to exhume the bones of the deceased some three years after burial, wash them with wine and place them in an ossuary. This takes place after the last in a series of memorial services for the departed has been offered by the priest and the family for the repose of the soul of the dead person.

245   On the eve of the Nativity of the Lord, vespers are chanted followed by the liturgy of St Basil. The hymn 'Lord, I called upon Thee', tak-en from Psalm 140, is the first hymn sung at the office of vespers. The liturgy of St Basil the Great is celebrated ten times a year.

248   The author is most probably referring to the first arrival on Skiathos of a group of persecuted monks who had fled from Mount Athos during the Kollyvades controversy (see first endnote to p. 163 above).

249   See first endnote to p. 16 above.

SHIPWRECK'S WRECKAGE

260　This popular story of the eye of the lake reflects the ancient myth of Arethousa, a nymph of Artemis, and Alpheus, the river at Olympia, who pursued her along the river bank. As the nymph prayed to Artemis for help, she was turned into a cloud which then dissolved into a stream that Artemis had caused to spring from the earth. Flowing underground the stream was united with the waters of the Alpheus, and emerged as a fountain at Syracuse in Sicily. This fountain in Syracuse still bears the name Fontana di Aretusa. It was also related that objects which had fallen into the river at Olympia would re-emerge at the fountain.

THE EASTER CHANTER

263　The Praises (*Engómia*) are the funeral hymns chanted while the *Epitáphios* is taken out in procession, not to be confused with the Praises (*Aínoi*) which are verses from the Psalms, beginning with 'Praise the Lord...', sung during matins.

268　See endnote to p. 148 above.

275　In monasteries the monks and nuns are called to prayer by the sound of a mallet striking an elongated plank of timber, the *sémandron*. The monastic assigned this task holds the wooden plank in one hand and with the other the mallet and goes around the inner court of the monastery striking the wood rhythmically to the measure of

　　　ton A dám, ton A dám, ton A dám, A dám, A dám
　　　‒ ‒ ◡　　‒ ‒ ◡　　‒ ‒ ◡　　‒ ‒　　‒ ‒

interchanging it with the rhythm of

　　　to tálan don, to tálan don, to tála, tála, tálan don
　　　‒ ◡ ‒ ‒　‒ ◡ ‒ ‒　‒ ◡ ‒ ◡ ‒ ◡ ‒ ‒

276　See endnote to p. 23 and the first endnote to p. 29 above.

277　Normally while the priest is vesting himself and reciting the special prayers that accompany this part of the preparation for the liturgy, the cantor is chanting the appointed *tropária* for matins; in the absence of a cantor here *Papa*-Dianelos is compelled to alternate the recitation of these prayers with the chanting of the *tropária*, a near impossibility.

278 Papadiamandis is referring to the *aspasmós*, the exchange of the 'kiss of love' between the members of the congregation which took place prior to the beginning of the liturgy, and which is evoked in the final *tropárion* of the canon of the feast: ' 'Tis the day of the Resurrection, let us be made radiant by the feast and let us kiss each other; let us call brothers those who hate us and forgive all in the Resurrection...'. This event of mutual embracing is also recalled in a poem by Greece's national poet, Dionysios Solomos (1798–1857): *Philithíte gliká cheíli me cheíli / péste Christós Anésti echthroí kai phíloi* ['Kiss one another sweetly on the lips / enemies and friends declare Christ is Risen'] ('*I Iméra tis Lambrís*' ['Easter Day'], *Ápanta* [*Collected Works*], Ikaros, Athens 1948, p. 186). It is possible that from this practice the 'Vespers of Love', held on Easter day, took its name.

286 In the nineteenth century time was still calculated in many places in Europe according to the rising and the setting of the sun, as it still is on Mount Athos, but with the proliferation of time pieces and the necessity of time tables imposed mainly by train schedules and work shifts in industrial establishments, a transcontinental agreement about time was made.

THE LADY'S HOUSE

292 The veneration of the Virgin Mary, who is usually called the *Panayía*, the 'Most-Holy' (the appellation meant as an intimate proper name and not a title), is manifested in all parts of the Greek Orthodox world. In Arta she is venerated as the Mother of Consolation, the *Parigorítissa*, in Kalamata as the Virgin Kalomata, in the outskirts of Trebizond as the *Panayía* of Soumela, in Skiathos as the *Kounístra*, but also the *Panayía* of Doman, Pyrgi, etc., according to the place where the particular icon is venerated. Often the name indicates not the locality but the conditions under

which the icon was miraculously found, as in the *Kounístra*, meaning the one who sways, because her icon was found amidst the branches of a pine-tree swaying in the wind. In this instance 'Salonikia' refers to the origin of the icon, which was probably brought to the island from Thessaloniki.

292 Hobgoblins (*kallikántzari*) appear throughout the Twelve Days of Christmas, but particularly on Christmas Eve. They are dark, impish creatures, invading human habitations through any ingress they can find, but mainly through chimneys, and once having entered a house create havoc by breaking pots, souring milk, and generally turning things upside down. See also the first endnote to p. 232.

293 At Epiphany, which commemorates the baptism of Christ, priests bless the waters on two occasions in simulation of the sanctification of the waters that took place when St John baptized Christ in the waters of Jordan. The first blessing takes place on the eve of the feast, which is known as the Lesser Blessing, and second on the actual day and is known as the Great Blessing. After the ritual the priests visit the homes of their flock and the public places of the village or town, sprinkling them with the holy water which is seen as averting all evil and engendering health not only in human beings but throughout all creation. See also endnote to p. 86 above.

Glossary

análavos: originally a sort of shawl worn by monastics, now a sleeveless vest worn over the cassock.

antídoron: bread that is blessed and distributed to the congregation by the priest at the end of the liturgy.

baklavá: a very sweet confection made of thin filo pastry, nuts and honey.

bárba: from the Italian for beard, a title prefixed to a man's name indicating a person of venerable standing in the community.

Epitáphios: a portable wooden representation of the tomb of Christ on which is laid, during the morning service of Good Friday, an embroidered cloth image of the dead Christ. The word *epitáphios*, which means 'on the tomb', refers to both the wooden representation of the tomb and the image of the dead Christ laid upon it. The *Epitáphios* is taken out of the church and carried in procession on the evening of Good Friday, followed by the congregation holding candles as in a funeral procession.

kataíphi: a sweet confection similar to *baklavá*, made from shredded filo pastry rolled in crushed walnuts and honey.

katavasía: the first *tropárion* of each ode of a canon that is sung in a particular tone, after which are modelled all the other *tropária* (plural) in that ode, and which is chanted at the beginning and end of the canon.

káthisma: meaning 'sitting', is a set of hymns chanted in one of the eight tones used in Byzantine chant, during which the congregation may sit.

Katholikón: the principal church of a monastic compound, usually situated in the centre of the main inner courtyard of the monastery.

kokorétsi: a much esteemed delicacy made from the inner organs of a lamb or kid, wrapped in intestines and slowly grilled over charcoal.

kóllyva: a mixture of boiled wheat, lightly toasted flour, nuts, pomegranate seeds, raisins, and a little parsley, heaped up in a dish, covered with sugar, and decorated with a cross formed with raisins, nuts and pomegranate seeds. It is offered at the memorial services for the dead, customarily on the third, ninth and fortieth day after a person's death, then on the third, sixth and twelfth month, and thereafter whenever the family wish to commemorate their dead. *Kóllyva* is also offered for the dead on All Souls Saturday which is set aside liturgically for the commemoration of the souls of those who have departed. See also the first endnote to p. 163.

koumbáros, *koumbároi* (plural): a designation referring either to the godfather of a child or the best man at a wedding, deriving from the Italian compare. In colloquial speech it is a friendly address inferring intimacy. See also the endnote to p. 136.

kyr: the shortened form of *kýrios*, meaning 'lord, master'.

kyrá: the shortened form of *kyría*, the feminine of *kýrios*.

laographía: composed of two words, *laós* (people) and *graphí* (written description), was first proposed as the Greek equivalent of folklore studies (*Volkskunde* in German) by Nikolaos Politis in 1884. It was officially adopted in 1909 with the publication of the first volume of the journal of the Greek Folkloric [*Laographikí*] Society which was given the title of *Laographía*.

lávra: a communal establishment comprised of several cells where monks live in autonomous isolation, derived from the ancient term denoting a narrow street flanked by small huts.

mastícha: a spirit drink flavoured with the resin of the mastic tree.

mástro: a popular form of address for a reputable craftsman or any skilled person, derived from the Latin *magister*, most often used as a prefix to a name. The English equivalent of 'master', or even that of 'mister', though of the same origin, does not convey the meaning it has in Greek. Another form of address akin to *mástro* is *mástoras*, the hellenized abbreviation of *magistoras*.

moscháto: a fragrant rosé wine made from muscat grapes.

myzíthra: a hard cheese made out of the whey left over from the first cheese-making, with good keeping qualities and frequently used grated over food.

papadía: the wife of a priest, and the name by which she is most usually addressed.

papás, vocative *papá*: the title of a priest.

rakí: an abbreviated form of 'rozaki', a variety of grape. *Rakí* is usually distilled from the skins, seeds and stalks remaining from the trodden grapes, but can also be made out of a variety of fruits and berries. In different areas of Greece it is known by different names. In Crete it also goes by the name of *tsikoudiá*; in the mainland of Greece mainly by the name of *tsípouro*. The Turks also call it *rakí*; to the Arabs it is known as *arak*. When flavoured with aniseed it becomes *oúzo* — *doúziko* in Constantinopolitan Greek.

sémandron: a wooden plank, or piece of metal, struck with a hammer, most commonly used in monasteries to summon monks and nuns to prayer. See also endnote to p. 275.

splinándero: a delicacy made out of lamb's spleen and other entrails.

svánziko, *svánzika* (plural): from the German *zwanziger*, an Austrian twenty-groschen coin that circulated in Greece in the years immediately following the Greek War of Independence.

syrtós: a general appellation for popular circular dances characterized by sliding side steps in distinction to other dances like *tsámikos* which are characterized by leaping steps. *Kalamatianós* is one of the most popular Greek dances of the *syrtós* type, taking its name from the town of Kalamata in the southern Peloponnese.

táler: from the German, sometimes spelt *tháler*, a silver coin in circulation in Europe for more than four hundred years, which gave the name to the American dollar, and also to the Greek *táliro*, meaning a five-drachma coin.

témpla: all manner of linen and bed furnishings which comprise a major part of a bride's dowry, a term particular to Skiathos.

tropárion, *tropária* (plural): a hymn composed for special feast days.

tserníki: a small single-masted sailing boat.

tsípouro: see *raкí* above.

typikón, *typiká* (plural): a liturgical designation describing various ecclesiastical books which contain the order of the services and detailed instructions as to how the many offices of the Orthodox Church should be conducted.

várda béne: probably a corruption of *guarda bene*, meaning 'pay attention'.

vlogoúdi: from *evlogoúdia*, meaning 'blessed small things', a diminutive of *evlogía*, meaning 'blessing'.

yéro: a prefix to a man's name, meaning 'old'.

Notes on Contributors

DAVID CONNOLLY has lived and worked in Greece since 1979 and is currently Associate Professor of Translation Studies at the Aristotle University in Thessaloniki. He has written extensively on the theory and practice of literary translation and translated over twenty books by leading Greek authors.

ELIZABETH KEY FOWDEN is an independent scholar who lives in Limni, Euboea. She is currently writing a study of education in the late Platonist tradition.

GARTH FOWDEN is a historian of late antiquity and early Islam, works at the National Hellenic Research Foundation, and lives in Limni, Euboea.

DENISE HARVEY lives in the countryside on the island of Euboea where she works as a publisher and editor.

GAIL HOLST-WARHAFT is a professor at Cornell University where she directs a programme of Mediterranean Studies. She has also worked as a journalist, broadcaster, musician and independent scholar, and her many publications include translations of Aeschylus as well as of modern Greek poets and prose-writers.

LAMBROS KAMPERIDIS is a priest serving an Orthodox Community in Montréal, Canada. He is also a Byzantinist specializing in the post-Byzantine period. He has written extensively on Papadiamandis and is preparing for publication his study on Nikolaos Mavrokordatos's *Treatise on Duties*.

PETER MACKRIDGE is Emeritus Professor of Modern Greek at Oxford University. His books include *The Modern Greek Language*, two co-authored grammars of Modern Greek, and *Dionysios Solomos*.

JOHN RAFFAN is a priest of the Orthodox Church of Scottish origin who lives and works in Greece.

PHILIP RAMP is an American poet who has lived and worked in Greece for many years. Among his translations are those of the Greek poets Nikos Karouzos, Tassos Denegris and Lydia Stephanou.

PAVLOS SFYROERAS, a classicist, and MARIA HATJIGEORGIOU, a Byzantinist, teach in the Departments of Classics and Religion at Middlebury College, Vermont. In their research and teaching, they look at the presence of the sacred in Greek literature, ancient, Byzantine, and modern.

AVI SHARON, who presently lives in New York, came to Greece a classicist and left it a student of modern Greek literature. Among his recent publications are a selection of the poems of C. P. Cavafy.

LIADAIN SHERRARD was born in Greece to a Greek mother and an English father, was educated in England, then subsequently made her home in Greece. She has translated books and writings from French and Greek on various themes, both literary and academic.

ANDREW WATSON works as an editor of the Oxford English Dictionary. He lived in Greece for a number of years, working for a publishing company and as a free-lance translator.

MAP OF SKIATHOS

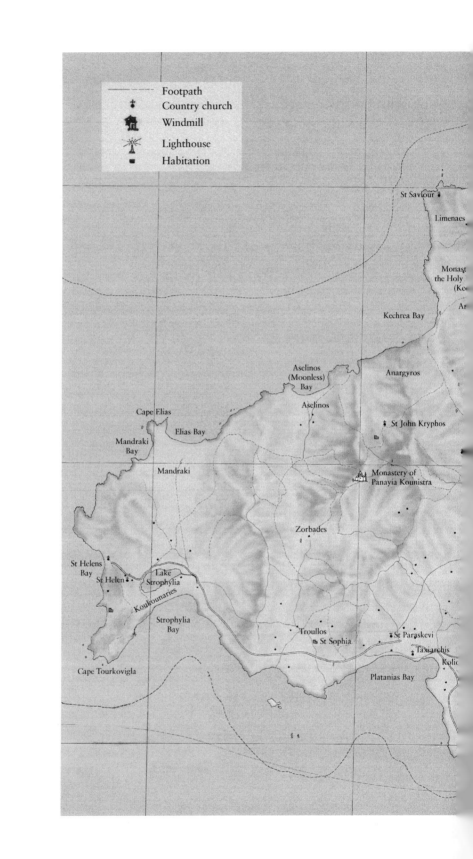

Footpath
Country church
Windmill
Lighthouse
Habitation

St Saviour
Limenaes
Monast
the Holy
(Kec
Ar
Kechrea Bay
Aselinos
(Moonless)
Bay
Anargyros
Aselinos
Cape Elias
St John Kryphos
Elias Bay
Mandraki
Bay
Mandraki
Monastery of
Panayia Kounistra
Zorbades
St Helens
Bay
Lake
Strophylia
St Helen
Koukounaries
Strophylia
Bay
Troullos
St Paraskevi
St Sophia
Taxiarchis
Kolic
Cape Tourkovigla
Platanias Bay

N

s Yialos

Cape Kouroupi

Tripia Petra

the Baptist   Klinias

mbia   Kouroupi

yia Doman   Stivoto

airimona   Monastery of

Stream   St Charalambos   Nikorsara Bay

ygdali   Vigles

K'fandonis   Megalos

arafiltzanaka   Yialos

Monastery of   Xanemos

the Annunciation   Deserted Village

Three Crosses   Kanakis's Spring   Kalivia   Cape Kephala

Cold Well   St George

St Dimitris   Christodoulitsa

St Athanasios   Stamelos's Spring

Prophet Elias (Elijah)

antine   Petralono

Matarona

Vourlidia

Doctor's Vineyard   Lagoon

Livadia

St Fanourios   St George

SKIATHOS
TOWN

Megali Ammos   Daskalio   Pounda
Bourtzi   Island

Cape Pounda

Maragos
Island

Arkas
Island

Black Scarf Rock

Tsoungria
Island

THE BOUNDLESS GARDEN, SELECTED SHORT STORIES
BY ALEXANDROS PAPADIAMANDIS, VOLUME I, EDITED
BY LAMBROS KAMPERIDIS AND DENISE HARVEY,
WAS SET INTO TYPE AND PAGINATED AT THE ATELIER
OF GRAPHICON, A. & N. KYRIAKIDIS, ATHENS.
THIS PRESENT EDITION WAS PRINTED BY ALPHABET S.A.
IN ATHENS IN DECEMBER 2018.
THE TEXT FACE IS SABON AND THE PAPER IS
ACID-FREE FABRIANO PALATINA.
3.